CW01206841

QUEEN OF HEARTS

EMPIRE OF SHATTERED CROWNS

4

MAY FREIGHTER

Port Lisza Academy

Port Lisza

Road to the Roya

The Docks

RKET

OCK
WER

Road to Heren

Orphanage

Garhue Mountains

Moonlit Mountains

Elisse

Arcane Ridge

Illermont

Vinmare

Mage Assembly

Legionare's Forest

Arcane Sea

Dresgan

Gosset

Morgan

Gisna

The Hollow Mountains
Northern Watchtower
Dragon's Heart Mine
Redford
Dragon Village
Grim Port
Newburn
The Royal Wood
Misty Sea
Port Lisza
Heren
Avonport
Drovia
Sinta
Avarea
Misty Peaks
Grenard
Vasa
Ashen Forest
Ponte
Crystal Sea
Reyniel
Setina

Copyright © 2024 May Freighter

All rights reserved.

ISBN: 979 8320616568

DEDICATION

To those of you who feel lonely or alone.

I hope my band of misfits can keep you company forevermore.

FOREWORD

This book is written in U.K. English.

Some spelling may be different to the U.S.

Author's website:

www.authormayfreighter.com

Interior and Exterior Illustration:

Cristal Designs, SonyaMoon

CONTENTS

	Acknowledgments	i
1	A Lonely Picture	1
2	Unpleasant News	9
3	Journey to the South	16
4	Eyes of Truth	25
5	Queen Cecilia	33
6	Moin Varetz	41
7	Support of the March	52
8	An Assassin's Promise	58
9	A Heart Long Broken	66
10	A Midnight Rendezvous	3
11	A White Lie	81
12	Fragments of the Past	88
13	The Young Prince	96
14	The Queen's Important Outing	108
15	Troublesome Rumours	119
16	Between Fire and Ice	127

17	The Shadow's Curse	136
18	Her Shield and Sanctuary	141
19	The Graveyard of Men	148
20	A Game of Crowns	155
21	Broken Bonds	162
22	A Rat in the Palace	168
23	Unnerving	180
24	Perfidy	190
25	Priorities	197
26	Bad News Come in Pairs	202
27	Greed of the Mages	213
28	Not Supposed to Die	220
29	The Cursed Bird	224
30	Till the Break of Dawn	233
31	The Cost of Protection	239
32	All That Remains	248
33	A Heartfelt Warning	258
34	Sealed by Magic	266
35	The Value of Friendship	273

36	Yearning of the Heart	280
37	Not a Hero	287
38	Prophecy Untold	298
39	The Villain	308
	The Game of Crowns Rules	311
	Language of the Beastmen	312
	Beastmen Dictionary (to date)	313
	About the Author	316

ACKNOWLEDGMENTS

A massive thank you to **Nicole** and **David Talbot** for trying out a game of Crowns and providing their feedback.

Thank you to **Nancy Zee** from **Cristal Designs** and **Jean W.** for the editing and proofreading the story.

Big hugs to my alpha reader and provider of useful medieval information—**my husband**.

My love and thanks to everyone in **The Lionhart Guild** for being my emotional support during the writing/editing/complaining/crying processes:

N. Talbot, N. Quinlan, K. Taylor-Gorman, S. L. Bloom, USAT Melissa Bell, Anaisu, M. Lewis, A. Williams, A. Eschweiler, Seren Nos, T. Morrisseau, S. L. Whiley, A. Stevenson, K. Grube, K. Meadows, K. Bergh-Lewendon, L. van der A., D. Willard, H. Rose, Author Ashlea Rhodes, D. Eyre, & Dominica.

Lastly, big hugs to all the readers and reviewers. Without you, this series wouldn't happen.

"Remember this, Emilia. While Lord Armel acts as your shield, I will be your sanctuary."
- Pope Valerian

1

A LONELY PICTURE

EMILIA

Emilia **peeled her eyelids open** to find a familiar ceiling of her bedchambers staring back. Her body felt weak and her head hurt. She tried to lift her arm only to find her hand was trapped under something warm.

Lifting her head off the pillow, she noticed Thessian's sleeping face on her bedside and his hand holding hers. "This is quite unexpected."

In the corner of the room, Ambrose stirred on a chair. The moment the head maid's eyes met Emilia's, they filled with tears. Disregarding all etiquette, Ambrose ran over to her queen and sobbed into the bedsheets. "Your Majesty! I feared you would never wake up."

Slowly, as her muscles obeyed, Emilia sat up and removed her hand from Thessian's before she couldn't feel her arm any longer.

How long did I sleep for? What happened?

Ambrose kept sobbing, showing so much emotion Emilia felt guilty for worrying her friend. After all, Ambrose was barely twenty years old and had experienced plenty of loss and pain in her short life.

"There, there," Emilia softly whispered as she patted Ambrose's shoulder.

The commotion woke Thessian who raised his head. He sluggishly reclined in his chair while sporting a light beard. He was also wearing a plain linen shirt tucked into his dark trousers which made it seem as if he was not concerned about appearances.

"Emilia..." He smiled. Her name sounded like a caress on his lips. "You are finally awake."

Emilia's heart raced, and she felt her cheeks suddenly getting warm. "Y-Your Highness."

Thessian rolled his shoulders and took in a deep breath.

Feeling her stomach hurt and her mouth parched, Emilia swallowed dry. Besides that, she didn't feel uncomfortable.

Wasn't I shot?

She gave him a quick study. "Were you hurt, Thessian?"

"You took an arrow for me, Emilia," came his reply. "Don't you remember?"

"I thought Your Majesty would die and then after healing, Your Majesty wouldn't wake—" Ambrose sobbed without finishing her sentence.

Emilia looked at her balcony while she kept patting Ambrose's back. "It's morning already. Stop crying, Ambrose. I'm awake and quite thirsty. Could you get me some water?"

Ambrose raised her teary face. "Of course."

Emilia smiled. "I was only asleep for a few hours."

"Two weeks," Thessian corrected her.

It took a moment for her to register his words. "What?"

"You were unconscious for two whole weeks." Thessian lowered his head in shame. "I regret not listening to you that night."

"Two weeks?" Emilia's voice rose, and she looked at Ambrose.

"That can't be right!"

Ambrose nodded as she poured water into a glass on the nightstand and offered it to her queen.

Accepting the glass and taking a sip, Emilia grimaced at the cold liquid, but she was too thirsty to wait for a cup of hot tea.

As she returned the glass to Ambrose, a million questions crossed her mind. "What happened with the duke's trial? And the smugglers? What about the serpentine powder? Please tell me the city is intact—"

Emilia was about to get up and go to her balcony to check the state of the city when she felt Thessian's hand on her arm.

"You've been sleeping for weeks. Your body is weak," he reminded her.

"How can you be so calm? Everything we've worked for…" The urgency in her voice made her lose her breath. Inhaling rapidly, she tried to calm down.

Thessian took her hand between his and spoke softly. "Count Baudelaire, Lord Armel, and I have dealt with everything in your absence. Duke Malette was hung for high treason and endangering the city. The smugglers were successfully captured and questioned by Lord Armel and his sister. You will have a report waiting on your desk when you are well enough to get up." His expression hardened, and he continued. "Regarding the arrow, Pope Valerian healed you."

Everything was solved, just like that? That's a bit anticlimactic…

"He did?" Emilia could not believe it. "What did he ask for in return?"

"Nothing as of yet."

Emilia looked at her head maid, who had dried her tears and seemed ready to comply with any requests. "Bring me some soup and tea, Ambrose. I will also require a change of clothes to hold an audience with His Holiness."

Ambrose shook her head vehemently. "No, Your Majesty! You must rest."

"I think I have rested enough," Emilia countered. "If it will make you feel better, bring Benjamin here to check on my condition."

"I have to agree with your head maid, Emilia. Your body needs to recover after such a long slumber." Thessian said firmly, holding her hand tighter. "I'm asking this as your friend. Please eat, drink, and rest before worrying about court affairs. Duty can wait."

Ambrose nodded with a stern gaze, and Thessian narrowed his eyes at Emilia as if daring her to disobey him.

He said he was asking as a friend, so why the mean face?

Huffing, Emilia fiddled with the quilt with her free hand. "Fine. I will rest for one day. Ambrose, ask His Holiness if he has time to have breakfast with me tomorrow."

With a scowl, Ambrose wiped away the remainder of her snot and tears with a handkerchief. She fixed her messy uniform and bowed her head. "I will return momentarily."

Emilia waited until Ambrose was gone and took a minute to stare at her hand under Thessian's warm, callused palm.

Is he so afraid I'll get up from my bed that he needs to keep my hand captured like this?

"Your Highness, I've promised to stay in bed for one more day. You can stop holding my hand to prevent my escape."

He pulled back, and she could swear that pink reached his cheeks.

Emilia instantly regretted the loss of his warmth. Having his hand on hers made her feel as if she was no longer dreaming and back to where she wanted to be.

Emilia pouted.

"What is it?"

"I didn't hear her answer." She reclined against the headboard, hitting the back of her head against the wood. "Ouch!"

Thessian was up in less than a second, placing his hand behind her head and rearranging the pillows so she would lean back without hurting herself.

She glanced at him with ambiguous feelings about what was happening. Why was the Imperial Prince in her bedchambers acting as her attendant? And where was Clayton?

Once Thessian sat back and smiled, she offered him a polite smile in return and perused the corners of her bedroom, looking for her shadow. Thessian said that Clayton had been busy while she was asleep.

"Is something wrong?" Thessian asked.

Clearing her throat, she wondered if she should ask the prince or wait for Ambrose to return. Would Thessian find her question odd?

"At least they didn't kill each other while I slept," she murmured under her breath as she reached for the glass and took small sips.

"What?" Thessian leaned in closer to her. "Are you feeling uncomfortable?"

She shook her head.

"Is my presence bothering you?"

"Of course not," she said immediately. "I'm very thankful for your concern and care. I'm sure you were worried about—"

"*You,*" he finished for her. "I was worried about you. Nothing else. Especially not about this kingdom."

Butterflies swarmed in her stomach. "Are you still mad?"

He frowned.

"I'm sure you are grateful to me for saving your life, but you were mad when I did, weren't you?"

He rubbed his chin. "How do you know me so well?"

"Your life is more important, so you shouldn't scold me. Let's move on and forget I was a tad reckless."

He arched an eyebrow and removed the glass from her hands. "Only if you promise you won't do this ever again."

"I wasn't the only one being reckless. You mingled with smugglers and joined them in a tavern."

"Innocent lives were at stake."

She stared at him in astonishment. "If you died, the— You can't die. You must become emperor."

"Not at the expense of the ones I care about."

"If it makes you feel better, I know I was foolish, but I would do it again."

"You were brave. Not foolish. Braver than many I know."

With a playful smile, she asked, "Am I forgiven, Your Highness?"

He took her hand in his. "You are, Emilia. I'll also make sure nothing bad will ever happen to you again."

A new wave of heat hit her like a wall of bricks. Removing her hand from his, she stumbled over her words. "S-someone might misunderstand our relationship if they come in and see you holding my hand."

"Does my touch displease you?"

She swallowed nervously. "That's not the point!"

"Anyone who dares to spread rumours about your honour will die by my blade," he assured her.

She waved her hands in panic. "No. No killing. It was a jest. I know you see me as one of your friends. You wouldn't hold my hand and worry about my life if you didn't see me as someone close." She swallowed her rising nerves and added, "I never knew what it was like to have a brother. My actual brothers bullied me and took pleasure in starving and humiliating me."

Thessian's face paled. "They starved and hurt you physically?"

She shrugged. "It's over now. They are dead and buried."

"I should have taken longer to kill them... What an atrocious family you had."

Despite the rage in his voice, Emilia couldn't help feeling pleased. "It would have been nice if you were my friend..." ...*In my previous life.*

"No one will ever hurt you again."

"I'm strong enough to protect myself. I have Ambrose and Lionhart. I have Clayton, and I have...you. I finally feel as if I belong somewhere. Maybe coming to this world was the best thing that has happened to me."

She lost her soft smile when Thessian's hand covered her forehead. "You don't seem feverish."

Pursing her lips tight, she scolded herself for talking too much.

She peeled his hand away. "I had a long dream before I woke up. A dream of another world where my friends weren't with me, and I missed them."

"I-we missed you, too. Everybody was concerned and kept busy, so they wouldn't go insane. Well, I'm not sure Clayton hasn't lost it."

"Why?"

He waved in dismissal. "We'll talk about that some other time."

Ambrose entered the room with a tray in her hands. "It's time to eat and then change clothes, Your Majesty." Walking to the opposite side of the bed, the head maid looked at the prince. "I have arranged for Your Highness' breakfast to be served in the dining hall. Please consider taking a relaxing bath beforehand."

Thessian narrowed his eyes at Ambrose but instead of calling her out on her behaviour, he grunted and got up.

"I'll be back in the afternoon." He adjusted his shirt. "Make sure Emilia does not leave her room. Call me if she disobeys."

Ambrose nodded.

"You answer to me, not him," Emilia protested.

"Not when Your Majesty's health is in question," Ambrose replied.

"All it took was two weeks for you to turn my personal maid on me," Emilia teased him.

"I'd never betray you," Ambrose pitched in with indignation.

Thessian's eyes lingered on Emilia's face. "You seem different."

"What do you mean?"

"Almost dying made you talk more, or perhaps you were always like this but hid your true self from me."

"Are you unhappy with anything I've said, Thessian?"

"I'm happy to know that you consider me a friend." Smiling, he turned around and waved. Shortly after, he paused and spoke over his shoulder. "I thank you for saving my life, Emilia. Next time, remember to never put yourself in danger on my account, or I'll be quite mad, indeed."

He strode out of the room.

Emilia grimaced at his threat while her heart squeezed painfully. In truth, she thought she could avoid the arrow and save him at the same time. Thessian was important to her and the continent's future. She had staked her survival on him.

How could I let him die?

A good man such as he deserved to live out the rest of his life with a beautiful wife and a litter of pretty children. He would care for his people and rule justly, and Emilia would be living her leisurely life away from the nobles and palace politics.

It was the perfect ending to a fantasy novel.

So why did the picture she painted make her feel lonely?

2
UNPLEASANT NEWS

THESSIAN

In his room, sitting on the edge of his bed, Thessian stared at the hand which not too long ago held Emilia's.

The girl who spent two weeks unconscious had awakened.

Never in his life had he felt so relieved as when their eyes met, and they shared everyday banter. Light was his heart and stress melted off his body. He managed to keep himself in check and not hug her out of sheer delight. With their size difference, he would probably crush rather than hug her.

The stuffiness in his chest dissipated, and he could finally breathe. Emilia had given him the Dante Kingdom and saved his life. She was extraordinary and a true friend. Although they had spent a short time together, he now knew he could trust her. Whatever she chose to do in the future, he would give her his full support.

Thessian owed her that much.

He was startled by the knock on his door.

Dame Cali announced her presence from the other side.

"Come in," he called.

Calithea entered his bedchambers and saluted him. "I came to report, Your Highness. I have completed the transfer of my duties as Guard Captain to Sir Jehan Wells. As of this moment, I can return to your side."

"Very good." Laurence and Ian's absence had caused quite a gap in the structure of the ranks among his knights. Calithea was the only one who could keep an eye on those at the camp and lead them in Thessian's absence. "Anything new to report?"

"I received word from our scout in the South. Despite the duke's execution and his son's and wife's escape to the Reyniel Kingdom, the draft for the army continues."

"Someone is paying a lot of gold to start a civil war," Thessian commented, balling his hands into fists. It was the worst-case scenario. He could no longer sit on his hands and wait for things to unfold. "Travel to camp and ready the men. The advance force will head for Marquess Rigal's territory come dawn."

"Are you planning on helping the marquess with border control?"

"Not yet. We will approach Duke Malette's territory without drawing too much attention. After all, during the trial, our camp was exposed and now we must move our forces to match the narrative. Otherwise, the nobles may suspect that we are not a mere band of mercenaries and question the Queen's legitimacy."

Dame Calithea's lips quirked at the corners. "I heard the good news. Her Majesty is awake and well."

"Not quite," he countered. "She has grown weak after the long sleep."

"I should visit her before I leave for camp. It may be a while before we see each other again."

"Good. Have Ronne on standby at the palace. Once I settle some personal matters, I will send a message and inform you of my plans. Dismissed."

Evening came, and Thessian headed to the Queen's room with a bottle from his personal collection to share with Emilia. His palms were sweaty. He had not been that nervous in years. Before leaving for the South, he needed answers to more questions than there were hours in a day. Alcohol was a good way to create a relaxed atmosphere, and it was Emilia's idea he shared his secret stash with her one day.

Instead of barging in, he informed the knights on duty of his wish to see her.

One of the knights knocked on the door, went inside, and came back with her permission.

Thessian entered Emilia's room.

She sat on her bed, dwarfed by the sheer size of it. The white bedding made her pale skin appear sickly and haunting.

On second thought, the alcohol may have been a bad idea...

Ambrose rose from her seat by the door and greeted Thessian with a respectful curtsy. "I will give you some privacy, Your Majesty, Your Highness." She slipped out of the room on feet as light as that of a trained assassin.

Emilia beamed at him upon spotting the bottle he held at his side. "Is that what I think it is?"

"Indeed." He marched towards the bed and offered her the bottle. "Though, I am in two minds about giving you alcohol in your current state."

Emilia's eyes twinkled as she gave the bottle a good study. "Oh, I have dreamed of a day I could taste the alcohol you make, Your Highness."

"Please speak casually like you did this morning. We are more than close enough, especially after you saved my life."

"Thessian," she said with a smile that made her appear her age.

Emilia was young, intelligent, and eye-catching. No doubt,

many noblemen will woo her after her coronation ceremony. That was not something he needed to worry about. Her spymaster, no doubt, would dig up any and all dirt on her suitors and have them scampering away like the pesky rodents they were.

He did not wish to sour her festive mood, but now was as good a time as any. "I plan to leave the palace for a while."

"Are you heading out to inspect your camp?"

"I am planning on marching the advance forces to Marquess Rigal's territory. It will allow me to assess Duke Malette's lands on the way there."

She laid the bottle beside her and knotted her hands in her lap. "You are leaving?"

"Yes. If I do not quash the budding rebellion, it will be harder to put a stop to once the men are trained and equipped with weapons. I plan to find out who is backing this treasonous plot and put a stop to it."

"You can't!" She raised her voice at him which was quite uncharacteristic for her.

He noticed her hands. They began to shake as she clutched the quilt. With a quick apology, he sat on the edge of her bed and gently took hold of her hand. "Why not? Did you see something in your visions?"

She bit her lip so hard that he worried she would cause injury.

"Emilia?"

With tears rimming her eyes, she met his stern gaze. "Do not leave. Let Dame Cali take care of it, or bring Sir Laurence back. You cannot go! Never!"

"Why not?"

"I fear you may die like you did in my vision."

Words failed him. Thessian had never been afraid of death. Yet, hearing about his approaching demise had him pause. "How do I die in your vision?"

She looked down, and her tears wet her strained knuckles. "You died when you left to quell the rebellion in the South. A trap was arranged for you and your men. The enemy set fire to your supplies, and you were forced to purchase food and drink from the local inns and taverns. You were all poisoned with an untraceable poison."

There was no need to question her further. She had seen his death in such detail that it could not be a mere dream or fantasy she created.

"I will be careful and have the supplies better guarded. I will carry food and drink with me just in case." He lifted her tear-streaked face. His heart gave a squeeze at how fragile Emilia looked. "Will that ease your worry?"

She sniffled. "You must travel separately from your men and hide your identity. Promise me!"

"I promise."

She carefully pulled his hand away and removed any traces of her tears with a handkerchief she hid under her pillow. "I worry that is not enough. After my coronation, I will travel to meet you."

"You would be leaving your castle open for an attack."

There was no room for argument. Determination lit a fire in her. "I will ask someone to act as my double. The nobles can easily be handled by Lord Baudelaire and Sir Rowell. If there is a need for a meeting with me, I could have my double act in my stead. At a distance, no one should be able to tell a difference. After all, I have not had my coming-of-age ceremony nor attended any social gatherings."

"Emilia, it could be dangerous. What if you get hurt because of me a second time?" The stuffy feeling in his chest returned. "What if you die?"

"I chose this path, Thessian. I will make you emperor and live to tell the tale no matter what." She picked up the bottle he brought earlier and uncorked it with a single motion. Taking a swig from the bottle's throat, she beamed at him and offered him a drink. "Let us not allow this wonderful alcohol to go to waste while we bicker."

He accepted her offering and took a few mouthfuls. The sweet citrus undertones of liquor had mixed well with the high-quality honey from the Empire. "I believe we have two weeks' worth of questions to catch up on."

Her good mood speedily recovered. Taking the bottle from him, she said, "I will go first. Why did you send Laurence away?"

"That is not a personal question, Emilia."

"It is. It will allow me to understand your thinking."

He had no will to argue with a patient. "It was partly a punishment for the fire my men caused under Laurence's supervision and the need to confirm something."

"What did you want to confirm?"

"Isn't that a different question?"

She pouted. "I do believe it should be considered as part of the first question as you have only given me half of an answer."

He laughed at her readiness to argue her point. "I have encountered a beastman in Redford, and Laurence happened upon a beastchild not long after. I thought there may be more of them. They can manipulate monsters and beasts around them. If their numbers are great, they could pose a threat. That is why I sent Laurence to find them. Whether beastmen become our enemies or allies is up to them."

The slight curve of the corners of the lips showed her approval.

He watched her drinking his liquor as if it was water. "Why catch an arrow for me? It was foolish and dangerous."

"No more dangerous than infiltrating a band of smugglers."

"I can handle a few smugglers. Most of them were non-combatants."

She tightened her grip on the bottle's slim neck. "I believe it is my turn. Inevitably, you must marry one day. Do you have someone in mind who could help you get the Crown Prince's position?"

He pondered her words as he rubbed his jawline. The noble ladies of the Empire were too delicate for him. If he had to marry someone, she needed to be strong, decisive, good at management, and able to defend herself when thrust into dangerous situations. Not like he would permit anything to happen to his wife. After the wedding, his first action would be to assign a whole regiment of knights to protect her.

"I have no one in mind." Thessian retrieved the bottle from her, allowing another three gulps to travel down his throat. He wiped his mouth with the back of his hand. "Why did you choose to support me to become emperor? Why not Cain or Kyros?"

"You are the only option where I survive," she admitted without reservations. "Prince Cain would never trust an unwanted princess from another nation. There was nothing I could offer him where he would not find me suspicious and kill me."

Her tongue seemed to loosen with strong liquor. He had omitted that a couple of sips of his alcohol could reduce a man of high tolerance to a bumbling fool in a matter of minutes. Due to years of drinking this brew, and Thessian's large build, he could consume half a bottle before he could feel its effects. Emilia was a different matter.

"Prince Kyros cannot take the crown while you are alive. That should prevent him from murdering the emperor…" Her speech slowed, and she sluggishly blinked. Her gaze became unfocused. She smiled widely upon seeing his face and cupped his cheeks. Squishing them together, she muttered, "You were my favourite character, Thessian. I fell in love with your bravery and honest heart. How could I let you die? You're such a cutie-patootie with 'ose kishable lips and wondarpul abs."

"Wha—"

He did not get the chance to finish as her eyelids fluttered shut, and she swayed.

Thessian caught her head and gently lowered it onto the pillow behind her.

As her drunken words replayed in his mind, his blood drained from his face and a heavy boulder settled in the pit of his stomach.

Is Kyros planning to commit treason?

To verify his conclusion, he wanted to shake her awake. But her peaceful expression stopped him in his tracks. Emilia said that as long as Thessian remained alive, Kyros would not go ahead with his plan to kill their father. With a heavy breath to calm his speeding heart, he decided to question her once he returned from the South.

Sparing one last glance at her angelic face, he asked out loud, "Just how much of the future are you keeping from me, Emilia?"

3
JOURNEY TO THE SOUTH

THESSIAN

That night, **Thessian could not sleep** and left his bedchambers early to visit the stables.

The sky lightened from the deepest shades of black and blue to the warming tones of purple and orange. As he walked through the quiet halls of Emilia's palace, he realised that he had grown fond of the kingdom and its people.

The people who surrounded Emilia were all colourful characters, full of life and grit. There was no better way to put it other than—they represented the best of the kingdom's citizens. They were the allies he wanted to welcome into the Empire. But he could not rush things, not until Emilia had a strong grip on the necks of the nobles in Dante.

The prince passed the guards, who acknowledged him with a

salute. Thessian would be away for weeks. Too many matters needed to be resolved in the South. He could only hope that nothing else happened during his absence that would shake the palace and its queen.

Thessian emerged outside. Dirt and small stones crunched under his boots. He inhaled a crisp breath of air, which pushed back his tiredness. Not long after, he arrived at his destination, only to spot his young scout sleeping with his back against the stables' doors and his mouth wide open.

"What are you doing here this early, Ronne?" Thessian asked.

The boy's eyes blinked open. Upon seeing Thessian, he jumped upright and groaned. Massaging his forehead, Ronne replied, "Greetings, Your Highness! I came to keep watch over your horse."

"Were you doing so with your eyes closed?"

Ronne's face turned as red as a ripe apple. "I-I may have fallen asleep."

Thessian patted his subordinate on the shoulder. "Are the horses ready for our departure?"

"Of course. I made certain to clean, feed, and water them, Your Highness."

"What of the stablekeeper?"

Ronne opened the door and pointed to an older man who was sleeping on a pile of hay with an empty tankard of ale at his feet. "He is indisposed, sir."

Thessian sighed and pulled out a sealed letter from his coat's inner pocket. He had dressed down to a mercenary's attire to keep attention away from himself. "Send a messenger to camp with this letter. It is for Calithea's eyes only."

"Yes, Your Highness." Ronne took the letter and ran off.

Before he could enter the stable, Thessian felt a chill travelling down his spine. He looked around but could not see anyone. Yet, there was no mistaking the unnerving feeling of being watched.

Grabbing the hilt of his sword, he drew it out of its scabbard. "Come out at once!"

The trees on his left shook as a figure clad in dark clothes jumped down.

Thessian narrowed his eyes on the unwelcome guest. "What are you doing here, Lord Armel?"

"Taking a nap?" Clayton responded matter-of-factly as he approached the prince.

"Somehow, I doubt that."

The assassin smirked. "Very well. I came to heal your thigh."

"And why would you go out of your way to do that?"

"My master nearly died protecting Your Highness. It must mean you are important to her plans. Therefore, if you leave here in top form, it would give her less to worry about."

Thessian sheathed his sword and crossed his arms. "You care a great deal about your master."

Clayton did not reply and waited expectantly.

Feeling a twitch in his eye, Thessian decided to avoid confrontation so early in the morning and sat on a barrel near the stables. "I hope I do not need to take my trousers off for this."

Clayton grimaced and sauntered over. "There will never come a day when I would willingly want that."

"Then you may begin."

With a shake of his head, Clayton hovered his hand over the prince's thigh. A golden light emanated from his palm, and Thessian could feel the tightness in his muscles melting away. Good thing he did not use his last healing potion. It would expedite the healing process of his thigh, but nothing could beat a healing mage's magic or a miracle of a high-ranking clergy member.

Clayton straightened up and stepped away. "I have finished. If you'll excuse me."

"Take care of Emilia while I am away."

"I intend to."

"And I suggest you do not let your feelings cloud your judgement," Thessian said with a cold undertone. "She may need to marry one day, for political reasons or because she simply does not return your feelings. It is best to keep a distance."

Clayton's expression remained blank, but Thessian knew that he hit a nerve as frost began to form on the assassin's shoulders and boots. "May your journey be long and fruitful."

Thessian watched Clayton's retreating form. He did not mean for his words to hurt the man. After all, he had been through an unexpected heartbreak and simply did not wish it on another. What he said was the bitter truth. One day, he and Emilia may need to sacrifice their hearts for political power or their ultimate goal. Such was the fate of those who wished to hold great power in their mortal hands.

It is a matter of time…

When Ronne returned from dispatching a messenger, they secured their belongings to the horses and rode out of Newburn. The streets bustled with life as people prepared for another busy day of restorations and work. He hoped the Queen would recover quickly and take charge. No doubt there were still spies hiding in her proximity.

Outside the city, Thessian halted his horse and peered over his shoulder. Over the past month, he came across many revelations and secrets. Some of them, he did not wish to know. A chance meeting with a foreign princess forced him to doubt his family and unearthed dangerous plots for the Empire's crown. Life always found a way to throw boulders in his path.

"Did you forget something, Your Highness?" Ronne asked.

"No. Let's go."

The prince secured his hood over his head and nudged his horse into a sprint in the direction of Countess Morel's territory. He had instructed Calithea to take the advance force through Baron Niel's and Count Alard's lands to reach the South. Although the baron was on Thessian's side for the coup, Count Alard remained a variable. If the count stalled Calithea at the border to Marquess Rigal's territory, that would leave Thessian unguarded for an extended period. Until they regrouped, the prince had to tread carefully and keep his identity a secret. There was also the matter of the poisoner who killed Thessian in Emilia's vision.

Without a doubt, he had enough on his mind to make the journey to the next town a short one.

By nightfall, they reached an inn on the side of a well-travelled road. Thessian's muscles ached all over, especially his legs. All he wanted was a meal and a comfortable bed to fall on. Hopefully, there were no rodents or bedbugs.

Unlike Laurence, who would be complaining about the dreary aesthetic of The Rusty Chalice Inn, Ronne was a quiet lad. He never once grumbled about being tired or hungry. If prolonged, such behaviour could be a concern and a problem for their mission.

They secured their horses to the posts and took their belongings with them. "From now on, I will be your older brother, Ronne. Call me Theo."

"Understood."

"You need to relax your speech too."

"I-I'll do my best, b-big brother?"

Thessian chuckled and ruffled the boy's mess of brown curls. "Come along."

Stepping into the weather-worn inn, Thessian was once more reminded that they had left Newburn and entered Countess Morel's lands. From his briefings on the Dante noble houses, House Morel extorted their farmers and workers through heavy taxation while making deals with merchants and other nobles.

The low ceiling felt claustrophobic as the tip of his hood almost touched it.

Uneven floorboards creaked under their weight with each step they made towards the busy barmaid. Aside from a group of four men at one table who seemed to be hired muscle, there was another table full of merchants.

At the bar, a row of patrons happily chatted away about the long day at work, some of them women.

The strong smell of ale, wood smoke from the stone fireplace, and the roast was enough to awaken the starving beast in Thessian's stomach.

A growl sounded behind him.

Thessian glanced at Ronne as the boy covered his stomach with his hands and gave the prince a sheepish smile.

Although Thessian would kill for a roast chicken, he had to remain vigilant. There existed poisons that even silverware could not detect. He was not about to try his luck.

Resting his elbow on the counter at the bar, Thessian waited until the barmaid came over.

She looked him up and down with a measuring stare. "Evenin'. What can aye do fer ye?"

"My brother and I are looking for a room."

She bent to one side to look past Thessian's hulking frame. Spotting Ronne, she asked, "He didn' kidnap ye or anythin'?"

Ronne's hands shot up. "Big brother would never do that!"

The barmaid finally smiled, which revealed her yellow teeth. "Aite den. One room. How 'bout hot soup? Made it meself this morn."

The boy's stomach let out another audible complaint.

Thessian replied, "One bowl of soup."

"Hav' a seat. Aye'll bring out a bowl fer tha striplin'." She shuffled away.

Looking around, Thessian selected a seat closer to the merchants. As his posterior touched the uneven planks of wood that were hammered together, he had to stabilise the chair that wobbled beneath him by grabbing the table.

Ronne had less trouble with his small size. He sat down and traced the old knife lines on the table's surface.

Thessian was not good at small talk. He often left the trifling conversations to Laurence. With a tired mind and body, he did not have much to offer to clear the obvious awkwardness between them. "Did Cali inform you that we finally took care of the man who hurt you and Renne?"

Ronne scratched the back of his neck. "She did."

"Do you feel better?"

The boy shrugged. "I don't remember much from those days, but Renne does. She never forgave that man for what he did to us and the rest of the children. She sometimes has nightmares and wakes up screaming."

Thessian reached over the table and patted Ronne on the head. "She will get better knowing that he is no longer out there."

"I hope so." Ronne looked down at his slender hands and asked, "But is revenge truly the answer? I have seen soldiers consumed by their hatred, and I don't want that for Renne."

The prince knew exactly what Ronne was talking about. People who lost close comrades or siblings to war often felt the need to take their anger out on others. Often, that anger was misdirected towards the innocent. Yet, in this case, Julio Grande paid for his crimes with his life. In Thessian's mind, Grande got off easy. He should have been drawn and quartered in a town square, so he would know how much suffering he had caused to others.

A bowl of soup was placed in front of Ronne by the barmaid along with a few slices of rye bread. She placed a hand on the boy's shoulder. "Yer quite glum fer yer youth."

"He must be hungry after the long journey," Thessian offered. "Why did you assume I kidnapped him when we arrived?"

The barmaid's face fell. "Tis been hard 'round these parts fer younglings. Mah brotha's uncle's cousin's boy went missin' two weeks prior. Naw one saw or heard nothin'. Been happenin' all 'round the smaller towns 'n' villages, I'm told."

"That is quite worrisome," he replied with concern in his voice.

"Aye. Not much we can do." She lowered her voice to a whisper and leant in. "Tha countess doesn' care fer tha commonfolk, so tha guards do nuthin'."

"Ah." Thessian nodded. Talking badly of nobility could make the barmaid's head roll should anyone affiliated with the nobles overhear her. To remain on the side of caution, he did not pursue the matter further. "Thank you for the meal."

"That'll be twenty coppers."

Thessian eyed her. "Quite expensive for a bit of soup."

"Ye look like ye can pay it."

"I've got holes in my coat and boots."

"Made 'em yerself, I suspect."

Thessian chuckled. "You've got a sharp eye."

"That aye do."

He made a mental note to write Emilia about the situation in Countess Morel's territory. The Queen could put some pressure on the countess to look into the issue of the missing youths.

After he paid her for the room and food, she asked, "Where ye headed?"

"South, in search of work."

"Judgin' by yer weapons, ye can fight. Best head ta Garlia den. Plenty of opportunities fer mercenaries der."

"Thank you for the suggestion."

Another patron raised their pitcher in the air and shouted, "More ale!"

With a huff and a grumble, she hurried away to attend to the needy customer.

Thessian patiently waited until Ronne finished his food before they headed for their lodgings.

On their way up the stairs, one of the patrons called out to Thessian, "My good sir, could you spare a moment of your time?"

"What is this about?" Thessian asked, stopping on the first step.

Under a woolly grey cloak, the man wore a red and brown cotte decorated with silver buttons and a fur collar. His leather girdle sported a metal buckle with an embossed lion biting its tail. Even his trousers seemed to be made of the finest wool and dyed black. Thessian concluded that the man in question was a wealthy merchant.

The man inclined his head in greeting and pulled down his fur hat. "My name is Delphine Leferve, and I work for The Emerald Swan Merchant Company. My colleagues and I are travelling to Garlia to present our goods to Countess Morel and require more guards to protect our caravan."

"What about those men at the inn?"

"They work for us, but we've received a worrisome letter and fear they may not be enough."

Travelling with a group of merchants would be a good way to hide Thessian's identity rather than acting on his own. Yet, if the goods they were carrying were expensive, they would be a target for bandits along the way. Protecting them could endanger his life more than necessary. The offer before him was a double-edged sword.

"We will pay you handsomely for your trouble," Delphine added with a silent plea in his tone.

"I will discuss this with my brother and give my response to you tomorrow, sir."

Bowing his head, Delphine sighed and put his hat back on. "Our caravan will be leaving after the morning meal. Please let us know by then."

Thessian nodded and watched the merchant ambling away. He turned to Ronne, who was a few steps above him on the stairs.

"Have you any information on The Emerald Swan?"

Ronne thought for a moment. "I heard some noblewomen in Newburn mentioning them. They supply luxury fabrics and jewels to nobles who can afford them. Someone named Marchioness Durand is one of their regular customers and this has annoyed some duchess to no end."

There was only one duchess in Dante—Duchess Feilitze Malette. Although she had lost her title and lands to the Crown after her husband's high treason charges, if she was anything like her husband, she would not let the matter rest. The merchant company might have a lot of information on the internal politics of the kingdom that even Lionhart was not privy to.

"We will travel with the merchants," Thessian announced and scaled the stairs.

"Yes, Brother!" Ronne ran after him.

4
EYES OF TRUTH

EMILIA

After a day of forced rest, Emilia felt much better, except for the slight hangover. Hands down, handmade alcohol by Thessian lived up to its name. The taste and aroma were divine.

Too bad she could not recall much of what they had discussed.

At least, she no longer walked like a newborn foal when making her way across her bedchambers.

Benjamin had visited her when she woke up and advised her to stay in bed for two more days.

Emilia refused.

She had been away from her office for two weeks. Just imagining the sheer volume of paperwork on her desk gave her chills. No matter what, she had to finish writing up proposals for the nobility to back and fund. The country needed to be brought out of the Dark Ages and into an era where the commoners got an education and could contribute to the country's improvements. The health and safety regulations for workers needed to be created and sturdy sewage systems had to be put in place in cities.

The most important proposal was personal hygiene for the commoners. They could not afford expensive soaps or healing from a priest and often got their wounds infected. She did not want a plague on her hands. To strike before the problem arose, she needed to find a way to produce soap for cheap and in large quantities.

Emilia also grew concerned about the Dragon's Heart gems. The mine would be depleted in a year or two and, with the recent trouble at the mine, she felt the need to investigate it. As she could not order Sir Laurence directly, she hoped he would notice her hint from the letter of introduction she gave him.

"Your mind is quite occupied this morning, Your Majesty," Ambrose commented as she brushed Emilia's hair.

"I was thinking about work."

Ambrose's mouth formed into a disapproving line. "The royal physician suggested Your Majesty rests. I may not be a doctor or a priest, but I feel that Your Majesty is yet to fully recover."

"We both know I cannot leave the throne empty for much longer. Instead, give me a report on the mood at the palace."

"Sir Rowell and I have completed a thorough clean of the staff and removed anyone who was suspected as a spy with Mister Lionhart's help. Those who stepped out of line in any way were reprimanded."

Emilia nodded. A clean palace was key to secret-keeping. "I need you to speak with Sir Jehan and recruit more guards for the palace. I cannot continue to rely on Count Baudelaire's men." Mentioning his name made her recall the promise of a duel between Sir Jehan and Sir Regis Lacroix. "Did the duel between Vice Captain and Jehan take place while I was asleep?"

"It did, Your Majesty. Sir Jehan won through experience." Ambrose finished tying the pale blue ribbons in Emilia's hair and stepped back. "Would you like to wear jewellery for your meeting with His Holiness?"

QUEEN OF HEARTS

"No. He does not strike me as a man who revels in lavishness."

"You may be right. During his stay here, His Holiness has not made a single request and ate what was brought to his bedchambers. He even healed the knights who got wounded during training."

"Have Pope Valerian and Sir Erenel acted suspiciously in any way?"

"I have the servants keeping an eye on them yet nothing of importance has been reported."

Emilia got off the stool and swayed a little on her heels. Shaking off the dizzy spell, she smiled at the nervous Ambrose.

"I am fine," Emilia assured her head maid.

Ambrose bit her lower lip and bowed her head. "I will escort you to the Drawing Room where breakfast will be served for your private audience with the Pope."

Emilia made her way through the familiar halls at a much slower pace than usual. She did not want to push her luck and faint. A round of healing from Clayton would be of help. For some reason, he did not appear since she woke up yesterday.

Over her shoulder, Emilia asked, "Have you seen Lord Armel?"

Ambrose was quiet for a long while, which got Emilia curious. She turned to find her maid had gone pale in the face.

Emilia rushed over and took hold of Ambrose's shaking hands. "What is the matter? Did something happen to him?"

"Lord Armel is perfectly fine."

"Then why are you so frightened?"

Looking around, Ambrose made sure no one was close enough to overhear her whispered words. "With each passing day that you were unconscious, Lord Armel became more and more terrifying."

"How bad could it be?"

"He took charge of torturing the smugglers for information, Your Majesty." Ambrose clammed up again as if speaking out would cause her head to roll.

"Go on."

Genuine fear reflected in Ambrose's large eyes. "You do not understand, Your Majesty. That was no simple torture. He brought them to the brink of death only to heal them and repeat the process. Screams from the dungeons could be heard all the way to the palace. They only stopped the day before you opened your eyes."

Emilia's empty stomach churned. Good thing she had not had her meal yet or she would have wasted it. From what Isobelle told her in the past, Clayton had a terrible childhood and was taught to kill and slaughter since he was a child. They were taught that empathy was a weakness. "What about the prince? How did he react?"

"His Highness was full of silent fury. No one dared approach him as they felt their lives would be cut short. Even Dame Cali walked on eggshells during her reporting."

Somehow, that answer pleased Emilia. "And what did they find out about the serpentine powder?"

"It would be best to hear it directly from His Highness or Lord Armel."

Emilia gave Ambrose's hands a final squeeze and let go. "Let us hurry. We cannot let my life's saviour wait too long."

Ambrose bobbed her head in agreement.

***

In the Drawing Room, Emilia was met with a curious sight.

Pope Valerian was leaning back in his chair, and Sir Erenel's face was close enough for them to kiss. The knight's hands gripped the armrests as he inched closer.

"Do not mind me," Emilia announced with a smile.

Sir Erenel jumped away from Valerian. "This is not what it looks like, Your Majesty!"

The Pope, too, waved his hands in front of him. "Sir Erenel was trying to see if I had something in my eye."

Great excuse.

"Worry not, I would support you two even if you were together. Love has no bounds where I'm from." She wanted to slap her forehead when she realised what she said. "I mean, it should not matter."

Valerian's eyes were full of curiosity she could not place. He got up and inclined his head in greeting. "I greet Her Majesty the

Queen of Dante. May the blessings of Luminos guide you."

When he mentioned the God's name, she cringed. Unlike every book she read where people would forget their meeting with the divine the next morning, her memory was intact. She even recalled the tedious promise to pray once a month.

Emilia politely recited the religious greeting. Taking a seat at the small table, she motioned for Valerian to join her.

He did so with a smile that would have melted her heart had she not heard a sobering tale about Clayton's torturing methods earlier. "I wish to speak with you privately, Your Holiness."

Sir Erenel's posture stiffened. "Your Holiness, you cannot!"

Valerian lifted his hand without looking at his escort. "Leave."

With a low bow, Sir Erenel grumbled, "As you command."

Emilia dismissed all servants after they finished serving the food and told Ambrose to wait outside as well.

Alone with Pope Valerian, she picked up a cup of her rose tea and took a tentative sip. She peeked at him over the rim, noting how relaxed he was in her presence. Instead of his cardinal garb, he wore a black linen shirt and white trousers that seemed tailored to fit his form perfectly.

"May I ask what it is you wished to discuss?" he probed.

Emilia set her teacup on the saucer. *I have to get it over and done with.* "You may not believe me, but I have a message from Luminos. The goddess wants you to stop praying so often. It is inconveniencing her..."

His eyes widened briefly, and he burst out laughing.

"I know this sounds far-fetched—"

His expression sobered. "Not at all. I believe you."

Her brows scrunched together. *Is he crazy? Who would believe such a story from a person they've just met?* "May I ask why?"

"You have a trustworthy face."

Emilia could not hold in her laugh. *Royalty and honesty do not go together.*

Valerian drank his tea quietly. "I am more surprised by the comment that Luminos is a female. If you could give me a description of the Goddess, I will propose to the cardinals a change to the statues."

She was at a loss for words once again. *Does his naive belief in what I tell him have something to do with being a Pope? That can't be it. He seemed cold and decisive when it came to punishing Bishop Lagarde. A man like that is no fool.*

"I did not see her true form."

He simply nodded.

Emilia finished her drink and sighed inwardly. "Your Holiness..."

"Valerian."

"Valerian, why did you heal me?"

He tilted his head to one side in confusion. "Was I not supposed to?"

"I am thankful for the healing miracle and will find a way to pay you for it, but—"

"Worry not about repayment, Your Majesty. I simply did not wish to miss my chance to go on a date with you."

Emilia froze. She had completely forgotten about their supposed date. "Why are you so eager to be with me?"

"Has Your Majesty never looked in the mirror? I think the reason is obvious."

Emilia raised a brow. She knew she was quite beautiful. Yet, that could not possibly be the whole truth. There were more than enough attractive women all over the continent who would jump at the chance to spend their day with His Holiness. As a man, he had no problems with his manners or appearance. His status was equal to that of a king. And if he could marry, as he claimed, then he was definitely on the most wanted bachelors list for noblewomen.

"You still doubt my intentions, I see." There was no denying the undeserved affection reflected in his warm green eyes. "Very well, I will tell you why I wish to court you."

She unconsciously leaned in.

"Since I was a child, Luminos has bestowed a blessing upon me called 'The Eyes of Truth'. It is an ability where I can easily tell truth from lies, which was the reason why I believed you when you spoke of the Goddess."

Once again, Emilia was stumped. She never read any of that in the original novel. As a character, Valerian never made an appearance or dealt with the Hellion's Imperial Family directly, which was why she knew next to nothing about him or his backstory.

"You wish to date me because I haven't lied to you?"

"It is because the moment I saw you, Your Majesty, I wanted to make you mine."

She frowned. *What kind of a cheesy pickup line is that?* "I am flattered by your feelings, Valerian, but I cannot return them."

"I wanted to give you the chance to get to know me through a couple of outings, but if I must, I could take you by force to the City of Light, Emilia."

All affection she may have had for the Pope was gone in an instant. "Should that happen, I fear you may find your city on fire one day."

"At least it would live up to its name. On more than one occasion, I have contemplated burning it all down to eradicate the sinners."

A chill crawled up her spine. He was serious. "I do not believe the Pope has the right to interfere with the Royal Family of Dante."

"I could proclaim you are the Saintess of Luminos and have people flocking to you day and night. The City of Light would become your sole refuge from believers and the members of the clergy. After all, a person who can speak to the Goddess is invaluable to the Church."

She stifled the urge to punch him by balling her hands in her lap. One word from Valerian could ruin all of her plans of helping Thessian become emperor. She could not let that happen.

Should I ask Clayton to assassinate Valerian when he leaves my territory?

The Pope left his seat and made his way to stand beside her. He lifted her hand to his lips and planted a soft kiss on her knuckles, just above her signet ring. "I hope you will reconsider. There is also your coronation ceremony…"

Emilia yanked her hand out of his loose hold and wiped it with a handkerchief. She stood from her chair and barely reached his shoulders at her full height.

Craning her neck, she held her ground and spoke with all the confidence she could muster. "If you dare threaten me again, I will ask Luminos to take your blessing and divine powers away." *Whether the Goddess will comply is a different matter.* "You will lose everything."

She could not tell what he was thinking. His expression remained a perfectly sculpted mask, which unnerved her.

Finally, Valerian's smile returned. Instead of warming her heart, it made her feet grow cold as if she dipped them in ice water.

"I wish to have you even more now, my lovely saintess."

5
QUEEN CECILIA

EMILIA

Emilia squared her shoulders. She would not be put down by Valerian, even if he could easily be a model or an actor in her former life.

"I am not an object Your Holiness can possess. I ask you kindly to step aside. This meeting is over."

His green eyes raked her stubborn expression before he gave her another cryptic smile and moved out of her way. "I would like for you to keep our agreement, Emilia. One date for my support of your coronation."

Emilia clenched her jaw so tight that her head hurt.

Giving up a day of her life to get closer to her goal was nothing. What she did not like was the feeling of being manipulated by the leader of the Church of the Holy Light. Before she could decide which side Valerian was truly on, she needed to learn as much as she could about him.

"One date, Your Holiness. I will choose the time and place and have the servants inform you."

"Are we back to being formal with each other?" He appeared slightly disappointed.

"Please enjoy your meal." As an afterthought, she added, "Thank you for healing me and saving my life."

She tried to walk to the door, and her legs gave out.

Valerian caught her with ease. The heat of his body permeated the soft material of the dress she wore.

Using his muscular arms for support, she steadied herself and lifted her head. "I must have tripped over some—" She stopped mid-sentence. The worry in his eyes could not be faked.

What is his true persona? A villainous, calculating Pope who wants to own me or the kind-hearted man helping me?

She looked away. "You may let go of me."

Reluctantly, he separated from her and stepped back.

With a courteous bow, he added, "I look forward to hearing from you, my saintess."

Emilia made her way to the door with care. Each step became more unstable than the last as strange emotions welled inside of her.

Why does Luminos need a good-looking Pope? Why couldn't he be an old man with rows of wrinkles and bad breath? Or is she testing me by throwing handsome men at me left, right, and centre?

After succeeding in her escape from the Drawing Room, she saw Ambrose outside the door. She turned to the Pope's escort knight, who seemed eager to get back to his guard duty. "You may go in now, Sir Erenel."

The knight bowed his head to her and hurried into the Drawing Room.

Emilia started making her way to her office at a slow pace with Ambrose trailing a couple of feet behind.

Maybe pushing myself to work isn't the best idea.

Her palace was not small by any means. Getting from one end to the other could take thirty minutes at a decent pace. With the way her limbs were beginning to tire after a short stroll, she briefly considered retiring to her bedchambers.

An image of her buried in a sea of paperwork came to mind, and her desire to relax for one more day dissipated in an instant.

In a quiet corridor, Ambrose asked, "Was your conversation with the Pope fruitful?"

Emilia stopped and whipped around. She grasped Ambrose by the wrists. "Do you think Pope Valerian could be bipolar?"

Ambrose scrunched her brows in incertitude.

Emilia went on. "He is decent and kind one moment and the next he talks of taking me to the City of Light as a hostage."

Ambrose's jaw fell open. "He threatened Your Majesty?"

"A little. I do not think he will act on it."

"I will inform Lord Armel and Lionhart to—"

Emilia shook her head. "Clayton cannot find out that Valerian wants to go on a date with me."

"Why not, Your Majesty?"

Emilia was about to speak but no words left her mouth.

That's right. Why not? Why do I want to keep my meetings with Valerian a secret from my shadow?

Clayton had members of House Escariot working in her castle. There was a high chance that her meeting with the Pope had reached his ears.

"Ambrose, I think I am feeling faint." Emilia touched her forehead for effect and pretended to sway. That was the surest way to have Ambrose forget about the conversation long enough to reach Emilia's office.

Ambrose's eyes grew wide, and she asked with a nervous edge in her voice, "Shall I assist you to your bedchambers?"

"Please assist me to the office, and summon Sir Rowell."

"Of course, Your Majesty."

Ambrose gently took hold of Emilia's right arm and guided her through the palace to the Queen's office. They received some concerned looks from the maids. Soon after, they had a handful of guards trailing after them, the royal physician, Sir Rowell, and even Antonio—the guard Lionhart had assigned to Emilia.

Her dramatic display turned into a parade of concern for her well-being. Not that she could blame them. After all, she awoke from a coma not too long ago.

Finally, taking a seat on a comfortable sofa in her office, Emilia dismissed everyone except for Benjamin and Sir Rowell. On their way out, she also noted the long adoring stare Antonio had for Ambrose, who treated the young man as if he were part of the furniture.

Looks like I missed out on a lot of interesting gossip while I slept.

Benjamin bowed his head. "May I take a look at your pulse, Your Majesty?"

Emilia sighed and offered her arm.

The physician stumbled over nothing as he rushed to her side to check her vitals, but Sir Rowell caught him before Benjamin's face could meet with the carpet.

"Sir Rowell, it has been a while," she said with a smile.

The head butler's usually serious face stretched into a warm smile. "I am pleased to see you out of bed, Your Majesty. I and the rest of the servants have missed you greatly."

The physician tutted. "Her Majesty should stay in bed! She has not fully recovered from her long slumber."

"I am fine. Sir Rowell, summon Lord Armel and Lionhart. I wish to get their reports on the smugglers and the events that took place while I was indisposed."

The butler inclined his head. "Yes, Your Majesty."

"Oh, and I would like for you to make time in my schedule for a...courting."

The two old men stared at her in disbelief.

Emilia nearly rolled her eyes. "Rather than courting, it is more of an outing with His Holiness." They did not seem impressed with her explanation, so she added, "As a token of my appreciation for healing me with a miracle."

Sir Rowell nodded. "I will inform Sir Jehan to make arrangements."

"There is no need for many knights," Emilia interjected. "We will be travelling in disguise. Tell Sir Regis Lacroix that he is to escort me on that day."

The butler seemed taken aback. "The Vice Captain, Your Majesty?"

"Everyone would expect the Queen to be escorted by the Guard Captain. Sir Regis is not well known around Newburn yet. To keep a low profile, I need someone like him."

At the same time, she could test Regis' loyalty to her. She could not afford to use him in dangerous situations if he would abandon his duty midway. Duke Malette's trial ended, and Bishop Lagarde paid for his crimes at the hands of Sir Erenel. Aside from Malette's family, who wanted Emilia's head, she hoped no one else was plotting her immediate demise.

Benjamin finished his checks and blew out a sigh of relief as he sluggishly straightened his back.

Pushing his glasses up the length of his nose, the physician said, "There is nothing wrong with Your Majesty. You should take it easy for the next couple of days, *as I have mentioned before*. But, seeing as Your Majesty is eager to disregard my advice, please do not overstrain yourself. Remember, no more than four hours of work a day." He turned to the head butler. "Make sure Her Majesty takes plenty of breaks."

Emilia peeked at her desk. Three thick stacks of parchments were resting on top similar to the three peaks of the Hollow Mountains.

Four hours a day will not make a dent in that...

Benjamin planted his hands on his old hips, and said sternly, "No more than four hours, Your Majesty!"

She raised her hands in defence. "I was not planning on doing more than that."

"Thank you, Your Majesty." Benjamin bowed his head and excused himself.

Sir Rowell had a relaxed smile on his face, which made Emilia curious.

"Are you finding this amusing, Sir Rowell?"

"I am pleased to see Your Majesty opening up to the servants. I still remember the first night you descended from your tower to escape its confines."

A frown creased Emilia's forehead. She left her tower in the morning to speak with the servants and deal with the events following the coup.

Unless...

"You knew all along?" Her voice came out frosty.

The memories of a nine-year-old child, who feared the world, were hard to shake. She was once a nameless, abused, and tortured princess. Maids did not like touching her for fear of getting cursed. Her brothers hated her because Emilia caused the former queen's death. Escaping her prison took every shred of bravery she could muster. Yet, the head butler knew everything, and not once did he say anything or help her in any way.

Her nails dug into her palms when she balled her hands in her lap. "Did you report this to King Gilebert?"

"I did not, Your Majesty." He lowered his silver head in shame and his voice filled with raw emotions the old butler tried hard to contain. "I served your father since he succeeded the throne and pledged my loyalty to the Crown. But the one person who truly brought laughter to this palace was your mother. Her death changed many people. It turned them cruel and unfeeling to the plight of a child who did nothing wrong. So, how could I betray her by participating in the pain you went through?" Sir Rowell lowered himself to his knees and lifted his face which filled with tears. "I may be late in saying this, but I apologise that I could not do more for Your Majesty. All I could do was keep your guards drunk and sated until your return."

Emilia felt water drops falling onto her knuckles.

She knew she was crying, but queens did not cry in front of others. Queens were strong and had a perfect image to uphold. Or so she told herself day after day.

The butler offered her his handkerchief without looking. "I am proud to be serving such a kind, caring, and brave queen. Your mother would be proud, Your Majesty."

"Thank you, Sir Rowell." She accepted his handkerchief with a trembling hand. "I wish to be alone."

He got up and bowed low. "Of course. Please have a good rest. And should you ever wish to see the former queen's picture, there is a painting of Queen Cecilia hanging in the treasury."

Emilia waited until she was alone. She wiped away her tears and blew her nose, unlike any lady of noble birth. To Emilia, the only mother she had ever known was in her previous life. Originally, her parents were excited about the idea that their daughter could be a genius. So, her mother boasted to all of her friends, who in turn, to test Emily's memory for fun, asked the child to read difficult passages from books she did not understand.

From then, Emily was enrolled in private schools.

No matter how hard she tried at Art, Music, or Sports, she was considered to be below average. Her eidetic memory became a boost in subjects where memorising mattered while the other subjects suffered.

Emily's mother pressed on. She forced her daughter to do Drama classes, which required a show of emotions—something else the girl struggled with as she did not have any friends. Any time she did manage to make a friend, her mother would question their parents' qualifications and the abilities of the child.

Soon, the teenage years came. Emilia became isolated from her peers. To keep up with the difficult subjects, she studied during her lunch breaks and at home. She went to any classes her mother chose to please her parents and receive a stray smile from them.

Not once did her parents ask her what she wanted or who she wanted to be. Her life was decided, and all Emily needed to do was walk the path they had laid out for her.

The only choice she truly made was on the day of her death—a choice to give up a life that was not her own.

Emilia crumpled the handkerchief in her hands and glided to her desk. Running her fingertips along the polished wood which was kept dust-free by the servants, she wondered what her life would be like with Queen Cecilia as her mother.

"A kind and loving mother, protective brothers, and a supportive father?"

It was such a difficult image to envision that she gave up the idea and began to work.

6
MOIN VARETZ

LAURENCE

Laurence carried Khaja back to the castle in his arms, ignoring the curious looks they received from the townspeople and the guards.

She hid her face in her hood and refused to look at anyone. Yet, he could hear her desperate attempts at stifling her sniffling and tears. That day, Laurence regretted being unable to go with Thessian to meet with their allies. Perhaps, if he was there instead of Ian, things would have turned out differently.

How am I to deal with a crying woman?

Aside from the noble ladies who faked their tears to get his attention or his mother who never shed a tear in front of a man, Laurence was at a loss. True grief needed time to heal. But time was not something they had a lot of. They had less than two weeks to find her tribe and assess whether or not they were a threat to

Thessian's plans for the kingdom. There was also a possibility of a dragon being on the loose in the Hollow Mountains.

A part of him wanted to return to Newburn and forget all about the mission.

They reached the castle as the muscles in his arms began to burn. As a gentleman and her temporary guardian, he pushed past his discomfort, opting to lengthen his stride and hasten his speed. Once Khaja was back in their room, she would be able to calm down and possibly explain who The Grey Wolf was to her.

On the way to their room, Countess Fournier and her escort maid spotted them in the hallway and glided over. "My goodness, what happened to Miss Khaja?"

Laurence groaned as the weight he carried did not get any lighter, especially now that he had to stop for a blather. "She is a bit upset, Lady Estelle. Please allow me to bring her back to her room."

The countess' kind eyes scanned the shrunken beastwoman in Laurence's arms. She nodded to her maid, and the woman pulled out a pristine handkerchief from the inner pocket of her dress.

Lady Estelle took it and pressed the silky material into Khaja's quivering hands. "If you need someone to talk to, Miss Khaja, I am more than happy to lend an ear." She moved out of Laurence's way. "I apologise for delaying you, Sir Laurence."

"Not a problem." He smiled politely.

Almost running past the countess and the rest of the servants in the halls, he scaled multiple staircases and reached the middle of a long corridor.

Finally, they arrived in their room, and he let her down. While supporting her around her middle with one aching arm, he opened the door with the other.

"Go in, Khaja." He gave her a gentle nudge.

She did not move.

"You may need to carry her inside," Ian commented behind them.

Laurence jumped. He forgot all about the elf. "Why do you care? Were you not happy to know that she was associated with The Grey Wolf?"

"Of course not," Ian retorted. "I know what it feels like to lose those important to me, Laurence. Or have you forgotten about my past?"

"I-I apologise, Ian. I believe it is time to begin making arrangements to travel to the Northern Watchtower."

"Are you going to leave Eugene behind?"

"There is no choice. He needs to heal, and those potions are too expensive to use on a broken wrist."

Ian gave a nod of approval. "We will make do without him."

The elf left Laurence and Khaja alone.

Taking a peek at the beastwoman, who had not moved or said a word, Laurence's concern for her rose. He took hold of her hand and led her to the bed where he got her to sit.

He briskly strode out of the room and asked a maid to bring some calming tea before returning to the beastwoman's side.

Khaja stared blankly at the handkerchief in her hands as tears silently rolled down her cheeks.

With each step he used to approach her, he had less and less to say.

What can I say? She won't understand me anyway.

Kneeling in front of her, he took her handkerchief and wiped her puffy face with it. His heart ached to see a fierce and strong woman such as her in low spirits.

Tentatively, he asked, "Khaja, sad?"

She lifted her gaze to his face. "Sad..."

"Was he your relative? No, that is too hard for her to understand."

Laurence combed his hand through his hair in frustration and looked around. Seeing the parchments they used to learn new words, he shot up and brought them over along with a piece of charcoal.

As a child, he spent a lot of time sketching the servants and the scenery during his free time. His parents considered it to be a pointless hobby, so he, eventually, gave it up to focus more of his energy on sword-fighting.

Who knew I would be using my childhood skills?

So, he quickly sketched what he remembered her appearance to be as a beast-child and outlined a tall man next to her. Since he knew nothing of The Grey Wolf's appearance, he decided to improvise and use knowledge from books. Beastmen were taller than humans. They did not bother keeping their hair short or cutting it. A beastman was typically muscular and strong enough to fight off a hundred soldiers with his bare hands.

As he focused on his drawing, Khaja slid off the bed.

Her fingertips ran over the freshly-inked image of the beastman, smudging it in the process.

"*Varetz,*" she whispered in a voice so low, he barely heard it.

Laurence scratched his head. "Does 'beastman' mean '*varetz*'?"

"*Moin varetz!*" she said with more energy.

"Loin?"

"*Moin!*" She pointed her index finger at herself.

"Oh, '*moin*' is 'my'." He mimicked her and indicated to his chest. "*Moin?*"

The beastwoman bobbed her head in acknowledgement and jabbed her finger at the drawing on the beastman. "*Moin varetz!*"

"My...lover?" He formed a heart with his fingers.

Khaja glared at him.

"Brother?"

She shook her head.

"Sister? Cousin? Uncle? Father—"

She pounced on him, pinning him to the floor. "Fa-zer."

"My father?" he asked, full of excitement.

Khaja's eyes watered again. "*Moin...varetz.*"

Laurence's smile melted away. Prince Thessian and Lady Riga killed Khaja's father to protect Redford.

At that moment, he did not care if she was a beastwoman or a pauper off the street. She needed comfort. A human's touch.

He pulled her down for a hug, allowing her to cry into his chest until she was satisfied.

Laurence gently laid Khaja on the bed. She had cried herself to sleep and did not stir no matter how much noise he made. His gaze travelled to his discarded sketch on the floor, making his chest tighten once again. He did not expect things to turn out the way they did.

If Khaja ever discovers who killed her father, she might want to take revenge. What am I to do?

He could not abandon her in the middle of the Hollow Mountains to fend for herself. Not that she could not kill an ogre or two, or rip their heads off with ease. Still, taking her back to Newburn would endanger His Highness. Leaving her behind in Redford was out of the question. She would track Laurence down to the end of the world while their mate bond existed.

There is a chance she will stay with her tribe if we can find them.

Yet, if there were more beastmen out there, why did The Grey Wolf attack Redford on his own? Why did he not ask for help from the other beastmen? Were they unable to help or did they refuse?

The only way to find the truth was to scour the mountains for her tribesmen.

He left the room in search of Lord Carrell. The marquess promised Laurence to show where he came upon the corpses of monsters on the map. As long as Laurence and his men could follow the clues, they should be able to find Khaja's people.

On his way, Laurence asked the guards for the marquess' whereabouts.

"I heard Marquess Carrell is personally questioning Baron Lucy in the dungeon," a guard on duty answered.

Equipped with directions, Laurence changed his route and headed to the dungeon. He passed through halls decorated with tapestries, stuffed monster heads, and an array of weapons that were neatly hung on the stone walls. Lord Fournier had no shortage of paintings of his daughters throughout the castle, but it was the paintings of Countess Estelle that occupied the key positions.

Lord Fournier must love his family a lot.

Laurence tried imagining what it would be like to be a family man. He spent too many years wasting his coin away at The Golden Suns and gambling dens to collect useful information on the nobles of the Empire. Women of the night, aside from being skilled in giving pleasure, were fantastic spies. The nobles who frequented them often turned into blabbermouths to impress the ladies with their achievements. For enough coin, the ladies Laurence visited gave him enough knowledge to survive among the Hellion nobles when they were back in the Empire's capital—Erehvin.

Unlike in Emilia's palace where the dungeon was separated from the main palace, in Fournier's castle, the dungeon was beneath them.

Arriving at the large doors beyond which should be the stairs that led below, he met with two more guards.

"Good evening, gentlemen," Laurence said with a cheerful smile. "Would you happen to know if Lord Carrell is in there?"

The guard on the left scratched at his scruffy beard. "Who's askin'?"

His colleague was slightly more polite and elbowed the other man in the side. "Can't ye see he's one of tha Lord's guests?"

"He didn' cum witha label," the first guard grumbled.

The second guard rolled his eyes and forced a light bow. "Greetings, sir. Marquess Carrell is currently questioning the Baron. As you do not have permission to visit the dungeon, I suggest you return to your room."

Laurence arched a brow. "Please inform Lord Carrell that Sir Laurence wishes to speak with him."

The first guard let out a displeased sigh and yanked the door to the dungeon open. He took a lit torch off the stone wall and shuffled down the long flight of stairs.

Laurence smiled again at the second guard, who seemed unhappy with his presence. Not every one of the Fournier guards seemed pleased that their lord was working with the Empire.

In awkward silence, they waited until Marquess Carrell emerged with the guard at his heels.

The Marquess wiped his sweaty brow with a gloved hand. "Sir Laurence, is there something I can help you with?"

"I do not have permission to enter the dungeon, it seems." Laurence glanced over the Marquess' shoulder at the guards. "Would you be kind enough to allow me entry?"

"Of course. These are the criminals we caught because of your efforts, Sir Laurence." Lord Carrell turned to look at the two men on duty. "Keep this in mind, men, do not hinder Edgar's guests unless you wish to see yourselves out of a job." Speaking over his shoulder, he added, "Follow me, Sir Laurence. There is much I must tell you."

On their way down the stone steps, the Marquess said, "I was planning to search for you if you did not come to see me. I have questioned Baron Lucy about his business with the slave traders. He claims they threatened him with his life if he did not help them." Lord Carrell let out a hearty laugh. "Too bad for him, his servants say otherwise."

"Bald Lucy must be a great playwright," Laurence said through gritted teeth. "His fibs are getting grander by the day."

"Worry not, Sir Laurence, I will make sure the evidence against the Baron is presented to the Crown. He will not escape his crimes."

Laurence forced his tense shoulders to relax. He could not wait to see Bald Lucy being in the same position Laurence and his men were in days prior.

They reached the bottom of the stairs.

Lord Carrell stayed put. "I did hear something interesting from the leader of the mercenaries. Among their victims, they found a wounded beast-child not far from the mountains. It would seem they sold her to a brothel."

From everything Laurence had learned in recent weeks, Khaja attacked Lord Fournier likely to protect her territory. She got hurt during the altercation and escaped with her life only to wind up in the hands of the slavers.

Laurence's face heated, and he felt his body trembling with rage.

"They sold a wounded child into sex slavery?"

The Marquess patted Laurence on the arm. "You are free to do with the slavers whatever you wish as long as they remain alive for their trial."

A sneer spread across Laurence's face. "Oh, I will keep them breathing…just barely."

Laurence's bleeding fists burned as he headed back to his room. He did exactly what he promised and left Ollie and his comrades barely breathing. Yet, after all that, his rage did not subside. The anger he felt reminded him too much of the last battle with the King of Darkgate.

Pressing his back to a wall, he closed his eyes and a suppressed memory of his final battle surfaced…

The sun slowly hid behind the hills, darkening the last fortress of the King of Darkgate.

At last, they managed to burst through the portcullis to the excited roars of Thessian's soldiers. Their men fanned out, attacking as many guards of the king as they could and clearing a path for Thessian and Laurence's entry.

Swords clashed all around Laurence. He ran over to his next target — a young man no older than eighteen. Swinging his sword with precision to make the kill as fast as possible, Laurence cut his enemy down.

Not far from him, Leo and Verena gave him a nod and split off from the main unit to secure the back of the fortress with their men.

Laurence briefly spotted Calithea to his right, plunging her sword into the gut of an unarmoured guard and quickly yanking it back out. She kicked him away and moved on, keeping her back to His Highness and acting as his shield.

Thessian raised his sword high and swung it with so much strength that the head of the soldier in his way came flying off along with his helmet.

For a second, Laurence wished he, too, was strong enough to cleanly cleave a head off.

"Break down the doors!" Laurence urged their men.

The soldiers who managed to advance past the dwindling number of enemies made their way to the last obstacle in Prince Thessian's path.

A little more and this war will be over. That thought gave Laurence a boost of energy with which he took down the king's soldiers that got too close.

Thessian yanked Calithea backward by the back of her breastplate and slashed the man who was about to pierce her with a spear. The prince ripped the weapon out of the soldier's hands and pushed him to the ground before finishing him off with a brutal stab to the neck.

"Thank you, Your Highness," Calithea said, breathless.

"Do not get distracted. Eyes on the enemy!" Thessian raised his voice for the others to hear. "Press on, men!"

With the prince's encouragement, the soldiers visibly showed more vigour in their attacks. The morale of the king's guards seemed to lessen with each passing minute their liege did not show his face to support them.

"We're through, Your Highness!" the soldiers at the doors yelled.

Laurence glanced at Thessian, who gave a curt nod.

Raising his fist in the air, Laurence yelled, "All units, charge!"

Inch by inch, they broke through the last defence of the king and made their way into the heart of the fortress.

High ceilings and cold grey walls surrounded them. Old cobwebs decorated the wooden beams above their heads and the decaying wooden furniture. In a rush to save his life, the King of Darkgate abandoned his main castle for this place.

Does not matter. He will perish here today.

Their soldier opened the doors to the throne room for Thessian and bowed low as he marched inside.

Following close behind, Laurence saw tension seeping into his friend's broad back.

Turning his head, he realised why. Up ahead, in front of an expertly carved wooden throne that had seen better days, stood an old man with a knife to his queen's throat.

The woman shook like a leaf but did not dare move. All she could do was keep her eyes squeezed shut.

Laurence's gut twisted with rage. Not only was the king old and weak, he had no respect for his queen. Not even in the last moments of their lives.

"You!" The king spat on the ground and glared at Thessian. "You better not come any closer. My wife is an imperial. Born and raised in the Hellion Empire. If you move, she will die by my hand."

Laurence felt his grip on his sword tightening to the point of pain. He was ready to storm over to the king and feed his blade through the foul swine's wrinkled neck.

Thessian scanned their surroundings before speaking. "There are no more men left to die for you, so you would use your innocent wife as a shield?"

The king let out a deep laugh. "Innocent? All imperials are guilty of something. Just look at what you have done to my kingdom!"

"You made your people miserable. You taxed them into starvation, sold my countrymen into slavery, and betrayed the trust of your aides because of your unquenchable greed!" Thessian snarled. "Yet, you dare preach about guilt?"

The king's sneer sent a chill through Laurence. "Do you believe I will let you leave here without sacrifice? A perfect victory does not exist!" His booming laughter flooded the throne room. "Listen! Listen to the sweet sound of your men dying."

As the king said that, the earth trembled with explosions that sounded in the distance.

Thessian's eyes grew wide as he looked over his shoulder. His blood-splattered face contorted with hatred.

During the commotion, the mad king had lessened his grip on his queen enough for her to flee, seemingly unnoticed by him.

Muttering something Laurence could not catch under his breath, Thessian strode over to the king and stabbed him in the heart.

The foul laughter of the king faltered with the growing stain of blood on his chest. "May you all burn in the depths of the Crimson Sea…"

The ground beneath the fortress shook violently with another explosion.

The walls encasing them fractured along with the wooden beams and stone that fell from above.

Laurence launched into a sprint and covered Thessian with his body in time for a chunk of the ceiling to collide with his back. He groaned in pain and looked down at the prince's deep frown.

"I never wanted to see you this close, Laurence."

"Believe me, Your Highness, I also prefer a casual distance between our bodies. I fear I may be too handsome even for the same sex."

The soldiers came over and removed the rubble from them. Thankfully, they managed to avoid any serious injury.

Stealing one final glance at the bloody corpse of the King of Darkgate, Laurence and Thessian fled the fortress before it caved in on itself with another ear-numbing explosion from the cellars.

7
SUPPORT OF THE MARCH

EMILIA

Not long after **Emilia composed** herself, Sir Rowell returned with a freshly brewed pot of chamomile tea on a tray. His eyes were a little red and puffy from crying earlier. She could not question his loyalty anymore. The head butler kept her outings from his former master a secret and even enabled her escapes as a child.

While pouring a cup of tea for her, he said, "Your Majesty, Lord Armel and Mister Lionhart are awaiting an audience to present their reports."

"See them in."

"Before that, Your Majesty, if I may, there is one more item of note. Marchioness Lucienne Durand is here to present her greetings to her new monarch."

Emilia's heart picked up the pace, but she kept her excitement off her face. Finally, things could begin moving in the right direction. After the meeting with the marchioness, Emilia would be able to know whether Lady Durand would be a useful ally or a terrible hindrance to her plans.

"Escort Marchioness Durand here. I will see her right away." Emilia got up and moved to her sofa. She sat in the middle, taking on her practised regal posture.

Sir Rowell moved the tea set over to her choice of seating before he bowed low and respectfully glided out of the room.

What seemed like forever later, Sir Rowell returned with a woman trailing behind. "Your Majesty, I present Marchioness Lucienne Durand."

Clad in the newest fashions, Lady Lucienne's black hair was pinned into a neat updo and her makeup was carefully applied to highlight her high cheekbones and full lips. Marchioness' masterfully tailored burgundy dress contained enough embroidered white flowers to cover a field.

Upon seeing Emilia, the older woman in her late forties effortlessly shifted her body into a deep curtsy. "I greet the Mistress of the Dante Kingdom, Queen Emilia Valeria Dante. May your reign be long and peaceful."

Emilia lifted her hand with the signet ring.

Marchioness Durand bowed low in front of Emilia and kissed the ring with no reservations.

So far so good…

"Take a seat, Marchioness Durand." Emilia motioned to the sofa opposite her. "I am pleased you have accepted my summons."

"It is a pleasure to finally meet you, Your Majesty," Lady Durand replied cheerfully.

Emilia could not sense any hidden meanings behind the woman's words. As a matter of fact, unlike almost everyone Emilia had to deal with, the Marchioness seemed to wear her emotions on her sleeve.

Or she could be a natural thespian.

"As you know, Marchioness Durand, I want your daughter, Lady Christine Durand, to become one of my ladies-in-waiting. I have called on you to discuss this matter." *And test your allegiance.*

The only thing that displayed Lady Durand's discomfort was the tightness of her lips.

"Does the news not please you, Marchioness?"

"That is not the case, Your Majesty!" Lady Durand lowered her head. "I ask that you rescind the request for my daughter to become your lady-in-waiting and take me in her stead."

Emilia's jaw nearly came undone. Getting Marchioness Durand to become a close confidant of the Queen would be of huge benefit, yet Emilia could not see why the lady would abandon her territory for which she fought tooth and nail after her husband passed away.

"And what would be your reason, Marchioness?"

"Christine is not strong enough to survive at court, Your Majesty. I beg of you to reconsider."

Not once did the woman raise her head. The only thing that told Emilia that Lady Durand meant every word was the raw emotion in her voice. She wished to protect her daughter who lived through betrayal and assault from a relative. As long as Emilia could have the support of House Durand, she did not care which of the Durands served her. What piqued Emilia's interest was that she gave them a way out in her appointment letter. Lady Christine could decline the invitation of her own volition. So, perhaps, the young lady felt pressed to accept as refusing the Queen could cause them problems with the Crown.

"Raise your head, Marchioness Durand. I will accept your offer to become my lady-in-waiting." Curious to know more, Emilia asked, "Do you have someone in mind to take over the march's management?"

Lady Durand lifted her head and smiled, making the laugh lines and wrinkles around her kind eyes more pronounced. "Yes, Your Majesty. My eldest daughter and her husband will take charge. They will have my secretary to support them."

If the Marchioness passed on the title to her eldest daughter, Emilia would be unable to use Durand's military power unless she received the support of the daughter, too. The only things she might receive in return would be the experience and political ties of Lady Durand. Not that she could fault the marchioness in any of that. Lady Durand was often seen as a trendsetter and a socialite among the Dante nobility along with Duchess Malette. There were rumours that Lady Durand was addicted to opioids, but judging by her clear eyes and pristine appearance, those had to be made up by the wagging tongues of high society and trouble starters.

Emilia rose from her seat, prompting the noblewoman to stand as well.

"I look forward to seeing you in your new position, Marchioness Durand."

"Please, call me Lucienne, Your Majesty."

"Then, Lady Lucienne." Emilia smiled politely.

The Marchioness gave another low curtsy which symbolised her strong respect for Emilia. "May you have a wonderful rest of the day, Your Majesty."

Sir Rowell escorted Lady Lucienne out and then let Clayton and Lionhart in. Before he could announce them, Emilia interjected, "That will be all, Sir Rowell. Thank you."

He gave a curt bow, turned on his heel, and left, closing the door behind him.

Lionhart broke into a grin once the door was closed. "I'm glad you are finally awake."

Emilia's smile grew wider. "I half-expected you to leave."

"Where would I go?"

"I apologize for worrying you."

"Some were more worried than others," Lionhart smacked Clayton's shoulder, forcing the shadow to steady his balance.

Emilia's smirked. "So I have heard."

"You seem happy. Did you receive good news just now or did you miss us?"

"Good news, indeed." Noticing that Clayton kept his gaze on the floor, Emilia decided to resume her seat on the sofa to prevent the men from having to stand during their report. "Take a seat, gentlemen."

They sat across from her, and Lionhart crossed his legs. A bit of his prosthetic showed under his trouser leg. "House Durand has been a shield for the Crown for many decades. It would be hard to lose their support. After all, the deceased marquess and his wife supported King Gilebert at his worst."

While Lionhart spoke, Emilia took note of Clayton's shaved face, dark circles under his eyes, and unwillingness to meet her gaze.

Giving her attention to her old friend, the Queen admitted, "Had I known she would be so easy to bring to our side, I would have spoken to her sooner."

Lionhart shook his head. "The Durands support the throne rather than the one sitting on it. So, if you had approached her before taking the throne, she would side with your father or the Crown Prince."

She thought about it for a second. "It matters not. With Duke Malette out of the way and the Durands on our side, the only remaining man who could be of concern is Marquess Sardou."

"Malette was working with King Araman of Reyniel," Lionhart informed her.

"Were they equal partners or was Malette used?"

Lionhart shrugged. "My guess is Araman promised the Dante throne to Duke Malette in exchange for territory or a high position in his court once the two kingdoms were merged."

"Lord Armel?" Emilia asked, glancing at her shadow who kept his eyes on his folded hands. "Do you have anything you wish to add?"

Before Clayton could utter a word, Lionhart sighed deeply.

"You should have a serious talk with your shadow," her mentor advised.

Emilia glanced at him. "Wait... Why?"

"I do not wish to hinder your reunion. I'm sure Ambrose has informed you of the most important events while you were asleep. Undoubtedly, Lord Armel has much to share from his—" he waved a hand in the air in search of a good word, "—interrogations." Clearing his throat, he added, "I will submit a written report on King Araman by the end of the day and look into Marquess Sardou."

Emilia glanced at Clayton, unsure if it was wise to be alone with him since he seemed uncomfortable in her presence.

QUEEN OF HEARTS

The last time they spoke was a short while before she caught an arrow for Thessian. Then, she recalled their conversation at the tavern the day before the duke's trial and felt her cheeks warming.

Lionhart was right. She needed to talk to Clayton and find out if he was mad at her or if his mental state was something she should be careful of and try to mend.

"Thank you, Lionhart," she said, still feeling the burn in her cheeks.

Her mentor acknowledged her words with a nod and limped out of her office.

8
AN ASSASSIN'S PROMISE

EMILIA

Once **Lionhart closed the door**, Emilia cleared her throat. "Lord Armel, are you upset with me?"

His answer came without delay. "I could never!"

"Then why do you refuse to look my way?"

She noticed his hands that had formed fists. "I'm afraid you might be the one disappointed in me, Master."

"And why is that?"

He raised his grey eyes, displaying guilt and sorrow. "I wasn't there to protect Your Majesty when you needed me the most."

"I had given you other orders. It wasn't your fault."

"I didn't arrive in time to heal you. Due to that, the Pope healed you, and you-you…"

Emilia's lips curled into a soft smile. "Did you miss me?"

"Master…" The confusion on his face and the pain in his eyes were the only answers she needed.

"If I died that night, you were free to live your life."

"I'd rather stay shackled to Your Majesty all my life."

"Because you're mine?"

"Yes."

She waved for him to come closer.

He stood only to kneel before her.

Cupping his handsome face, Emilia looked into his emotional eyes. "I was informed of the things you did to the prisoners while I was unconscious."

"Is Your Majesty disappointed?"

His voice was soft and harmless as if he could never hurt anyone. But she knew that wasn't true. Clayton only showed that side of him to her. And all he had done was for her because she almost died. If it weren't for magical healing, she would certainly be no longer among the living or reincarnating into another hellish life.

"When I was…dreaming, I feared I'd never come back. All my life, I thought I was living a terrible nightmare, suffering for my sins."

"Master could never do any wrong," he claimed, leaning into the warmth of her hands on his face.

"I'm not perfect, Clayton. I have killed, lied, and had my family slaughtered to gain this power."

"None of that changes my opinion of Your Majesty."

Emilia smiled despite the sadness that had settled in her warring heart. "I'm not mad at you. I'm not disappointed either. I don't know what I would do to the ones who dared to hurt you or any of my friends. You might have overdone it, and I know that's how you were raised, but I also know that there's more in you than just killing and torturing." She placed a finger over his lips before he could say anything else. "I'm back. Alive and well. Now promise me that you won't lose your humanity if anything else happens to me in the future."

"Nothing will happen. I'll make sure of it."

In a joking manner, she asked, "Would you destroy the world

for me if I asked you to?"

"I'd freeze it until there is nothing left."

She could feel the honesty behind his resolute response. "What about the innocent?"

"I only care about you."

Emilia hesitated. "Because I'm your master?"

He shook his head. "Because you are you, and I won't ever let anyone else harm you."

Sliding down the couch, she sat on the floor next to him. Clayton tried to help her up, but Emilia stopped him. "While we're alone, I'm not your queen."

"Who are you then?"

"Emilia."

His eyes were vacant as he seemed to process her words. "Are you not afraid of me?"

Emilia tilted her head to the side, taking note of his gorgeous features and the warmth coming from his body. Her hands returned to her lap now that Clayton didn't fear looking at her from what she could assume was shame mixed with guilt.

A part of her was glad he took revenge in her stead. It saved her time in paying back their dues to the smugglers for trying to murder her subjects. She was also fine with receiving a sword wound from Lionhart to get him onboard her team, but she did not enjoy being pierced with an arrow and nearly meeting the maker.

Scratch that.

She did meet the Goddess, who dragged her into this world for amusement. Just thinking about Luminos reminded her of how the Goddess saw them all as pawns.

Inhaling sharply, she asked, "Is it foolish of me to believe you when you say that you'd never harm me?"

"Even if someone else was my master, I'd rather kill myself than harm you."

"Yet, we barely know each other. Before my family's death, I didn't even know of your existence."

Clayton looked down. "Let's not talk about the unpleasant past. You're free from that awful tower, and I'm with you now."

Emilia's heart beat faster as her lips curved into a soft smile. She slipped her hands into his cool palms and nodded. "You are right. I'm not alone anymore."

To avoid another display of emotions, she asked, "I believe you have a report for me."

Clayton adjusted his posture and met her eyes. "The leader of the smugglers, Sara Sayeed, claimed she worked closely with a sage, who is often seen advising King Araman as of late. The sage goes by the name of Lina Galleran. She is known throughout the continent as an individual who holds dangerous knowledge."

"What kind of knowledge?"

"She is the creator of the serpentine powder and an untraceable poison called 'Wicked Grudge'."

Emilia felt blood draining from her face. "Did you say Wicked Grudge?"

"Yes, Mas-Emilia."

Despite feeling safe so close to him, the mention of the poison reminded her of her goal and of the implications of lowering her guard while pursuing a romantic relationship with her shadow.

The Queen got up and began to pace around the sofa.

If memory served her correctly, that was the poison used to kill Thessian in the original novel. Her mind raced with possibilities and their outcomes. Lina Galleran had to be eliminated before her brew could reach Thessian's lips. Although, if that woman came up with explosives, Lina could also be a useful ally if she changed sides.

To make a final decision, Emilia needed more information on the sage.

Turning around to see Lord Armel on his feet and looking at her with concern made her feel less alone and powerless. "Clayton, House Escariot has dealings with the poison market, correct?"

"Is there anything you would like to purchase?"

She stopped behind her sofa and rested her hands on the backrest. "I would like for you to arrange a meeting with Miss Galleran."

"As far as I am aware, the sage is not open to private audiences.

She is only interested in the unusual."

Unusual? Emilia smirked. "I think Miss Galleran will want to meet the people who buy enough Wicked Grudge to murder a city."

He smiled at her creative plan. "Yes, that could gain her attention. I will make arrangements at once."

"Wait!" Emilia swallowed nervously as she approached him. Stopping in front of him, she craned her neck to see his face better. *Ah…the sight of a handsome man is still the best medicine for the heart.* "Did you mean what you said the other night at the inn and today?"

His voice came out soft. "About only being yours?"

"And about liking my kiss."

"I have no reason to lie to my master."

She swallowed dry. "I'm not good at displaying my emotions."

"I understand."

"I never knew the love of parents, friends, or… Well, until now."

"I know."

She couldn't stop her insecurities flowing out. "I don't want to use my position or your curse to force you to do something you don't want."

His lips curled into a soft smile.

"Therefore, you don't need to pretend that—"

Her speech was cut short when his lips covered hers. To her disappointment, he leaned back almost immediately.

Fluttering her eyelashes, she tried to understand what had just happened. After all, she was a girl with zero dating experience in two lifetimes and was truly at a loss for what to do.

"May I kiss you again?" he asked with a sultry voice that made her knees almost give in.

She nodded, unable to speak.

Clayton moved closer, circling one arm around her waist and pulling her against his body. With closed eyes, he kissed her gently on the lips, and Emilia eagerly responded.

As the kiss deepened, the world around them faded away, and all that mattered was this moment, this connection between them. Clayton's hands trailed down her back, pulling her closer.

Emilia felt a rush of desire wash over her. For a moment, she forgot about her responsibilities and her duties as a ruler. All that mattered was this man, this kiss, this feeling of being wanted and loved.

When he broke away, she tried to gasp for air and stop her legs from trembling.

She could no longer deny that he made her feel things she had never felt before. Maybe what brought them closer was the fact that they were merely two wounded beasts who protected their weak hearts by wearing a mask of strength. Or it could be a pure and deadly attraction.

Whatever it was, Clayton seemed willing to pursue it without restraint.

His words awoke her from her reverie. "I will report as soon as I know more about Miss Galleran. She may be tricky to separate from King Araman's side. No doubt he has her watched at all times."

Emilia clutched the material of his coat, trying to fight back the yearning to kiss him again and forget about their responsibilities. Her eyes widened with realisation. *What if this is more than attraction?*

"Your Majesty?"

Emilia snapped out of her derailing thoughts. "Yes?"

"Can I be so bold to ask you something?"

"Of course," she whispered, feeling her cheeks get warmer as their eyes met.

He lifted his hand yet stopped short of touching her cheek. "Is Your Majesty planning a date with His Holiness?"

His question after such a passionate kiss left her confused. Still, if that was a display of jealousy, something inside her made her feel happy about it. If, at first, she wanted him to know about it since he hadn't come to visit her, now she didn't want him to misunderstand. "It is a business transaction, nothing more."

"May I escort you?"

"No!" Her voice came out too harsh, and she mentally chastised herself.

He furrowed his brows.

"You can protect me from the shadows. We cannot be seen with too many escorts or our identities would be exposed."

He let out a sigh of relief and lowered his hand. "Of course, Your Majesty."

Emilia did not wish to see him go. In a voice barely above a whisper, she asked, "Did you kiss me to prove that you belong to me alone?"

"I will forever belong *only* to you."

Her breath hitched. "Even after the curse is broken?"

He nodded. "I'll never leave you."

In the back of her head, her mind cautioned to mistrust men's promises.

Oh, sod it!

As a final barrier broke inside Emilia, she threw caution to the wind and pulled him down by the lapels of his coat for a fever-inducing kiss, which he returned with eagerness.

Her skin tingled with warmth every time his hands roamed her back. Being pressed against his hard body felt so good. So right. She never wanted to leave his tight embrace that seemed to suck her in and not let go. Running her hands over his chest, she felt the hard muscle underneath his clothes and smelled a hint of cedarwood. Being able to touch his body, even through the barrier of his clothes, felt like an achievement after weeks of secretly drooling over it.

Pausing to gasp for air, she looked up with hooded eyes, noticing his closed ones.

Cupping her face, Clayton opened his eyes. "What's the matter?"

"I feel guilty for leaving you alone for so long. I don't want you to turn into a monster."

"I'm an assassin."

"Not by choice."

"I need to be ruthless to continue to be useful to you."

Emilia wrapped her arms around his neck.

Caressing her face and planting a kiss on her forehead, he whispered, "Since I've met you, I no longer curse my fate. Our paths would never cross if I hadn't become who I am today."

She nodded. Before she could kiss him again, a slight knock on the wall panel behind the late king's portrait made Emilia jump.

Oh, Gods! It's Ambrose... How much did she hear or see?

Reluctantly, the Queen stepped away from Clayton and fixed her dishevelled appearance.

She cleared her throat. "I hope to hear your report on Lina Galleran soon, Lord Armel."

He lifted her hand, bowed low, and gave a tentative kiss to her exposed wrist. "I will return with good news." Leaning in close so only she could hear him, he whispered in her ear, "My one and only master."

9

A HEART LONG BROKEN

THESSIAN

Thessian groaned when the morning rays reached his sleeping face. He covered his eyes with his hand to hide from the invasive brightness and forced himself into a sitting position.

"Brother, are you awake?"

Turning his head to one side at the query, Thessian spied Ronne standing in front of their luggage. The lad was changing into a warmer shirt for the journey, which revealed deep knife scars on his side and back that were left behind by Julio's research.

Ronne finished lacing up his shirt and tried to comb his locks. However, his hair pointed in different directions no matter how much he brushed it. Giving up, he put away the comb and sighed. "Should I fetch our breakfast?"

"No need. I will eat what I have brought."

"Are you afraid of being poisoned, sir, I mean, Brother?"

"I was told there may be an attempt on my life through poison, yes."

Ronne's face hardened. "I will pay closer attention to our food from now on!"

Thessian got out of bed and stretched his stiff muscles. The mattress he slept on felt like a pile of rocks covered with a sheet. Even covering the straw mattress with his cloak did not help get rid of the smell of dampness and mould that emanated from it.

"You need to call me Theo, not Brother."

"Yes, sir, Bro-Theo. I-I will check on our horses," Ronne replied and ran out of the room.

That boy is more spirited than Laurence. I wonder how my friend is doing on his mission...

Thessian dressed and secured his weapons to his belt. The journey to Garlia would take two days, possibly three with the merchant's caravan.

He rummaged through his knapsack for food. When he came across the storage cloth, he took out a few strips of dried meat and a bread roll.

I just need to tolerate these rations until I return to Newburn, he thought as the chewiness of the meat hurt his teeth.

After polishing off the food, he pushed it down with some water from a silver flask.

Then, the prince retrieved a piece of parchment, a quill made from a goose's feather, and a sealed ink pot. Taking a seat on the bed, he used the wall to write Emilia about Countess Morel's territory and the recurring child kidnappings. Although he did not wish to burden Emilia with too much work after her only recently waking from a coma, he knew that she would want to get to work as quickly as possible. Her stubbornness and dedication were unmatched when it came to paperwork. Something he lacked a great deal.

Rather than sitting in the office, he preferred to train with his knights or inspect his territory.

He chuckled to himself. *Hence why Ludwig is planning to quit working as my secretary if I do not return soon... I should wrap things up in Dante as soon as possible.*

The prince waited until the ink dried and folded the parchment three times before sealing it with some wax and his seal. As he was about to slip the letter into his inner coat's pocket, Ronne returned and closed the door behind him.

"I have checked on the horses and fed them, Theo. Also, the merchants are downstairs, having their breakfast. Should we let them know we wish to travel with them?"

Thessian put everything away, except for the letter, picked up his knapsack, and threw it over his shoulder. "I will find Delphine Leferve while you bring our horses out front. Oh and —" Thessian handed Ronne the letter. "Have this sent to Queen Emilia."

"I will inquire with the barmaid about any messengers headed to Newburn." Ronne bowed his head, collected his belongings, and followed Thessian out of their room.

On his way downstairs, Thessian could already hear the excited voices of the men gathered for their meal. On the last step, he scanned the area for Delphine. It was not hard to spot the man dressed in extravagant and colourful attire.

In a way, Thessian wondered if the man wanted to be pickpocketed or kidnapped. Yet, no noble would purchase goods from a merchant who did not appear as if they were drowning in gold. After all, nobles were all about appearances. As long as they outwardly displayed wealth, the others would believe in the false image and think they were doing well financially.

Ronne nodded to the prince, took all of their belongings, and hurried to speak with the barmaid.

In the meantime, Thessian approached the table with the merchants and inclined his head in greeting. "Good morning, Mister Leferve. Does the offer to travel with you still stand?"

Delphine wiped his mouth with a handkerchief and bobbed his head while he finished chewing. "It does! I am so pleased to know you will be joining us. As I have mentioned earlier, I promise to pay you a decent sum for your trouble." He looked around Thessian.

"Are you travelling alone?"

"With my brother. You saw him yesterday."

Delphine smiled widely, forming deep laugh lines on his cheeks. "Wonderful! Why don't you have a seat?" He pushed a spare chair out for Thessian. "Have some food as well. I would like to introduce you to my colleagues."

Thessian produced a well-practised smile he often used for the nobles in the Empire and sat at the table in the last available chair. This time, he sat with caution in case the chair was as wobbly as the last.

Delphine picked up his tankard and took a long drink of his ale. He blew out a contented breath. "Allow me to introduce you to everyone. This is Henri Leclerc." The merchant pointed to a slender man dressed in muted greys and browns. His hair colour resembled fresh ashes, and his weary eyes sported a muddy shade. "He is in charge of record-keeping for The Emerald Swan and will also be the one distributing everyone's pay when we reach Garlia."

Henri produced a grunt instead of a greeting and continued to chew his stew.

Delphine motioned to the second man sitting at the table whose body was on the skinny side. The young man ducked his head before Thessian could get a good look and savagely dug into his bowl.

"T-that's Sacha... He's a bit shy." Delphine drew Thessian's attention back to him by patting Thessian on the shoulder. "What do we call you and your brother?"

"I'm Theo, and my brother is Ronne."

Sacha choked on his food, quickly muttered, "Excuse me," in a pitchy voice, and ran out of the inn.

Thessian raised a brow. "Your friend is very shy, indeed."

Delphine let out a nervous laugh. "Sacha is not usually like this. He is new to travelling with us, but he does great work by keeping the accounting books in check."

Thessian turned in his seat to see the four mercenaries who were nursing their tankards or cradling their heads after what appeared to be a long night of heavy drinking. "Your guards are looking under the weather."

The merchant rubbed the back of his neck. "They were a last-minute hire. That is why Henri and I decided to hire you for additional security."

In truth, Thessian would have done the same thing had he been in Delphine's shoes. After all, a band of mercenaries who got drunk on the job were useless. Instead of protecting the goods and the merchants, they were busy wasting their coin away.

Getting up from his seat, Thessian said, "My brother and I will wait for you outside."

"But you haven't eaten anything," Delphine replied, full of worry.

"I ate in my room." Thessian inclined his head. "If you'll excuse me."

Without waiting for a reply, the prince left the inn in search of Ronne. The boy must have finished talking to the barmaid because he could not be seen at the bar.

Stepping out into the cold morning air, Thessian was met with the harsh rays of sunlight that briefly blinded him. He covered his eyes with his arm and lowered it in time to see Sacha's wig falling off with a strong whip of wind.

Long golden hair swayed in the wind and familiar violet eyes looked back at him.

Thessian stood there speechless for what seemed like forever. His eyes were drawn to the one woman he wished to never see again yet could not forget no matter how many years had passed.

"Lady Clarissa von Leutten?" Thessian's words came out as a strangled whisper, and he did not know if she could hear him. His throat grew dry and his palms sweaty. "I-I..."

She fixed her wig and ran over. Covering his mouth with her hand, she hissed, "Come with me, *Your Imperial Highness*!"

Before he could react, she captured his wrist and pulled him after her to the side of the inn.

The second they turned the corner, she let him go and crossed her arms. "What is His Imperial Highness doing in the middle of nowhere?" As if finally realising her impropriety towards a member of the Imperial Family, she curtsied and lowered her head. "I-I apologise and greet Your Imperial Highness, The Second Star of the Helli—"

"Enough of that, Lady Clarissa!" He closed the gap she had created between them and looked down at her. "I could ask you the same thing. What is a married woman from the Empire doing in the middle of the Dante Kingdom?"

Lady Clarissa lifted her defiant face. She had not changed one bit since their last meeting ten years ago. A splash of light freckles covered her rosy cheeks, her long, blonde eyelashes framed her sparkling eyes that resembled exquisite amethysts, and her full red lips reminded him too much of a kiss they shared under the oak tree on the eve of his sixteenth birthday. She was and forever will remain the beauty who got away from him.

"I do not see how it is any of His Highness' business."

He frowned. She acted offended, yet it was she who broke the engagement only to announce her marriage a month later. "Are you married to Delphine Leferve?"

She scowled at him. "He is my employer!"

"Then perhaps Henri Lec—"

Lady Clarissa slapped her hand to his mouth. "We will speak of this no further."

"Sacha? Where are you?" It was Delphine's voice coming from the inn's entrance.

She stepped away and adjusted her wig once again, making sure the stray strands of her blonde locks were well hidden beneath the brown mess of curls.

Delphine came around the corner. "Is something the matter?"

"Everything is fine." She pointed to Thessian over her shoulder. "Theo was asking for directions after we reach Garlia."

The merchant visibly relaxed. "Ah, I can help you with that. Where are you headed?"

Thessian watched as Lady Clarissa marched away from them. Tightening his jaw, he finally replied, "We are headed to Dresgan."

"Duke Malette's territory?" Delphine rubbed his smooth chin. "It is unfortunate he betrayed the Crown with his schemes. I heard Her Majesty resembles Queen Cecilia a lot and has been kind enough to allow him a fair trial. Oh, I am talking of useless things again!" He came over and patted Thessian on the back. "The best way to Dresgan from Garlia is to take the merchant's road. As a matter of fact, after Countess Morel's home, we were planning on visiting the nobles in the South. You could continue travelling with us."

Thessian considered the offer. It would allow him to find out exactly what Lady Clarissa was doing in another kingdom and disguised as a man. "That may not be such a bad idea."

10
A MIDNIGHT RENDEZVOUS

EMILIA

In the reflection of the vanity's mirror, Emilia watched Ambrose's stony expression while the head maid brushed the Queen's hair. Ambrose had never been so quiet during their private time. She always had something to talk about or inform Emilia of. Yet, today something seemed to be off.

Do I bring it up?
Will she do it?
How much did she see of what happened with Clayton?

Emilia mulled over the options and decided to approach the subject with caution. "How are you feeling, Ambrose?"

"I take good care of myself to not become a burden to Your Majesty."

"I—" Emilia turned around on her stool and took hold of Ambrose's hands. "Is something bothering you?"

"It is nothing of importance, Your Majesty."

"So something *is* bothering you." Giving the head maid's hands a light squeeze, Emilia finally got Ambrose to look her in the eye. "Please tell me what's wrong. I want to help you in any way I can."

Ambrose cast her gaze downwards once more. "Does Your Majesty love Lord Armel?"

Emilia's words were stuck in her throat. Love was a strong word. She was attracted to him, and they had shared miserable childhoods, but love was a feeling that grew and changed with time. She and Clayton did not know each other long enough for such deep feelings to develop. Not yet, at least.

"I do have some feelings for him," Emilia managed after a long pause.

"Does that mean Your Majesty no longer wishes to help the prince?"

Emilia's brows drew together. "Why would you think that?"

"Love blinds people and forces them to make decisions they would not normally make. I fear that you may sacrifice your goals for the momentary pleasures."

A mirthful laugh escaped Emilia. Ambrose was worried over the silliest things. Emilia's goal to be free from the confines of the palace, ranks, and the weight of a kingdom never changed. Just because she sprouted feelings for someone would not diminish the need to help Thessian become Emperor of Hellion. If she abandoned her quest, every mage on the continent would be culled by Kyros, including Clayton and Lady Riga.

She could not let that happen.

Rising from her seat, Emilia smiled at Ambrose. "My desire to change my fate remains the same, I promise. If Clayton cannot follow me—or will not—I will not blame him."

Ambrose gave a slow nod.

"Is that everything that's on your mind?"

"There is another matter…"

Emilia's expression sobered as she noticed Ambrose's nervous demeanour. "What is it?"

"Ivy sent a letter. She claims she is doing well at the academy, but I can tell from her writing that something is wrong."

"Do you believe something happened to your sister?"

"I cannot be certain, but I wish to take a short leave to see what the problem is... Only if Your Majesty permits it."

"Of course, I'll allow it! Ivy is someone important to you and is like a younger sister to me. Inform Sir Rowell of your leave, so he can assign someone else to take care of your duties while you are away."

Ambrose blew out a heavy breath, and her lips curved upwards. "Thank you, Your Majesty."

"Now that I think about it, should I go with you?"

"No! I cannot ask you to abandon your duties for my baseless worry."

"Ambrose, you are more important to me than the nobles or even the crown. Never hesitate to ask me for help. I will do whatever I can for you and your family, no matter what it takes."

Tears escaped Ambrose's eyes, and she wiped at them. She went down on her knees and pressed Emilia's hand to her forehead. "I thank the gods every day for allowing me to find such a perfect mistress as you."

"I am not perfect, Ambrose. No one is."

Emilia urged her maid to stand up and gave her a warm hug. She patted Ambrose on the back until she calmed down and stopped sniffling.

With another quick hug, Ambrose left the Queen's bedchambers to make arrangements with Sir Rowell.

Emilia wrapped her satin robe tighter and approached the balcony. She had sensed someone's presence there for a while. Ambrose must have been too distraught about Ivy to notice.

Pushing the doors open greeted her with a cold breeze that greedily wrapped around her.

Paying it no mind, she smiled. "Good evening, Lord Armel. Are you here to make a report?"

"Am I only permitted to visit Your Majesty when I have something to report?"

She took a step towards him, and he mirrored her movement.

"Not particularly, however, I was under the impression you were busy looking into Lina Galleran."

"I have left the task of tracking Lina Galleran to a trusted member of the household." His warm smile reached his eyes which reflected the candlelight in her room. "May I be permitted to visit Her Majesty whenever my whims allow?"

Emilia caught him by the lapels of his coat and pulled him flush against her. "I fear you may never leave my side if you do, Lord Armel."

"I fear you are correct."

Despite the evening chill, her body warmed from within. She could almost taste the sweetness of his words and felt her heart picking up the pace.

Clayton never rushed her or demanded anything in return. She liked that about him—a little too much.

Her fingers climbed up to his neck, and she secured her hands behind it, drawing his face closer to hers.

As she did that, she felt his large hands cautiously, at first, landing on her waist. When she didn't push him away, his hold on her tightened.

He rested the side of his head against hers and breathed in her scent. "What can your humble servant do, Your Majesty? You smell sweeter than Goddess Mel."

She let out a giggle as his soft hair tickled her cheek. "That's the bath oil you are smelling."

"Beyond the oils and perfume, the scent you carry envelopes me with strange warmth. It is driving me to disobey my vow of service, to keep you in my arms, never letting go."

Emilia's face was on fire, making her bury her face in his shoulder. "You are exaggerating, Clayton."

He lifted his head enough to see her. "I wish to kiss Her Majesty."

Ambrose's words from earlier snaked into Emilia's head. She knew that falling in love with someone could destroy her plans. She had never loved anyone enough in her two lifetimes to make a great sacrifice. Every boyfriend she ever wanted was a fictional character or well beyond her reach.

Strangely enough, looking into the depths of his eyes—that were as honest as he was—she could not deny that Clayton's feelings were undoubtedly there. He did not shy away from them.

His expression changed to concern. "My apologies. Have I upset you?"

She shook her head and felt hot tears streaking her cheeks.

"No, my mind wanders to unnecessary concerns."

How she wished to be free from the binding chains of power. Yet, without power, she could not help Thessian. She could not change the horrid future. She had to step up and be someone strong, someone worthy of people's admiration and support. And every morning, she had to hide her nagging feelings that created doubt after doubt.

Clayton took Emilia by the hand and led her to her bed. He helped her take a seat on the edge and knelt in front of her. While never breaking eye contact, he collected the salty teardrops resting on her smooth face and turned them into tiny crystals on his palm.

Then, smiling, he pressed his hands together. Upon opening, the crystals had merged. A light blue glow emanated from his palms, with more ice forming until it shaped into an ice figurine of her standing tall and regal in a wide flowing gown.

"Please accept this gift, my precious master."

Emilia was so engrossed in the magic that she hadn't even noticed she had stopped crying.

Even after showing him her weaknesses, he did not budge. Like never before, she wanted him for his sincere heart that called out to hers.

"I don't want to hurt you, Clayton. You know who I am and my position. A day may come when I have to make a choice that tears us apart. If you think you cannot handle that, then we need to stop."

He set the figurine on the floor and placed his hands on the hard wood. Closing his eyes, ice rapidly spread around her figurine and more figures started to surface from the sheet of clear ice that coated the floorboards and rugs. She recognised the people as they formed one by one—Ambrose, Lionhart, Thessian, Count Baudelaire, Sir

Rowell, Sir Jehan Wells, Lady Isobelle, and finally Clayton himself.

Looking back at her, he spoke softly but sternly. "I will forever stand behind you and the choices you make. As long as I draw breath, I will protect this piece of your generous heart that you have so graciously bestowed upon me and will never feel hurt or abandoned. I ask nothing from you but that you are true to yourself."

"You truly have a way with words…" She sniffled, trying not to burst into another embarrassing crying session.

"My master deserves nothing less than everything I have."

I guess, I should thank Luminos for giving me a second chance at life. "I think you may kiss me now."

His lips stretched into a smile.

Moving closer to her, his eyes fixated on her lips as she held her breath. When his lips touched hers, she was unsure of what to do. Should she close her eyes and allow him to take charge, or should she guide their kiss?

The shadow's kiss started as a soft brushing of her lips. Soon after, it was full of urgency and yearning.

She fell back onto the bed as he climbed on top of her. All the while, he kept his attention solely on her reactions as if afraid she would change her mind at any second.

Emilia deepened the kiss while her hands roamed his broad chest. The buttons on his coat were a nuisance, but she did not plan on going further that night. They had more than enough time to explore each other in the future. Hopefully, next time there would be no guards outside to worry about who could overhear.

Maybe I should ask Sir Rowell to clear the corridor in advance…

Gasping for air, she broke away and studied his face. He truly was too eye-catching to have never dated anyone. It was a loss for the ladies of the kingdom and a huge win for her.

"Are you truly not hiding a fiancée in some secluded mansion?"

He chuckled. "I am only able to devote myself to one woman, and that woman occupies my mind day and night."

"She must be quite beautiful."

"Her hair is as black as the darkest night, lips as red as the

Dragon's Heart, and her eyes could easily be compared to the clear skies after a storm."

"You should have been a poet, Lord Armel."

"Surely Your Majesty jests?"

She giggled and pulled him down to meet her lips and end the conversation there.

Emilia rested her head on Clayton's chest and listened to the soothing sound of his steady heartbeat. During their lengthy session of getting to know each other better without words, he had removed his coat without her realising it. This allowed her to get a proper feel of his upper body through the thin material of his shirt.

If only I could use him as a pillow for the rest of my life...

"You know, I have been wondering this for a while. How old are you, Clayton?" He was a judge in the kingdom's legal system, so he could easily be a thirty-something-year-old with a baby face. Not that she would mind either way.

"I am seventeen, Your Majesty."

Emilia sat up and stared at him in disbelief. "Well, then I am sorry to inform you that the years have not been kind as you look to be in your twenties."

He let out a laugh that wet the corners of his eyes with tears. "It was a jest. I am twenty-five as of last autumn."

The Queen playfully swatted his thigh, which was like hitting a stone wall with her palm. "I am pleased you have relaxed around me enough to joke."

"And I am glad I got to kiss my master until her lips grew swollen."

She touched her aching lips and smiled. In her previous life, she missed out on a lot of fun by focusing on studying and pleasing her parents.

This time around, I plan to live for myself and those I hold dear. As the

Queen thought that, she could not stop her worry over Ambrose's sister and her troubles at the academy.

"Is something the matter?" he asked.

"I think I should follow Ambrose to Port Lisza, and I have the perfect excuse for this outing."

"Are you planning something dangerous again?"

She faced Clayton and gave him a peck on the lips. "I'm certain my shadow will be there to keep me safe."

"I am forever at your disposal."

11

A WHITE LIE

LAURENCE

Another day had passed since Khaja learned about the fate of her father.

Laurence tried to cheer her up in any way he could. He brought her tasty meat skewers, showed her his favourite dagger, and even gifted her new clothes for the journey to the Hollow Mountains. She could not wear Countess Estelle's frilly dresses for hiking.

Yet, none of his gifts brought a smile to her face.

Seeing her, sitting quietly in front of the fireplace in their room, caused his chest to feel stuffy. Rubbing his chest to ease his heart, he thought about what else he could do and frowned. After all, they had to leave for the Northern Watchtower with Lord Carrell and Lord Fournier in an hour. Any more delays could not be permitted. Laurence had to return to His Highness' side as soon as possible. Thessian was not helpless by any means, but he was also not immortal. His skills with the sword would not save him from a dragon's flames or an arrow to the chest.

Taking a seat next to her on the floor, he crossed his legs and used his arms for support as he leaned back. "Is Khaja still sad?"

The beastwoman pouted and nodded once.

He looked at the slow dance of the flames above the charred logs in the fireplace. Again, there was nothing he could say that she would understand or that could cheer up a woman who lost her father. Grief forever remained with those who kept on living. It surfaced from time to time as if to force the dagger deeper into the wounded heart.

"I once had a comrade named Eli Godwin. We were not the best of friends, but he was hard to miss among the stone-faced soldiers. The man smiled all day long. It did not matter if we lost hundreds or thousands of soldiers in a battle—friends or allies. He would smile and say, 'We're alive. We made it another day. Let's pay those—'" He cleared his throat. "Well, some swearing was involved. What I am trying to say, is that there will always come another day, another battle, another scar to heal, and...another loss. It is inevitable in life. You just need to find someone you can rely on and be yourself with, Khaja. Someone you can share your sorrow and grief with."

Laurence rubbed the back of his neck. He said a lot of things, yet she most likely understood none of them.

"*Mir*, Laurenz."

"I don't know what that means."

She pointed to her heart. "*Mir*." And then pointed to him. "Laurenz."

"My?" He thought that 'moin' meant 'my'. *Is it a synonym?*

Khaja jabbed her index finger at her heart again. "Mi-rrrr. Laurenz mir."

"Heart?"

Looking at where she was pointing, his speech faltered slightly. "Uh, chest?"

Khaja did not respond and kept waiting for him expectantly.

"Love?"

Tilting her head to one side, she seemed to think about that word. He taught it to her only yesterday when she managed to get up and eat something. Any chance he got, he tried to increase her vocabulary, so they would have an easier time communicating with each other.

"Love Laurenz? Love Laurenz!" Khaja smiled and pointed to her chest one last time. "Khaja love Laurenz."

As a distinguished knight in Prince Thessian's army and a son of a marquess, Laurence was never short on confessions. Yet, Khaja's simple words made his ears burn. Scrambling into a standing position, he rubbed the sweat off his palms on his trousers. "I think we should finish packing for the trip to the Hollow Mountains."

Khaja followed his lead and stood. She folded her arms under her breasts, which was something she picked up from observing others. "Laurenz love Khaja?"

Laurence opened his mouth and the words were stuck in his throat. He could easily shoot her down. He had no feelings for her. At least, he thought he didn't. Khaja was of a different species. She needed to be with a beastman, not a human. And Laurence had promised to marry Calithea on their next break from their missions. Cali was important to him. She was a comrade, a friend, and a woman who did not wish to use him for his family's name. Her bravery shone on the battlefield, and he could not ask for a better partner who understood and accepted him.

So why am I hesitating?

The beastwoman's patience must have run out. She moved to stand in front of him and pointed at his heart. "Laurenz love Khaja?"

"Love is a complicated word for humans, Khaja."

"Yez or n-no?"

Stuck between a rock and a hard place, he nearly jumped out of his skin when someone knocked on the door. Taking this as a sign from the gods that he could avoid the topic for a while longer, he launched to open the door for his life's saviour.

Ian raised a brow at Laurence's wide grin. "Are you having a wonderful time in there, Laurence?"

Laurence's smile turned into a scowl. "Are the preparations complete?"

"Yes. Everyone is gathering outside."

"We will be down shortly."

Ian peered past Laurence and sighed. "I pray we locate her tribe soon for I fear for my health."

Laurence looked over his shoulder and noticed Khaja's burning glare which was directed at the interrupter of their conversation. "You are quite resourceful, Ian. I am certain you will be fine."

The elf did not take kindly to the jest and stalked off.

There goes my safety net.

"We have to get going," Laurence announced as if nothing happened.

He secured his weapons to his hips, stashed two daggers in his boots, and pulled on a fur coat made of the ice wolves' pelts. Lord Fournier had plenty of them in his storage since the last monster attack on Redford.

Once he finished packing his knapsack, and checked if he took everything of importance, he started for the door.

Khaja did not move when he prompted her to leave with him.

Running his hand through his hair, Laurence could tell his choices were shrinking. He also knew that if he told her that he did not love her, Khaja would take off to never be seen again.

What can I do? Should I listen to Ian's advice and lie?

But if I do, I will, indeed, become a lowlife unworthy of Calithea...

He let out a heavy sigh and strode over to the beastwoman. Placing his hand on her shoulder, Laurence said, "From now on, we are friends, Khaja. I love Khaja as a *friend*."

"Laurenz love Khaja?" Her expression brightened, and she beamed at him.

His lips tugged into a weak smile.

I am going to burn in the Crimson Sea for this...

The gathering of knights outside of the castle was hard to miss with the growing crowd. Laurence tugged on his horse's reins and brought his steed closer to Khaja. As he was about to tell her to climb on, Lord Fournier buoyantly walked over.

Khaja let out a low growl, and the lord's stride faltered. The Count let out a nervous laugh. "I suppose she has not yet forgiven me for slashing her."

Laurence stepped in front of Khaja and bowed his head. "I apologise on her behalf, Lord Fournier. Khaja lost someone close to her recently and has been a little upset."

The Count stroked his long beard and gave a slow nod. "I understand. The lady's heart needs time to heal. I came to invite you and the lady to ride in the carriage with us."

As warm and inviting as a carriage ride was, Laurence did not trust Khaja's self-control enough to leave her in the presence of the nobles she disliked. She managed to survive a few meals in Lord Fournier's dining hall, but that did not mean she would behave in a cramped space with three men. She was thrown into a brothel against her will not too long ago. That fact kept gnawing on Laurence's conscience. He was no better than the men who mistreated Khaja by fooling her.

"I—" Laurence looked over his shoulder at the beastwoman who snuck up behind him and wrapped her arms possessively around his waist.

"I won't interrupt your time together," Lord Fournier said with a chuckle before he returned to his carriage and climbed inside.

Laurence let out a long sigh. He no longer cared if people misunderstood their relationship. Correcting everyone they met took too long.

Sergey and Yeland approached him. The two men looked better after some rest. The colour had returned to their faces and the bruises had faded a great deal.

Sergey spoke first. "Commander, can't we give one of those healing potions to Eugene to help with his wrist?"

"It would be a waste. What if we need them in an emergency? Also, if possible, I'd rather not use them at all. His Highness spent a lot of coin to acquire them."

The duo solemnly nodded.

"What about Sir Ian?" Laurence spied the elf on horseback, blending in with the group of two dozen knights that were escorting the nobles. Most of the men seemed to belong to Lord Carrell, as Lord Fournier only brought with him four knights from his main guard, including the Guard Captain—Neil Gagnon. The numbers made sense as they would be travelling to Lord Carrell's territory where the Northern Watchtower rested at the foot of the Hollow Mountains.

"Sir Ian seems eager to leave Redford," Sergey muttered.

"That man cannot sit still for too long in one place," Laurence replied, thinking of Ian's need to keep moving to avoid detection by anyone related to Shaeban. Hiding within the ranks of Thessian's army was the best place to stay out of sight. "No more idle chatter, gentlemen. Get ready to leave."

The men climbed atop their horses, leaving Laurence with Khaja who had yet to let him go.

He awkwardly turned in her arms and indicated to his horse. "We need to get on."

She shook her head and buried her face in his chest.

Laurence was beginning to think the journey north was going to take a lot longer than he anticipated. Peeling her arms away from him, he slipped his boot into the stirrup and pulled himself into the saddle. Leaning over, he offered her his hand.

Khaja peered back in the direction of the small forest where The Grey Wolf died and clenched her jaw. She whispered something under her breath that Laurence did not catch and took his hand.

Once she was securely seated behind him, Laurence draped her arms over his stomach to prevent her from toying with his hair or sniffing him.

Before he could urge the horse to move, Lady Estelle pushed past the guards and walked over to Laurence. She smiled at him. "I have good news, Sir Laurence. Riga said the Queen is finally awake."

"That is good news." *She can read my report in full and know how much trouble I went through to secure Bald Lucy.*

The countess pulled out a silk handkerchief from her fur coat's pocket and handed it to Khaja. "May your journey be free of troubles and tears, Miss Khaja."

"*Daszik*," Khaja replied, accepting the gift.

"Thank you for your hospitality, Lady Estelle. It was a pleasure staying in your castle." Laurence inclined his head in respect and followed the rest of the knights on horseback out of the castle's grounds. They passed the now familiar houses, the stalls in the marketplace, including the butcher's. The burly man lumbered around his stall to wave to Khaja, which made Laurence grip the reins harder.

To the sound of hoofs battering mud after the rain, they passed through the final gates and emerged beyond the stone walls that protected Redford.

Laurence felt Khaja's hold on him tightening. She had to be nervous, leaving for an unknown destination with strange men and after finding out that her father was killed. In truth, Laurence did not know what he could do for her other than help reunite Khaja with her people. Once she rejoined her tribe, she would be happier.

Or so he hoped.

The horses picked up the pace, and Laurence put his worries to the back of his cluttered mind.

12
FRAGMENTS OF THE PAST

EMILIA

Clayton must have left after Emilia had fallen asleep as she was greeted with the cool sheets next to her in the morning. She sat up in bed and combed her tangled hair away from her face with her fingers.

Bright light streamed in through the gap between the curtains. The weather was perfect for a trip to Port Lisza where she originally recruited Ambrose as a maid from an orphanage. There was no way Emilia would leave Ambrose to deal with Ivy's issues at the academy on her own. Nobles were often rude and intolerant of commoners, especially those who studied alongside them. Emilia had paid quite a hefty sum to the owner of Port Lisza Academy to take in Ivy as a student while keeping her origins a secret.

After everything Ambrose had done for her over the years, Emilia wanted to do all in her power to support the two sisters. She owed them that much, perhaps more.

A knock on the door pulled Emilia from her thoughts.

Instead of Ambrose, however, it was Marchioness Durand who came to attend to the Queen's needs.

Lady Lucienne gave a deep curtsy. "I greet the Mistress of the—"

Emilia raised her hand. "No need for that, Lady Lucienne. I prefer to keep my mornings simple."

The Marchioness fluidly resumed her proper posture and neatly folded her hands in front of her. "Good morning, Your Majesty."

Emilia smiled. "Good morning to you, too, Lady Lucienne. I presume you are here in the head maid's stead?"

"That is correct, Your Majesty. I have taken it upon myself to speak with Sir Rowell about the Queen's budget for dresses and jewellery and was unpleasantly surprised that there isn't one."

Emilia got out of bed. "There have been more pressing matters to deal with than fancy clothes and fanfare."

Immediately, Lady Lucienne picked up the cloak off the back of the chair and draped it over Emilia's shoulders. Since Emilia did not see it there the previous night, Clayton must have left it out for her in case the morning was cold.

He's very sweet for an assassin.

"It is my understanding that Your Majesty wished to have ladies-in-waiting to manage such boring tasks. If you permit it, I would like to take charge of Her Majesty's wardrobe."

Usually, Ambrose was the one to pick the tailors and order the dresses Emilia wore, but Emilia had to blend in with the constantly flowing fashions of nobility. Lady Lucienne was a socialite whom the noblewomen of Dante respected and followed. Passing up on such an offer could cause a rift in her freshly-established relationship with the Marchioness.

Lady Lucienne added, "I promise to take Your Majesty's tastes into account at all times. I know all of the kingdom's best tailors, jewellers, and shoemakers. If Your Majesty wishes for any design to be made, I will see to it that it is completed in a timely manner."

"Thank you, Lady Lucienne. I look forward to your counsel."

The Marchioness' makeup was light enough for Emilia to see a blush colouring the older woman's cheeks. "I appreciate Your Majesty's trust and will do all in my power to live up to your expectations."

Emilia thought of the best test for the noblewoman. If their tastes clashed too much, she could come up with an excuse and place Lady Lucienne in charge of organising the royal events instead. "Please choose two sets of clothes for me today. I wish to have a pleasant breakfast with His Holiness to discuss some business and then we will travel to Port Lisza in commoners' disguise."

Lady Lucienne's expression soured. "This may sound impertinent, Your Majesty, but it could be dangerous to leave the palace without proper protection."

"You needn't worry. I am not going alone."

The Marchioness did not seem convinced. She guided Emilia to the stool in front of the vanity and began to brush the Queen's hair with an ornate bone hairbrush made with boar bristles. With feather-light and practised strokes, the lady gently combed Emilia's hair.

"Your Majesty's beautiful features remind me of Queen Cecilia."

Emilia stiffened at the mention of the former queen. She heard from Sir Rowell that Queen Cecilia was a kind and loving individual, but she did not expect Lady Lucienne to be on friendly terms with Emilia's mother.

"May I have permission to speak freely, Your Majesty?"

There were no downsides to learning what Marchioness Durand was eager to get off her chest. After all, the more Emilia learned about Lady Lucienne's goals, the quicker she could make up her mind as to what duties she could entrust to the marchioness.

"You may."

Lady Lucienne's lips curved into a meek smile. "Your Majesty may not be aware of this, but Cecilia and I were good friends before her marriage."

Thinking back on the past brought life to Lady Lucienne's eyes, and her tone overflowed with fondness. "Cecilia was a free spirit. She wanted to venture out into the world—to see the sights of the

Arcane Sea, or the Mage Assembly, or go as far as the Kingdom of Asmor. She read books written by travellers and often wrote me of her secret desire to run away from her royal duties and join an expedition."

Lucienne's lips pressed into a line, and she sucked in a breath. "I can finally say this now that her husband is no longer here. Cecilia deserved better than a man who left her to rot in a palace only to be attacked by the vipers who prey on weak hearts."

Thinking back, Emilia did read over a hundred books related to travel around the Hellion Empire, the recently fallen Kingdom of Darkgate, the ruins of the fallen Kingdom of Tzidan, the Kingdom of Drovia, and some accounts about the pilgrimages to the City of Light.

Those belonged to the former queen?

It was unexpected since most noblewomen were more interested in appearances than education. Just like the mother Emilia never got a chance to meet, she too felt stifled in the palace and wanted to do away with it.

"Why are you telling me all of this?" Emilia asked, studying the Marchioness' face intently in the mirror's reflection.

"I apologise, Your Majesty. I was rambling."

Their eyes met in the mirror, and Emilia knew that Lady Lucienne wished to speak more about Cecilia. The young queen did not know how to feel about a mother she never got to meet. Just hearing the word 'Mother' in passing made Emilia shudder, and the memories she recalled during her deep sleep made her heart ache.

"Lady Lucienne, prepare my attire and inquire with His Holiness if he is able to attend breakfast. Also, inform Sir Rowell to make the necessary arrangements for the outing." There was little chance Valerian would miss the opportunity to go on their date. As long as she could convince him to go to Port Lisza, she could kill two birds with one stone—the date with Valerian and find out how Ivy was doing.

Hopefully, he won't mind spending the day tailing the head maid of the palace...

"Of course, Your Majesty."

Emilia felt the inquisitive stare from Valerian who sat next to her instead of taking the seat of honour at the opposite end of the dining table. Today, he seemed comfortable sporting a turquoise doublet with intricate golden embroidery worn over a white shirt that peeked out at the untied collar. A nobleman's clothes suited him too well. Somehow, he managed to blend in with any style and place with unnatural ease.

Did Luminos bless him with outward tranquillity, too?

Emilia chewed on her apple pie and could taste none of it. Swallowing her food, she looked at him. "Your Holiness, aren't you going to eat your meal?"

His mouth curved downwards when she used his title.

"Valerian," she corrected herself.

His name on her lips brought his charming smile back. "I do not eat in the mornings. All members of the Church of the Holy Light fast until noon."

Emilia set her cutlery down. She should have done more research into the customs of the Church. "I hope I did not offend you by inviting you here for a meal."

"Not at all. I am more than happy to be by your side, Saintess."

She did her best to keep a straight face as she clutched her knife and fork with an iron grip. "Would you mind not using that title in front of the servants?"

Leaning back in his seat, Valerian raked his eyes over the three maids who stood against the wall with their eyes cast to the floor. "Nancy, Leelah, and Karine—you ladies won't share my endearment for the Queen with anyone, will you?"

The maids nodded vigorously.

Emilia assessed him with interest as she wiped her mouth with a napkin. The Pope spent barely over two weeks in her palace and was on the first name basis with the help. He was a force to be reckoned with, especially since the maids had rosy cheeks after hearing him speak to them.

Valerian's too charming for his own good.

He gave her a cheeky smile that made her unconsciously smile back. "See? All is well again."

"Yes. You have ingrained yourself in this palace faster than I ever could."

The Pope must have picked up on the edge in her tone as he reached over the table and patted her hand. The warmth from his calloused palm made her jerk her hand away.

"It is a habit of mine," he replied. "I try to get along with everyone no matter where I am."

"Would you get along with prisoners if you were thrown in a dungeon?"

He let out a laugh. "It has happened before."

Emilia's brows inched upwards. *The Pope was thrown in prison? When? By whom?*

As if reading her mind, he rested his chin on his hand. "When I was first granted the gift of healing by the Goddess, not many were as welcoming as they are today. It was in part thanks to Sir Erenel who kept me safe that I managed to survive and reach the City of Light."

"Isn't a holy knight assigned to the Pope after they take the position?"

"We met in a fishing town while Sir Erenel was on a mission to escort Cardinal Maynard. I was but a carpenter then, trying to make ends meet."

Emilia inched closer to listen to his fascinating backstory. She would never have expected that a commoner could become the Pope. It was no wonder the Cardinals were up in arms about it. "How did you go from being a carpenter to a prisoner?"

Valerian locked gazes with her. "Cardinal Maynard was asked to perform a miracle and heal a fisherman's wife. Unsurprisingly, he refused to help without getting a hefty donation for the temple. I got so angry that I saw red. As I stormed over to speak my mind to the pompous man who pretended to be a dutiful follower of Luminos, my body grew heavy. My mind filled with knowledge I never possessed and bright light emitted from my flesh. It engulfed the town and healed everyone in it regardless of their ailment. Before I knew what was happening to me, Sir Erenel was on his knees in front of me, muttering something about a miracle."

She clenched her jaw. The cardinals of the Church were as bad as the common nobles. They would not move an inch unless their financial desires were met. And to kidnap a man who awakened his holy powers? That was beyond her. She briefly mused about hopping on a ship across the Misty Sea to the City of Light and punching Cardinal Maynard in the face.

Valerian reclined in his seat. Although he tried to smile, it did not reach his icy eyes. "After expending all of that godly energy, I fell unconscious for days. At that time, Cardinal Maynard claimed I was a heretic mage and had me arrested by the local baron. Thankfully, Sir Erenel did not leave my side the entire time and kept me from harm for he believed that Luminos had chosen me."

"If you were imprisoned, how did you become the Pope?"

"After I was transported to the City of Light, the cardinals took their time deciding on how to execute me." He clenched his fists and let out a laugh that sent a shiver through her. "What they did not expect was an uprising of believers. Those who were healed did not trust Maynard's words. They spread the word about the miracle I had created from village to village, town to town, city to city, until thousands flocked to the City of Light before the papal election. They demanded to be healed…by the man chosen by Luminos."

Finally, he lifted his gaze. It was filled with so much warmth and kindness, that her heart gave a squeeze. She had undergone her struggles in life and knew what it was like to be blamed for the things she did not do.

"What did you do?" she asked, completely enthralled by his melodic voice.

"I healed the people, day and night. Rich or poor—it did not matter to me. Luminos granted me the power of healing, and all I could do was follow Her will. And every night, I collapsed from exhaustion, just as every night there was an assassin waiting to take my life."

Emilia gasped. "You fought off assassins?"

"Sir Erenel never left me alone. Staying by my side, his prowess with a sword grew, fed by those who wished me death. Not soon after, the twelve cardinals could no longer deny my powers or the voice of the endless stream of pilgrims flocking to the High Temple."

"I...I am sorry that happened to you," Emilia said and meant it.

Valerian gently lifted her hand to his lips. "T'was but a fleeting suffering that has led me to you, Saintess."

Ah, my heart nearly jumped out of my chest! He's a perfect flirt.

Having extracted her hand from his hold, she asked, "Your Holi—Valerian, would you join me for an outing this afternoon?"

He beamed at her, bringing out his dimples that were hard to ignore. "I will always make time for you, my beautiful saintess."

Emilia smiled back and clasped her hands together. "Wonderful! Please dress down as we are going to visit Port Lisza."

Valerian raised a brow. His captivating eyes seemed to see right through her scheme, but he simply chuckled and finished the water in his goblet. "I look forward to our *outing*."

13

THE YOUNG PRINCE

THESSIAN

The gusty wind turned into a storm by evening. Battered by the harsh elements, the merchant's caravan rocked from side to side on the road.

Thessian was faring no better on horseback as he wiped the rainwater from his face. He could not wait for an inn or a village to take refuge, and, at this point, he would settle for an alcove on the side of a hill.

His horse, although not typically the nervous kind, was huffing and treading along the now mulch of a dirt road with great effort.

They all needed a break after the long journey.

The merchants' caravan pulled to the side of the road.

Delphine peeled back the canvas and jumped out of the back. This made Thessian tug on his horse's reins, drawing the animal to a halt.

The merchant approached the mercenaries first, shouted something over the storm, and made his way to Thessian and Ronne, who were bringing up the rear.

"Theo, we will rest in the nearest village before the storm gets worse," Delphine yelled.

"Very well," Thessian replied, eager for a break.

Delphine glanced at Ronne. "We should be out of this miserable weather soon enough, boy."

The merchant returned to his caravan, and they urged the horses to pick up the pace.

In Thessian's view, the caravan rocked on the road—the wheels struggling to maintain speed on the muddy, uneven roads. He hoped it would last until they reached a safe place, for Lady Clarissa was never fond of storms. She often yelped when she heard a thunder's roar in the distance.

I should not think in such a way. That was over a decade ago.

They passed a handful of farms until they pulled to a halt in front of an inn which was surrounded by five houses and a general store.

The merchants went inside to enquire about the rooms while Thessian and Ronne secured their horses in the wooden stables which appeared to be slapped together haphazardly. Thessian could not help overhearing the hired guards groaning about the weather.

As he tied his horse to a post, the doors of the stables reopened, and the four mercenaries they travelled with waltzed in.

Thessian noted that three of the men seemed to be in their thirties while the last one was a lad no older than his late teens.

"Can't believe we're stuck out here!" One of the men grumbled as he ran a beefy hand through his wet clumps of dark hair.

"Better 'ere than out der, War'n," the second man, with a thinning hairline, replied in a more cheerful voice.

Warren snorted and finally took notice of Thessian and Ronne. "And who're you supposed t'be?"

"We were hired by Delphine to protect the caravan on the way to Garlia."

"I know that much!" The man studied Thessian and then Ronne with a raised brow. "Is he your boy?"

"Brother," Thessian corrected.

Warren bobbed his head in acknowledgement. "I had a brother once. Tha swine-lick'r got killed by the guard of some noble for disrespecting him. You've got a face of a noble."

"Is it because I'm handsome?" Thessian rubbed his jawline thoughtfully, feeling the beginnings of a beard there. "I must admit, I get that a lot."

Warren let out a loud guffaw. "Guess men like you get hired often by dem nobles. You look too clean-cut to be running with the cut-throats."

"I'm not here to justify myself."

All the questions were beginning to get on Thessian's nerves. He did not have the time or the desire to get friendly with some mercenaries he would not be seeing in a couple of days. What he needed was to get changed out of his wet clothes.

Thessian unstrapped his knapsack from the horse and draped it over his shoulder. He ignored Warren's barrage of questions, strode out of the barn, and headed for the inn.

Ronne ran after him. "Do you think it wise to ignore them, Theo?"

"They are of no consequence to us or our mission. Just stay alert."

They entered the inn to find Delphine, Henri, and Lady Clarissa standing in a circle with sour looks on their faces.

Thessian approached them and eyed the merchants. "Is something the matter?"

Delphine smiled his usual smile, but it did not reach his eyes. He let out a nervous laugh. "It would appear there is only one room available. Due to the storm, we are not the only ones seeking shelter from the elements."

Any chance of a hot bath went out of the window. Most likely, the merchants would take the room for themselves and leave the mercenaries to stay in the barn.

Delphine spoke with resignation. "Sacha has poor health and

will take the room while we will stay with the goods in the stables."

Thessian could not help his confusion showing. Delphine was considering Lady Clarissa's comfort above his own. That, or the goods needed to be protected at all times.

"If you don't mind me asking, what goods are you delivering to Countess Morel?"

Delphine was about to reply when Henri interjected, "I will retrieve Sacha's baggage from the caravan and escort him to his accommodations."

With evident relief, Delphine nodded. "Good idea. I shall pay the innkeeper for the food and see if he has any spare blankets we could use."

Thessian's eyes met with Lady Clarissa's for a second. Her complexion was on the pale side. Her eyes were weary. As thunder rumbled outside the inn, she squeezed her eyes shut and hurried after Henri.

I guess, she hasn't gotten over her fear.

The night dragged on.

Thessian had changed into dry clothes and sat on a heap of hay next to Ronne.

A handful of oil lanterns were spread out around the stables to illuminate the space. The howling wind and the pummelling of rain against the roof and flimsy walls kept most men awake.

From his spot, Thessian assessed the merchants—Henri and Delphine. With everyone's help, they managed to bring the caravan into the stables, which occupied almost all of the free space that the horses didn't use.

The merchants had their backs resting against the wheels and were drinking from their flasks.

Warren and his band of men had taken off their wet cloaks and coats, wrapped themselves in blankets the merchants had passed out from the caravan, and were happily consuming another barrel of ale they purchased from the innkeeper. They seemed to care little about the threat to the merchants or their merchandise, which seemed strange, as it was their job. It was almost as if it was of no consequence if their employer lived or died.

Thessian got up, which drew Ronne's attention.

"I am going to speak with the merchants," Thessian informed him. "Rest." He briefly glanced at the rowdy mercenaries. "If able."

The boy settled down on the hay and closed his eyes, all the while keeping his hand under his knapsack where he most likely was holding on to a dagger or a knife.

Thessian approached the merchants. "Would you mind if I sat down?"

Delphine nervously glanced at Henri and then waved for Thessian to come closer. "Are you having trouble sleeping?"

"I do not sleep well in a noisy environment," Thessian lied.

Years on the battlefield taught him how to fall asleep in five minutes. It did not matter if meteors were falling from the sky or hundreds of soldiers were having a drinking party outside of his tent. At war, the worst thing that could be heard was silence as it often was followed by death.

"Oh, I completely understand that," Delphine replied cheerfully. "I myself prefer a bed to the rough dirt."

Henri screwed the lid onto his flask and shot up. "I will rest in the caravan."

The slender man nodded to Thessian, shuffled around, and clambered into the back of the caravan, which was covered with a thick sheet to keep the prying eyes at bay.

Taking this opportunity, Thessian sat near Delphine, his eyes focused on seemingly nothing in front of him while deep in thought. He wanted answers to many questions.

Why is Lady Clarissa travelling with merchants? Do they know her true identity? Are they concealing her from someone?

And the question that bothered him the most. *What happened to her after our engagement fell apart?*

"You seem to have a lot on your mind, Theo."

Thessian turned to the man. "If it is not a secret, how did you meet Sacha?"

Delphine took another tentative sip from his flask. Lady Clarissa had spent all day in the caravan with him and possibly had shed some light on her connection to Thessian.

"It happened four years ago when I was in Vinmare. As you may know, it is Count Baudelaire's territory and is filled with vineyards. I thought it would be a good idea to do some research on wine for my customers. Duchess Malette and Countess Morel were incessantly asking me to find a winemaker as good as Baudelaire. So, in one of those vineyards, I discovered Sacha."

"You stumbled upon him in a vineyard?"

Delphine clutched his flask. "The tale is a slight more grim, but yes."

Grim? "How does a vineyard worker become an accountant for a merchant company?"

The merchant wheezed out a sound similar to a pained laugh. "Sacha proved his abilities to me rather quickly." Turning directly to Thessian, the man narrowed his eyes. "You are awfully interested in my employee, Theo. Are you two well acquainted?"

"We are acquainted enough."

"Sacha did not think so when I asked him."

"He is a shy person," Thessian countered.

Delphine furrowed his brows, making the wrinkles on his forehead stand out. "I do not know what relationship you and he may have had in the past, Theo, but I suggest you let the matter rest here. Sacha is no longer the person you once knew. Many things have happened to him, most of which were not pleasant."

Thessian ground his teeth and climbed to his full height. "I think I should retire for the night."

"I thought you could not sleep due to the noise…"

"I will have to make do."

Equipped with new information, Thessian returned to Ronne's side. The boy's breathing came in rhythmic succession, letting the prince know that his subordinate was deep in the realm of dreams.

He lay on his back next to the lad and closed his eyes. As he did so, all he could see in his mind's eye were the long blonde locks and eyes as captivating as violets.

Musical laughter came from the Rose Garden in the Imperial Palace's West Wing. Streams of sunlight filtered in through the glass dome of the vast greenhouse the emperor had built for his beloved empress as a token of his undying affection. Roses from all over the continent bloomed and painted the view different shades of red, yellow, and white—all colours of the Hellion Empire's flag.

Thessian halted his stride and turned to Alvin Crumb—the Head Butler of the Empress' Palace. The man, although still able to fulfil his duties, grew visibly old after Thessian turned fourteen.

"Must I do this today? I have sword practice..." Thessian grumbled.

Alvin's lower lip twitched as it did when he was about to drone on about imperial duties. "Your Imperial Highness, meeting your fiancée is of utmost importance to the Empire. Lady Clarissa von Leutten was hand-picked by Her Imperial Majesty for you, just as Lady Vivienne Becker was selected for His Imperial Highness, Prince Cain."

"But Cain is of age to get married. I do not plan on it."

"You never know what the future holds, Your Imperial Highness. Please put forth your best manners for Lady Clarissa. She may not enjoy your talk of sword-fighting techniques and rolling in the mud with the knights."

"We weren't rolling in the mud, Alvin. We were wrestling!"

"Yes, that. Please do not mention it to the young lady of House von Leutten."

Thessian rolled his eyes. Not only was he stuck with a fiancée he did not want, he had to listen to Alvin's incessant nagging.

"Thessian?" The empress' sing-song voice called out. "Come closer and meet Lady Clarissa and her mother!"

Thessian stifled a groan and put on his best smile. After all, imperial duties were everything to the prince. He had to appear perfect, be an *example, and never allow others to grasp his weaknesses. Which was why he did not wish for a lady to be a part of his life. If they did manage to form a good relationship, she may be in danger due to his status. Although House Leutten were historically a family of knights and generals, they may not be able to protect her until their wedding day.*

"Your Imperial High—"

"I'm going!" Thessian muttered under his breath.

At the age of fourteen, he was taller than most men in the palace. He was even as tall as his older brother, Cain, who turned seventeen last spring. Thessian could not wait to grow taller still. As his body grew in muscle, his ability to swing the heavy steel sword got better. Soon enough, he may even defeat the Knight Commander in a duel.

The paved path led the prince to a circular gazebo carved from the finest white marble. There, with a smile on her face, his mother sat in an ornate chair carved out of the elder wood and shaped to perfection by the most skilled craftsmen in the Empire. A golden dessert table between the empress and her guests held up a plethora of cakes and pies.

Upon seeing her son, Empress Leandrys' smile grew wider. For a woman in her late thirties, she remained a steadfast beauty that no woman could match with her long golden hair that was pinned up with intricate pearls and flowers, delicate features, and kind green eyes.

Thessian stopped a polite distance away from his mother, placed his right hand over his heart, and bowed at the middle. "The second prince greets the Moon of the Hellion Empire, Empress Leandrys Debrianna Hellios."

"Come closer my son," the Empress announced.

Thessian straightened up and approached the table.

At the same time, Marchioness von Leutten jumped up from her seat with her daughter doing the same. He could not see their faces as they kept their gazes locked on the floor.

Diving into a deep curtsy, the Marchioness said, "I greet the Second Star of the Hellion Empire, Prince Thessian Alexey Hellios."

"I greet you also, Marchioness von Leutten. It is a pleasure to see you again. Please be at ease."

The Marchioness finally lifted her face as she fluidly adjusted her posture. "It is my pleasure to introduce my daughter, Lady Clarissa von

Leutten, to Your Imperial Highness." Noticing that her daughter did not leave the curtsy, the Marchioness nudged the girl with her sharp elbow. "Come and greet the prince, Clarissa."

With equally practised movements as that of her mother, Lady Clarissa resumed an upright posture, smiled politely at Thessian, and parroted the same greeting as her mother. "I greet the Second—"

The rest of the greeting was lost on him. His breath caught in his throat at the sight of the lady's mesmerising violet eyes that shone with rebellion and determination. She was no simple lady who enjoyed embroidery and hid behind a quiet disposition.

Thessian took hold of the lady's hand and gave it a faint kiss on the back of her hand. "It is a pleasure to meet you, Lady Clarissa von Leutten."

The Empress let out a giggle. "Thessian, Lady Clarissa has not had the opportunity to take a stroll around the Rose Garden. Could you give her a tour?"

Thessian glanced at his mother. She must have picked up on the fact he found Lady Clarissa eye-catching. "It would be my pleasure, Your Imperial Majesty."

Thessian offered the lady his arm. "Please allow me to escort you, my lady."

Lady Clarissa pursed her lips and draped her arm through his, placing her hand ever so lightly on his forearm.

Alvin followed behind them a few paces while Thessian walked away from the gazebo and guided the lady to the quiet, winding trails of the hedge maze beyond the walls of the greenhouse.

Lady Clarissa tucked a stray lock of her blonde hair behind her ear. "His Imperial Highness must be thinking a great deal of things as the silence that has befallen us continues to stretch."

Thessian felt his ears burning. He did not spend much time talking to ladies at the imperial balls or formal events. Instead, he preferred to engage in conversation with Laurence Oswald, who was a breath of fresh air among the nobles' children. Despite the two-year gap, Laurence did not treat Thessian as if he were an unreachable idol or a stepping-stone to power.

"I do apologise for not being entertaining, my lady. I was told not to talk about the things I enjoy."

She snorted, and he struggled not to gape. "Mother told me all talk of unladylike hobbies is forbidden also."

"Would you be interested in listening to a boring lecture on sword-fighting while we walk?"

"I prefer sword-fighting to talk of doilies, ribbons, and coloured threads."

He let out a laugh. "I think we will get along quite well, you and I."

Lady Clarissa finally smiled for the first time, which made his heart thump rapidly in his chest.

Thessian swallowed nervously. Perhaps Mother did choose a partner most suited for me.

"And what of the lady's hobbies? What is it that makes them unladylike?"

"I enjoy sparring with my older brother when Mother is not looking, of course. According to her, women with a fighting form are unattractive, and would make it hard to find a husband in life."

"Since I am to be your fiancé, I find your hobby to be admirable. It does not diminish your worth in my eyes."

"Then we should spar to see who is stronger."

Thessian was taken aback. He was at least a foot taller than the lady. "Lady Clarissa, are you saying you are stronger than me?"

"It is the easiest way to find out. For all I know, Your Imperial Highness spends his afternoons idling under an oak tree and chewing on straw."

He could not help laughing. She had described Laurence to a fault. "I assure you, my lady. I take my position as Prince rather seriously. I hone my sword skills to be able to defend our land from invasions and those who wish ill upon our countrymen."

Lady Clarissa came to a stop and studied his face with intent. "Your Imperial Highness may find that taking the life of another is not easy, be it for the defence of the Empire or the protection of one's body."

"Does the lady speak from experience?"

She waved his comment away. "I do not need it. I saw my father's haunted expression after his first war. He left a jolly man only to return a broken one."

Thessian had nothing to add. House Leutten was one of the shields that protected the Emperor and the Empire. They often engaged in warfare to protect the western borders. Thessian overheard his father mentioning Marquess von Leutten's bravery on more than one occasion during dinnertime and knew that taking a life was no simple matter. The Knight Commander told him that a million times. Yet, hearing it from such a young lady who was barely fourteen made his heart squeeze.

"I thank you for your candour, my lady. Shall we resume our stroll? I suspect the Empress and Marchioness von Leutten are waiting for us to return."

Lady Clarissa sucked in a deep breath at the mention of her mother and gave a reluctant nod. "Please lead the way, Your Imperial Highness."

In the shade of the oak tree near the Imperial Knights' Training Grounds, Thessian sat on the grass next to his chatty guest.

"Do you fancy her then?" Laurence asked as he picked a piece of an apple out of his teeth.

Thessian nearly cut his hand while oiling his sword's blade. "Lady Clarissa is my fiancée, Laurence. I will marry her regardless of my feelings as she is someone the Empress chose for me."

"Come now, no need to act coy. I knew the second you started talking about the lady's pretty face that Your Highness was a lost cause."

"How would you know that? You're barely twelve!"

Laurence put his arms behind him and leaned back. "I have two brothers, remember? All they do is talk about the ladies who took their fancy at the balls. I think Dion was the one to comment on Lady Clarissa's striking charm the other day."

Thessian clenched the oily cloth he was using to spread the oil on his sword. "How dare he eye the fiancée of the Imperial Family?"

"Calm yourself, Your Imperial Highness. Dion would not dare touch her now that the engagement has become official, and you are to wed her when you come of age. He has bigger problems, like keeping up with his succession classes. The idiot still struggles with history and territory management."

"You speak as if you are taking them alongside him."

"No. I'm not allowed. Only Dion and Florence are permitted to attend those. We are the heir, the spare, and the pawn. I am but a trading tool for my family to spread my seed and create more Oswalds."

Thessian stared at his new friend in disbelief. Laurence certainly had a pessimistic outlook on life.

The prince took out a clean cloth from a leather satchel beside him and wiped the excess oil off the blade. "Unlike in the Oswald household, my brothers and I are all vying for the throne."

"Does that mean you will end up killing each other one day?"

"Of course not! We are a family, and we get along."

Laurence remained silent and scratched his dark-brown mop of hair. "It appears, Dion is not the only one not taking his history lessons seriously…"

The prince grasped the hilt of his sword, and Laurence was upright in the blink of an eye. "I think I hear my father calling. Till next time!"

As if sensing imminent danger, the marquess' son ran off, leaving Thessian to ponder the many things he never wished to think about.

14
THE QUEEN'S IMPORTANT OUTING

EMILIA

Emilia, **Sir Regis, Sir Erenel,** and Valerian rode on horseback to Port Lisza, which was the closest port to Newburn as well as Ambrose's hometown.

The Queen did not want to draw too much attention, so she put on a short brown wig and a woolly hat. To look as plain as possible, she asked Lady Lucienne to remove all makeup. To her surprise, Marchioness Lucienne complied without as much as a hint of displeasure. If Marchioness Durand truly could be trusted, the takeover of the kingdom's nobility was a short stretch away. Emilia could almost taste victory on the horizon. Once her plans bore fruit, she could hand the Dante Kingdom to Thessian, which would help him get the position of Crown Prince. From there, the path to the

Empire's crown could take a couple of years.

Then again, Kyros won't let Thessian take the throne without a fight.

As they travelled through the Royal Wood, Emilia's eyes settled on Valerian's broad back. He had knowledge bestowed upon him by Luminos, which held her interest.

What kind of information did he receive? Just how many blessings from the Goddess did he possess? Why Valerian?

Although he was hard to read on most days, she could not say that she did not find herself thinking about him from time to time. Unlike Clayton who opened his heart to her and would happily turn against the world for her, Valerian's empathy towards others drew her in. He did not seem to care whether someone was a king or a street urchin. He would use his healing powers as long as the people needed him. It was an admirable trait, and possibly the reason why Luminos chose him as her representative.

"We are almost there," Sir Regis announced from the front of the line.

Emilia smirked. It had been two years since she last visited Port Lisza, and every time she was blown away by the jaw-dropping view.

Pulling her horse to a trot when they broke through the forest's never-ending treeline, she admired the shimmering sight of the vast Misty Sea. Lazy clouds drifted above the busy town that overflowed with merchant ships docking and leaving the port. Rows upon rows of log houses spread farther back than the last time she was there, and she could see the spire of the clock tower at the heart of it all, in the market square.

She turned her gaze to the northern part of Port Lisza, spotting the red-tiled roof of the academy where Ivy was taking her classes. The fifteen-year-old wanted to become a teacher in the orphanage where Ivy and Ambrose grew up after losing their parents to sickness. It was a simple goal that Emilia wished to support.

"Your Ma—" Sir Regis stopped himself as he turned his horse around to speak to her.

"Call me Lady Em while we are here," Emilia instructed. "And I shall call you Regis in turn."

The Vice Captain of the Royal Guard blushed and gave a nod.

Valerian inched his steed closer to her other side. "Is this where we will have our date? I must admit, it is quite picturesque."

"I am pleased you like it," she replied. "There is one place I wish to visit before we can commence our date."

"I expected as much."

Emilia studied the Pope's serene face. He did not seem to mind that she was using their date as an excuse. He was much easier to deal with than a royal prince or a king. "Thank you for your understanding, Valerian."

"In return, while we are here, let us play a married couple."

Sir Regis's brows shot up while Sir Erenel nearly fell off his horse. The holy knight managed to steady himself at the last moment.

Emilia shrugged. "Very well. For the time being, you are my husband, Val."

The Pope grinned and leaned over until he planted a soft peck on her cheek. "You may take me anywhere you wish, my lovely wife."

Ever the flirt...

Sir Erenel, still recovering from the last shock, involuntarily jerked his horse to the right, causing him to slide halfway down to the left. He clambered back up as his confused horse started to spin in a circle.

Emilia let out a mirthful laugh at the whole situation and urged her horse into a trot down the hill that led to the core of the town.

Along the road, they passed newly built houses and stores. She recognised a smithy attached to a weapons shop peeking out from one of the alleys and made a mental note to visit at some point. The smith was a kind-hearted, family man who sold Emilia her favourite dagger when she was short on coin. Since that first awkward encounter, she decided to visit every chance she got and even paid extra for his services. Hopefully, he had not forgotten her over the past few years.

Emilia sucked in a breath of fresh, salty air. Although Newburn was merely two hours away on horseback, the stifling feeling that the city brought made her feel as though she was suffocating. Here, in a town full of hard-working sailors and merchants, she could be herself.

Turning at the crossroads, she headed south in the direction of the orphanage. The children there had suffered on her account during King Gilebert's funeral parade, so she dared not visit them right away. In her stead, Ambrose was often the one to go and get the updates from the nuns who worked tirelessly to keep the place going.

She pushed her horse uphill until she came to a white house with a picket fence. There, she hopped off her steed and pulled him by the reins as she approached the gates.

The men followed along in silence, most likely pondering, what on earth the Queen of Dante was up to? Not that she could blame them.

She handed the reins to Sir Regis. "Wait here. I will be back shortly."

"Lady Em, it is too dangerous for you without an escort," the Vice Captain complained.

"That may be for a noble or a queen, but I am a commoner right now."

"If I may be so bold, commoners do not have escorts," the knight grumbled back.

Emilia crossed her arms and tapped her chin in thought. "I suppose they do not. While I have a husband over there—" she nodded towards the Pope, "—perhaps you and Sir Erenel could act as my over-protective brothers?"

Valerian snickered and patted Sir Regis' back. "Brother-in-law, I hope we are on good terms."

"If it will make you feel better, Regis, Val can come along. He does not look as imposing as you or Sir Erenel."

"Please, call me Eren. The Sir may attract unwanted attention," the holy knight suggested.

She peered over her shoulder, noticing that the nun in charge had come out with a perplexed expression on her haggard face. Ambling over to the group, her wrinkle-framed eyes widened in surprise. "Lady Em, is that you?"

Emilia waved the knights off and approached Sister Sabianna. "Good day to you, Sister. I assume Ambrose has come by this morning."

The nun visibly relaxed and fondly replied, "Yes, she did. Ambrose is a wonderful example to all of the children in the orphanage. They love seeing her and often miss her when she's not around."

"I apologise for stealing her time away." Emilia took Sister Sabianna's aged hands in hers. "I hope it is not too much to ask, how are the children doing? I—er—heard what happened to them during the king's funeral parade."

The nun grimly hung her head. "It may be best for you to come inside for a cup of tea in my office." She studied the men accompanying Emilia. "Do they work for your father's merchant guild?"

"I am her husband, Valerian, and they are her brothers, Eren and Regis." Valerian draped his arm around Emilia's shoulders.

Sir Regis visibly twitched as though he was about to leap forward.

Sister Sabianna looked from Emilia to the supposed brothers who did not resemble each other in the slightest.

"We have different mothers," Emilia clarified.

The nun's mouth formed an 'o', and she gave a nod in understanding. "I apologise for questioning your family, Lady Em."

"No need. We get that a lot. Right, brothers?" Emilia asked over her shoulder.

Sir Erenel and Sir Regis nodded in unison, giving each other a side glance afterwards.

"Then please," Sister Sabianna began in a warm tone, "come in, all of you. Any family of Lady Em's is a family to us at the orphanage."

"Thank you kindly for your hospitality, Sister." Valerian flashed one of his killer smiles.

Emilia was tempted to smother his face with a thick cowl. The

Pope even made the old nun blush.

How am I supposed to survive as his pretend wife for a day?

The head nun led them around the side to the back of the house and brought them into a cramped office that was decorated with simple wooden furniture, including a desk. As she offered Emilia to sit, the two plainly-dressed, broad-shouldered knights bumped into each other in their attempt to enter at the same time. Eventually, they squeezed in, one at a time, while struggling not to step on each other's toes.

Once Sister Sabianna left to bring tea, Valerian broke the silence. "To think my wife has been helping the orphans of this town. I never knew you were such a generous lady."

"You will find that there are a great many things you do not know about me."

"And I look forward to finding them all."

The Pope beamed at her, and Emilia nearly rolled her eyes.

Sister Sabianna returned only a couple of moments later with a hot cast-iron pot of steaming water, some nettle tea in a ceramic jar, and a teacup. Pouring the tea for Emilia with trembling hands, it was obvious that the tremors which had visibly gotten worse over the years hadn't abated. Emilia wished she could help in some way, but no amount of gold could fix time's affliction.

The Queen stole a peek at Valerian. *Could the Pope's miracle cure Sister Sabianna's illness?*

No doubt, he would willingly agree to do it, yet that would give away his identity to everyone in town. A healing miracle was as flashy as it was visible from a distance.

Valerian winked at her and bent down to whisper in Emilia's ear, "I could ask Eren to heal her if that is your wish."

Emilia mulled over her options. He could read her so easily, it was frightening. Yet, she was thankful that he could understand her without her needing to utter a single word.

"On our way back," Emilia replied.

Their eyes met before he retreated to stand behind her, between the two knights.

"It is nice to see that you and your husband are very much in love," Sister Sabianna commented.

Emilia felt a chill washing over her. She was not actually married to Valerian. In the same vein, she only recently accepted her feelings for Lord Clayton who promised to protect her from a distance today.

"You were going to tell me about the children," Emilia said to divert the conversation.

Sister Sabianna lowered herself into an old, creaking chair behind her desk and rested the teapot on its worn surface. "Some of them have become frightened of strangers and refuse to leave the orphanage. The only one who has been a brave boy is Gabriel. He even wishes to join the Royal Guard and serve the new queen after he was rescued by Her Majesty."

Emilia's brows rose a notch. *Is Gabriel the boy the bandits' leader used as a shield during the negotiations?*

"Tis but a dream. To become a royal knight, one must be a noble or of noble birth," Sister Sabianna commented sadly.

Sir Regis cleared his throat. "I have a friend who works as a royal guard. He said, Her Majesty does not discriminate based on rank or birthright."

The nun's smile returned. "Then there is hope for Gabriel to one day realise his dream!"

Emilia balled her hands in her lap. In a few years, she would no longer be the Queen of Dante. She would not need guards or attendants who followed her around. Hopefully, by then, the young lad would find a different goal to strive towards.

"Is there anything I can do to help the children?" Emilia asked.

The nun shook her head. "They need time to heal and overcome their fears."

"I see," Emilia replied, deflated. "What about Ivy Blanc? Do you know how she is faring at the academy?"

Sister Sabianna opened a drawer in her desk and pulled out a thick stack of letters with neat cursive handwriting. "Ivy has been such a good child. She wrote me almost daily about her studies and how interesting every subject was. As of recent, her letters arrive rather infrequently. What once was excitement sounds akin to forced repetition. I fear she is having a hard time, but I cannot visit her. As you know, entry into the academy's dormitories is restricted to family members."

And high-paying patrons.

It was not uncommon for wealthy nobles to sponsor a promising child and expect them to return the favour by working for the household as a servant later on.

No wonder Ambrose left her duties as Head Maid to visit Ivy. If even Sister Sabianna began suspecting something was amiss then Emilia had no choice. She had to investigate the matter fully. And if some noble's son was giving Ambrose's younger sister a hard time, Emilia would be more than happy to expel the noble's child and their family to the countryside.

"I think I will pay Ivy a visit." Emilia stood and reached into the inner pocket of her woolly coat. She retrieved a small coin purse which she pushed across the table to Sister Sabianna. "My donation for this month."

"Oh, Lady Em, there is no need for this! Ambrose has given us more than enough to last until the Harvest Festival."

"There can never be enough gold when young ones are involved." Emilia gave the nun a reassuring smile. "Take it and feed the children something tasty that could ease their troubled hearts."

Sister Sabianna reluctantly accepted the coin purse and, with a strain, and a groan from the chair, rose from her seat. "I cannot thank you enough for your patronage, Lady Em. Truly! It is as if the gods sent you to us."

"Perhaps one of the goddesses did," Valerian offered with a cheeky grin.

Emilia fired a glare at him over her shoulder, and Valerian raised his hands in mock defence.

Turning back to Sister Sabianna, Emilia said, "It was a pleasure to see you again. I may not be able to come for a visit in the future, but know that I will continue to support the children."

On their way out, Valerian whispered something in Sir Erenel's ear, and the holy knight marched over to Sister Sabianna with purpose in his stride.

Offering her his hand, Erenel asked, "May I please have your hand, Sister?"

The nun appeared confused yet placed her shaking hand in his.

Erenel encased her hand with his and closed his eyes. A moment later, golden light spread from his palms.

The nun's eyes grew wide. No doubt she had never seen a true healing miracle as those were only provided for the wealthy. She glanced at Emilia, her surprise still fresh on her face.

"It is a gift for your hard work, Sister," Valerian said as he inched closer to Emilia's side. "May the blessings of Luminos guide you."

Sister Sabianna's mouth fell open. "I have seen you somewhere—"

Valerian placed his index finger to his lips, and the woman gave a slow nod in understanding.

Sir Erenel's healing light faded, and he took a step back. "May the blessings of Luminos guide you."

Sister Sabianna stared at her hands which no longer shook. Tears welled in her eyes, and she wiped them away with a beatific smile on her face that no longer appeared haggard. "I thank you, Lady Em, your *brothers*, and, of course, your *husband*."

"We best be on our way." Emilia turned around.

As she started for the door, it opened, and the boy she remembered from the funeral parade stared up at her with his brown doe eyes. He studied her face intently and shouted, "By the gods, you're the Que—"

Emilia covered his mouth with her hand and smiled kindly.

The boy could hardly contain his excitement but managed to do it by squeezing his lips shut.

Pulling back, Emilia straightened her posture.

"Gabriel, the guests were just leaving," Sister Sabianna announced, coming closer.

The boy's excitement plummeted only to be replaced by a scowl. He grabbed Emilia by the hand and pulled her after him with a lot of force.

The Queen nearly stumbled over her feet. Somehow, she

managed to follow along to the frantic calls of Sister Sabianna and Sir Regis.

Gabriel opened a door which led to a room where the children were either working on improving their sowing skills or learning to read with Sister Pailin who was much younger than Sister Sabianna.

"Look who's here!" Gabriel announced to the other children.

The children turned their heads from their tasks. Some appeared confused while others froze on the spot.

A girl no older than ten, with two thin braids resting on her shoulders, dropped her needle on the table as her eyes bulged in their sockets.

Sister Pailin shot upright. "Lady Em, have you come for a visit?"

"I—"

Emilia was cut off by one of the children screaming and cowering in fear behind Sister Pailin. Three of the other children followed suit and hid behind the table and chairs.

Sister Sabianna burst into the room and took in the unfolding scene. "Oh my, what a mess!"

Gabriel squared his shoulders and pointed at the crying child. "No need to wail like a wee babe, Chrys. She saved our lives. The Queen of Dante saved us!"

The room fell silent.

Emilia slapped her hand to her forehead. *Children truly have no filter on important matters.*

Sister Sabianna rushed over to Sister Pailin, and they curtsied low.

"Hurry now, children, all of you!" Sister Pailin urged.

"I-I apologise for any disrespect Your Majesty has suffered," Sister Sabianna said in a shaky voice. "If Your Majesty permits it, we will correct our behaviour—"

Emilia sighed while Valerian and their escort knights entered the room.

With a soothing smile firmly planted on his face, Valerian approached the two nuns. "Lift your heads, Sisters. Today, we are Valerian and Emilia—a husband and his lovely wife. There is no need to treat us any differently."

Emilia could not help being astounded by his relaxed demeanour.

Sister Sabianna and Sister Pailin did not move.

"Please raise your heads." Emilia used a tone as kind as Valerian's. The sooner she left the orphanage, the quicker the situation would be resolved. "Thank you for the tea, Sister Sabianna, and your hospitality. We will be on our way now."

The head nun cautiously peeked up. Whatever she saw on Emilia's face, made the older woman relax at last. "Thank you, L-lady Em. For everything."

Emilia nodded and turned around. A small hand caught her by the hem of her coat and tugged a few times, drawing the Queen's attention.

Looking down, Emilia saw the same girl with the braids holding an embroidered handkerchief in her small hand.

The child offered it to Emilia. "Please take this, Your Majesty. Thank you for saving us."

Emilia's eyes stung with unshed tears when she accepted the messily embroidered handkerchief. She was not used to people acknowledging her efforts. More than that, she was not used to people outside of her inner circle seeing her as anything other than a Cursed Princess or a Cursed Queen.

"Thank you, little one. I will treasure this gift you have given me."

Before Emilia turned into a cry-baby in front of the nuns and the children, she smiled one last time in reassurance to Sister Sabianna and left the orphanage as fast as manners permitted, her left hand clutching the child's embroidery of the red delphinium flower.

15
TROUBLESOME RUMOURS

EMILIA

Ready to leave, Emilia looked at the sky from the top of her saddle. Stormy clouds drifted towards the port town from the south. They had to pay a visit to Ivy's academy next. As long as they hurried, they could make it in time to question the dean about the situation. With the sun commencing its downward trend, the odds that Ambrose had finished her business at the academy were high. It would prevent Emilia from getting caught spying on her head maid.

"Where to next?" Valerian slid his boot into the stirrup and pulled himself onto his horse.

She remembered that they were supposed to be on a date, yet he had not complained once or demanded they do anything that would resemble a lovers' outing.

"I have business at the Port Lisza Academy. I could meet with you and Sir Erenel at the Laughing Clam, which is just off the main road, for supper."

"No need to part ways. I'm having a good time."

"Are you serious?"

"Of course. I learned more about you today than I have from the entire time I spent at the palace."

She studied the Pope's expression for any tells that could indicate he was lying. He seemed sincere. "You are a strange man, Valerian."

"Is it wrong for a husband to want to know more about his wife?"

"We are only pretending for a day."

He chuckled. "I can officiate our wedding at a moment's notice. All you have to do is say 'yes'."

Emilia dismissed his shameless flirting and spoke to Sir Regis. "We are heading to the Port Lisza Academy."

"Understood," the royal knight replied.

Her Vice Captain became much more tolerable since Sir Jehan took over as Guard Captain. Perhaps the young knight's pride was tempered when a man whom he considered to be old and decrepit beat him in a fair fight.

Too bad I missed the show.

Emilia wanted to judge Sir Regis' prowess with the sword with her own eyes.

Her gaze travelled past Valerian and Sir Regis to Sir Erenel. The man did not reveal much about himself. He seemed to go along with whatever Valerian decided and executed his orders like a robot. She could not help wondering if there was more to his story than the mask of a holy knight serving the Pope.

For now, Ivy's trouble was more important than any curiosities she had. Emilia patted her horse's glossy brown mane, feeling the soft fur beneath her fingers and urged the animal to pick up the pace.

The men wordlessly followed along.

On the other end of town, Port Lisza Academy stood tall. A thick brown-brick wall surrounded the academy and its two dormitories that were separated by gender. Instead of approaching the academy right away, Emilia and the rest of her companions secured their horses at the nearest posts and headed to the main gates on foot.

The guards on duty eyed their approach with smirks.

"Halt!" the man in a mud-coloured woolly coat with a sword strapped to his hip said as he raised his arm. "You are in the wrong part of town."

Emilia reached into her coat's pocket and retrieved a silver entry seal in the shape of a rose given to her by the dean. Only sponsors received the seals while the direct family members of the students had to ask for entry by proving their identity.

The guard stiffened and changed his tune in an instant. "Is the lady here to see the student she supports?"

"No. I wish to speak with the dean." Emilia slipped the seal back into her pocket. "These are my guards. They are coming as well."

"I will inform Baron Eggart of your wish to see him, my lady. May I have your name?"

"Tell him Lady Em is here."

In his panic, the guard bowed down and shot back up. "Lady Em! He instructed us to allow you entry anytime you wish. Please,"—he hurriedly opened the gate for her and motioned for her to come in—"follow me to Baron Eggart's office."

Emilia had paid a lot of gold over the years, partly as an investment in education and to encourage the students to work for the Crown later on. This way, when Thessian took over, there would be plenty of suitable candidates for different ministerial positions to choose from. So, checking in to see if her money was well spent was a good idea.

She glided through the gate and was faced with a snaking cobbled road that led to the main entrance of an impressive estate with stone walls and arched windows. The baron's estate sat on a bed of vibrant grass and was encased with manicured hedges. If memory served, the academy covered everything from heraldry and swordsmanship to mathematics and horseback riding for the nobles' children. At the age of seventeen, they could graduate and have their debut in high society. If Ivy wanted to participate in that kind of life, Emilia was ready to sponsor the girl.

It took less than ten minutes to reach the entrance and another fifteen to get to the dean's office. Most of the students had returned to their respective dormitories which were built behind the main estate, leaving some stragglers that were still on their way out of the main building.

Emilia felt the judgemental eyes of the passing students on her. She was young—graduation age. They were probably curious as to how a commoner got into their expensive halls. Baron Eggart would have a lot of explaining to do to the students' parents to ease their worries later.

Arriving at the door, the guard escort knocked and waited for the door to open before taking his leave.

A man in his mid-fifties appeared in the doorway. His tired eyes settled on her face before his mouth unhinged. "Lady Em, it is good to see you!"

The baron opened the door widely and warmly welcomed her in. "Have you come for an inspection? Do you need anything?" He rubbed his hands together, full of eagerness to please. "Tea, perhaps?"

Emilia was getting a bit hungry, but she was not keen on eating or drinking anything that wasn't made by the people she trusted explicitly. "No need for that, Baron Eggart."

She entered his office which was on the smaller side compared to the classrooms and sat on a plush green sofa without being prompted to. She kept her expression blank, but the accusation of wrongdoing soured her tone. "Baron Eggart, sit down. We have much to discuss."

The older man studied her entourage of three muscular men and ran a hand through his long, thinning ivory hair. He nervously ambled to sit opposite her in his leather armchair.

"Tell me, Baron, what has been going on with Miss Ivy Blanc?"

"Whatever do you mean, Lady Em? Nothing! I think the girl is safe and content with her studies. I often check in on her academic performance, and she is a wonderful student. All instructors think so."

"Then why did I hear that she is unhappy?"

Eggart stilled as if trying to find the right words. At that moment, rain pummelled against the floor-to-ceiling windows of the dean's office. The sky darkened, giving life to the growing shadows in the room.

Baron's attention was drawn to the windowpanes. "It is good you came when you did. I heard this morning a storm is headed this way."

"Baron Eggart..." Emilia spoke in a much colder tone.

The baron dropped his head and sighed. "I-I apologise, Lady Em. To answer your question, there are rumours that Miss Ivy was asked to attend the academy's spring ball by Countess Morel's son, Cyrus."

"And?"

Baron Eggart swallowed as he looked Emilia in the eye. "The young lady turned his offer down. Since then, rumours of her being of common birth have begun to spread."

Emilia's hands turned into fists in her lap. She never got involved with Countess Morel because that woman supported King Gilebert's corrupt rule. Lionhart's investigation uncovered plenty of moral wrongdoings by the countess and her lavish lifestyle, but nothing Emilia could use to eliminate her. At least, not yet.

"What have you done to quell the vicious rumours?"

The dean shifted uncomfortably in his seat. "I did not get involved for the fear of worse retaliation against the young lady."

Emilia clenched her teeth hard enough for her jaw to hurt. She could not entirely blame the baron for sitting on the issue. Most nobles would if the choice came down to closing one's eyes to the misdeeds of a powerful noble house or protecting a commoner.

With Ambrose finding out about the situation, she would want to deal with Countess Morel's son in one way or another.

To squash those rumours, there was only one solution. Emilia had to give Ambrose a noble rank. It would also raise her status among the servants and those who visited the court. The only problem with that was the possible backlash from the nobility who did not support Emilia. After all, randomly allowing commoners to join the ranks of nobility would make them nervous.

"Silence the rumours and keep an eye on Countess Morel's son," Emilia said in a honeyed voice. "Or I will be forced to transfer Ivy to the Royal Academy in Newburn, along with the generous funding I provide."

The baron nearly flew out of his seat and bowed his head. "Lady Em, I would never allow for anything bad to happen to Miss Ivy! Trust me when I say this, I will do everything in my power to keep her happy here."

Emilia glanced at Valerian who stood by the door with the knights. Since he could tell the truth from lies, he was a perfect lie detector.

The Pope seemed to wordlessly understand her message and gave a light nod of his head.

"Very well. I will entrust this matter to you, Baron Eggart," Emilia replied to the visible relief of the noble.

She got up and studied the fat drops of rain sliding down the windowpanes. They needed to get to an inn before the weather got any worse. "We will be leaving now. I will return and, by then, I do hope you have dealt with the problem effectively."

The baron straightened his posture, gingerly took hold of her hand, and gave a light peck to the back of Emilia's hand. "Thank you for putting your faith in me."

Emilia extracted her hand and nodded to the men waiting for her. Once they were all outside of the office, Emilia ordered, "Regis, when we return, inform Jehan and Lionhart to look into House Morel. I want to know of everything that's going on in their

QUEEN OF HEARTS

territory, and to pay special attention to Cyrus Morel."

"Yes, my lady," Sir Regis replied with a bow of his head.

"Are you going to meet Miss Ivy in person?" Valerian inquired, his green eyes shining with interest.

"No. She and Ambrose are very much alike. They refuse to burden me with anything involving them."

"Then is our date over?" Valerian couldn't hide the disappointment on his face, or perhaps he didn't even try.

Emilia could not deny him after using him and his feelings as an excuse to leave the palace for a day. "Baron Eggart mentioned that a storm is on the way here. We should take refuge at the nearest inn."

The Pope brightened up. "That's a great idea, my dearest wife."

She laughed at how easy it was to get along with Valerian beyond the formality of the palace walls. His easy-going personality and incorrigible flirting suited him much better.

While on their way to where they had tied up their horses, Emilia and the others had gotten completely soaked. As they turned a corner, she felt a chill climbing up her back, as if someone was watching them. Since the weather got worse, and the wind's savage whip assaulted the port town, the people had retreated to the safety of their homes. The only ones who were out could not be considered good company.

"I think we are being watched," Emilia told Valerian.

His body stiffened. "Should we return to the palace, after all?"

"We would need to ride through the Royal Wood, meaning we would be an easy target for an ambush. Our best option is to find a place with as many people as possible and hope that our new friends wouldn't risk showing their faces in public."

"Very well." Valerian turned to Sir Erenel. "We have company, Klaus. Stay alert."

Sir Regis drew his sword from his scabbard just as five cloaked figures, with weapons drawn, ran out in front of them.

Emilia pulled out a dagger from her boot. "Let's retreat to the academy!"

"Too late," Valerian informed her.

She spun around to find another eight men, in armour and murder in their eyes, assembling behind them.

So much for a relaxing day out of the office!

"Sir Regis and I will keep them busy while Your Holiness and Your Majesty make your escape."

"There are too many of them for you to handle," Emilia countered, gripping her dagger's hilt.

"It matters not. Our priority is your safety and survival," the holy knight replied.

Valerian raised his hand, palm up. "Your spare sword, Klaus."

Emilia was once again stunned by the Pope. *Valerian knows how to fight? Wasn't he a carpenter? Did the Goddess bless him with fighting knowledge, too?*

She looked up at the sky and muttered under her breath, "I wish you'd have given me as many boosts!"

Valerian grabbed Sir Erenel's spare sword and took hold of Emilia's hand. "Our guests are not the patient kind. We must hurry. Klaus, Sir Regis, clear a path!"

The knights charged for the smaller group of the cloaked assassins ahead.

Emilia did not get a chance to do anything when Valerian pulled her along right behind their guards.

16
BETWEEN FIRE AND ICE

EMILIA

E**milia panted from running** as she had not yet fully recovered after her deep sleep. Sadly, her pursuers did not suffer in the same way.

Valerian must have noticed her slowing down, because he turned a corner and yanked her into an alley, pressing their bodies flush against the inlet wall of a house.

Despite the urgent need for more air in her burning lungs, she held her breath.

The mercenaries that escaped Sir Erenel and Sir Regis ran past the alley.

The rain grew heavier, and her body shivered from the cold.

She lifted her head to find Valerian staring down at her.

"They must be after me," both said in unison.

Emilia covered her giggle with her hand, even though the heavy rain probably muffled most of the sounds they made. "The Cardinals?"

"Most definitely," he replied, still keeping his ardent gaze trained on her face. He brushed aside the wet strands of her wig's hair that were stuck to her forehead and cupped her cheek with his cool hand. "Are the nobles after your life, Emilia?"

"There are a few who do not agree with me being on the throne."

"Who would not wish for such a god-like being to be above them?"

Emilia cleared her throat to hide her embarrassment. First, it was Clayton who could turn her face beetroot-red with a handful of words and now the Pope was spouting equally cheesy lines.

"There they are!" someone shouted from the entrance to the alleyway.

Emilia and Valerian turned their heads.

She could hear her heart thumping in her head as her pulse rose with her nerves. The cold numbing her was forgotten in seconds with the rising levels of adrenaline preparing her for a fight.

Gripping her dagger, she separated from Valerian and took on a fighting stance.

"Emilia, it may be best if you stand behind me. I would not want for you to get a scratch on your lovely body."

She smirked as three men charged at them at full speed with their shortswords at the ready. "I can take care of myself in a fight, Val."

To prove her point, she bent backwards to avoid the violent swing of the first mercenary's sword, ducked down, and drove her dagger into the man's armpit.

Valerian had easily parried the attacks of the two assailants with his sword and kicked one of them in the chest, knocking the man down.

Before her opponent had the chance to grab her by the hair, Emilia yanked out her dagger. Red coated her blade and hand. She had no time to think and stabbed her dagger into her enemy's throat.

Sputtering, he collapsed to his knees and then onto the dirt.

Emilia wiped her blade on his soaked cloak as his blood pooled in his wounds and left expanding rivers of crimson in the alley. By the time she was finished, Valerian had dispatched the man on the ground and mortally wounded the final assailant in the gut.

"They didn't tell us you could fight—" the mercenary with short, soot-coloured hair grumbled under his breath. He dropped to his knees and cradled his bleeding wound.

"Who sent you? If you answer honestly, we may spare your life," Emilia offered, moving to stand beside the Pope.

"Our guild was hired by the duke's family."

"I was right," she said, narrowing her eyes on the mercenary. "They were after me." As an afterthought, she asked, "What about the cloaked men?"

The man groaned in pain. "I-I don't know who they are."

"I suppose they were after my life," Valerian interjected, with a smug look on his face.

Emilia got little more out of the mercenary before he careened to one side and fell unconscious from blood loss. She was not about to risk her life saving an assassin who tried to kill her.

"We should find Erenel and Regis." It did not sit well with Emilia to abandon their knights to fight off that many enemies.

"They will be fine," Valerian assured her. "Klaus can heal himself and your escort if they get hurt."

Ah, I forgot about that.

She sneezed and sniffled. Her body was colder than ice.

"We should get you somewhere safe and warm you up, Emilia." He was about to take her hand when an arrow blew past his shoulder and lodged in the wall beside him.

Emilia's eyes darted around the rooftops in search of the archer.

"Move!" she snapped, taking hold of his hand.

She did not get far.

Valerian wrapped his arms protectively around her and pressed her against him. "I hope you will forgive me for this brief rudeness."

She gaped at him. Valerian was acting as a live shield to keep her safe from the arrows.

"You're insane!"

"The Goddess' messenger cannot come to any harm on my watch."

Another arrow seemed to hit his back, and he let out a low grunt.

Emilia's eyes watered. "Valerian, please do not get hurt because of me!"

He smiled down at her. "No need to worry. These things cannot kill me. No mortal weapon can."

Something heavy fell off the roof of the nearby house with a thud.

Emilia cautiously stuck her head around Valerian's muscular arm to find the frozen corpse of a cloaked man with an arrow still drawn in his bow.

A second later, Clayton jumped down from the rooftop and lunged at Valerian with an ice dagger. To Emilia's shock and amazement, the ice weapon smashed into tiny pieces upon contact with Valerian's skin.

"Let Her Majesty go!" Clayton snarled, forming another ice blade in his right hand.

Emilia jumped in front of the Pope to defend him with her hands raised. "Clayton, he is not our enemy. His Holiness was only trying to keep me from harm."

Clayton's expression softened when their eyes met, and he replied with a hint of bitterness in his tone, "I should have come sooner. It was hard to locate Your Majesty due to the storm."

She took a step towards her shadow and smiled. "You're here now."

"As much as I enjoy the outdoors," Valerian began with mock cheer, "I think it best we get Emilia to a place where she can warm her body before she falls ill."

"Did you just refer to Her Majesty by name?" Clayton growled.

"Am I not permitted to call my wife by her name?"

"Wife?"

Emilia placed her hands on their chests to stop them from killing each other. "Gentlemen, I must admit, I am quite cold and hungry. Shall we find an inn to rest?"

Clayton glanced at her hand on his chest and sighed. "I will escort you from here. Sir Regis and the Holy Knight eliminated most of the assassins before I found them."

"See? I told you Klaus and your knight would be fine," Valerian added with a cheerful smile.

Emilia blew out a sigh of relief. "Let us regroup quickly and get warmed up."

A short while later, they reunited with the two knights close to where they had split off and found an inn that was overflowing with people, eager to escape the awful weather.

As Emilia stepped through the threshold and into the safety of the cosy seaside inn, she considered her ridiculous situation.

The Queen, the Pope, and an assassin walk into an inn... How is this not a joke?

"I will enquire with the innkeeper about the rooms, my lady," Sir Regis informed her and pushed past the crowding merchants who were busy complaining about their goods getting ruined by the storm.

With the way things went that day, Emilia was not expecting any good news. She rubbed her chilled arms. Her fingers had gotten completely numb from the cold.

Lifting her gaze to Clayton, she noticed he was standing farther away from her than usual. It did not take long for her to realise why. His hands were covered with frost. He was probably struggling to control his emotions.

Emilia gave him a reassuring smile and fought the chattering of her teeth. "I am f-fine, Clayton."

Sir Regis pushed through the merchants and returned with his shoulders slumped. "It appears there is only one room available, my lady. The innkeeper said we won't be able to find another in this weather."

Emilia pursed her lips. There were five of them. All of them couldn't fit in a small room, no matter how hard they tried. She also needed a bath, which would need privacy. She did not mind Clayton's company, but the others…

"The lady should take the room, and we will remain on guard," Clayton offered, although he looked just as drenched as the rest of them.

"I agree. My wife needs some hot soup and a cosy blanket to warm up her body," Valerian joined in, receiving another death glare from Clayton.

Politically speaking, it would be beyond rude for Emilia to take the room for herself and leave the Pope to sleep on the dirty floor of a tavern. Staying up all night was also an option. She could keep the Pope and her shadow in the room with her and pass the time by playing a game or two.

"Valerian, Clayton, you can stay with me. Regis, Erenel, I am sorry, you will have to spend the night guarding the room."

The knights nodded.

Valerian smirked while Clayton frowned. Neither said a word about her impulsive decision.

One by one, they took turns taking a bath behind a wooden screen and having their wet clothes hung in front of the fireplace.

Dressed in her undergarments and wrapped up in a grey woolly blanket for warmth, Emilia sat on a chair with her knees tucked close to her chest, and her eyes trained on two flawless male specimens who only sported a pair of trousers to keep some decency.

They paid extra to have the innkeeper bring a table into the room along with three chairs and three bottles of Baudelaire wine. Emilia even asked for some parchment and charcoal to draw. Since the only game she knew how to play was Poker, she decided to make a deck of cards.

Valerian poured their drinks and studied Emilia's work. "What is that?"

"A game," she replied. "It is fun, I promise."

"What would we stake?"

Clayton narrowed his eyes at the Pope across the table as he crossed his arms over his chest.

Emilia ignored their battle of wills and completed her chicken-scratch doodles of the four suits. She handed the parchments to Clayton. "Could you evenly cut these up into cards for me?"

Her shadow summoned an ice dagger which seemed as sharp as any fine blade when he easily cut through the parchments one by one. His arm muscles flexed and relaxed, briefly making her fixated on them.

She tore her gaze away and studied the Pope.

Valerian took a sip of his wine from his goblet and sat back in his chair. "This is certainly not what I was expecting when I decided to get to know you, Emilia."

She let out a laugh. "Why? Do you find me boring?"

"Quite the opposite. You are so mystifying and beautiful. I cannot take my eyes off you."

"I could help and pluck your eyeballs from their sockets," Clayton warned.

"Are you threatening the leader of the City of Light, Lord Armel?"

"I merely offered to resolve your problem."

Emilia cut in, "I am more interested in how the assassins found out the Pope and I would be visiting Port Lisza today."

"Did Your Majesty tell anyone?" Clayton asked.

"I let Marchioness Durand know, but she did not seem the type to betray me so quickly."

"The Marchioness is not the only one who knew of our date," Valerian muttered over the rim of his goblet.

Emilia raised a brow. "Who else?"

"Every servant in the dining room was also aware of where we were going."

That seems plausible. The maids changed all the time in the palace. One of them could easily be a mole for the Malettes. "Do you think it was one of the maids?"

The Pope shrugged. "If we question them, I will know for certain."

"Something more concerning then..." Emilia picked up her goblet and tasted the rich sweetness of the wine in it.

Valerian leant in, eager for more information. "What could worry the Queen more than a spy in her court?"

She licked the wine off her lips. "How did Sister Sabianna figure out who you are? No posters or heraldry ever portrayed the appearance of the new pope."

Valerian seemed pleased with her curiosity about him. He leaned in closer to her. "When Sir Erenel and I first arrived at this port, I may have performed a few healing miracles on those who needed them."

"You are terrible at keeping yourself hidden," she commented.

"It is not as if anyone can stop me. Many have tried."

Clayton finished his task and handed her a perfectly uniform deck of cards.

Emilia murmured her thanks and awkwardly shuffled the card-sized parchments. Since they were quite thick, it was a little difficult to manage all the cards at once. Amidst the process, Emilia explained the rules of the game to them while pushing the possible betrayal of a new ally to the back of her mind.

It did not take long for the two bickering men to turn into serious players. Emilia's nervousness around them melted away with each goblet of wine she consumed. By the time they finished the third bottle and asked for more, she was no longer cold. On the contrary, she felt hot and ready to ditch the stuffy blanket around her shoulders.

So, she did just that, letting it fall to one side and off the chair.

Much better!

Resting her chin on her fist, she eyed Valerian's well-defined upper body. He unquestionably had spent a lot of time doing manual labour. His arms were muscular but his waist was slim. In contrast, Clayton's abs seemed to be more toned. His six-pack reappeared every time he moved forward.

If she was still in her previous world, the chance of her sitting with two hunks and playing a card game till dawn was zilch. Her mother would never permit her to even be in the same room with two men when she was seventeen, not to mention date an older man who killed others as his profession.

"Your Majesty, are you tired?" Clayton's concern broke through her hazy thoughts that drifted towards more than just a card game with the men.

Emilia waved his comment away. "How can I be tired when my eyes are so well entertained?"

Valerian burst out laughing.

"Your Majesty should lie down," Clayton offered kindly.

How can I say no to that handsome face? To my handsome face. He's mine. He-he.

Emilia pouted and abruptly shot up from her chair. The world swayed around her, or she did. She could not be sure.

The men automatically did the same, making her smile. They were so adorable, she could cuddle their abs all day.

"Men, let's go to bed!" she ordered and turned on her heel towards the bed behind her.

"Your Majesty—" Clayton began.

"I will not say no to *that* kind of invitation," Valerian added.

"How could you even consider it?" Clayton snapped.

Emilia attempted to put her hands on her waist and failed, so she whipped around instead. "This is an order. Don't keep your queen waiting!"

The men clammed up and looked at each other nervously.

With that, Emilia smiled to herself and clambered onto the bed, where she curled up in the middle of the comfortable sheets before abruptly falling to sleep.

17

THE SHADOW'S CURSE

VALERIAN

Port Lisza. Night at the inn.

Valerian watched Emilia in astonishment. At what he initially thought was a joke, the Queen of Dante brazenly ordered that he and her shadow should join her in bed. Before anything could happen, however, she was asleep faster than either could respond.

With a shrug of one shoulder, he said, "You heard the Queen's order. We should get in bed."

Lord Armel's malicious gaze could set the inn ablaze. "I hope that was a jest, Your Holiness."

"Why? Are you planning another attempt on my life?"

"It has crossed my mind."

Valerian laughed as the truth spoken by the man was clearly visible above Clayton's head in ancient text. On the day of his awakening as Luminos' servant, Valerian received knowledge of all languages in existence. He could even read the pesky curse on the shadow's back. "As you have seen with your own eyes, I cannot be killed by any weapon made by a mortal."

The assassin's lips tugged into a half-smile that made Valerian doubt his Blessing of Steel Skin for the first time. "If a blade cannot kill you, perhaps poison or starvation will. I could lock you up in a dungeon and keep you there until you are nothing but bones."

"That would hinder my plans to purge the Church of the filth it has collected, so I must decline your extended invitation."

Lord Armel's hands emitted a low blue light as an ice blade formed in his grasp. He pointed it in the direction of Valerian's throat. "Whatever your intentions towards Her Majesty are, they better not be a hindrance or a danger to my master."

Raising his arms in defence, Valerian replied, "Believe it or not, it was love at first sight."

Clayton moved the ice blade down and brushed it against Valerian's bare arm, where the tip of it crumbled. Not wanting to admit defeat, the assassin fired another glare at the Pope.

Valerian continued as he lowered his arms. "Do you not see the Goddess' glow around Emilia? She shines as bright as the sun sometimes. Only the blind cannot see that she is a special existence in this world. What is there not to love?"

"That is not love. It is mere fascination." Clayton shattered the ice weapon and indicated to the space in front of the fireplace that was not occupied by their wet clothes. "Sleep on the floor, Your Holiness."

"Then what do you feel towards her? Fascination? Curiosity? Love?"

"My opinion of Her Majesty is none of your concern."

"Have you told her how you can break your curse yet?"

Clayton grasped Valerian by the throat and forced him back until the Pope's back hit the wall. "What do you know of the curse?"

"Answer my question first."

"Why do you want to know?"

"Shouldn't your master know your opinion of them?"

"Her Majesty does not need to be burdened with irrelevant information."

"Oh, I think she does. Something that involves her life would certainly be of interest to her."

Clayton's fingers dug into Valerian's throat despite the blessing. The action made it hard to breathe but not enough that Valerian thought he should act in his defence yet.

"She will soon find out one way or another. Why hide it?" Valerian probed.

"Her Majesty is too kind-hearted and may do something she regrets. I will bear this curse until the day I die."

"You will go mad before then, Lord Armel." Valerian captured Clayton's wrist and peeled the shadow's hand away from his throat. As he did so, he recited the curse one line at a time,

"For ten generations, the cursed will suffer,

And their damned minds will easily shatter.

Should they defy fate and ignore their summons,

The Death's bell will ring,

Claiming them and their loved ones.

So tirelessly serve your Master of Vows,

The holder of Dante's purest of bloods.

Yet should the Master's desires turn dark,

Destroying the shackles of fate can be done

By ripping their foul heart out."

Valerian did not get the chance to finish when he noticed that Lord Armel was looking at the floor in shame. All fight had left him.

"It is an interesting curse," Valerian commented. "As you know, all curses have a way out."

"I do not plan on killing my master if that is what you are suggesting."

Valerian raised his hands. "I would never willingly endanger the life of my saintess."

"Then there is no way out for me."

Does he not know about the last three lines? I see no reason to tell him everything at once.

Valerian offered Clayton a hand in the form of a handshake. "If you are willing to cooperate with me, I will help you resolve your curse without bloodshed."

Lord Armel seemed sceptical as he eyed the intrusive hand. "Why should I rely on you?"

"Because we share a goal—to protect Emilia." He nudged his hand closer to the assassin. "Do you accept?"

It took a long minute before Lord Armel shook hands with Valerian, who was beginning to feel foolish standing there with his hand out.

"Now then, shall we join our master on the bed as ordered?" Valerian asked cheekily.

Clayton shot the Pope another glare and then sighed. "As long as you do not touch her."

"I will be the perfect gentleman."

"If you're not, I will test if the ice blade can pierce your eyeballs next."

"That's quite worrisome. I was planning on performing a healing miracle on her in case she falls ill."

Clayton did not seem happy about the suggestion. "I can heal her with my magic."

"A Goddess' blessing is stronger than any mage's magic trick."

"Then let us work together. The combined effects would be far better than any old miracle."

Valerian felt his lips tugging into a smile. He was beginning to like Lord Armel, although the viscount did not feel the same as of yet.

Motioning to the bed, he started moving over. "Shall we?"

They sat on the edges of the mattress.

Lord Armel placed his hand on Emilia's hand while Valerian bent down and lifted her soft ebony locks to his lips, garnering a quizzical look from Clayton.

The Pope closed his eyes and muttered a prayer to Luminos in a language long abandoned, but it was the most prominent one among the tongues he came to know upon awakening. It was also the language of Lord Armel's curse.

He felt his body welling up with the Goddess' warmth and guided the healing energy out through his fingertips. Just like the first time he healed her, the energy Luminous supplied was tremendous and pure to the point where his limbs grew heavy and his mind weary.

Once the process came to an end, he opened his eyes to find Lord Armel was in a similar predicament—exhausted and low on mana. The competitiveness with the viscount was a refreshing feeling he had not felt before. They each wanted Emilia, yet Lord Armel was the one who needed her.

Too tired to think for much longer, Valerian lay next to the Queen and let out a long sigh as he closed his eyes. Before sleep claimed him, he felt the bed shifting as the shadow gave in to his desire to stay beside his master.

Valerian smirked.

18
HER SHIELD AND SANCTUARY

EMILIA

After a good night's sleep, Emilia rolled onto her side and hit something solid with her face. She furrowed her brows and rubbed her aching nose better.

When she opened her eyes to see what the hard object in her bed was, she was met with the naked chest of a man with a spray of light hair on it. She followed the chest up to a pair of mesmerising green eyes that were looking back at her with amusement dancing in them.

With her heart in her throat and, suddenly wide awake, she tried to scoot away from the Pope's chest.

He grasped her around the waist to keep her in place. Lowering his lips to her ear, he whispered, "Be careful, dear wife, or you could push Lord Armel off the bed."

Dread filled Emilia as she turned her head to find her shadow sleeping on the other end of the bed, shirtless and handsome first thing in the morning.

I swear I am not going to drink a single drop of alcohol after this!

"I—wait, I am not your wife, Your Holiness," she hissed back. "It was a pretend play for a day. Or have you forgotten?"

"Truly a pity. But, as I have said before, just say the word, and I will officiate our wedding before the gods."

She gazed at his face, seeing no humour there. *He's serious.* He could wed them at a moment's notice. With all the strange blessings Luminos had given him, who knows what getting married by him would do?

"I do not think we are well enough acquainted to get married, Your Holiness."

He smiled, revealing those dimples again that made her heart do another nervous jump. "At least, it wasn't a 'no'."

Emilia pushed his arm away and sat up. Rubbing her face, she tried to get a sense of the situation and how they ended up in it. No. Perhaps, pretending none of it happened was the best solution.

Good thing Ambrose is not here to see any of it.

Lifting her gaze towards the table and chairs, Emilia's entire being stilled. In one of the chairs sat none other than her head maid with a look of disapproval carved onto her face.

"Ambrose!" The word that left Emilia's lips was but a squeak.

The head maid stood and bowed her head. "Good morning, Your Majesty. I have arrived not long ago with a change of clothes for you."

"I can explain!" Emilia scrambled off the bed, realising how it must have looked—the Queen of Dante lying in her nightdress between two topless hunks.

Wait, how hot the men are is not the problem here!

"Your Majesty needn't explain anything to me. I have come to look after your needs."

Emilia winced, feeling as if she was being scolded by a school teacher. Ambrose tended to talk more about work and distance herself from the topic at hand if she was seriously unhappy with something.

"You are finally awake, Lord Armel." Ambrose's stony expression and chilly words were hard to miss. "May I ask how did Her Majesty end up in this predicament? I heard from Sir Regis that Her Majesty was completely *drenched, cold,* and had to *share* a room with *two men*. This is beyond impropriety."

Clayton combed his fingers through his hair as he got off the bed. He sauntered over to the dead fireplace where he took down his shirt and pulled it over his head.

"Lord Armel?" Ambrose demanded, in a harsher tone this time.

"Ambrose, it was my idea to stay up," Emilia added.

"Her Majesty can do no wrong," Ambrose replied kindly. "It is the duty of His Holiness and Lord Armel to keep the tongues from wagging all over the kingdom."

Emilia fiddled with her hands in front of her. She had no excuse for getting blind-drunk twice in the same week.

No wonder Ambrose is upset.

Now dressed, Clayton approached Ambrose. "Head Maid, my duty is to protect Her Majesty and fulfil her wishes. I have no desire to ever hurt her in any way. So, stay your anger and help Her Majesty prepare for the journey back to the palace. We must not delay her return any longer." He half-turned and nodded in the direction of the Pope. "If you are unable to quell your rage, His Holiness is mostly to blame for the situation. It was his idea to demand a date from Her Majesty in the first place. Now, if you will excuse me, I will secure transportation."

Emilia covered her snicker when she saw Valerian's utter surprise at Clayton's getaway.

The Pope scrubbed a hand over his face and sat up in bed. "Your shadow is proficient at making a speedy escape."

"He would not be a good assassin if he were not."

Ambrose draped a cloak over Emilia's shoulders to cover her. "Please wear this until His Holiness is ready to leave."

Emilia wrapped the cloak around herself and smiled at Ambrose. "Thank you. I know you must have realised why His

Holiness and I came to Port Lisza."

Ambrose gave a curt nod. "I will deal with Ivy's problems, Your Majesty. There is no need for you to trouble yourself."

"I heard from Baron Eggart that Cyrus Morel may be involved in the trouble with Ivy. This is not a matter that can be easily solved by you alone. Please, Ambrose, rely on me more."

"I do not wish to burden you with—"

"It's not a burden!" Emilia grasped Ambrose's arms. "I want to help. After helping me and supporting me for years, I would like to repay you even if just a little."

Ambrose shook her head from side to side. "You have taught me everything I know and supported my sister. Without you, I would have no hope in this life." Her eyes filled with tears. "How could I selfishly ask for more from Your Majesty's kind and revered soul?"

Emilia was ready to join in on the waterworks. She sniffled and, out of the corner of her eye, saw that Valerian was quickly donning his shirt.

"There are some things I need to say to His Holiness in private before we head downstairs," Emilia said softly.

Ambrose bobbed her head—her anger from earlier had completely dissipated. "I will wait outside."

When the head maid was gone, Emilia faced the Pope. "Will you hold up your end of the bargain, Valerian?"

He ran a hand through his sandy hair with practised movements that suited a model and moved to stand in front of her. "Of course. I would not dream of lying to you, my saintess."

"As someone who can easily tell truth from lies, you could also be the most cunning of liars."

He chuckled at that. "That may be, but then I would never be able to reach your heart."

"My heart already has someone in it," she countered, taking a step back.

Valerian's warm gaze did not change. He easily diminished the distance between them with a single stride and cupped her face. "Remember this, Emilia. While Lord Armel acts as your shield, I will be your sanctuary. Tell me anything, and I will believe it. If the world is against you, I will welcome you into my arms and hide you away."

The heat from his body so close to hers sent tingles through her, and she could not tear her eyes away from him. "You would believe that I came from another world?"

"Without a doubt." There was no shred of hesitation from him. He took her words at face-value and accepted them.

What a strange man...

Slowly pulling away from her, he inclined his head. "I will travel to the temple and make certain the crown is placed upon your beautiful head."

"Thank you, Valerian." She meant every word.

Although they met under strange circumstances and with much suspicion, Valerian never once tried to hurt her. He had his goals and heavy burdens just as she had hers. However, she did not wish to hurt Clayton's feelings by running off with another man right after they decided to express their affection for one another. Be it friendship or a political alliance, she no longer minded what kind of relationship the Pope wanted to form with her. If he could give her the temple on the platter, she would gladly take it.

"This one time, I won't hold back," he muttered.

Before Emilia could fully leave her train of thought, his lips met hers, and she froze on the spot. His arm snaked around her waist while the other cupped her cheek with such tenderness, that she couldn't find the strength or will to push him away. No one could fake such strong affection, not even the best actor on the continent. At least, she hoped. Instead of the urgency and passion that Clayton displayed when they were kissing, Valerian's kiss was slow and methodical—a reverence almost.

She closed her eyes to enjoy the moment.

After what seemed like a long minute, he pulled back, and breathed the next words, "I will protect you, Emilia. Luminos has chosen us for a reason."

Half-jokingly, she replied, "She may have merely chosen us for amusement."

"It does not matter. Life of those chosen by the gods is never easy, and I will do what I can to clear the path you wish to take."

"Just don't start any crusades in mine or Luminos' name."

"I cannot promise that." Valerian grabbed his coat from the back of the chair and waved goodbye before leaving Emilia alone to her thoughts.

Just how much are the gods manipulating us?

Is the path I'm on the right one?

Ambrose stuck her head around the door. "Your Majesty, may I come in?"

"Yes, of course, Ambrose."

The head maid slipped into the room and closed the door behind her. From her satchel, she pulled out a fresh set of clothes for Emilia along with a hairbrush, perfume, and ankle boots.

"You came prepared," Emilia commented, eyeing the items spread out on the table.

"When it comes to Your Majesty, I must do all I can."

Taking a seat on one of the chairs, Emilia said, "Valerian will force the temple to proceed with my coronation. We must begin preparations with haste."

"Then the outing must have pleased him."

Emilia thought back to the day prior—their breakfast where she learned of his previous vocation, the visits to the orphanage and the academy, the dual assassination attempt, and then a night of alcohol and card games with two topless men. It was a day to remember compared to a casual date full of strolls through a garden and dull talk.

"He is not someone easily deterred once he sets a goal," Emilia fondly replied.

"Does His Holiness please Your Majesty?"

"We are allies, for now." Emilia slipped off the cloak she was wearing and, with her head maid's help, changed into the dress that Ambrose had brought. Her thoughts drifted, still feeling Valerian's lips on hers. Never in her wildest dreams did she think she would have her pick of men.

Am I becoming as bad as Thessian? Bringing back women every time he leaves the palace.

Is he going to bring another one from the South? Should I start the construction of the harem, after all? One for me and one for him.

The Queen shook her head at her silly idea. The palace would have plenty of rooms to spare for the time being.

Once she was fully dressed in a plain navy dress and a wig disguising her natural hair, Emilia finished up by securing her cloak with a metal clip.

"Ambrose, should Baron Eggart fail to fix the problem with Countess Morel's son, I will deal with the matter."

Lowering her head, Ambrose replied, "I pray it will not come to that, Your Majesty. Ivy and I wish to become your support not an obstacle to your goals."

"Getting on the bad side of House Morel may put me at a disadvantage with the nobles who supported the former king. So, as long as I can find any wrongdoing on their part, I can pressure them to fix their behaviour."

"I will ask Mister Lionhart for more information on Countess Morel," Ambrose offered.

"No need, I've asked Sir Regis to inform Lionhart."

"Very good, Your Majesty."

"Let's set off. As nice as it was to see Sister Sabianna and Sister Pailin, I think I have had enough adventures in Port Lisza."

19
THE GRAVEYARD OF MEN

LAURENCE

The journey to the Northern Watchtower was much shorter than Laurence had anticipated. After a full day on horseback, they had made great time and arrived at the huge steel gates just as the storm from the south reared its head.

One of Marquess Carrell's knights dismounted his horse and proceeded to shout up to the top of the enormous fortress' gatehouse. "Hail, the Marquess arrives. Open the gate!"

From above, three heads peered over the battlements, took in the sizeable entourage, and scrambled away.

Several dragging moments later, the ominous gates peeled apart, permitting them entry into the dull courtyard which appeared to double as a training ground for the knights.

Laurence nudged his horse to follow the lords' carriage. He felt Khaja's arms around his middle clutching him tighter as the fort loomed over them, its dark walls dappled with dying moss.

Once inside, and upon closer inspection, Laurence noted that the knights of the Northern Watchtower had seen better days. Most were missing a limb or were heavily scarred and eyeing them with suspicion. The mood of the place was on par with a starved garrison under siege and for a good reason. Although assumedly made of volunteers and locals, it would be expected that not all were there by choice. Those who were charged to protect the Northern border from the monsters that descended from the Hollow Mountains often had their lives cut short.

In Darkgate, before the construction of a chain of defences and lookout posts at the base of the mountains, plenty of villages were destroyed by the ever-growing number of ogres and goblins. It was not a perfect defence against all beasts, but this fortress was an invaluable place to coordinate and gave some relief, or at least some warning, to those who could not relocate away from the mountains.

Over his shoulder, Laurence whispered, "Keep your hood up, Khaja."

She hid her head behind his back, and he patted her hands on his stomach. There were no women in the Northern Watchtower, and he'd seen first-hand what happens to women when discipline breaks down. Although Khaja was a beastwoman with the strength of several men, these men were veterans of fighting monsters more powerful than her. With some possibly having nothing to lose, he worried about his charge.

Is it only because she is my charge?

Get a hold of yourself, Laurence! What are you even considering? Of course, I would protect any woman in danger! Khaja still counts, right?

They were greeted with a perfectly formed five rows of soldiers who had assembled at a moment's notice. Their captain—a man in his late thirties with a crooked nose and deep-set eyes—stood tall and proud at the front to greet the lords. His raven hair was short and his face red from the cold.

Laurence pulled his horse to a stop and hopped off. He took Khaja's hand and helped her down, all the while taking in the sudden uplifting mood as Lord Carrell stepped out of his carriage.

Unlike most nobles who came for inspections and scrutinised everything and everyone, Lord Carrell approached the captain of the knights and gave him a firm hug.

"Carver, it is good to see you, old friend!" Lord Carrell cheered.

Carver grinned. "It's been too long without the ale you bring, my lord!"

Lord Carrell peeled back and let Lord Fournier have his turn in greeting the commanding officer with another friendly hug.

"What brings you here, my lords?" Carver asked, looking from the lords to the sizeable military entourage. His eyes settled on Khaja, and his brows pulled together into a scowl.

"You may not believe me, but we are searching for a dragon," Lord Carrell replied.

"A dragon?" Carver's eyes, although on the small side, bulged. Then, he scrubbed a hand over his face. "Best to speak of this inside. I'm afraid we won't have suitable accommodation prepared for the lady. Please give us some time to prepare."

"She is going to accompany us up the mountain," Lord Fournier added quickly.

It was the second time that Carver's shock was written all over his face. "I know some women can be strong, but the Hollow Mountains are not a safe place for the fairer sex. She may want to reconsider after seeing the state my men are in."

Lord Carrell draped his arm over Carver's shoulders as the rainfall began to cover the snow-sprinkled ground. "We shall confer inside."

Carver bowed his head low. "Yes, my lord." His voice took on a commanding tone, and he yelled, "Men, return to your stations!"

The soldiers dispersed, which allowed for the rest of Lord Fournier's men and Laurence's team to secure their horses at the stables and head into the internal stronghold.

Taking Khaja's hand, Laurence made his way to Sergey, Yeland, and Ian who had gathered to one side.

Laurence spoke low. "We will head up the mountain after the storm passes."

"What if it lasts for days?" Sergey asked as a growl of thunder could be heard even through the thick walls of the fort.

"If it does, we will wait here."

Ian let out a heaving sigh. "I will inquire about Khaja's accommodations. Until then, she should not roam about."

"Are you worried for the men?" Sergey joked.

Laurence flicked Sergey's forehead. "Khaja is still a woman."

Rubbing the freshly sore spot, Sergey muttered, "You sleep with her every night, Commander."

That deserved Sergey a second flick before Laurence diverted his attention to Yeland. "You are quieter than usual."

Yeland's dark hair was slick with rain, so he brushed it away from his eyes which reflected his nervousness. "I have heard this place is full of criminals and knights who had wronged the Dante Crown. It may not be the safest place for Miss Khaja, nor us."

"It certainly is not," Laurence agreed. "I will keep her by my side, and we must be on our guard."

"That may be more difficult than expected, Commander," Sergey stated.

Laurence whipped his head around from the emptiness he felt in his hand to the busy entryway of the fortress.

He cursed. *Khaja's gone.*

Lord Carrell had graciously granted Laurence a room next to his and Lord Fournier's on the second floor. After sending Sergey to drop off his and Khaja's belongings, he scoured the inside of the fortress for the beastwoman near where she had disappeared from his sight like a ghost two hours prior.

Yeland and Sergey were then sent to gather information on the Hollow Mountains from those in the Northern Watchtower, and Ian did what he did best—disappearing off on his own.

Coming to a halt at a sturdy door to the outside, Laurence grasped the metal handle, feeling the cold seeping into his skin. He pushed the door open only to be met with strong winds and a downpour.

"Where have you gone, Khaja?" he grumbled, taking a step onto the battlements.

From his marred view, he could see five of the Watchtower's knights lying on the ground.

His gut twisted with panic, and Laurence rushed to their side. Squatting next to the first knight, Laurence noted that the man was knocked unconscious, as were his other comrades. No blood or wounds were visible, so Laurence assumed he was on the right track to find his illusive beastwoman.

He lifted the men to lean against the wall and followed the battlements until he spotted her, sitting on the merlon and staring into the distance, towards Redford.

Khaja was soaked. Her red hair turned a darker shade as her tresses were weighed down with rainwater. The black clouds that had gathered above them did not seem to bother her, nor did the harsh snaps of the chilly wind that crept under Laurence's layers.

He took a step forward, which finally drew her attention. "Come on, Khaja." He waved her over. "This is not a place to be during a storm."

She stood atop the merlon and gazed at him with her unnaturally silver eyes. From where he stood, Laurence could see the sadness was still reflected in their depths. Her usual smile seemed almost a mirage and the knowledge that he was using her to find her tribe wedged a dagger in his chest that seemed to twist farther in with each passing day.

Balling his hands at his sides, he lowered his head in shame.

Laurence never had to make the hard decisions. Those rested on the shoulders of His Highness, who accepted his burdens and those of others with silent grace.

But Laurence was not Thessian.

He had nothing to give Khaja. Aside from some skill with the sword, he was a powerless man, betrothed to another. His heart wavered every time he saw Khaja's face streaked with tears of loss for her family. And every time, he beat his emotions back in check, put on a mask of cheer, and pretended that everything was going swimmingly.

He heard her jumping off the merlon and lifted his head.

Khaja approached him and cupped his cheeks with fingers that were as cold as ice. She must have been cold and never said anything.

Can she feel it?

His heart ached more.

"Laurenz, sad?"

He managed a wry smile. *If only she knew...*

"Khaja love Laurenz."

Laurence tried to free himself from her, but she would not let him. Her grasp on him tightened until his head was trapped between her palms.

"Khaja love Laurenz," she repeated as if seeking some sort of confirmation.

"There is nothing to love, Khaja!" he snapped at her. "I am not worthy of your affection. As a matter of fact, it is best no one truly falls in love with me." He captured her wrists and forced her hands away from his face. "How can I ever love another when I am but a pawn for my family? Calithea, too, will soon realise this. She will leave me. I cannot have hopes. For my life, I cannot hope for love. Not now, not ever!"

A long silence stretched between them as he sucked in deep breaths. He had no right to take his frustrations out on her, not when Khaja did nothing to deserve it.

As he was about to apologise, she rose on her tiptoes and kissed him.

The kiss stunned him. It was not forceful. It was merely a peck that could shatter with a tilt of his head.

He did not move.

Couldn't.

They were two people twisted with agony that gnawed at their bleeding hearts. His will to keep her away kept shrinking with each passing day, and his attraction to her was harder and harder to fight.

"Sir Laurence, I would advise you to continue in your bedchambers. The unconscious guards won't remain so forever." Ian's voice came from behind Laurence, making him jerk away from Khaja.

Laurence felt his ears burning and let out a nervous laugh. "Nothing's going on, Ian."

"Oh? I must have been having a vivid night terror, seeing the commanding officer of this expedition exchanging bodily fluids with the ladies every chance he gets."

That pesky el—wait a second... Laurence gaped at him and ignored the blatant insult. "Did you just admit I am your commanding officer?"

Ian wiped the rainwater from his face with a drawn-out sigh and started to leave. "Get out of the rain before illness befalls you."

"I definitely heard you say 'commanding officer'!" Laurence chased after the retreating elf.

"Lord Fournier is looking for you," Ian informed him and sped up.

Coming to a stop, Laurence smirked. Ian's hard exterior was cracking. There may come a day when Iefyr allows others to get close to him.

Khaja looped her arm through Laurence's, bringing him back to the situation at hand. They were like sewer rats, wet and in need of a hot bath.

He nodded towards the fortress. "Let's go inside."

Khaja's eyes raked his face. She smiled again and snuggled in closer to him, making their clothes squelch.

As they headed back to the door, Laurence heard the grunts and groans of the knights who were regaining their consciousness. He hurried her along to get away before they were caught.

20
A GAME OF CROWNS

LAURENCE

Having escorted Khaja to their accommodation on the second floor of the fortress, Laurence changed his clothes and left the room to visit Lord Fournier.

In front of the Count's door stood his Guard Captain and another knight that Laurence never could remember the name of.

"I was told that Lord Fournier wishes to speak with me," Laurence informed Captain Gagnon.

The captain gave a swift nod and proceeded to knock on his lord's door before announcing Laurence's presence.

Once granted permission to enter, Laurence ventured into the room where Lord Fournier and Lord Carrell were engaging in a game of Crowns. From a glance at the board, Laurence could tell that Lord Carrell was a few moves away from winning.

"Good evening, my lords."

QUEEN OF HEARTS

Lord Carrell waved him over. "Care for a game of Crowns, Sir Laurence?"

"It has been a long time since I last played. I would hate to disappoint you." That was partially a lie. Prince Thessian enjoyed that game all too much during the campaign against Darkgate's king, which forced Laurence to be his opponent most of the time.

"You would prove to be a better challenge than Edgar who is of the opinion that the king should fight his own battles."

Laurence stifled a chuckle. Moving the defensive pieces away from the king piece was the same as compromising the king's safety net. After all, the capture of the king was the main goal of the game. "If you will have me, I will gladly join."

Lord Carrell grinned and motioned to the empty chair near the table the lords occupied. Through the window behind Lord Fournier's burly frame, Laurence saw a bolt of lightning carving its way through the sky and striking the mountainside.

Settled in his seat, Laurence rolled back the sleeves of his shirt and, at Lord Carrell's behest, lifted the velvet screen into place which separated the view of the two sides of the board from each other.

Laurence arranged his nine pieces into a defensive formation. He did not peg Lord Carrell as someone aggressive when it came to strategy. The Marquess seemed the type to ponder his moves well in advance rather than dive straight in and lose his knights and archers in the hasty pursuit to topple the opponent's king.

Lord Fournier, who could see both sides of the board, rubbed his beard in thought and grinned. "Oh, this will be interesting!"

"Are you prepared?" Lord Carrell asked.

Laurence nodded, and Lord Fournier removed the screen. Taking a careful study of Lord Carrell's arrangement, Laurence learned two things about the Marquess.

One—Lord Carrell did not place the king behind the fortification piece but rather surrounded it with the four knights. That was not the common play Laurence had seen from the other nobles in the Empire. Two—the lord's advisor piece was hiding behind the fortification and two archers. It rendered the advisor unable to move forward, and, simultaneously, protected him from Laurence's knights that were placed on either side of his centralised fortification to protect his king.

"You seem to be at a loss for words, Sir Laurence," Lord Carrell said.

"I did not think anyone would protect their advisor as much as they would a king," Laurence commented, finally taking in the calm demeanour of his opponent. "By the lord's reaction, I can assume you have expected me to play defensively."

"It seemed fitting for your character." Lord Carrell moved an archer forward by one square. A slight trembling of the Marquess' right hand caught Laurence's eye. If it was any other noble, Laurence would have attributed the action to nerves, but he had seen the same tremor before. It must have been related to the scar in the shape of three deep claw marks the Marquess had on his wrist. "Have you considered my offer to travel together through the Hollow Mountains? They are quite dangerous for a small party."

Laurence matched Lord Carrell's move by sliding the leftmost archer forward. "It would be safer to travel in greater numbers, as you have suggested, but I fear that could deter the beastmen from coming out of their hiding."

"It is not as if you can engage in meaningful dialogue with them."

"Khaja can speak with them."

They continued to move the pieces on the board until Lord Carrell eliminated one of Laurence's knights.

Lifting his stern gaze from the board, Lord Carrell asked, "What if she tells her people that you are a danger to their tribe? Or that the Fournier family killed one of them?"

Laurence had never considered such an eventuality. If Khaja did not want to be around Laurence and his comrades, she would have run away a long time ago. There was no way they could restrain her or keep up with her if she chose to disappear for good. Everything was her will, including the kiss from earlier.

As for the possibility of retribution, I can only hope Khaja will not pursue it.

Avoiding the subject, Laurence replied, "My advisor will spread false information and move the lord's knight away from the king."

Lord Fournier let out a loud yawn, drawing their attention. "With how slow this match is moving, I could go for a nap."

"Do you not feel nervous, Edgar?" Lord Carrell turned in his chair and rested his arm on the backrest. "What if the beastmen in the mountains attack Redford? One of them can control nearly fifty ice wolves. What do you think a hundred of them could do?"

"The answer is simple, Lenard," Lord Fournier said with an edge. "I will fight to defend my land, my family, and my people."

"Ever the soft-hearted fool... Eliminating a threat before it appears is a better course of action." The Marquess turned back to the game, moving another piece.

Laurence cut into their discussion. "Are you saying I should kill Khaja and abandon my mission, Lord Carrell?"

The Marquess remained silent for a moment as he tapped his index finger against the board next to which were the discarded knights and archers from both sides. "My words may seem harsh, Sir Laurence, since you hold feelings for the beastwoman, but her tribesmen are a threat to Dante and the kingdom's people."

"So is the dragon in the Hollow Mountains," Laurence fired back.

Lord Carrell pushed his knight to advance towards Laurence's king that was hiding behind the fortification piece. "That is why we plan to take care of it, if able. While the dragon is still young, the beast is manageable with the right tools and weapons."

"The dragon can shape-shift, has the scales stronger than the finest steel, and can even read the minds of men. What tools could stop a creature so powerful?"

"Magical tools must be used for magical beasts, Sir Laurence." As Lord Carrell spoke, lightning struck close to the fort, invading the room they were in with brighter light than the oil lanterns could ever produce.

Too focused on the discussion with the Marquess, Laurence had lost his concentration on the game. By the time he looked down to take note of the pieces he had left, his king was trapped in the corner of the board with nowhere to run.

Rising from his seat, Laurence announced, "It's my defeat, Lord Carrell. I should retire for the night."

"Not going to stay for a drink?" Lord Fournier pulled out a small barrel of ale he had sitting next to his feet the entire time.

Laurence inclined his head. "Thank you for the invitation, Lord Fournier, but I must return to Khaja."

The Count nodded in understanding.

Lord Carrell's face hardened. "Do you still plan to go your separate way in the mountains?"

"It is the mission I was given by His Highness, Lord Carrell. I will not abandon it."

Laurence's mood had turned sour since the Marquess brought up killing Khaja and dismissing the mission entirely. The beastmen may be a strong race, but humans had defeated them in the past. He also needed to find a way to break the mate bond Khaja had created with him. With it in place, she may never find a suitable spouse.

At the door, when Laurence reached for the iron handle, Lord Carrell called after him, "We will leave for the First Peak after a day's rest, assuming the storm allows."

"Understood."

Laurence could feel the veins in his head throbbing as he escaped from the lords' room. His mission came first.

How could Lord Carrell even suggest I abandon it?

Arriving in front of his door, he rolled his shoulders to rid his body of the built-up tension and ventured inside.

His eyes rounded, and he nearly fell backwards out of the room.

Khaja was stark naked and sitting near the lit fireplace. Her damp hair ran down her back. Her curves and valleys were completely on display for him to see.

Covering his eyes with his hand, he shuffled into the room and closed the door behind him before any of the guards outside of the lords' room could take a peek.

"Khaja, why are you naked?" He stole a glance around the room through the gap between his fingers, finding her wet clothes scattered unceremoniously on the floor.

Oh, it's my fault. I should have been more attentive.

Keeping his eyes squeezed shut as he passed her, Laurence approached their knapsacks that were propped up against the wall. "You must be cold. I will find something for you to wear."

He untied the sack in which he kept Khaja's clothes and came across the white nightdress Countess Estelle insisted every lady had to own.

This'll have to do!

With the soft linen brushing his fingers, he pulled it out of the sack and turned around only to yelp in surprise.

Without making a single noise, the beastwoman had moved behind him.

Immediately, he covered his eyes with his free hand and offered the nightdress to her.

When she did not accept it, he groaned and waved it at her. "Khaja, get dressed. I cannot keep my eyes shut all night."

I was originally planning to sleep, but how can I do that when there's a naked woman right next to me?

His knuckles brushed against a mound of soft and warm skin. If he had to guess based on their heights, his hand was touching her chest.

Laurence swallowed nervously as he became tethered to the spot.

Is it a breast? It could be a breast. What if it's a breast?

Get a hold of yourself and think of Calithea's breasts instead!

Hmm, they were certainly not as big as Khaja's...but they were quite perky.

Oh, what am I thinking? This is not helping me calm down in the slightest, especially down there!

Khaja snickered. "Laurenz shy?"

"Yes, I am quite shy." He moved his hand away from whatever he was touching. "Clothes. On!"

Laurence nearly jumped out of his skin when her hands landed on his waist.

"Ha-ha, Khaja, you are a very beautiful woman. Very! To the point where my nether region reacts to you without me wanting it to. So—" He wiggled away from her. "I will be the perfect gentleman and extract myself from this situation as fast as my legs can carry me."

After throwing the nightdress in the direction of where he assumed she was standing, he turned on his heels and sprinted for the door and beyond. Even with the distance between them finally growing, all he could hear was Khaja's playful laughter.

21
BROKEN BONDS

THESSIAN

At the peak of dawn, the storm had subsided to a drizzle. The dirt road the merchants used had turned into a muddy mess, forcing them and other travellers to remain in place for the day.

Thessian sat at a table in a hearth-warmed inn and ate the vegetable pottage Ronne had sampled for him. He could not help wondering how Dame Cali was doing with the movements of the troops through Baron Niel's territory. If things were on schedule, and the storm had not slowed them, the advance forces should have arrived in Heren. From there, they would head to Avarea and then west towards Dresgan where Thessian would coordinate with them to assess the threat of the Malettes' rebel forces.

Since the Malette ducal family began recruitment just under a month ago, there should not be more than a few hundred men. Unless the news Thessian received was outdated.

His appetite disappeared at the dreaded thought that he could be headed for a trap, just as Emilia had warned. With her ability to See, her words could not be dismissed as mere worry.

And yet, I often pray she is wrong about Kyros...

Pushing his bowl away, Thessian stood, drawing Ronne's attention.

The boy began to shovel the food into his mouth to finish eating as fast as possible.

Thessian raised a hand. "No need to hurry. I am going to stretch my legs. Once you're finished, bring our belongings back to the stables."

With his mouth stuffed full of food, Ronne gave a bob of his head.

Taking the opportunity to clear his mind, Thessian scanned the dining area. Since he did not see Lady Clarissa eating with Henri and Delphine, he decided to check in on her. He could not shake his worry ever since he learned of how she and Delphine met.

What grim tale is she hiding?

While everyone was busy chatting among themselves, especially the caravan's guards who were, once again, too rowdy to seem concerned about their charges, Thessian took to the stairs and scaled the rather small steps two at a time.

Reaching the first floor, he looked around. There were six rooms and only one of them belonged to Lady Clarissa.

He ran a hand through his mussed hair and adjusted his ashen coat to appear somewhat presentable.

Lifting his hand at the first door, he knocked.

A man's holler came from the other side, complaining of the noise, so Thessian moved on to the next door. His fist collided with the worn wood for three raps. The silence from the other side was palpable. The prince was about to move on when he heard something clattering inside.

It would be rude to intrude... But what if Clarissa is in trouble?

He tested the handle, noting that the door was unlocked.

I could always act drunk.

Adding a wobbling shuffle to his gait, Thessian leaned on the handle and pretended to be surprised as the door glided open. He readied the apologies for whoever was inside but the words did not leave him when a sharp blade of a knife pressed to his throat, and he was pulled into the room by a slim figure.

"Is barging into someone's room a new hobby for Your Imperial Highness?" Lady Clarissa's hiss was harsh on his ears.

That made him think back to the times he had erupted into Emilia's bedchambers unannounced. "And is your hobby, my lady, to greet guests with a blade to their throat?"

The lady moved the knife away and sheathed it in her boot. Her long blonde hair, tied in a ponytail, glided over her shoulder when she bent down. "*Uninvited*. What are you doing here, *Theo*?"

"I came to see how you were faring after the storm."

She speared him with a glare. "I am not a child who is scared of a little thunder!"

"I never said you were."

Relaxing her shoulders a notch, she invaded his space. From such a close distance, he could smell thyme soap on her body and hair.

"I thought you were a thief or a scoundrel." Lady Clarissa measured him with a scrutinising stare.

"If it makes you feel any better, I did not plan to steal or do anything scandalous."

She broke into a grin. "I, too, cannot imagine Your Imperial Highness doing anything inappropriate. You were ever the perfect prince."

Thessian did not like the sound of that. "I was never perfect, Lady Clarissa."

She looked away and sashayed over to her bed where her wig and coat were. "I am no longer a lady of House Leutten."

"What happened to you? Why did you break our engagement? What happened to your wedding?" He had to stop himself from shaking the answers out of her.

"Theo, we are but a merchant's accountant and a mercenary. What happened in the past does not matter."

"It matters."

Her slim fingers straightened out the messy locks of her wig as she picked it up. "My father owed a great debt to my would-be husband's family. To pay it off and keep his prestige, he decided to sell me."

Thessian's hands formed fists at his sides. He held great respect for Marquess von Leutten in the past. Now, after hearing that he was willing to sell his daughter to cover a debt, Thessian's opinion of the man completely changed. "The emperor would not agree to dissolve an engagement because your family changed their minds at a moment's notice."

In drawn-out silence, she redid her hair and put the wig on.

"Lady Clari—"

"Sacha!" she snapped at him. Her voice softened as tears glistened in her eyes. "I am Sacha now. Nothing more and nothing less."

He took a tentative step towards her. "How did the engagement get broken? Father refused to tell me the details, and Mother pretended the engagement never happened."

"My father lied to His Imperial Majesty. He said I was...*tainted*. That I threw myself at men left and right. His Imperial Majesty was angry but, because of his friendship with my father, he dissolved the engagement and pardoned me for my supposed crimes." She sniffled and rubbed at her eyes with her sleeve. "I wanted to marry you, Thessian. I did."

With a full-blown ache in his heart, Thessian enveloped her in a hug and patiently waited until her tears subsided. Lady Clarissa was more than just a fiancée to him. She was a kindred spirit who enjoyed swordplay and talk of knights' expeditions to fight off monsters or put down rebellions. After he got the news that their engagement was over, he could not think straight for a week, or, possibly, a month. Laurence had to take the drink away from Thessian's tent and went as far as throwing a bucket of cold water at the prince to bring him out of his drunken stupor. Thessian could never fault his friend for any of it. Their soldiers were dying on the battlefield all because his mind was elsewhere.

There is no way to turn the time back, just as there is no way to restore what was once broken.

Thessian massaged her back, feeling how slim she was through the loose-fitting and rough material of her shirt, then gently nudged her away by the shoulders.

"Let's start over," he said. "My name is Theo, and I am a mercenary for hire from the Hellion Empire. I have a younger brother, Ronne, and we are travelling south."

Lady Clarissa seemed to regain her composure and lifted her face. Her eyes were red from the tears she had shed. "I am Sacha. I work for The Emerald Swan Merchant Company and am proud of the work I do."

To give her some room, he moved to the door and rested his back against it, arms crossed. "How did you meet Delphine Leferve?"

"It is a sordid tale. Do you still wish to know?"

He nodded.

Sacha sat on the edge of her bed and stared blankly at the wall for a while. Sucking in a deep breath, she said, "After I abandoned my former name, I fled from Hellion. At first, I did not realise that my actions would haunt me even to Dante." She sneered and wiped away the remnants of tears from her damp cheeks. "Foolishly, I used my first name and did not change my appearance in the beginning. I travelled from town to town until I settled in Vinmare three years ago. The local grape farms needed labour, and I needed the coin to survive. Two months into my job, I was captured by the men my would-be husband hired. He did not believe I was dead, and to this day is still searching for me."

Thessian's brows rose. "Did Delphine save you?"

"Not exactly. Delphine came to the storehouse for an inspection, which allowed me to steal a sword and fight back."

"You fought against a band of mercenaries on your own?"

Sacha shrugged. "What was I to do? Let them take me back to my fiancé who wants to kill me with his own hands for disgracing him?"

"Should I kill him for you?"

She gave him a stern look an etiquette teacher would give to a hopeless student. "You cannot. He is not someone a wandering mercenary can fight against."

"You know exactly what I mean," Thessian replied as he lowered his arms and gripped the hilt of his sword. "I could easily remove him from your life."

"Even if that someone is the Crown Prince of Vare?"

Thessian went silent. The Crown Prince of Vare—Risseniel Iberteus Letille—and Thessian used to be amicable in their childhood. The bond of youthful friendship had waned over the years. Thessian dedicated more time to wars and the defence of the Empire, and Crown Prince Risseniel no longer wrote him. As a Sovereign State bordering the far west of the Hellion Empire, Vare also shared its borders with Kyros' territory. They were an ally and a trading hub that connected the Hellion Empire to the kingdoms in the west. Killing Crown Prince Risseniel would no doubt cause a war to break out with the entire western side of the continent.

"There is no fixing this. All I can do is hide until he loses interest in me," Lady Clarissa said glumly.

"What if you hid in Darkgate? It is my territory and there is no need for Risseniel to visit."

Her mouth curved downwards, and she got up. "I could never place such a burden on you. Hiding a wanted person could put you in grave danger or cause political strife."

I am already hiding the exiled Crown Prince of Shaeban. What's one more fugitive?

"My offer remains nonetheless," he said, pushing away from the door.

Her violet eyes twinkled when she smiled, but from her tone, he knew that she would never accept his helping hand. "Thank you. I think it's time to eat. Will you escort me?"

"It would be my pleasure."

22
A RAT IN THE PALACE

EMILIA

A day after returning to the palace, Emilia held a meeting with her closest aides in the Drawing Room. Comfortable in her chair at the dessert table, she observed the tawny Naguruan tea Sir Rowell poured into her teacup before effortlessly placing it in front of her on a saucer.

Ambrose and Lionhart sat across from Emilia, their expressions grim.

Sir Jehan Wells, who was the new addition to her inner circle, stood guard by the door.

Although invited, Clayton and Lady Isobelle could not attend the meeting.

It's for the best. I still can't look him in the eye after how I behaved at the inn. His image of the ideal queen must have shattered after that drunken ordeal.

She lifted the cup to her lips and inhaled the malty scent of her tea to push away her future relationship problems. She had a much bigger issue to deal with.

Someone had leaked her schedule to the assassins. Not only that, they leaked the Pope's outing as well. Had Valerian been any other king or ruler, he would not have been so forgiving.

Emilia sipped her tea hoping that Marchioness Durand had nothing to do with it.

Finally, she placed her cup down and folded her hands in her lap. "There is a spy within these walls."

Ambrose's face turned ashen. "Is that the reason for Her Majesty's attempted assassination in Port Lisza?"

"Quite so," Emilia replied.

Lionhart rubbed his eyes and then pinched the bridge of his nose. "And things were going *so well* for us."

His words, laced with sarcasm, brought a chuckle out of Emilia. "Valerian suspects it to be one of the maids while I cannot also discount the possibility of Marchioness Durand having a hand in it."

Sir Rowell bent down to her level. "If I may, Your Majesty, Marchioness Durand spent that afternoon with me. She had many queries about you and would not let me go until the sun had long taken refuge beyond the horizon."

Emilia gazed into the head butler's earnest eyes. "Lady Durand could have arranged for the messenger to deliver word to the assassins after attending to me that morning."

"It would be foolish for Marchioness Durand to assassinate someone she wishes to grow close to," Lionhart pointed out and crossed his arms. "The Durands follow whoever wears the crown."

"Malette also had royal blood in him. He was King Gilebert's cousin," Emilia retorted.

Ambrose spoke up. "Your Majesty, it is almost as if you are hoping it was Lady Durand instead of the maids. And, if it is one of them, I will take full responsibility and bring the traitor before you."

Emilia pondered Ambrose's words.

Do I want it to be Lady Lucienne? Is it because she was close with the former queen?

Lady Lucienne's presence had stirred a lot of memories Emilia wanted to erase. Just the thought that Queen Cecilia could have been a loving mother who brought up Emilia with care and affection made her heart heavy. All of those what-ifs did not suit any purpose, yet she could not help her mind straying from time to time.

"I have kept tabs on Lady Lucienne since she arrived in Newburn," Lionhart offered, drawing Emilia's attention away from her reverie. "From my information, she is not a threat to you. Her focus appears to be on her daughters and forming a bond with you."

"When I spoke with Lady Durand, she did not seem to have any ill will towards Her Majesty," Sir Rowell said.

"Very well, we will assume the Marchioness is innocent. Without solid evidence, it would be difficult to place the fault at her feet." Emilia gave Ambrose a sympathetic smile. "Could you look into the maids and see if any of them had left the palace during my excursion?"

Ambrose slapped her hand to her chest. "Of course, Your Majesty! I will investigate the maids immediately."

Turning her head to the Guard Captain, Emilia asked, "Could you check with the guards who were on duty regarding this matter, Sir Jehan?"

"Aye'll report any findings as soon as I have 'em, Yer Majesty," the Guard Captain replied with a bow of his head.

Emilia finished her tea after dismissing Ambrose, Sir Rowell, and Sir Jehan to begin their inquiries. Soundlessly setting her cup on the saucer on the table, she said, "Lionhart, my coronation will take place in three weeks."

He leaned in and rested his elbows on the table. "Are you prepared? After the crown is on your head, there is no going back. It is not too late to take your fortune and escape into obscurity. Leave this wretched place and start a new life. Preferably one where your life is not endangered every day."

Emilia knew he wanted what was best for her. Otherwise, he would never urge her to abandon a seat of power for a simpler life. "I cannot. I have a promise to keep with Thessian."

"Is the Empire's prince that important to you? I thought your heart yearned for another."

"My heart and my goals are not in conflict."

He scrutinised her with a long stare. She could see a flurry of emotions swimming across his face—from concern to fret to displeasure. He settled on mild annoyance and patted his false leg. "Do you know how I got this?"

"Not for the lack of trying. You never let anyone know, not even Sally."

Lionhart grimaced. "Oh, she tried to get the answers out of me many a time. She even got me drunk to see if that would force me to talk."

Emilia arched a brow as she rested her back against the chair. "Are you going to tell me?"

"I am considering it."

"Is it related to nobility?"

"Close."

"Royalty?"

"Yes."

A knot formed in Emilia's throat. She never heard of a royal punishment where a man's leg was cut off. Not in Dante or the Empire, at least.

"You do not need to tell me if you do not feel ready," she told him.

Lionhart must have taken note of her discomfort and closed his eyes. His fingers dug into his knee, and pain showed on his face. "I...I hail from Asmor." He opened his dark eyes. One look into their anguished depths halted all responses from Emilia. "More specifically, Kharam—the capital city of Quiyn. From the day I was born, I was chosen to become one of the king's shadows. It was the greatest honour for my parents and the harshest curse for me."

Lionhart sucked in a shaky breath as he cast his gaze to his false leg once again. "Train. Obey. Kill for the Crown—that was the mantra our teacher taught us. During a mission, he disappeared without a trace. No one but me and those in our unit knew of his demise. So, we mourned our loss in silence and, as his best student, I became the new leader of Verhalra."

"How old were you when it happened?" she asked tentatively.

Lionhart briefly looked up. "Fourteen. I was but a pup, eager to please his master for that was all I knew, all I cared about."

"It could not have been easy."

"Taking a life is not hard. A stab of a blade in the right place and they're gone. They weren't people. They were targets without a name. In my mind, they were no different from the wooden dummies we trained on."

"Do you feel the same to this day?"

He paused and then a pained laugh escaped him. "Not since I broke the rules and fell in love with my wife. I could not pass her by. She had the brightest smile, the kindest soul, and the softest heart. Anyone would fall for her and give up their everything. Isran became my world." His voice quivered and a lone tear travelled down his cheek. Wordlessly, he wiped it away.

Emilia did not like where the story was headed, but she remained silent and allowed him to continue at his own pace.

"Years passed. I learned my wife was with child. Then and there, I decided to leave the Verhalra. To show my resolve, I trained my successor—the best student of mine. I reported to my master and begged for his understanding. The king granted me his blessing along with one last mission."

The spymaster's shaking fist hit the table, making Emilia's bouncing teacup clatter against the saucer.

One of the guards peered into the room.

Emilia smiled calmly and waved him away and placed her hand over Lionhart's as gently as she could. "Did you fail?"

He produced a sound similar to a laugh that twisted her gut and pulled away from her touch. "Of course not! Having assassinated the enemy king, I returned victorious to find my wife's throat slit and the Verhalra waiting for me in our home."

Emilia felt sick. She covered her gasp with her hand.

"They bound me, cut off my leg, and threw me on a rickety river boat at the docks. My successor—Ahwen—made a show of cutting my throat, but not deep enough to kill me. He pushed off the boat with his foot and told me to survive while, in the distance, my master watched the whole time." Lionhart's eyes flared with hatred. "I can still see his smile in my mind's eye to this day…"

Emilia's hot tears streaked her cheeks and dripped onto her hands. She fished out a handkerchief from the inner pocket of her dress and dabbed at her face. There were no words that could soothe or change the atrocities that happened to Lionhart. His past was his to bear.

Once she managed to regain control of her emotions, she asked, "Are you planning to take revenge on the King of Quiyn?"

"It was the reason why I formed an information guild. To take down any opponent, one must be armed with their weaknesses. That is, until you came into my life, Emilia."

"I-I do not understand."

"When we first met, you were the same age my child would have been if they were alive. I took it as the gods granting me a second chance to atone for the lives I have taken and to quell the raging storm in my heart."

She got up from her seat, glided over to him, and hugged him. "No matter your past, you are my important friend. I could not have asked for a better man to stand by my side."

He sniffled and wiped at his runny nose. With his hand, he covered his eyes, and his shoulders trembled as he silently mourned the loss of his wife and child.

Emilia rubbed his back in circles and cried alongside him. They did not have familial ties or blood to share. Yet, she felt closer to him than anyone else. If he was her father instead of King Gilebert, she might have had a much happier childhood.

After a while, he wiped at his face with the damp sleeves of his coat and stood up, which forced her to take a step back from him.

His eyes and nose were tinted red and swollen from the emotional display.

Clearing his throat, he said, "Let us never mention this for the rest of our lives."

She smiled kindly. "Don't you think Sally should know you cried like a newborn babe?"

"Never tell Sally. As a matter of fact, I never cried. I had dust in my eyes."

"In the Queen's Drawing Room? Ambrose will be upset to learn that the maids are not doing their job."

"Quite right."

They laughed and hugged for the last time.

"Thank you, Emilia, for being who you are and for helping me grow and move past the desire to seek vengeance. Without you in my life, I might have remained in the darkest of pits till my last breath."

"And I thank you for teaching me how to fight and stand up for myself. Your teachings have saved me on more than one occasion."

With a smile still in place, he stepped away from her. "Do you feel well enough for a sparring session?"

After her stay at the inn with Clayton and Valerian, Emilia felt better than ever. No hangover, either. Her muscles regained their strength, and she did not tire as easily as she did after initially waking from her coma. It was truly a mystery.

Grinning back, she replied, "With you? Anytime!"

A good sparring session with Lionhart had been what she needed to take her mind off of her troubles with men.

Focused and adamant about not shedding another tear that day, instead of returning to the office, Emilia retreated to the Royal Library.

The knights on guard duty saluted her and opened the intricately carved double doors for her to pass.

She waltzed inside and dismissed her guards for a moment of peace.

Once the doors shut behind her with a booming thud, calm washed over her as she inhaled the earthy scents mixed with leather and wood undertones.

The Royal Library was the largest room in the palace. It had over forty rows of specially crafted bookcases from the finest of Ash trees from the Ashen Forest in the south of Dante. Each towering bookcase required a stretching ladder to retrieve the books from the top shelf.

Her surroundings dwarfed her as if letting her know that all the knowledge stored in that room was too much for one person to hold. Yet, she had read the vast majority. However, she did fib a little to Duke Malette when he first arrived to voice his protests. After she realised she wasn't dreaming, and the visits from her brothers became less frequent, she read any content that sparked her interest—books, journals, poems, ballads, or any tales the kings deemed important enough to keep on a shelf, excluding the obviously explicit material, of course. At least, some of it. She had read book after book, sometimes staying in the library's shadows for days with nothing but a cup of water.

Waving her memories aside, Emilia picked up a lantern off the table by the door and made her way down the straight path carved ahead for her. The clacking of her heels echoed with each step to the point where she found it a bit distracting.

Halfway down, she paused and turned her head to read the golden plaques on the bookcases in search of the one she once procured.

As her heart picked up speed with her nervousness, she resumed her sauntering along the aisles while contemplating on giving up on her purpose. After all, there was no valid reason for her to find out more about the kind of person the former queen had been. They had never met, and the deceased queen hadn't truly given birth to her. Emily only became The Cursed Princess of Dante when she was a small child, not a baby.

Although her heart was filled with friendship and affection for those around her, nothing seemed to be able to replace a mother's love. She craved it along with the acknowledgement of her struggles.

Once she found the aisle she was looking for, Emilia hung the lantern on the hook above her head and diverted her attention to the books. Her fingers brushed the dusty vellum spines of the bound travel manuscripts and the journey accounts hand-written by the kings and scholars of old. They had not been touched in years, possibly since the day she returned them. The secret escape passage at the back of the thirteenth aisle, behind Queen Athela's statue, was only known to the royal family. Emilia will forever be grateful that the second prince, and her supposed brother, was a chatterbox. He spilt royal secrets without prompting while he played his tricks on her. He thought she was too stupid to understand anything since she stopped talking for the second time. At least, his jests did not involve poisonous fruits and berries that the first prince often forced her to eat.

She tilted her head to one side. Now that she thought about it, she could not even remember their names. They were always, Prince One and Prince Two. With her memory, that had to be an achievement or a major failure. Though, victims of abuse often suffered from loss of memory and other maladies. If Emilia wasn't an adult mentally once she reincarnated, her sanity would have shattered with everything that she had to endure. Luckily, her eagerness to survive after abandoning her former grim life gave her a purpose. Her knowledge of another, much more advanced world made her more cunning and resourceful.

Again, her thoughts kept her distracted. When she focused, her eyes caught the sight of a travel journal of a pilgrim. She removed it off the shelf and ran her fingers over the sable leather cover with silver corner pieces. Popping the metal clasp open, the Queen peeled the smooth vellum pages apart and traced her fingertips along the beautiful cursive writing of the man who recorded his perilous journey through the Shanha Desert on the Asmor continent.

Did Queen Cecilia also read his account? Did she enjoy it?

The scattered facts about the former queen were giving her vertigo.

Emilia could easily relate to Cecilia's desire to flee from the palace and see the vast world out there. Soon, that could become an impossible dream. Too many responsibilities and the lives of others had a chokehold on her movements. Each person she added to her side became an additional chain that held her in place.

Suddenly, the doors to the library opened and closed with a loud thud.

The clacking of someone's boots drew closer.

Emilia put the journal back on the shelf, lifted her skirts, and unsheathed the dagger she kept strapped to her thigh. It could not be Ambrose or Sir Rowell. Their footsteps had a different pattern. The person's stride was too noisy to be a maid and too quiet to be a man.

It must be a noblewoman.

Click, clack. Click, clack.

Only those of royal blood or high nobility could enter the Royal Library.

For a second, Emilia considered leaping out with a dagger in hand and attacking first, in case the person was after her life. Yet, that would be foolish since the guards had granted entry to the person in question.

Unless they were killed.

Her constant brushes with death were making her extra paranoid.

Reluctantly, she gritted her teeth, hid her weapon in the sleeve of her dress, and assumed her royal stance as if she were expecting the intrusion on her private time.

Lady Lucienne came into view, holding something in her hand. She spotted Emilia and gracefully glided into a swan-like obeisance. "Greetings, Your Majesty. The maids told me you were here."

Emilia lifted a dark brow. *The maids are chattier than ever since Thessian left the palace.*

"You may lift your head, Lady Lucienne." Emilia's eyes were focused on the object the Marchioness was holding. "What is that in your hand?"

Resuming proper posture, Lady Lucienne asked, "May I have permission to approach Your Majesty? I have something I need to give you."

"Is it something so important that you felt the need to interrupt my time alone?"

The Marchioness must have picked up on Emilia's foul mood and lowered her head. "I apologise for my thoughtless behaviour. I will come back another time."

Emilia took a step towards her. "What is it you wish to give me?"

Lady Lucienne lifted a small stack of letters that were bound with a thick ebony string. "These are the letters I have received from Queen Cecilia in the past. I-I thought you may want to read them."

"What led you to such a conclusion?"

"As Your Majesty knows, I have three daughters. It may be presumptuous of me, but I can see Your Majesty is hurting."

"You are correct. It is presumptuous."

Lady Lucienne lifted her gaze as her fingers fidgeted with the stack. "Will Your Majesty accept this gift of mine?"

Emilia could not tell why Lady Lucienne was so determined to do this. There was no benefit for the Marchioness or House Durand from what Emilia could see. If anything, it could alienate her from the Crown if the Queen took it as a direct insult for bringing up the painful past.

Still on guard, Emilia replied, "I will accept your gift, Lady Lucienne."

Blowing out a breath, the Marchioness came closer and handed the letters to Emilia.

Once Emilia held them in her left hand, Lady Lucienne stepped away. "I will leave you to your thoughts, Your Majesty."

Before the lady could turn away, Emilia asked, "Do you think Queen Cecilia would have been happy to have a daughter?"

"The answer you seek is in those letters."

Emilia toyed with the string binding the letters for a long time after the Marchioness had left her side. She felt the tightness in her throat.

Should I burn them?

What if Cecilia never wanted a daughter? Boys make better heirs in the eyes of the nobility.

Grabbing the lantern off the hook, she made her way to the cushioned sofa by the arched stained window. She sat down, placing the lantern on the floor. The dagger's blade warmed against her forearm, becoming a nuisance, so she returned it to its sheath.

Her mind whirled with possibilities as she studied the letters that seemed to become heavier in her lap with each passing second.

What harm could a stack of letters do? They're just old letters by someone who's no longer around.

That someone is also a mother I never got to meet.

How much time had passed, Emilia did not know.

Her fingers clutched the end of the string. She was about to pull on it when Ambrose's voice came from the entrance of the library. "Your Majesty?"

Emilia had never been more relieved to hear from her head maid. Her trepidation was replaced with a bubbly feeling in her gut.

Tucking the letters into the inner pocket of her dress, she called back, "Over here!"

A minute later, Ambrose rounded a bookcase, red in the face and out of breath. "We have found them!"

The Queen smiled. "Perfect."

23
UNNERVING

EMILIA

At the doors that led to the courtyard, Emilia slowed her haste, straightened her back, and folded her hands in front of her. She gave a curt nod to the guard, who proceeded to open the door for her.

Ambrose draped a cloak with a fur collar over Emilia's shoulders, and the Queen glided out of the palace into the courtyard.

After the storm had passed, the sky was clear and dyed a myriad of hues from orange to pink and purple. The evening was upon them, and she had not gotten much done other than stare at some old letters.

In front of Emilia's Guard Captain and Vice Captain, on the paved path, were three people bound with rope and on their knees. One was a guard still in his armour. The other two were a palace maid and a laundry maid. Their uniforms were different and easy to distinguish.

The plump palace maid with two blonde braids caught Emilia's eye first. It was Nancy—the girl who served the meal during breakfast with Valerian and the one who was terrified of the "ghost" in the West Wing. For a simple servant, Nancy certainly had been drawing attention to herself too often.

Clenching her jaw, Emilia held in her temper. In her mind, she counted to ten all the while drawing out the time for the punishment. She had hoped the servants would plead for mercy or proclaim innocence.

That did not happen, which meant they knew the weight of their crimes.

Emilia spoke over the heads of the criminals to Sir Jehan and Sir Regis. "Did all of them commit treason?"

The maids started to shake while the guard remained motionless.

Sir Jehan stepped forward and lowered his head. "It would appear so, Yer Majesty."

Without turning, Emilia asked, "Ambrose?"

"I have queried the maids and have gathered their statements," Ambrose readily replied.

"And I have a written record that Sir Sraid Rod was missing his guard duty shortly before an attempt on your life, Yer Majesty," Sir Jehan piped in.

Emilia pinched the bridge of her nose. She thought they had cleaned up the palace enough to get rid of the spies. Yet, no matter how hard Ambrose or Lionhart tried, there were always people willing to sell out others for a few gold coins. All she could do now was find out who was the mastermind behind the spies.

Lowering her arm, she stood in front of Nancy. "Who hired you?"

She bowed as low as the ropes permitted and sniffled. "I didn't do it, Your Majesty! I'm innocent, I swear."

"How so?"

Nancy dared not raise her head. "The information slipped out when I was talking to Clara about how elegant His Holiness was during breakfast."

Hearing the maid's admission made Emilia's voice come out even colder. "You dare share information that was spoken privately between His Holiness and I?"

The maid's excuses withered away. She burst into uncontrollable tears and shrunk in on herself.

The name of the laundry maid rang a bell, so the Queen moved on to her next. "What say you, Clara?"

Clara whipped her head up. Her long tresses of chocolate-coloured hair were carefully secured with a white cotton hat. Her skin was so smooth and unblemished, that it made Emilia frown.

The brunette had tears in her dark eyes but all the right emotions were missing. "Oh, Your Majesty! *Please* spare me! I am a breadwinner for my poor family. My sister's taken ill as of late—"

Nancy's head snapped up. "You don't have a sister!"

Clara rolled her eyes. The maid would have made a terrible actress. "And you forgot to mention how you wanted to fondle His Holiness' private parts."

"I-I did not!" Nancy's cheeks flushed despite her denial.

"What else did you say?" Clara licked her lips. "Imagining him above you could drive you to ecstasy in under a minute? You also said that if you were as pretty as Her Majesty, you'd keep him in your bedchambers until he ran out of stamina."

Emilia glanced at Sir Jehan and Sir Regis who, too, appeared uncomfortable with the direction the conversation took. She had to admit, Valerian was hard to ignore. If she was a maid who caught his attention, even for a second, she may have fantasised about him as well.

He's a good kisser, too.

To push away unwanted memories, she cleared her throat. "Who hired you, Clara?"

The laundry maid finally stopped yammering away and lifted her dead eyes. "What's it matter? I'll be gone before sunrise."

"It would spare you the torture of the dungeons," Emilia replied.

Clara thought about it with a tilt of her head and peeked at Sir Sraid Rod next to her. "He got me into this mess. Ask him."

Clara was acting unbothered for someone who would soon be burned at the stake for treason against the Crown. Her accomplice would receive a less dignified death. He would be hung, drawn, and quartered for high treason. Emilia could order a beheading instead, but those were not necessarily successful on the first try if the executioner was incompetent or the blade was dull.

The guard did not need to be prompted. Sraid Rod lifted his head, his mouth twisted in utter disgust. "You're one to talk! You said you admired me, tellin' me I just needed to pass on a message now and again."

"Don't listen to him, Your Majesty," Clara cautioned with a dramatic shake of her head. "That's how I fell for his charm."

Emilia tried to find the charm Clara mentioned and completely failed in doing so. If Sir Sraid Rod stood next to Thessian, Clayton, Valerian, or even Sir Laurence, he would blend in with the background or the dirt beneath their feet.

Could he have a pleasant personality?

Sraid growled, "You wretched wench! I should never have listened to your grovelling no matter your skills in bed."

I suppose not.

Emilia's head began to ache. Out of the trio, Nancy seemed the least guilty. Other than being a blabbermouth, she had no malice to her actions. Yet, there was no escaping punishment. The one Emilia seemed most concerned with was Clara. That laundry maid made Emilia's skin crawl. Every time Clara looked at the Queen, their eyes met, which was a grave disrespect to the ruler of the kingdom, but the corners of her mouth were also strangely quirked up in a clear display of a challenge. That woman had no love for the Crown, and her appearance and body language told Emilia that she was no servant. Clara was probably not only a spy but also a trained assassin. She used her charm to seduce one of the guards and pretended to be friends with Nancy to get her to talk and share what was going on inside the palace walls.

Even as Emilia pondered, Clara boldly looked at her as if death meant nothing to her.

Completely brainwashed by her master. She won't say a word.

"Take the criminals away," Emilia declared and turned on her heels.

Behind her, she could hear Nancy breaking down into an ear-piercing wail while Sir Sraid Rod spewed curses at Sir Regis and Sir Jehan. Clara remained completely quiet, which made ants crawl up Emilia's spine. She could almost feel the laundry maid's malicious stare burning a hole in her back.

When the traitors were dragged away by the palace guards, Emilia could not shake the bad feeling that twisted her gut into knots.

"Ambrose, inform Sir Jehan that Clara needs to be watched at all times and look into who recommended her and her past. There is something about her that makes me uncomfortable."

"Does Your Majesty also think her to be odd?"

Emilia hugged her middle and rubbed her arms in an attempt to soothe her nerves. She had seen assassins fear for their lives when they were faced with death. Clara seemed undaunted and emotionless. On second thought, perhaps emotions were not the problem. What surprised the Queen was the clear defiance Clara displayed as if the maid knew something Emilia didn't.

"Odd is an understatement."

Even after dinner and a hot bath, Emilia's body did not release its tension. She sat on her bed in her nightdress, arms and legs crossed, and scrutinised the stack of letters Lady Lucienne had gifted her.

This is ridiculous! I should open one and see what's in it.

Marchioness Durand did not appear to be there to cause harm. She was also proven innocent of an attempt on Emilia's life.

So, what's holding me back?

A light tap came on her balcony's windowpane.

She turned her head to find Clayton standing on the other side of the double doors, one hand hidden behind his back.

Did he bring something for me?

Climbing off her bed, Emilia padded barefoot to the balcony's doors and peeled them apart. She could not help a cheeky smile forming on her lips. "Good evening, Lord Armel. Are you here to make a report?"

He smiled back and moved his arm to unveil his gift. In his hand, he held a palm-sized plant pot with a single indigo flower that resembled a water lily but not quite. The stem and leaves were closer to anthurium.

"What is it?" she asked.

"It is a Wishing Flower." Clayton glanced at the night sky and the drifting clouds that hid the moon. His smile stretched as he placed the pot on the balustrade and took a step back.

Emilia tucked her hair behind her ear. "It is a pretty flower, but I fear it may fall on a passing guard's head if it remains there."

"Give it a moment, Your Majesty," he assured her, his attention still firmly on the sky.

Amused by his determination, she waited patiently and curled her toes from the chill. "I hope it happens soon for I am getting a little cold."

He froze and then bowed his head to her. "My apologies, Your Majesty. Please go inside to warm up near the fireplace."

The flower on the balustrade twitched as a sliver of moonlight peeked out from behind the clouds. The plant expanded to twice its original size and a silver glow emanated from its petals, making Emilia's eyes grow wide.

"It's beautiful," she said, breathless.

He slipped out of his coat and draped it over her shoulders. "I am pleased you like it. There is a legend with this flower. If you make a wish on its final day of life, it will come true no matter what."

"Then shouldn't you make a wish and break your curse?"

"Your wishes are much more important than mine." His reply

came in a sultry voice that made her chest all fuzzy. He offered her his hand, which she took without hesitation.

"I do apologise for this—" He scooped her into his arms and carried her closer to the flower.

Emilia covered her giggle with her hand and breathed in his woody scent.

"Please make a wish before the flower fades."

The Queen gave it a quick think. She had everything at her disposal to achieve her goals. What she needed was time, and she had plenty of that on her hands.

"Do I need to make a wish and keep it a secret until it comes true?" she asked.

"I am not aware of such a custom."

She clasped her hands together and spoke dramatically. "O Wishing Flower, please grant me a wish." Her tone turned serious when she looked up at Clayton. "Please break Clayton's curse soon."

His eyes widened, and their eyes met. "It is a waste of a wish. Do you not have any desire of your own?"

"I have plenty but nothing a mystical flower can help with."

The Wishing Flower, as if hearing Emilia's request, pulsed three times before its petals began to deteriorate at a rapid pace. They turned into shimmering dust that was carried away by the wind, leaving behind a vacant stem.

"Now that you have given me this magical gift," she said, cupping his cheek. "I have to wonder what I will receive on my birthday."

"When is it?"

"A day before the Festival of Life."

Clayton appeared deep in thought as he carried her back inside her bedchambers. He set her down on the bed and went back to close the balcony doors.

Upon his return, he noticed the letters. "Are those from your admirers?"

She burst out laughing at the winds of jealousy that were blowing his way. "No, they are from the former Queen of Dante."

"Queen Cecilia?"

"Marchioness Durand thought I should have them."

He picked up the stack, turning it every which way before taking a whiff. "They do not appear to be poisoned."

"You can smell poison?"

"It's not hard when you grew up mixing poisons from young."

Emilia's heart gave an uncomfortable squeeze. She took his hand in hers and intertwined their fingers.

Just how much of myself can I reveal to him before he realises how fragile I am on the inside? Every relationship required a leap of faith. She could trust him with her life, knowing that Clayton would not betray her. She would even go as far as to risk her life to save him.

Does that constitute that we are truly in love? Or is it a temporary affliction of the mind?

She may be living in a fantasy novel, but the world she had witnessed with her eyes was harsh and cruel. *The Cruel Empire* was no romance, by any means.

"The letters," she muttered, taking them away from him, "they make me uncertain about many things."

"Should I destroy them?"

Emilia considered his offer while looking at the orange flames bustling in the marble fireplace. "No. I think I should face my fears."

"Would it please Your Majesty if I read them out?"

"It would please me more if you used my name instead of my title."

His cheeks reddened a little and he faced away. Clearing his throat he said, "I could do that, E-Emilia."

Emilia bounced off the bed. He was too cute, and she couldn't hold back from wrapping her arms around him and pressing her body against his.

She lifted her head while resting her chin on his chest. "Are you shy by any chance, Lord Armel?"

He refused to look her in the eye.

Since he did not cooperate, she peeled away and climbed back on the bed. Patting the space next to her. "Read them to me one at a time."

Clayton ran a hand through his raven hair and sauntered around the bed. Taking the offered seat next to her, he pulled on the ebony string that bound the letters and picked the first envelope off the stack. With practised elegance only nobles could display, he removed the topmost letter and unfolded it in front of him.

His eyes skimmed the first few lines. Then, leaning his back against the pillows, he began to read in his smooth voice while she rested her head on his thigh.

"*My dearest Luci,*

In recent days, my existence has been enveloped in an unsettling hush. My parents have ceased their reproaches regarding my temperament, and Madame Rissou, in her instructive endeavours, has softened her approach. Astonishingly, she even bestowed praise upon my lamentable dancing skills.

Can you fathom such a transformation?

Something peculiar is afoot.

At the esteemed tea party hosted by Lady Fleur Morel, new tidings reached my ears—news that you, dear friend, are to wed Lord Durand. Curiously, why did this revelation come from the lips of that preening peacock rather than your own? Despite my mild vexation, I extend heartfelt felicitations. Lord Durand's unwavering gaze upon you during the Winter Ball did not escape my notice, nor did your apparent lack of objection.

Should he ever vex you, rest assured that I shall engage him in a stern discourse when next our paths intersect. My boots have been polished, and I do not fear to employ them.

Warmest regards,

Cecil."

Emilia gasped for air between her busts of laughter. Queen Cecilia was not what she expected. The way King Gilebert and his sons treated Emilia, she believed the former queen was on the same wavelength as them. In truth, Cecilia was seemingly a spirited lady with a strong will. No doubt high society and her parents had a hard time containing her.

When her laughter finally settled, Clayton smiled down at her.

"Do you feel better now?"

"Oh, I certainly do." She reached up and pulled him down for a kiss.

A crash from the balcony startled them.

Clayton paused. A second later, he separated from her and leapt over the bed towards the balcony, flinging the doors open. In his right hand, an ice blade was forming.

Emilia's heart was in her throat. She reached under her pillow for her dagger.

Armed with her weapon, she asked, "What is it?"

"A mage was here," he hissed, scouring the balcony for something. "There are traces of mana."

"Can you tell the kind of magic they used?"

He looked back at her, his grey eyes ablaze. "Teleportation."

Did the Malette's change their tactics? Are they planning to use mages against me now that the mercenaries failed? "Weren't mages with that ability captured and killed on sight?"

"Only in the Empire," Clayton corrected her and approached her with haste. "Whoever was here is gone for now, and I doubt they will return tonight. I shall follow their trail and have Isobelle stay by your side."

"How long will you be gone?"

"I am uncertain." His brows drew together into a pained expression. "Should the mage appear again, go to the temple where the Pope is."

"Are you telling me to run into the arms of another man?"

"He cannot be killed easily and has pledged to keep you safe."

Emilia slipped his coat off her shoulders and handed it back to him. She felt almost naked and a little lonely when the warmth was replaced with the chilly air.

"My coronation is in three weeks. Be back by then."

Clayton bowed low and left a kiss on the back of her hand that was still clutching her dagger. "As you command, Master."

24
PERFIDY

THESSIAN

Over his second breakfast, Thessian could tell that Lady Clarissa had let down her guard around him, if only by a smidgen.

In his mind's eye, he vividly remembered the day he received the letter from his father that the engagement was dissolved. Back then, Thessian could not bring himself to seek her out for answers. He had foolishly believed the rumours at face value—that she had left him for another man. With the truth that had surfaced today, he had no idea what to do. As things stood, they could not be together.

Too much time has passed. Feelings had changed. Or had they?

"Theo, you have been rather quiet," Sacha pointed out from across the table.

Thessian pushed his second bowl of pottage away. "I think I have had enough food for one day."

Concern bled into Sacha's voice. "You hardly ate anything!"

Should I tell her this is my second serving? "This is plenty."

Sacha gave Thessian's muscular frame a sideways glance. "Must be nice to survive on air and sunshine."

Thessian laughed. In the past, after days of eating nothing but bread and dried fruits on the front lines, Thessian and Laurence would hunt for a good meal. The last time, they caught and engulfed half a boar. "If only that was the case."

Delphine stiffly approached their table with a forced smile. "Sacha, there is something we need to discuss."

She swiped at her mouth with the back of her hand and gave Thessian a nod before disappearing with the merchant to her room upstairs.

Assuming that Sacha was not coming back to keep Thessian company, he headed back to the stables next door.

The stench of horse manure and cow dung overpowered the strong smells of hay and piss when the flimsy door was pulled open. Wrinkling his nose, he squeezed past the caravan only to receive a puzzled stare from a horse nearby.

His attention was drawn away from the animal as he picked up a faint rattle of a cage behind the thick canvas of the caravan. Upon closer inspection, the material was thicker than normal canvas, as if the merchants were desperate to hide the contents.

Leaning his ear against the canvas, he heard the sound of claws or talons hitting against the metal.

Henri languidly came around the corner of the caravan and scrutinised Thessian with a look of distrust in his tired eyes. "Is there anything you need?"

Tempting as it may be to pin the spindly merchant to the caravan and question him about the creature they were transporting, Thessian dismissed the idea. If he angered Sacha's employers, he would no longer be able to travel with them.

I will keep this pretence going a while longer.

"No." Thessian pushed past Henri to get to Ronne and their belongings that seemed to be tucked away behind the heap of hay used to feed the animals.

Even with all of the animals awake, it was too quiet in the stables. Soon, he realised why.

The boisterous mercenaries hired to guard the caravan were, once again, shirking their duties.

I hope Delphine won't pay them a single coin once we reach Garlia.

Without turning around, Thessian heard Henri clambering into the back of the caravan. The man did not seem to rest, and it was not surprising with guards as useless as those they had hired.

"What shall we do now?" Ronne asked upon Thessian's arrival.

"Clean our weapons and do what we were hired for."

The lad peered at the caravan and then back at Thessian. "Should I polish your weapons for you?"

"No need. We have plenty of time on our hands, and I need to keep busy."

"Is it to stop thinking about a certain someone?"

"And who would that be?" Thessian's tone held an edge to it, making the boy shut his mouth.

The prince picked up his scabbard that was resting against the wall and drew his sword. The steel blade subtly reflected its years of use. Despite the careful maintenance, some deeper scratches and chinks had formed here and there which were not easily ground away. In due time, the blade would be too thin to grind and would need replacing. As a military man of stature, Thessian kept multiple weapons at camp and routinely swapped out his damaged swords whilst on deployment. With all the chaos since coming to Dante, he had neglected to swap his weapon back at camp. That turned out to be a positive for this mission as the worn sword looked more feasible for a mercenary.

The familiar heaviness in his hand had become an extension of his body. A soldier could do without an arm or, sometimes, even a leg, but he could not survive without a weapon.

He sat down on the hay, pulled his knapsack close, and took out a clean linen cloth and a palm-sized ceramic jar of clove oil to clean the blade.

Slowly but surely, his mind calmed with every methodical movement.

Before the cockerel's call the next morning, they packed their belongings, fed the horses, and set off with the caravan to the faint brightening of the sky.

Sacha and Delphine were inseparable since their talk, which prevented Thessian from querying her about their cargo. All he knew was that they were headed to Countess Morel's estate in Garlia. The countess had a reputation for enjoying a lavish lifestyle, so he assumed the creature in the caravan had to cost a fortune.

His eyes narrowed on the thick canvas. *Whatever they are transporting, I hope Sacha won't needlessly put herself in danger.*

Once the horses passed the last house, they were pushed to hasten their speed.

Thessian's stomach was in knots. The closer they got to their destination, the sooner he would need to part with Lady Clarissa. His trip down memory lane was not as unpleasant as he had imagined. If anything, seeing her again had his heart race more than once—a fact he would never admit to anyone.

At the end of the day, Clarissa was a wanted woman by the Crown Prince of Vare. Thessian could not tarnish the political relationship with them. Not yet. The Empire was in the process of recovering from the prolonged war with Darkgate. It may have been two years since most of the soldiers rejoined their loved ones, but the heavy loss of lives was still fresh on everyone's minds. A full-scale war with a friendly state would diminish the morale of the troops, especially if the Vare Royal Family were loved by the people. At the next Imperial Ball, which the delegates from Vare were likely to attend, he would speak with Risseniel.

The matter with Dante was a gamble on Thessian's part. It was a political takeover with minimal casualties. To that day, he was thankful for Emilia's help and the information she provided. No matter how their relationship began, she made a perfect partner for him. With her by his side, he felt as if nothing could stop him from achieving the position of Crown Prince. And if Kyros was, indeed, scheming to kill their father, and words could not reach his younger brother, Thessian may need to close his eyes to their brotherly bond. As much as it would pain him to do so.

I hope it won't come to that...

The day wore on and the stretching farmlands turned to rolling hills. The snow had melted completely, removing its chilly blanket from the stubborn grass. In the distance, with a backdrop of the Steel Peaks mountains, the stone walls of Garlia could be seen, which made Thessian blow out a breath of relief. The altercation the merchants were expecting had to have been a humbug.

From the back, Thessian saw Warren nodding to his friends and urging his horse ahead of the merchants' caravan.

The action startled Henri, who nearly diverted the horses into a ditch.

Once the caravan returned to the middle of the road, Warren still pressed closely to the two horses at the front. The second mercenary pushed ahead on the other side, which forced the caravan's horses to flick their ears back and forth.

"What is the meaning of this?" Henri shouted at Warren.

Warren pulled out a dagger from its sheath at his hip. Leaning over, he jabbed the blade into the horse's hip, causing the animal to buck and neigh in agony.

The remaining two mercenaries promptly stopped their horses to block Thessian and Ronne, keeping them separated from the caravan at the rear.

Thessian looked to Ronne. "Be on guard."

Ronne's face hardened. "Understood!"

Thessian pulled out his dagger in preparation. For now, he had to keep his distance.

The caravan's horses lost themselves to the fear. They lurched wildly ahead.

The frame of the caravan creaked and cracked. Almost immediately, the back wheel snapped from the burden. No longer balanced, the caravan careened to one side, throwing Henri off.

Warren and his partner kept up with the caravan until it toppled into the ditch on the left with a loud crash.

Clarissa!

One glance past the mercenaries blocking his path let Thessian know that Henri was not moving. The man lay in a mangled heap short of the toppled caravan, possibly dead.

Gritting his teeth and squeezing the hilt of his dagger, the prince nudged his horse to slowly approach the men, Ronne following beside him.

The man who seemed no older than Thessian on the left offered, "Get out of here with your life and your brother."

The youngest of the mercenaries on the right seemed uncertain of what to do. He looked to the older man and then back at Thessian. He must have been a new hire and not yet witnessed any bloodshed.

In the distance, Thessian spied Warren and his friend getting off their horses to advance on the caravan. Sacha and Delphine were assumedly buried within the unmoving mess of canvas and cargo.

At the same time, from behind a hill about five miles ahead, a cluster of men on horseback raced towards them at a pace which told Thessian that they were not coming to help. The bandits would reach them in less than ten minutes at the speed they were consuming the road.

"How could you betray your employers?" Thessian growled.

The youngest blanched. "I-I—"

His partner sneered. "Guess you've never owed a debt. We are all sellswords. Honour is not something we can eat."

Glaring at the young mercenary, Thessian asked, "Boy, do you agree?"

"Leave Lyr out of it," barked the man, unsheathing a knife from his waist and pointing at the road behind Thessian. "Go. Now! Or

I can't guarantee your life."

Thessian's body radiated with heat. At any moment, the other bandits would join, and he would be killed or sold off somewhere. He had to think of his goals, of Ronne, of the Empire's future. He could escape and later track down the bandits.

Yet his body refused to move and abandon Lady Clarissa, albeit temporarily.

Killing Lyr and his companion would not be a problem. He could charge them, kick them off their horses, and, once on the dirt, aim for their vitals.

That would take too long.

Ronne must have sensed Thessian's uncertainty and drew his horse closer, wordlessly giving his support.

Sheathing his dagger to feign retreat, Thessian replied, "We will leave you to your spoils."

Before they could turn their horses around, Warren yelled, "Stop wasting time, Igren, and capture him!"

Igren groaned and waved his knife at Thessian. "You've missed your chance."

25
PRIORITIES

LAURENCE

At the crack of dawn, Laurence, Khaja, and their companions gathered in Laurence's room.

Every time the beastwoman entered his field of vision, he recalled the image of her naked form that his mind stubbornly refused to dissolve. So, opting for the safest option, he avoided looking at her entirely.

From the chair near the dying fireplace, Sergey asked with a big yawn escaping him, "Is somefin' wroangh?"

Laurence scrubbed a hand over his face. *What isn't?* "When we reach the First Peak, we will need to split away from Lord Carrell's men sooner rather than later."

Ian locked eyes with Laurence. The elf, currently cross-armed, had his back against the wall. Despite his relaxed demeanour, Laurence knew that Ian was observing all of the potential entrances and exits as normal. "Do elaborate."

"Marquess Carrell asked me to kill Khaja and abandon our mission."

Sergey gaped at Laurence. "Abandon our mission?"

The elf drummed his fingers against his arm, his expression stayed unreadable. In a tone that could be used to talk about the weather, Ian added, "This mission is partially of our own making. His Highness would be disappointed with us only finding the girl and not the village. No doubt he would send others to look for it."

"We are not going back. That is not an option!" Laurence's voice shook with anger. "Khaja must be returned to her tribe." *And I need to get rid of this bond.*

"She could stay with us," Yeland suggested next to Sergey. "Khaja likes Commander a great deal, and she can fight somewhat, too."

Laurence shot a glare at Yeland, and the knight shut his mouth.

"There is no need to get emotional," Ian interjected, incurring more of Laurence's wrathful stare. He let out a long sigh. "We were given a mission to find her and evaluate the threat her people pose. With our delay in the Dragon Village, we could spend weeks in the mountains, longer if Khaja does not cooperate. So, we need to decide when to withdraw from the mission since the mountains are dangerous and the conditions assumedly harsh."

Sergey chimed in, "Our current provisions will last about a week, two if we stretch it. We would need to gather more before we go. Foraging may be hard on the mountain."

Laurence massaged his eyelids with his thumb and index finger. He sucked in a calming breath and then observed his comrades in the room. Some of the tension he felt left his stiff shoulders. None of them wanted to fail Prince Thessian, and Ian had a point. They would be dawdling in the dangerous mountains with a dragon, monsters, and there was a possibility of wrathful storms.

Getting up, Laurence bobbed his head, his decision made. "We will travel up the Hollow Mountains with the lords and split off when opportune. If we cannot find Khaja's tribe within two weeks, or at least signs of where to go next, we will head back."

Yeland spoke in a hushed tone. "What do we do if Lord Carrell tries to kill Khaja before we split up?"

"I will deal with the situation if it comes to pass," Laurence replied.

Sergey slowly stood and lowered his head. "Commander, there is something I wish to request."

Laurence eyed Sergey, who appeared five years older with his unkempt beard. "What is it?"

"Before we left, I received a letter from my mother. My father is in poor health, and my older brother will be taking on the baron's title in two months. I wish to return to the Empire after this mission to congratulate him in person."

"Transfer of a noble title is an important affair." Laurence approached Sergey and squeezed his comrade's shoulder. "We will have you return to your family in one piece."

Sergey grinned from ear to ear. "Thank you, Commander!"

Bending to see Yeland on the chair, Laurence asked, "What are your plans after this?"

Yeland's face turned bright red. "I plan to court a lady I got to know in Newburn."

"It better not be Dame Cali," Laurence said with false annoyance. "I plan to marry her."

Yeland waved his hands in front of him. "I would not dare court Dame Calithea, Commander!"

Laurence chuckled and faced the elf. "The last one left is you, Ian. Any plans?"

Ian scowled at Laurence as if he did not expect the question to ever be directed at him. "I have no plans that you would find entertaining."

"That cannot possibly be true," Laurence countered.

"I do not make plans as I do not know if I will be alive to see them through." With those parting words, Ian pushed away from the wall and marched out of the room.

I should have been more careful with my words.

Sergey pointed to the door with his thumb over his shoulder. "We will prepare for the journey, Commander."

Laurence nodded and glanced at the bed where Khaja was lying on the fur blanket and blowing bubbles with her mouth. Sensing his attention, she stopped what she was doing, lazily rolled onto her side, and propped her head up with her hand.

"*Zaotuo yille kablenen kur kai vosie,* Laurenz," the beastwoman stated matter-of-factly.

"I hope you are not judging me with a straight face, Khaja. I know perfectly well that I have misspoken."

Come morning, after a hearty meal provided by Marquess Carrell, Laurence's group, the noble lords, and their escorts mounted their horses in the courtyard. At the exit of the courtyard, some spearmen in thick armour were preparing their packs, no doubt Captain Carver had sent additional men to protect his lord in the mountains.

Meanwhile, Lord Carrell and Lord Fournier had abandoned their carriage for two sturdy brown steeds.

A supply train was also arranged by Captain Carver, which would follow closely behind with its own contingent of soldiers from the Northern Watchtower.

From the information gathered by Sergey and Yeland, Laurence learned that the First Peak of the Hollow Mountains was three days away, the Second Peak was two weeks away, and the Third Peak could take nearly six weeks to reach. The location Lord Carrell had vaguely provided in Redford of the suspicious monster corpses was somewhere above the First Peak's midpoint, so, hopefully, the beastmen were hiding on the first mountain.

Khaja's arms wrapped around Laurence's middle—an action he had grown used to throughout their journey together. He could feel her pressing up against him, including her plump bosom.

Haaaaah! Please let us find her tribe soon. I do not know how much longer I can act as a gentleman.

Lord Carrell nodded to Captain Carver, who signalled to his men in the gatehouse to open the gates.

The men scrambled to their positions to turn the heavy mechanism and lift the gate bit by bit.

The spearmen assembled into a formation and followed after the lords.

Laurence patted Khaja's hands. "We will bring you home soon. Wait a little longer, Khaja."

"Hommm?" she asked full of uncertainty.

He smiled at her over his shoulder. Seeing her silver eyes gazing at him with brimming affection had his smile falter. He swallowed. "It's a place where you belong."

26
BAD NEWS COME IN PAIRS

EMILIA

A **sleepless night followed** Clayton's exit. Emilia had to call Ambrose to spend the night in her bedchambers in case the mage with the ability to teleport returned. Having her good friend nearby gave her some comfort, but her mind could not rest.

What if the assassin comes while I'm using a chamber pot? What if they are waiting for me to fall asleep only to jump out and stab me in the heart before Ambrose can help?

With Queen Cecilia's letters forgotten, Emilia got out of bed, washed up, and dressed with Ambrose's help. Clayton would track the mage for her, and she had to trust he would be successful in his pursuit. All Emilia could do was wait patiently and do some more research on mages.

Once the sun broke through the horizon, there were multiple knocks on her door.

Emilia glanced at Ambrose.

The head maid bowed and went to open the door to their uninvited guests.

On the other side, Sir Jehan's tired eyes were cast downward, and his mouth was set in a tight line. He approached Emilia with Sir Regis at his heel.

The two men went down on their left knee with their heads hung low.

"Yer Majesty, we bring bad news," Sir Jehan said with a crack in his voice. "Clara Voylan has escaped from the dungeons."

"And what were the guards doing at the time?" Emilia inquired, unable to contain her irritation from seeping out.

Sir Regis replied, "Her cell was locked and none of the guards had seen her, Your Majesty. I, too, spent the night alert and awake but did not see that maid. It's as if she escaped by—"

"Magic," Emilia finished for him. "Teleportation magic to be precise."

That solves the mystery of who the mage was last night.

At the same time, Sir Rowell appeared in the doorway. His usual greeting was nowhere in sight as he joined the knights in a row and bowed low. "You Majesty, Lady Diane is missing."

Emilia raked her mind and came up with nothing. "Who?"

"The wild noble lady Prince Thessian escorted through the castle on his shoulder, Your Majesty," the head butler offered.

Blood drained from Emilia's face. *Thessian's hostage is gone?*

Unconsciously, she covered her mouth with her hand as she began to pace the length of her bedchambers. It could not be Lady Diane Walden who wielded the power of teleportation. Otherwise, she would have made her escape a long time ago. No. She would not get caught by Thessian in the first place. The only conclusion was that when Clara failed to attack Emilia last night, she took Lady Diane with her instead.

This complicates matters. A lot.

Since Diane witnessed too much, she cannot be permitted to return to the Empire, or even to write a letter to her family. Otherwise, Thessian's cover-up would fall apart.

"We need to find them!" Emilia announced as she stopped in front of Sir Rowell and the knights. "Sir Rowell, summon Lionhart to my office."

"At once, Your Majesty. Furthermore, correspondence from Prince Thessian of Hellion and Sir Laurence Oswald of Hellion has arrived. I have placed them in your office." The head butler excused himself and ambled out of the room at a hurried pace.

There're also my coronation preparations that must begin as soon as possible. "Ambrose, send a messenger to Count Baudelaire and Marchioness Durand. Invite them to my office in the afternoon. Also, have Lady Riga come see me."

As a mage, Riga could shed some light on magic and its limits.

Emilia directed her attention to the kneeling knights. "Sir Jehan, double the patrols around the palace. Be on the lookout for Clara or anyone resembling her. Remember that she can teleport so do not hesitate to scrutinise someone that is already inside. Sir Regis, visit the Lionhart Guild and have them look into mages that can use teleportation magic. I want to know everything about them and the extent of their abilities."

The Guard Captain and Vice Captain stood up and saluted her.

"Your Majesty," Ambrose began with uncertainty, "who will guard you in our absence?"

Emilia smiled at the new guest in the doorway.

"It appears, I have arrived in time for the festivities." Lady Isobelle was clad in another curve-hugging black dress that drew the surprised attention of the guards at the door as though she had suddenly appeared. After a moment of them scrutinising her, the noblewoman was permitted entry into the Queen's room.

Isobelle flawlessly curtsied. "I came to guard Your Majesty at my brother's behest."

Emilia's bedroom had become a gathering place for bad news. It was time to move things along. "Wonderful. Let us speak in my office."

QUEEN OF HEARTS

An hour later, Emilia was sitting on a sofa in her office across from Lionhart, Lady Riga, and Lady Isobelle. They barely squeezed altogether into a two-seater, despite there being another seat nearby, but held in their discomfort.

Emilia skipped her meal that morning. She could not stomach even a morsel of food with the ever-increasing list of problems.

Why can't I have a nice, quiet day without someone trying to kill me? Should I pray to Luminos for some peace?

Keeping her hands folded over her lap, the Queen sat rod straight. "There are several matters that need to be resolved post haste. Lionhart, have you any information on Clara Voylan?"

"I don't, but any good spy would use an alias. I suspect such is the case here." He rested his elbow on the armrest. "I have lost contact with my spies in Marquess Sardou's estate in Elisse. There is a high possibility they were caught and executed by the marquess. As for the marchioness of House Durand and her daughters, I found nothing of concern. They have not engaged in anything illegal or brow-raising."

"Yes, I am starting to believe that Lady Durand may be on our side," Emilia admitted.

"She is a socialite," Lionhart added. "Be cautious still."

Emilia gave him a weak smile and studied the young lady as she fidgeted with her fingers between the two adults that dwarfed her. "Lady Riga, how much do you know about the mages and their abilities?"

"I only know what I've read in the books my father bought for me. Mages of the past possessed weak abilities. None could conjure a fireball as big as mine or revive a person from near death like Lord Armel. Truthfully speaking, and I may be wrong, but I have noticed a pattern." Lady Riga nibbled on her lower lip. "In more recent accounts and journals of mages, they describe their powers differently. I believe the mages are becoming stronger with each passing year. My magic, too, is harder to control than before. It has gotten stronger over the years and takes greater effort to control."

The mages are getting stronger? This could shift the power balance on the continent and possibly the entire world.

Emilia mulled over the original story of *The Cruel Empire*. The mages were killed by Kyros when he assumed the Empire's throne, but she never stopped to ask why. Every character in the story had reasons for their actions, which meant that Prince Kyros had his reasons for the slaughter, too.

Did the mages rebel? Want more power?

Emilia thought hard about the events after Thessian's death. The story followed a commoner mage—Emmeric Bellfyre—who awakened his magic at eighteen. It was considered unnaturally late for a mage, so no one suspected he had any powers. Emmeric was a low-ranking soldier within the ranks of Darkgate's military. Along with his friends, whom Emmeric met on his travels over the years, he took on the cruel and unjust Emperor Kyros. If she calculated the timeline correctly, at present, Emmeric would be a sixteen-year-old boy. When Thessian died, the hero was about to turn eighteen. And at twenty-two, he defeated Kyros. There was no mention of mages vying for the throne from Emmeric's point of view. They only wanted to be left alone. At least, the characters who surrounded the hero.

But what of those who weren't in his inner circle? Mages like Clara would not sit still if their power grew exponentially, and I learned first-hand how quickly things spiral out of control due to a small change in the narrative.

So, if Thessian takes the Empire's throne, would there even be a need for Emmeric to emerge as the hero? Have I taken his path away from him?

Maybe I should have him monitored closer to his supposed awakening in the original story to see if it still happens.

If I'm alive by then...

"Is everything alright?" Lionhart asked, breaking Emilia out of her thought process.

Emilia was stuck for words. She had spent all of her time

thinking only of how to survive and make Thessian into an ally. If the mages fought for power, Thessian would have no choice. He would defend the Empire and his people.

A war might be inevitable.

Massaging her temples, the Queen inhaled deeply. "I may have realised something too late."

"Is it important?" Lionhart probed.

"I'm uncertain." Turning her attention to Lady Isobelle, Emilia asked, "Does House Escariot have any records on mages or teleportation magic?"

"Is Your Majesty asking if we have killed any?" Lady Isobelle queried. "Sadly, the answer is no. Brother and I have not received any contracts for a mage with such troublesome ability."

"What of your predecessors?" Emilia pressed.

Lady Isobelle draped her arm over the back of the sofa as she got comfortable in her seat, which squished Riga against Lionhart. "I would need access to the family's vault of records. Only the head of the house holds the key, and he is away."

Lady Riga shifted uncomfortably at the mention of mage deaths.

"There is nothing for you to fear, Lady Riga." Emilia gave the young lady a reassuring smile. *Except for assassins who can pop out of nowhere, a possible war in the near future, and the Church of the Holy Light should Valerian's plot to purge the corrupt cardinals come undone.*

"Your Majesty, when will you introduce me to Lord Armel?" Lady Riga asked.

Oh, it has slipped my mind.

Riga probably wanted to be of use to Thessian. Being left behind while the rest of the soldiers travelled to the south of Dante must have hurt her feelings and pride.

"Lord Armel is away on a mission. He may not be back for some time," Emilia replied.

Lady Isobelle smirked and hugged Lady Riga to her side. "I could keep you company when I am not guarding Her Majesty if you'd like."

With eyes gleaming with hope, Lady Riga asked, "Are you also a mage, Lady Isobelle?"

Isobelle poked Riga's turned-up nose with her index finger. "No, but I have seen my brother practising his magic. Clayton is as boring as he is meticulous. I am surprised we have not killed each other yet with how different we are."

Emilia raised a brow. *Boring?* He brought a glowing flower to her balcony the other night and created miniature ice statues, all to bring a smile to her face.

The fire behind Riga's eyes ignited. "What techniques did he use to control his powers better?"

"He took a cold bath." Isobelle grinned. "There were also times he fasted for a week. My personal favourite was when he was so angry, he stabbed himself in the wrist with a dagger, though I would not advise that for someone who is not a healing mage."

The young lady bobbed her head as if soaking in all of the insane ideas Lady Isobelle was suggesting.

Emilia raised her hands. "Perhaps it would be best to have Clayton here, in case the lady needs a healer."

"We could ask a priest from the temple to come by," Isobelle countered eagerly.

"Better yet—" Lionhart jumped on the bandwagon, "—we can invite the Pope for tea and healing practice."

Isobelle and Lionhart smirked at each other.

Emilia could see a strange bond forming before her eyes. "Best not rely on healing magic in case the damage becomes irreversible."

The young mage erupted from her seat. "I will go and take a cold bath!"

"But the winter is barely o—" Emilia did not get to finish her sentence when Lady Riga fled from the room.

A heavy sigh escaped Emilia. The duo responsible for this mess sat there, pleased with themselves for having given a child some terrible ideas. "I hope you two will keep an eye on her. I do not want the palace to burn down. But, is what you've said true, Lady Isobelle? Is that how Clayton trained?"

Isobelle's mirth waned, and she sat properly in her seat to face the Queen. "I did not fib, Your Majesty. To become a mage with great control requires an in-depth understanding of one's body.

Oftentimes, suffering is involved—be it of the body or the mind."

During the meeting with Luminos, the Goddess did mention something about my life being worse if I was born a mage. Is this what she was talking about?

A cold bath and starvation were the things Emilia was used to as a child.

Could the trials to master magic be harder?

None of it made much sense to her. Why did the Goddess choose *her*? Why give her a miserable existence? With each day, more questions sprouted like axillary buds on a branch in spring.

Emilia had to stop the thought train there and rose to her full height, prompting Isobelle and Lionhart to do the same. Waving them to sit back down, she went to her desk and picked up the letters Sir Rowell mentioned earlier that morning that lay atop the large stack of parchments. The first letter had a wax seal with a letter T surrounded by a wreath of leaves while the other was signed in ink at the same place with a slightly exuberant letter L.

Sir Laurence and Thessian even have a similar way of marking their letters. She hoped their working relationship would be restored once Laurence returned from his mission.

Taking Laurence's letter out first, she read the contents to herself.

To Her Majesty the Queen of Dante,

I am pleased to inform you that one Bald schemer has been caught by yours truly (and friends).

My companions and I have suffered a great deal during this mission. We had to defeat three hundred bandits, got to experience life in a cosy dungeon, and almost became the property of a fighting arena.

Next time, I implore you to provide more information.

Separately, I've included a full report.

With respect,

Sir L

Her brows arched but not at the number of bandits Sir Laurence had to fight, nor the impoliteness of the letter. She did not think Baron Bald Lucy was more than a swindler. "Lionhart, have you heard of Baron Bald Lucy?"

"The Shuffling Boar?" Lionhart asked with amusement. "I received word from the Dragon Village that Bald Lucy was taken into custody by Count Fournier. Why? Is he important?"

"Was he involved with the kingdom's slave trade?" Slavery in Dante was legal but most of the nobility she dealt with frowned upon it. As someone who came from the Modern Age of another world, it was a concept that made her sick to her stomach. Without solid footing among the nobles, she could not push for slavery reform. After her coronation, she could convince the majority to outlaw it and push the law through. In the meantime, Emilia had to decide on a suitable replacement and send them to the village to secure the mine and Bald Lucy's assets. "How prevalent is it in Dante?"

Her spymaster's face hardened. He left his seat and sauntered to the window that overlooked Newburn. Peering into the distance, Lionhart folded his hands behind his back and forced the words out. "Do you want the truth or the anecdotes the nobles tell one another?"

"It must be worse than I've imagined," Emilia muttered under her breath.

He pried his gaze away from the peaceful view. "There are five major houses of Dante's nobility who push for slavery: House Sardou, House Malette, House Bonett, House Morel, and House Jullien."

"The Malettes were dealt with," Emilia countered. "That makes it four."

"The duke may be dead, but his family are very much alive. Although they were stripped of their title and branded as traitors, the grip House Malette has on society remains in place."

Lady Isobelle joined in by saying, "We have Marchioness Durand and Count Baudelaire on Her Majesty's side. Their opinions will carry a great weight if they begin to openly speak of the dissolution of slavery. Many nobles who respect them or have business ties with them will quickly step in line."

"They could equally be ostracised for their extreme beliefs if the nobility is not ready to hear them," Lionhart replied.

Emilia sat behind her desk. "Lady Isobelle is not wrong. We will start small and build up the idea that owning slaves is something to be admonished for. The faction on Thessian's side will also side with us."

Lionhart seemed sceptical. "I disagree. This will only work if the houses that support the idea have the kingdom's gold in their hands. Prince Thessian's faction are all military men with little to no influence on the economy."

"I have Count Alard, Baron Lebhan, Marquess Sole, and Baron Niel on my side. They hold a sizeable piece of the trading pie."

"I hate to disappoint you, Emilia, but I recently learned that Baron Niel is playing both sides. He supported the coup and sided with you at the same time."

Emilia's hand wrinkled the letters she was holding. Baron Niel had not been the most vocal of her supporters. She assumed him to be a typical noble who was sick of the regime in power. Knowing that he quietly played her and Thessian lit a fire in her chest. "That sneaky fox!"

"For that reason, I am keeping watch over his trade deals in recent weeks. We don't know if he is also helping King Araman."

"Give me the command, Your Majesty, and I will plunge my dagger in Baron Niel's smug face," Lady Isobelle suggested nonchalantly. Having the sofa all to herself, the lady had completely relaxed by crossing her legs and resting her pretty face on her palm, all the while taking a generous study of Lionhart's posterior.

"I will think of a way to deal with him." Emilia used the letter opener to lift Thessian's wax seal off his letter. Without looking up, she asked, "Anyone else I should be wary of?"

Lady Isobelle giggled. "Only every noblewoman in the kingdom, Your Majesty. They are vicious snakes beneath their makeup."

Lionhart snorted. "And every nobleman who wishes to wed you for the status of King."

Emilia's hands froze on the letter she was reading while half-listening to them. There were child kidnappings in Countess

Morel's territory which were worrying enough that Thessian had to bring it to her attention. Neatly, she folded the letter back into its envelope and lifted her gaze.

"We will start with House Morel and House Sardou. I am also concerned that your spies went missing. Marquess Sardou must be hiding something, and I am eager to know what it is. As for Countess Morel—" the Queen waved Thessian's letter in the air, "—she has been ignoring the plight of her people." *And I need her to remove her son from Ivy's life.*

Isobelle smirked. "Your Majesty, why not invite the high-ranking noble ladies for a tea party? You can assess their allegiances and see who can turn. The women may even act as your agents and whisper in their husbands' ears whatever ideas you impart on them."

"Lionhart?"

The spymaster rubbed a hand over his freshly grown beard. "Yes. It could work, and I would love to attend purely for the entertainment value of Emilia trying to talk about the latest fashion and needlework. Though, I must admit, some noble women prefer hunting."

Equipped with new ideas, Emilia beamed at him. "You are quite right, Lionhart. Some of them *are* fond of hunting, and that is precisely the event I will be hosting." *After my coronation, of course.*

27

GREED OF THE MAGES

EMILIA

Since their discussion, **Lionhart** strode with purpose out of Emilia's office to return to his duties, leaving the Queen to ponder the repercussions of *accidentally* shooting a noblewoman with an arrow.

Archery was not Emilia's strong suit. Ambrose excelled at it while Emilia preferred the dagger. She enjoyed the weight of it in her hand and its versatile use.

Lady Isobelle sat up straight on the sofa when a knock came on the door, and Sir Rowell announced that Count Edmund Baudelaire and Marchioness Lucienne Durand were due to arrive at any moment.

Emilia pushed all worries aside. Her coronation came first. No matter what, she had to complete the event flawlessly to gain the acknowledgement of the people, Dante's nobility, and, hopefully, the monarchs of the neighbouring kingdoms.

Too much to do and too little time. I suppose that's my fault.

Valerian would not be around forever. He would need to return to the City of Light sooner or later. Having the Pope presenting her with the crown and sceptre would wipe away any misconceptions that the pious might have about her curse. The Church would no longer be able to publicly dispute her claim to the throne, which should keep them quiet for a bit. She couldn't hope the cardinals would stay silent for good. They would inevitably try and frame her subsequent actions as grounds for excommunication. If they learned of Valerian's strange attachment to her, they might try to twist that somehow, maybe claim bewitchment.

Ambrose came into the office with a teapot and cup on a silver tray. She effortlessly lowered the tray on the edge of Emilia's desk and began to make the drink. "I thought Your Majesty would be parched after a long discussion with Mister Lionhart."

A soothing rose scent filled the office for the Queen's contentment.

"Thank you, Ambrose," Emilia murmured, her smile growing.

"It is my pleasure to serve." Ambrose carefully placed the porcelain teacup on a saucer in front of Emilia and picked up the tray before backing up against the wall.

Emilia closed her eyes to enjoy the scent a second longer. It soothed her nerves and the panic that riddled her since she learned of the teleportation mage and Lady Diane's disappearance. Opening her eyes, she asked, "Lady Isobelle, are you versed in the matters of event organisation?"

"I am often left in charge of fifty unruly shadows, Your Majesty. If you need me to put someone in their place, it would be my pleasure."

Emilia lifted her teacup and took a tentative sip, allowing for the soft taste of rose tea to linger on her tongue. "No, that won't be necessary. Not yet, anyway."

"I believe Lady Lucienne is more than capable of organising events. Whilst her husband was alive, she hosted plenty of gatherings at her estate in Illermont. Brother and I have attended once or twice, and she never disappointed."

"That puts me at ease, Lady Isobelle," Emilia replied.

Sir Rowell came back with Count Baudelaire and Lady Lucienne in tow. The head butler proudly puffed up his chest and announced them with great gusto.

Emilia smiled. "Thank you, Sir Rowell."

The old butler inclined his head in understanding and shuffled to a spot next to Ambrose.

The Marchioness glided into a curtsy, and Count Baudelaire bowed low to Emilia.

"We greet Her Majesty the Queen of Dante," Lady Lucienne announced cheerfully.

The Count had echoed the sentiment with equal cheer.

Emilia smiled at them. Although Edmund Baudelaire could not use his ducal title until after her coronation, Emilia had to mentally remind herself not to put him before Lady Lucienne. "Marchioness Lucienne Durand, Count Edmund Augustine Baudelaire, thank you for coming on such short notice."

Count Baudelaire came back to his full height. "Call on us day or night, Your Majesty, and we will heed the summons."

Lady Lucienne returned Emilia's smile as she resumed proper posture.

Deciding not to stretch the news out for too long, Emilia said, "My official coronation will be held at the Temple of Light in three weeks—a day before my birthday celebration to be exact. I need your help and guidance in arranging everything."

Count Baudelaire's eyes seemed to double in size. He turned stiffer than a mountainside rock.

Lady Lucienne, despite wearing some makeup, turned as white as flour and began to fan herself with her hand. A nervous laugh escaped the marchioness. "Surely, Your Majesty means a year and three weeks."

"I'm afraid not. Three weeks are all we have," Emilia assured her.

Lady Lucienne swayed on the spot, and Sir Rowell effortlessly appeared beside her and steadied her by the elbow.

Count Baudelaire cleared his throat. "Your Majesty, if I may be so bold, arranging a coronation of a new monarch of a kingdom is no simple matter."

"One is aware," Emilia replied, her jaw set. "We do not have the luxury of another year. Duke Malette's family has escaped to Reyniel and is plotting a rebellion. The coronation will succeed in quietening the Church, who prey on the people's fears, and bend the nobility's ever-changing positions more in my favour."

The Count lowered his head. "Since Your Majesty has thought of it to such an extent, who am I to question this decision? House Baudelaire and all those affiliated with us will donate generously to the occasion and will urge the other nobles to do the same."

Lady Lucienne seemed to finally push past her shock. She folded her hands in front of her, as she separated from Sir Rowell, and said, "I will invite the best tailors, designers, shoemakers, jewellers, and craftsmen to the palace. House Durand will take responsibility for executing the event flawlessly and making Her Majesty shine brighter than the sun."

Lady Isobelle stood from her seat and bowed her head. "House Armel will provide protection."

Emilia clasped her hands together. "I cannot thank you enough for your support. I'm sure it will be an event for the ages."

"We are here to serve," Count Baudelaire assured the Queen.

The noblewomen nodded.

"If there is anything you require —" Emilia motioned to the head servants, "—please let Head Butler Sir Rowell and Head Maid Miss Ambrose know. They will accommodate you."

Lady Lucienne spoke up. "Has Your Majesty considered which kingdoms should attend? I fear that with such limited time, without asking the Mage Assembly for help, getting the word out to the kingdoms beyond Reyniel and Drovia will be difficult. The messengers will not arrive on time and the monarchs might feel slighted."

"You have the most dealings with the Mage Assembly as they often trade with Illermont, Lady Lucienne," Emilia replied with a tilt of her head. "Do you think they will cooperate?"

The Marchioness' right eye twitched. "They're a curious bunch. Reclusive, too. I fear they will refuse to help unless lured outside of their tower with gold."

"You mean a bribe?" Lady Isobelle snickered. "How about we starve them? Cease all trade with their island and let them take up fishing. That'll be a sight!"

Lady Lucienne did not seem amused by Isobelle's suggestion. "The mages could curse the people of Illermont. *My* people, Lady Armel."

Something bitter had to be brewing on Isobelle's tongue as the corners of her mouth twisted into a sneer.

Emilia interjected, "Cutting the Mage Assembly off would not bring us closer to our goal. We need their cooperation, not another enemy."

Isobelle's aggression towards Lady Lucienne simmered away, and she quietly sat back down on the sofa.

The options were limited. Emilia could invite the King of Drovia and the King of Reyniel. It would take a month to send a letter to the Hellion Empire's capital, but she had to do it to not tarnish the relationship between Dante and Hellion. Anyone beyond the Moonlit Mountains and Garhue Mountains would be unable to attend due to the time limit. She could also invite a representative from the Mage Assembly and try to establish a good relationship with them. With Pope Valerian in Newburn, there was no need to send anyone to the City of Light.

Having reached a decision, Emilia concluded, "I will write the invitations to Drovia, Reyniel, and the Hellion Empire, sending our fastest messengers tonight. We'll also issue an open invitation to all lords from the same, so they don't feel alienated. In the meantime, Lady Lucienne, contact the Mage Assembly and let them know that I wish to invite their representative to the palace at their *earliest convenience*. They need our food as much as we need their magical knowledge."

I could inquire about a tutor for Lady Riga as well.

"Of course, Your Majesty," Lady Lucienne chirped.

Emilia gave Count Baudelaire, who was still frowning, a

reassuring smile. "Count Baudelaire, do you have any suggestions?"

He placed a hand over his heart and bowed. "If I may, I believe it is high time to hold a meeting of the lords, Your Majesty."

Emilia pulled back into her seat as her fingers knotted on her lap. She wanted to avoid directly meeting all of the major houses of Dante's nobility until after her coronation. At that time, Count Baudelaire could flaunt his ducal title, which would become a powerful shield for her. With Thessian's faction and her nobles, the remaining houses could be persuaded, especially since Marchioness Durand was also supporting Emilia openly.

I can't think like a coward.

Emilia gathered her courage. King Gilebert kept the nobles out of his decisions. Those who were friendly with him often came to whisper in his ear while the nobles who opposed him in any way were sent back to their territories in disgrace.

She had to do better than that.

Uniting the lords under her banner would be difficult but not impossible. While in office, she had been preparing for weeks, writing up proposals to improve the kingdom and its internal systems. Knowing the nobles, if she brought with her the stack she had in storage, they would bail without a second glance.

Baby steps. Let's test the waters first. "Re-open the House of Lords, Count Baudelaire. I will host the first meeting in two weeks."

Count Baudelaire beamed at the Queen, making his laugh lines more pronounced. "A wise decision, Your Majesty."

Emilia left her seat and glided around her desk. She stopped in front of Count Baudelaire and Marchioness Durand. They were her pillars now. With them by her side, she felt courage filling her chest to the brim.

"Please do your best and begin the preparations for my coronation."

They bowed low and unanimously said, "We will, Your Majesty."

Emilia made her way to the window while the nobles exited her office. She looked out at the view of Newburn she had grown accustomed to. As a matter of fact, in her short time on the throne, Emilia had become fond of her kingdom's people and the land. Before she disappeared from their sight completely, she wanted to leave behind a legacy—a place filled with laughter and joy rather than starvation and misery.

"I hope Thessian is doing well," she mumbled under her breath.

28
NOT SUPPOSED TO DIE

RIETTE

Riette stepped out of the fourth portal she created with an unconscious Lady Diane on her shoulders. The foul noble lady would not stop fighting the entire time. So, at their previous stop, Riette resorted to silencing Diane with a trusty punch to the face. T'was not as if the imbecile was treated any better at the palace where she was a mere hostage for the Queen and Empire's Prince.

"*Be patient, Riette,*" she reminded herself in her best attempt at Marquess Sardou's sultry voice. He had a grip on her heart and a noose around her neck. No man could control another as well as he did. No man deserved the throne of Dante but him.

No matter, the Queen will die soon enough.

Discarding Lady Diane on the filthy floor of an abandoned house in Wellens, Riette massaged her aching shoulders and glided to the dusty window. Her mana was low, and her body was drained of energy. Using another mana potion would only waste the Marquess' kindness. She would wait instead. The Queen's shadow would take a while to track her this far anyway.

She ran a hand over the sheet of dust, removing it in one swipe, and peered beyond the thin pane of glass.

Daylight bathed the busy trade town with its multitude of stores, stalls, and shops. Decorations made of spring flowers were being draped over every doorway, arch, and shop sign for the looming Festival of Life.

Riette clicked her tongue. *A pointless tradition. No life exists without death.*

Lady Diane's groaning reminded Riette that she was not alone.

The noble lady shrieked when she saw Riette. "You filthy servant! You dare to strike my beautiful face!"

Diane touched every groove and crevice of her visage, especially her pointed nose. "Thank the gods it's all there. How dare a mere maid even consider touching my precious being! When my father learns of this—"

Riette let out a wicked laugh, halting Diane's words. Tilting her head to one side, Riette stared at the lady sitting on the floor in a dress so out of fashion, that even the poorest of nobles would not be caught dead wearing it.

"Your father? The *dead* Marquess Walden?"

"De-dead?" Diane stammered under the intense stare. "That's not true. His Highness wouldn't do that."

"He killed the King of Dante in cold blood and put a puppet queen on the throne. He set fire to Newburn to force the panicked populous to rely on their new monarch for safety and support. Killing your father was nothing but a pebble tossed in the wind to *His Highness.*"

Diane's nails clawed at the floorboards as she fisted her hands. "What do you wish of me?"

Riette scratched her messy dark hair. She hated pretending to be a servant, yet servants had the best information. She was no noble, either.

A pet? Am I a pet?

Scrambling into a standing position, Diane's panic bled into her voice when Riette did not reply. "Answer me at once!"

Riette's patience was wearing thin. The lady was pushing for another punch to the face. This time, possibly a sowing of the mouth, too.

"Be kind to those above and ruthless to those beneath," she quoted Marquess Sardou. "You are beneath me, my lady."

"You are insane! I will not stay in this filthy house with a crazed laundry maid." Lady Diane strode for the door.

Riette's mouth twitched with every feeble attempt Lady Diane gave at yanking open the locked door.

When the pulling didn't work, Diane resorted to kicking and then punching. Eventually, puffing like a chimney, and completely red in the face, the lady faced Riette. "Open this door…immediately."

Riette only responded by watching with contempt.

"Are you deaf or dumb? Must I repeat myself?" Diane's shrieks filed away at Riette's string of patience.

Remember the good times, Riette, she thought to block out the barrage of curses that flew her way.

Diane lost her composure and threw herself at Riette, grabbing her hair.

An arrogant and useless girl, this one.

As Diane's nails scraped Riette's scalp, Riette's mind turned blank. On impulse, she punched Diane in the gut, causing the woman to peel away and fall onto her knees while gasping for air.

Without stopping, she kicked Diane in the face.

Once. Twice. Four more times.

Crimson streamed from the once noble lady's nose and was smeared all over her face. The woman was suffocating on her own blood, which brought a smile to Riette's lips.

Such filth deserves much worse for touching the property of Marquess Sardou. So, die! Die for the honour of touching what belongs to someone else. Die for the future King of Dante.

Amidst the flurry of kicks directed at Diane's midsection, Riette noticed that Lady Diane had stopped her struggling. On second thought, she ceased moving altogether.

"Did she die?" Riette bent down and checked the lady's pulse on her slender neck.

Nothing.

She checked the wrists.

Again, no pulse.

"You weren't supposed to die," Riette grumbled in her displeasure. "Why didn't you hold out like I did?" She lay next to Lady Diane's corpse and hugged it from the side. "That is why I am above you. Above the weak."

She revelled in the fading warmth of Lady Diane's flesh. Although noble, Diane smelled of sweat, fruity perfume, and chalky makeup powder.

"It may be for the best that you die now," Riette murmured. "More bloodshed is coming."

29
THE CURSED BIRD

THESSIAN

Time was of the essence.

"Ronne!" Thessian barked at his subordinate.

The lad pulled out throwing knives from his coat's sleeves and cast two of them towards Lyr to create a distraction.

Simultaneously, Thessian undid the clasp around his waistline that held his scabbard, pulled his sword out over his horse's head, and shed the sheath on the dirt. With sword in hand, he urged his horse to sprint towards Igren, who dropped his knife in his panic.

Out of the corner of his eye, Thessian noticed Lyr cradling his shoulder where one of the knives had lodged. The mercenary careened to one side too far and slipped off his horse with a loud thud followed by anguished moans.

Thessian manoeuvred his horse. He managed to get behind Igren and hit the man hard on the back of the head with the rounded pommel. Swinging his sword around would affect his balance and create too many openings for Igren to counter-attack.

The mercenary's mouth slackened. He blinked several times as if to clear his vision.

Thessian used the hilt to drive it into Igren's side with enough force to knock him over and off the animal.

"Deal with these two and check on Henri. I need to help Sacha." Thessian told Ronne.

"Understood!" Ronne jumped off his horse and ran over to Igren as the mercenary fought to get back up. With a stone-cold look that Thessian had never seen on the boy's face, Ronne kicked Igren in the temple and picked up the fallen mercenary's knife.

Igren cradled his head and vomited to one side.

One glance from Ronne had Lyr scrambling backwards on all fours, his shoulder wound forgotten.

Ronne has the situation under control.

Thessian diverted his attention to the toppled carriage and forced his horse into a gallop in that direction. There was movement under the canvas. Just as Warren began to lift the sheet, his partner prepared to block against Thessian's incoming attack.

With Thessian's hold steady and true on the sword in his right hand and the reins in his left, he quickly tapped his horse with his heel to urge the animal into a standing position for a second.

The mercenary fell backwards on the dirt when flying hooves were directed at his head.

Once the horse came down, Thessian jumped off his saddle and swung his sword at the mercenary's arms that were raised in defence. The prince kicked the enemy in the side with enough force to make the man double over, which allowed the prince to slice the distracted mercenary's throat open.

Thessian heard the hasty approach of the stampeding horses. *There's no more time.*

Picking up the pace, Thessian ran over to Warren who had his sword drawn.

"Who d'you think you are?" Warren spat.

One look at Warren's shaky hold on his dagger let Thessian

know the man was not expecting retaliation.

Behind Warren, Sacha crawled out from under the canvas and indicated for Thessian to be quiet. With a slim dagger in her hand, she approached Warren, yanked his head back by the hair, and shoved the blade into the side of the mercenary's neck.

Crimson painted Warren's throat as he fought his way out of her reach and away from them. His hands covered the gaping wound in a futile attempt to survive while he started to run in the direction of the incoming mercenaries, falling over his feet shortly after.

"We must leave. Now!" Thessian urged, offering Sacha his hand.

"Not without Delphine and Henri." She peeled back the canvas to uncover Delphine, who was cradling a golden cage. Inside was a bird with flaming feathers that emitted a golden light and possessed the most striking and shimmering diamond eyes.

"A fire bird? That is what you were transporting?" Thessian hissed in disbelief. "Have you lost your mind?"

"This is not the time," Delphine tried to smooth things over.

Thessian returned to his horse, shoved his foot in the stirrup, and hoisted himself into the saddle. He offered his hand to Sacha with great urgency. "Leave the bird and let's get out of here."

"What about Henri?" She stole a glance in the direction of where Ronne was checking on the merchant.

From what Thessian could see, the man had not moved an inch. At the same time, Ronne lifted his head and shook it.

"He did not make it," Thessian informed Sacha and Delphine.

Her lower lip quivered. Grabbing Thessian's hand, she was pulled into a seat behind him.

Once Thessian felt that Sacha's hands were securely around his midsection, he turned his horse around and ordered Ronne, "Get Delphine and follow me."

The boy was back on his horse in a matter of seconds and helping Delphine get on. With a nod to Thessian, they set off into a sprint.

To the sound of gruff yelling and the hasty battery of hooves behind them, an arrow whizzed past and got stuck in the mud ahead of his horse.

The wind whipped around Thessian's face as he leaned forward in his seat, feeling Sacha's arms tightening around him and pressing her face against his broad back.

Ronne with Delphine followed close behind.

Briefly glancing over his shoulder, Thessian noticed that the arriving mercenaries were more interested in the discarded fire bird and the crates of spoils that were left behind for them to loot. It was, after all, what they came for. If the merchants got away, not much loss on their part. They would be drinking heavily tonight in celebration.

Thessian's heart raced in his chest as much as it did when Emilia got hurt. His palms ached from the grip he had on the leather reins, so he uncurled his fingers a little.

I should have suspected the mercenaries from the start... They were too lax for men supposedly hired to guard important merchandise. A fire bird at that!

He huffed in disapproval. Everyone knew of the terrible luck the fire birds brought to their captors. The only way to avoid bad luck was to kill them on sight or leave them be. Too many cases of the fire bird's owners dying in dreadful accidents turned into anecdotes to be dismissed as mere superstition.

Delphine should have known better. Or, perhaps, he did know and decided to endanger his friends regardless.

They rode until the horses slowed and had their mouths hanging open to suck in as much air into their lungs as they could. Since the animals needed a break, they stopped near a farm they had passed earlier that day.

The sky began to darken, taking away another day with it.

Sacha released him. She swung her leg around and hopped off, all the while remaining quiet.

Thessian could not fault her. She had lost a companion.

They were lucky to get out of that situation with their lives. If the mercenaries reached them, especially since they had an archer, Thessian and the rest would not live another day.

He got down from his saddle and patted the steed. "You did well today."

Thessian never dared to name any of his horses, not since his horse was poisoned when he was but a child. He had to be careful about the things he enjoyed and the people he kept close. If they were not strong or cunning enough, they would end up dead as the enemies of the Hellion Empire were numerous.

Ronne and Delphine joined Thessian and Sacha. The lad wordlessly took the reins of the two horses and led them away to a nearby stream for a drink.

Thessian studied the head merchant with a scowl. "How will you proceed?"

Delphine lowered his head. His shoulders slumped along with his usually cheerful exterior. "I...I think I should return for Henri's body tonight." He glanced at Sacha. "Alone, of course. I could not possibly think of endangering you, Sacha."

She crossed her arms, her left eye twitching with evident irritation that exuded from every pore in her defiant body. "I will go. I am faster and can defend myself."

"It is too dangerous," Thessian warned them. "The bandits may be lying in wait for you to return. You could be sold off or killed."

"Do not get involved in this, *Theo*," Sacha snarled back.

He took a step towards her, looming over her as she barely reached his shoulder. "As the man who saved your life, you should at least consider keeping it."

"My life is my own. I can do with it whatever I want."

"Perhaps I should have spared myself the trouble and allowed you to perish at the hands of Warren and his friends."

Her burning glare did not waver. "I could have taken care of those feeble men myself!"

Thessian covered his eyes with his hand. Lady Clarissa had not changed. She always remained obstinate even in a losing situation. "My lady—"

She punched Thessian in the arm, drawing his gaze. This time, she appeared ready to kill him.

Delphine sighed and patted Sacha on the shoulder. "Theo cares a great deal about you, I see that now." Looking up at Thessian, the merchant continued. "I think you are right. I believe I will travel to the nearest town and inform the guards of what has happened. I should write a letter to the Merchants Guild in Newburn and Henri's family." He paused and cast his gaze to the ground. "Ah…It would be prudent to inform them in person." Nodding as if to confirm his plans, he gave Sacha a fleeting smile that did not reach his sorrowful gaze and shuffled towards the spot where Ronne was feeding the horses some fruit.

Thessian blocked Sacha's attempt to leave. "You are not going after Henri's body."

"How are you going to stop me?" she hissed much like a cat who feared for its life.

Raking his fingers through his hair, Thessian lowered his voice so only she could hear him. "Was Henri your lover, Clarissa? Is that why you are stubbornly determined to reclaim his body?"

She gasped and kicked him in the shin. "Have my head for hurting the Imperial Family if you must, but I will not tolerate you twisting my words. A friend is a friend. You would do the same."

Ignoring the shooting pain travelling up his leg, he grabbed her by the arm. "Have it your way! *Tomorrow*, we will go together when the odds of those bandits being there are at their lowest. Tonight, we will rest."

"The nearest inn is not for miles!" she countered.

He pointed to the farmhouse not far from them. "We could ask to stay in there."

Sacha was about to respond but then changed her mind. After a long pause, she grumbled, "Tomorrow it is."

They had paid the farmer and his wife a hefty sum to stay in the two-storey farmhouse and to keep the horses in the barn for the night. Delphine seemed almost pained to relinquish his hold on the coin during the exchange. Undoubtedly, he had a merchant's heart.

The farmer, Fin, and his wife, Fern, invited everyone to dinner with wide smiles after they glimpsed the amount of gold they received.

Crammed around the rickety table made of what appeared to be sanded-down pickets, Thessian forced a pleasant smile he often used on the people at royal balls. "Thank you for allowing us to stay. It was kind of you."

At the head of the table sat Fin—the sturdy man with a frowsy beard and matching copper hair. His eyes crinkled around the edges when a grin spread on his tanned face. "Naw need fer thanks. We're 'appy ta help."

Fern brought out stew in faded wooden bowls and carefully placed them in front of her guests. Lastly, she came out with the food for herself and her husband before taking a seat at the table. She had a thin frame encased in a dress that seemed too loose as if she had lost a lot of weight in recent months.

Fin readily dug into the vegetable stew his wife had prepared. Pieces of stew fell on his beard as he shovelled the food into his mouth.

Delphine, across from Thessian, eyed the farmer with great interest before taking a sip of the stew. His eyes widened before he, too, dismissed the formalities of polite company.

Fern's grey eyes twinkled with glee. "Is tha food ta yer lik'n, Mista Delfine?"

Delphine paused, swallowed, and wiped his mouth with the back of his hand. "I've never tasted a better stew, Madam."

Ronne was next to sample the meal. He bobbed his head in agreement. "This is some great stew!"

Sacha glanced at Thessian from across the table. They had their apprehensions about eating the food prepared by others. Since Emilia shared her vision with Thessian, he could not discard the possibility that even the kindest of people could add a drop of poison to his meal.

Ronne gasped and pointed to a dried flower wreath on the wall, drawing everyone's attention to it. At the same time, he effortlessly swapped his proven bowl with Thessian's. "That's one dazzling wreath!"

"Oh, ye jest!" Fern murmured, her cheeks gaining more colour.

"No, I swear!" Ronne assured the hostess. "Best I've ever seen."

Delphine rubbed his jaw in thought. "The flowers may be common, but the arrangement is balanced and has an artistic flair to it. I believe you have talent, Madam."

Fin could not contain his booming laughter. "I told ye, Fern! Once spring comes, we shood sell dem at tha market."

"We shood, shoodn't we?" his wife replied with a giggle of her own.

When Fin's excitement calmed, he turned to Delphine. "How come yer out 'ere in tha middle 'o nowher? Coold o' made it ta Garlia before mid-niht."

Delphine struggled to keep a straight face. Most likely, the thoughts of losing a friend were fresh on his mind.

Thessian interjected, "We were attacked by bandits along the way. Lost one of ours in the fray."

The farmer's face fell. He cleared his throat and motioned to the food. "T'was rood of me ta ask. Le's eat and pray ta tha gods f'yer friend."

For the remainder of the meal, only the quiet sounds of eating were heard.

Thessian stole a few glances at Sacha. She had retained the indifferent mask she often used at the imperial balls and tea parties. All emotions were hidden. No one would be the wiser she was mourning.

No one except him.

Thessian could see the slight wrinkles of stress around her eyes and the tiniest downward curve of her plump lips. It was a rare sight, indeed, since Marchioness von Leutten was known for hiring the strictest of teachers when it came to her children's education.

After the meal, with a rusty oil lantern in one hand and his belongings in the other, Thessian and Ronne headed to the room assigned to them by Fern.

Sacha came up behind Thessian and caught him by the sleeve. "I wish to have a long talk with Theo." She directed her gaze at the lad. "You can stay with Delphine tonight."

Ronne wordlessly peeked at the prince who gave a curt nod. With a slight bow, the lad skipped towards the room at the other end of the hallway.

Using fluid movements, Sacha brushed his hand with her calloused fingers and took hold of the lantern. She smirked and led the way to their room, all the while keeping her hips swaying in the most distracting manner.

Thessian raised a brow. *What could she possibly want to talk about? It better not be about going back for Henri's body...*

30

TILL THE BREAK OF DAWN

THESSIAN

Thessian and Sacha entered the simply decorated, quaint room that had minimal furniture—a bed, a stool, and a storage chest. Not that there was space for any more furniture. Dried flower wreaths decorated the gloomy stone walls along with a handful of messy wooden carvings.

She set the lantern on the stool and removed her wig, allowing her blonde ponytail to fall down her back. Without a care, she tossed it on the bed before planting her hands firmly on her hips. "I suppose I owe you for stopping me earlier."

"Think nothing of it."

He made his way to the wooden storage chest and lowered his knapsack next to it. Then, he rested his sword against the wall. Without a sheath, it would draw too much attention, so he planned to visit a smith in Garlia as soon as they arrived there. For the time being, it would be best to keep it wrapped in a spare shirt and bound with rope. A dagger was often more than enough to kill a man and a better choice for combat in close quarters.

"Ever the perfect prince," she muttered.

He turned his head her way, suddenly irked by the statement. "I am but a man. The perfection you see is lacking in the eyes of every noble of the imperial court."

She lowered her arms and sashayed towards him, shedding all pretence of being a man. "They are fools. You've spent years at war—killing, sacrificing, bleeding while they drank wine and spent their coin on new fancy garments and jewels. Many-a-time I heard stories of your achievements among the commoners. They praised you, hailing you as the hero who brought victory to the Empire and saved those who were enslaved by the King of Darkgate. So, think nothing of those portly cats whose only joy in life is tearing each other down with veiled insults."

"Did you take up poetry on your travels?"

Sacha smirked as she stopped beside him. "Among other things."

Thessian was not blind. He knew she was up to no good. Sacha—or Lady Clarissa—had an uncanny ability to get into trouble. He could try to dissuade her or offer to protect her, yet none of that was what she wanted.

"What was the important matter you wished to discuss with me?" he asked, completely aware of how her pupils dilated when she looked at his body.

"You must have guessed it was a lie."

"Indeed." *Especially with all the practice Emilia has put me through in recent weeks.*

"Then you also must have figured out that I find you agreeable." Her fingers walked up his arm until they cupped his cheek. "We are no longer children, Thessian."

"That we are not," he agreed with an edge to his tone and gently covered her hand with his. "You must realise the repercussions of spending a night with me."

"Whatever do you mean? We are but a man and a woman. No

noble titles or families involved."

Thessian frowned. "It is never that simple."

"It can be." Clarissa wrapped her arms around his neck and drew him down for a kiss. Her mesmerising eyes were locked with his, and for the life of him, he could not break out of her enchanting spell.

Their lips met. Unlike his first-ever kiss with Lady Clarissa in the Imperial Capital, this was no chaste endeavour. Electricity coursed through him. He could taste the sweetness of mead on her breath as their tongues intertwined. His hand wrapped around her silky hair while the other roamed her back. Through her shirt, he felt uneven bumps and grooves on her shoulder blades and carefully parted from her enticing lips.

"Is something the matter?" she asked, breathless. Her eyes were still unfocused from their kiss.

"Were you hurt?"

Clarissa blew out a breath. "Does it bother you?"

"Of course not, I—"

"I will show you mine if you show me yours."

His jaw slackened from shock.

Clarissa snorted after seeing his reaction. "I meant the scars, Thessian."

She stepped back and lifted her linen shirt over her head. Her ample breasts were tightly wrapped with strips of fabric. Where her porcelain skin was visible, he saw old deep scars on her shoulders, collarbone, and arms that could have only been caused by slashes of a blade. He could also see the forming bruises she must have suffered during the carriage wreck.

His heart went out to her. She did not deserve such pain to be inflicted on her. No woman did. That was why he fought in the wars. To take on the burden and protect his people.

"How did you get them?" he asked, unsure if he wanted to hear the answer.

"It's a dull story not worth our time."

He did not budge, and she rolled her eyes.

"Fine," Clarissa grumbled, crossing her arms. "You know what happened at the vineyard where I worked. I was caught and had no place to run. The mercenaries—" her nails dug into her arms, "—did more than capture me before Delphine arrived."

Balling his hands at his sides, Thessian snarled, "Are any of them alive?"

"No." There was a dark twinkle in her eye. "They have paid for what they've done." Drawing close to him, she tugged on the lapels of his coat. "I did say you had to show me yours."

Changing the subject? It may be for the best.

Thessian sucked in a calming breath and managed a smile. Slipping out of his coat, he dropped it on the storage chest. Then, he grabbed the hem of his shirt and pulled it over his head in one swift movement before discarding it in the same manner.

He straightened up, taking in her reaction.

Clarissa's cheer was replaced with pity. She circled him, laying her eyes on the many scars he sported on his back.

"How many times were you stabbed?" Her voice was barely above a whisper.

"About two dozen times thus far. Somehow, I have escaped with my life each time, often thanks to Laurence or Ian."

Her fingertips traced the largest scar on his back as she said, "Is Laurence Oswald still serving you?"

"He is a good friend."

Clarissa snickered. "Some ladies at court believed that you were more than friends with how often you preferred each other's company over those same ladies."

Thessian felt his ears burning as he covered his face with his hand. *Me and Laurence? Best not to imagine it for I may expel my dinner.*

"Worry not," she assured him, her mirth returning to her melodic voice. "I never thought for a second you fancied Laurence. He was the best of the Oswalds—a boy without their rigid countenance and dull humour."

Lowering his hand, Thessian found her standing in front of him again. "Laurence hasn't changed."

"Where is he?"

"Away on a mission."

Clarissa smirked and pulled on the bow that held the binding around her chest in place.

As the long strips of fabric became loose and cascaded to the floor, Thessian swallowed nervously.

Her voice took on a sultry note when the last of the binding was removed, exposing her ample breasts for him to see. "One night is all I ask for. No feelings or commitments."

By no means, was she the first woman he had seen naked. Yet, she was the only one who could make his heart jolt into a nervous sprint and his palms sweat.

"And you are certain you will not regret this?" he asked, grappling with the last shred of his sanity.

Clarissa licked her lips and pressed her body against his. "Oh, I am more than certain."

"So be it." Discarding all remaining reservations, Thessian hoisted her up into his arms and covered her mouth with his.

The night was young, and he had more than enough energy and desire to keep the lady entertained till the break of dawn.

Thessian's sleep was interrupted by rushed steps approaching his room. He sat up in bed, noticing that Clarissa was nowhere to be found, and reached for his dagger under the pillow.

A second later, panting and with sweat dripping down his red face, Ronne burst into the room. "Theo, your horse was stolen by the merchants!"

So that's what she was up to.

"Good thing I did not name it," Thessian grumbled under his breath.

"Should we pursue them?"

Thessian dismissed the suggestion with a wave of his hand. "We will continue our journey to Dresgan. The meeting with Calithea and the advance forces is fast approaching."

Ronne gulped down some air and grinned from ear to ear. "I will ready our horses, I mean, horse."

Thessian climbed out of bed and chuckled when he saw a hastily scribbled note on the floor. He picked it up and read out loud,

"*Dearest Theo,*

I am no thief. Inquire about the payment for your horse at the Emerald Swan Shoppe in Newburn, though I have my doubts you are short on coin.

Till we meet again.

Sacha

P.S. Last night was incredible."

He covered his laugh with his hand to not disturb the farmer and his wife.

Lady Clarissa, you never cease to amaze me.

31

THE COST OF PROTECTION

LAURENCE

After two days on horseback, Laurence and the rest were forced to dismantle their horses and walk on foot due to the rough terrain. The uneventful journey up the First Peak had made his stomach into a tight fist.

At night, they had camped out with one eye open, and not even a growl of a beast sounded in their vicinity. However, a harsh squawk of a bird or a mating call of an owl in the sea of evergreen trees had plenty of men on high alert and nervously clutching their weapons with a steel grip.

Where are the monsters?

The lack of beasts to slay had saved them time and lives, but Laurence's worry did not settle. There were no bodies, as if all of the ogres and goblins decided to leave the mountain through a secret passageway no one was aware of.

Or, they all perished without a warning.

With the third night falling over the snow-covered Hollow Mountains, Laurence kept his stinging, cold hands near the roaring campfire that Sergey and Yeland managed to light with great effort. The gusts of wind had his breath catching every time the flames dimmed to barely a flicker before resuming their strength above the logs. They had resorted to pouring oil on the logs to keep them alight.

A fire mage would have been a great boon on this journey.

Sergey and Yeland huddled together, their youth written on their faces and hands probably as frost-bitten as Laurence's. Even the woolly gloves were of no help on the First Peak.

Ian, who normally preferred solace, chose to stay with the group. His eyes scanned their surroundings every couple of minutes, evidently unnerved by the quiet they were enveloped in.

Khaja, who appeared to be completely unaffected by the cold, was picking at her teeth with the nail of her index finger. She seemed fond of the stew Laurence prepared. Although, she had never complained about any food he had given her.

Her trust in me weighs heavily on my heart.

"C-c-commander," Sergey said through chattering teeth, "I'll b-be b-blunt-t-t. It's a litt-le bit c-c-old up h-he-here."

Laurence shoved his hands into the pockets of his coat that was made from ice wolf pelts. The warmth from the fire managed to stay long enough for him to sigh in contentment. "I'm aware."

Ian sniffled and wiped the snot under his nose. He shot up as if an arrow pierced his buttock. "I will check the perimeter."

Even the elf is cold.

"Sir Ian," Yeland piped up, jumping off his knapsack. "I will go with you."

Ian scanned Yeland with a cold gaze but said nothing as he hurried past him.

With evident confusion, Yeland looked to Laurence who muttered, "Go."

A smile spread over the young knight's face, and he chased after Ian.

"I t-t-think Sir I-Ian is g-get-ting s-s-soft," Sergey commented.

Laurence thought back to how hard it was to approach Ian in the beginning. That elf would never eat with them or sit at the campfire. The distance certainly had shrunk. "What's not to love about us?"

Sergey chuckled. He got off his knapsack and rummaged in it for a metal flask that he uncorked and swallowed a few mouthfuls of the liquid inside.

Blowing out a satisfied sigh, he offered the flask to Laurence. "Best ale I could find in Redford, Sir."

"Must be quite the ale. Even your stuttering has calmed." Laurence accepted the drink and took a swig. The burn of the malty alcohol was welcome to the cold air that made his throat ache.

Sergey's eyes widened. "It has, hasn't it?"

Laurence was about to hand the drink to Khaja and paused. He had no idea about her alcohol tolerance or how it would affect the beastwoman.

The decision was made for him when she plucked the flask from his hand and inhaled the contents.

Wiping her mouth with the back of her hand, she peered into the hole of the flask. "No drink?"

Sergey and Laurence looked at each other. A silent prayer that alcohol would not cause her to go on a rampage was not far behind.

Sergey extracted the flask from her and turned it upside down. A single drop fell off the neck onto the snow between his legs. Dejected, he returned to his makeshift seat and sighed. "I-it's s-s-such a pi-t-t-ty."

Wrapping his coat tightly around him and hiding half of his head inside, Sergey looked like a ball of fur with a tiny head.

Laurence did not sport a better appearance.

After a long pause, Sergey unburied himself from the cosy fur. "Sir, what if we can't find Khaja's tribe?"

"We have to," Laurence countered in a tone that was harsher than he meant it.

Sergey winced. "The monsters are missing. What if the beastmen also disappeared?"

Laurence felt his brows knitting together. He lowered his gaze to the flames and gnawed on his lower lip. Without the beastmen, the mate bond with Khaja could not be broken. Worse still, it would mean that Khaja's family was gone.

If there were no more beastmen, what was he to do? Should he leave Khaja in the mountains and hope she does not cause any trouble to the surrounding towns or take her back to Newburn? Lady Riga and Prince Thessian were responsible for her father's death. He peeked at Khaja who looked back at him and smiled sweetly.

How will she react when she learns who the killers are? Would she want revenge?

Turning back to Sergey, Laurence replied, "I pray to the gods your guess is wrong, Sergey."

A crunching of snow drew Laurence's attention.

Captain Neil Gagnon approached them with a stern look on his face. He stopped near Laurence. "Lord Fournier wishes to speak with you."

Laurence's jaw clenched at the mention of one of the lords. He rose to his full height and pointed to Sergey. "Khaja, stay with Sergey."

She ignored the command and got up as well.

Laurence shook his head and pointed to his comrade a second time. "Stay."

At that, she stepped back and shuffled towards Sergey. Even under her hood, he could tell her ears hung as low as her mood.

Sucking in a steadying breath, Laurence followed Captain Gagnon to Lord Fournier's tent. Snow crunched under his boots. As they passed a group of three soldiers who were shuffling to their tent, Laurence picked up on their words.

"I cannot believe Her Majesty sent us here!" the first soldier grumbled.

"Calm yourself, Rem. We will eventually return to serve at the palace," the second soldier assured.

"Not if that she-ogre, Captain Louberte, is still there!"

Laurence's heels dug into the ground, causing Captain Neil to pause, too. He turned around and stormed over to the trio.

"Good evening, men." Laurence put on his best smile. "I could not help overhearing the name Louberte on your tongues. Are you acquainted with the dame?"

The blond soldier named Rem eyed Laurence with distaste before his eyes settled on Captain Gagnon. For a second, he seemed to consider the situation. "We are, indeed, acquainted with her. She is the reason we are here in the first place."

Laurence raised a brow. "How so?"

Rem scowled. "If I remember correctly, you are also one of them."

"One of whom?" Laurence asked, his fingers itching to punch a face that had been staring him straight in the eye without a shred of respect.

"Hellion swine." With a grimace, Rem spat on the floor.

It was not the first time that Laurence had to put up with disobedient soldiers. The best way was to discipline them until their spirits were broken, only to remake them anew into men who served their cause. Yet, this was not a man in Thessian's army. It was a foreign soldier who boiled with hatred for the Empire. Not just that, Laurence could see the anger Rem held for Calithea, and it rubbed him the wrong way. His hands balled into fists at his sides, and his face burned despite the cold air.

Laurence snarled, "Say that one more time."

Captain Gagnon grabbed Laurence's shoulder and gave it a squeeze that could be felt through the thick coat he was wearing. It was a warning. "Sir Laurence, my lord is waiting."

Forcing a long breath through his flaring nostrils, Laurence kept his jaw locked and resumed the march to Lord Fournier's tent. Queen Emilia must have sent those men to the Northern Tower as punishment. Too bad no monsters were appearing on the Hollow Mountains, as those weaklings would not survive a single day under attack.

Once they were a safe distance away from the soldiers, Captain Gagnon said, "Pay them no mind, Sir Laurence. They are young and foolish."

"Men their age should be able to take responsibility for their words."

Captain Gagnon stopped in front of a tent that had been covered in pelts to keep in the warmth and gave Laurence an understanding look. "Worry not. There will come a day when they will see what death in battle is, and they will change their tune. I will announce your presence to my lord."

With a nod, Laurence waited until Captain Gagnon entered the tent. Shortly after, the captain peeled back the door and motioned for Laurence to enter.

Laurence shook off his irritation with a roll of his shoulders. He strode into the tent with a smile plastered on his face. "Good evening, Lord Fournier. How may I be of service?"

The Count sat on a chair in a thick red vest over his white shirt. His hulking frame reminded Laurence of a fully grown bear who was ready to defend his territory at any given moment. In his hands, he held his sword which he was cleaning with a white cloth. He set the sword and cloth against the storage chest beside him and raised his bushy brows.

"Sir Laurence, it is good of you to come see me so quickly."

Laurence's smile never faltered. "I would never deny a request from His Highness' ally."

Lord Fournier grinned as he stood. His head nearly touched the ceiling of the tent. "You are a loyal soldier. I respect that." The Count stroked his dark beard as he considered Laurence. "I wished to speak with you about the beastwoman."

Laurence felt the tension building in his back. *Has he changed his mind? Does he want me to kill Khaja?*

Lord Fournier chuckled. "No need to be on guard. I simply wished to know if Miss Khaja has shown any signs of familiarity with the area?"

"Not yet, my lord."

"When I encountered her in the mountains last time, she was not far from this place. Little ways to the west, I believe." He moved his sword away from the storage chest, placed it on the chair, and opened the chest. From there, the Count retrieved a rolled-up parchment that was sealed with a sturdy string. He untied the seal and unravelled the map of the mountain trails so that Laurence could see it as well.

In black ink, next to the many trails, that were marked and signed by Lord Fournier's cursive writing as dead ends or monster dens, was a small circle not far from their current location. "I believe you should head there tomorrow morning."

"Are you truly not concerned with the beastmen and their strength?"

"To say that I am completely unbothered would be a lie, but I cannot think of hurting that child any more than I already have. Miss Khaja did not deserve the fate she was dealt. If it was one of my daughters who ended up wounded and sold into slavery, I, too, would go and attack the men who hurt her. The Grey Wolf might have damaged my town and hurt my people, but he was a father who loved his daughter dearly. I see that clearly now."

Laurence committed the location on the map to memory and swallowed in an attempt to clear the sudden tightness in his throat. Other than reuniting Khaja with her people, there was nothing else Laurence could do for her. He wanted her to be happy, to find a good partner, and to one day overcome her grief. As a human man, there was little he could offer her, especially since they could not understand each other. Not fully, anyway.

"Thank you for doing this, Lord Fournier." Laurence stepped back from the lord and folded his arms behind his back. "I appreciate it."

As Count Fournier rolled the map back up with his hands, he added with a strain in his deep voice, "Do not mind Lenard's hasty words. He has been a true warrior his entire life. He protected his people alone when King Gilebert refused to send more troops to Lenard's territory for defence against the monsters. No friend of mine has sacrificed as much as he for those he cherishes. That includes his right arm."

That piqued Laurence's interest. He had noticed Lord Carrell's right hand shaking, yet could not bring himself to ask the marquess for details. Such matters were best left alone as the nobility did not enjoy sharing their weaknesses with the others. "What happened, if you don't mind me asking?"

Lord Fournier put away the map and went back to occupying his chair and cleaning his weapon. The shiny blade reflected the orange light of the lantern that rested on a barrel not far from where the lord sat.

"My apologies. It was rude of me to ask," Laurence muttered.

With a faraway look in his eyes that were focused on his sword, Lord Fournier dove into another story. "Two years ago, Lenard left for an inspection to the Second Peak. His expedition was attacked by a pack of ice wolves that were hiding in the nearby cave. Lenard got away with the help of his men but not before he hurt his right arm. It may have healed externally, but there are times when I see him struggling to hold his sword up." Lifting his gaze that seemed to be as heavy as his tone, Lord Fournier added, "As his friend, I ask that you do not hold his words against him. Lenard's only goal is to protect his people."

Laurence shifted his weight from one leg to another. He understood all too well the implications of a proud warrior losing his ability to fight. On the battlefield, he had witnessed plenty of men broken by the loss of a limb or irreparable damage to their bodies. Yet, he could not push down the concern that Lord Carrell may try something before they must go their separate ways and hurt Khaja. She was innocent in all this, and her people also deserved a chance.

"That is everything I wanted to share tonight, Sir Laurence," Lord Fournier said. "I pray you find what you seek."

Laurence inclined his head. "Thank you, my lord. I pray your search for the dragon is equally as fruitful."

The Count let out a loud guffaw. "I've never fought a dragon. A wyvern, yes, but dragons are creatures of myth and legend. Their scales are said to be as thick as steel, their minds with knowledge of days long past, and their breath's so powerful that they could burn a city to the ground in a matter of hours."

"They can also read your mind and change their form."

The Count's eyes widened. "I've read that in the report given to me at the palace, yet I did not believe it."

"It is true, my lord. I have confirmed it when we fought it."

"Then you are lucky to be alive." Lord Fournier resumed the cleaning of his sword. "Have a good night, Sir Laurence."

Taking the hint, Laurence excused himself and left the Count's tent. He respectfully said goodbye to Captain Gagnon outside before making his way back to Khaja and Sergey.

Most of the soldiers who were not on watch duty were turning down for the night.

He paused to look up at the stars above, each one brighter than the last.

I hope we'll find her people soon.

32
ALL THAT REMAINS

LAURENCE

At dawn, a light mist had settled over the mountain which would cause some concern if it became too thick. Laurence and his men wouldn't be able to locate the place Lord Fournier had shown on the map.

Hastily, Laurence and his companions began packing their belongings, preparing to separate from Lord Fournier's and Lord Carrell's forces.

Sergey proudly proclaimed, "Commander, everything is packed."

Yeland stood next to him and inclined his head in agreement.

Laurence nodded at his men while he finished stuffing his knapsack with his food provisions. "Say your goodbyes now as we will depart promptly. Hopefully, we will be able to find the right trail before making camp."

Sergey bumped Yeland's shoulder in excitement. "Finally! I cannot wait to get off this mountain and return to the Empire. Just thinking about the taste of mead there has me itching to get moving."

Yeland's cheeks reddened. The knight was probably thinking about the lady he was interested in, or he was just cold.

Ian rested his back against a tree and scowled at the sight before him. Seeing that, Laurence sauntered over. Khaja wordlessly followed along, her head turning at every loud sound made by the Northern Watchtower's soldiers.

Laurence caught her by the hand and gave it a light squeeze.

With a smile on her face, her worry visibly retreated.

Stopping in front of Ian, Laurence couldn't help asking, "Why the long face?"

"This place is all wrong." Ian rubbed his upper arms as if his skin was crawling.

"The lack of monsters bothers you also?"

The elf grew serious as he lowered his arms. "When I checked the perimeter last night, I found no traces of monsters or beasts. This mountain is as dead as can be, apart from the wildlife."

"What do you think happened to them?" Laurence asked.

"I suspect the dragon played a part in this extraordinary event, if it is here." He paused as if searching for the right words. "It is a good thing for us if so, and yet I cannot shake the feeling that something is wrong."

Laurence had to agree. The Hollow Mountains were never quiet. It was unnatural. Although monsters that resided in the mountains were just as unnatural to begin with. No one truly knew why they appeared. One day, the monsters were simply there, attacking unsuspecting travellers and unprotected villages alike. Their patterns were not yet discerned by even the greatest of scholars.

Where did monsters come from?

He studied the elf with interest. "Do you know anything about monsters and their origins?"

"We do not have them in Shaeban."

Laurence sighed. With limited information, they could only

engage in guesswork. Some scholars in the Empire theorised that the monsters were summoned by the mages with the power to raise the dead. Yet, the monsters were never seen with the mages who were supposedly controlling them. It was a logical fallacy. After all, necromancers had to stay within the range of control, and hardly anyone could raise more than two or three undead at a time. Any such mages were often caught and put on trial before they could cause any damage.

So, what is the truth?

Yeland and Sergey ran over.

Sergey was the first to inform them, "Lord Carrell is here!"

Laurence spared a nervous glance at Khaja when Ian placed a hand on Laurence's shoulder and leaned in close.

In a low voice, the elf said, "I will keep an eye on her. Deal with the marquess."

Resuming his outwardly relaxed and friendly demeanour, Laurence waltzed over to where Marquess Carrell and his guards were standing. The marquess sported a stern expression that could not hide his displeasure.

I suppose we will not be parting amicably...

Laurence stopped a safe distance away and bowed briefly. "Greetings, Marquess Carrell. Have you come to wish us safe travels?"

Lord Carrell's penetrating gaze dug into Laurence's skull. "Will you not concede your position?"

Laurence eyed the guards. They were prepared for battle as their hands hovered close to the hilts of their swords. He had to tread carefully as the odds were not in his favour. Most of the men at the camp belonged to Lord Carrell. Although Khaja was strong, and Laurence's companions were no weaklings, they would not survive a confrontation with nearly one hundred seasoned knights.

"My lord, I regret that I must apologise. I intend to carry out my orders," Laurence said in a silky voice.

Lord Carrell let out a disappointed sigh. "I, too, must apologise. I cannot let you risk the safety of my people."

In a flash, Marquess Carrell drew his sword, as did his guards.

On instinct, Laurence did the same, and with their swords pointing at each other, the air at camp grew still with anticipation of orders. All soldiers were ready to attack Laurence and his friends.

Behind him, Laurence heard Khaja's growl which was filled with anger. Ian, Sergey, and Yeland were probably having a hard time holding her back.

The Marquess' eyes burned with resolve, but there was a tremor to the hand in which he held his weapon. "Will you not consider the innocents who could be murdered by the beastmen? They are a danger to all of Dante."

Laurence considered his options. He had to smooth things over before they got out of hand. "How many beastman attacks have taken place in Dante till now? For all I can guess, the attack on Redford happened because the Grey Wolf believed his daughter was killed or captured by Lord Fournier. Would you not seek the same of your people?"

The Marquess' mouth was set. He mulled over Laurence's words, yet his sword did not lower an inch. His next words were as sharp as the blade he was holding. "I will see to it that you and your men are held personally responsible if a single man, woman, or child is hurt by your actions. Of that, you will have my word."

Laurence swallowed hard. He did not take promises lightly. If this ended poorly, he was guaranteeing his head on a pike or a war with Darkgate at the least. He needed to carry out his orders. Would Thessian want him to give up?

Is this too much of a risk?

There was nothing Laurence could do other than agree and believe in Khaja and her tribe's willingness to cooperate.

Lowering his sword, Laurence placed a hand over his racing heart. "You have my word that I will give everything in my power to prevent such an outcome."

Lord Carrell's tremor intensified until the sword slipped out of his hold. The nearest guard to him quickly placed his sword on the ground, picked up the fallen sword, and dusted off the snow before handing the weapon back to Lord Carrell on a bent knee.

There were murmurs among the soldiers and vicious questions asked in hushed tones.

One piercing glare from Lord Carrell silenced the onlookers. Their faces were fearful of the consequences of questioning their marquess.

Returning his attention to Laurence, Lord Carrell spoke in a clipped tone as he sheathed his sword, his men following suit. "You may be on your way, Sir Laurence."

Laurence glided his sword into its sheath, adopted a straight posture, and inclined his head in respect. "I greatly thank you for your generosity, Lord Carrell."

The Marquess spared one last glance at Khaja over Laurence's shoulder and strode away, leaving Laurence with a bitter taste in his mouth.

Once the situation was over, Laurence felt like he would topple from a breath. His legs were made of cotton, and he felt sweat on his back despite the cold. He had taken on a responsibility greater than he alone could shoulder. And, deep down, Laurence knew that Thessian would truly be the one who would have to deal with the fallout should the beastmen turn against the humans. Once again, Laurence had put a great burden on his friend's shoulders without intention.

Sergey ran over, his eyes wild and full of fret. "Commander, your orders?"

Laurence had to be strong and give reassurance to his men. For morale, a weak leader was worse than no leader at all.

Draping his arm over Sergey's shoulders, Laurence put on a smile. "We depart immediately lest we take advantage of the lord's generosity." He spared one last glance in the direction of where Lord Carrell went. "And may the gods be on our side."

Heading west, they did not need to climb as much. Hours

passed in silence. No one wanted to bring up what had happened at camp.

Laurence's mind was too preoccupied with the litany of disasters which could arise from his hasty decision.

Should I have killed her after all?

But then, one look at Khaja's face was enough to spring doubts to mind.

He could not raise a sword against her. She had been through enough suffering without him adding to it. In truth, there was a part of him that hoped the beastmen would stay in the Hollow Mountains and never descend. Their presence would not be welcomed by other humans, and they would forever be perceived as a threat.

Unless Queen Emilia chooses to protect them. He sighed. *That wouldn't happen.*

Emilia was a regent for His Highness. The other kingdoms may consider her to be a threat if she openly sided with the beastmen which were supposed to have been eradicated centuries ago.

The situation is grim.

Laurence slipped his knapsack off his shoulder and rummaged until he found the map of the First Peak. He studied it intently, having marked the place Lord Fournier had shown him.

Ian stopped next to him and peered over Laurence's shoulder. "How much farther?"

"I cannot be certain, but I think we are close."

As he said that, Khaja removed her hood. Her furry ears perked up. With a wide smile spreading across her face, she sprinted ahead.

Muttering a curse under his breath, Laurence slipped his knapsack over his shoulder and chased after her along with the others. His breaths came in heaving pants as her speed could not be matched by them. No matter how hard they tried, for every step they made, she seemed to make two.

She came to a halt in front of an evergreen tree and stroked the rough bark with her fingers.

When Laurence and his companions caught up at last, they were so out of breath that Sergey collapsed on the snow and gasped for air.

Yeland fell onto his knees and wiped the sweat off his brow.

Ian seemed unaffected, or he pretended to be since his face revealed exertion also.

"What is it, Khaja?" Laurence asked, inching closer to her.

She stepped back and pointed to the claw markings on the tree while smiling fondly at the four deep scars in the rough bark. "Khaja fa-zer."

The Grey Wolf made those markings? They had to be close to the beastmen territory. He turned to Ian and the others. "Stay alert."

Sergey and Yeland wordlessly got up, their eyes searching the other trees for faults.

Ian was no different. He glimpsed their surroundings, but most likely he was trying to listen out for incoming threats.

Khaja tapped Laurence on the arm, drawing his attention. She took a hold of his hand and smiled. "Go."

She wants me to follow?

Laurence gave her a nod, and her smile blossomed.

Stepping away from the tree, she skipped ahead, this time at a pace the men could follow. With each new step in the undisturbed snow, Laurence's nerves frayed and his shoulders hurt from the tension rising in them.

In under ten minutes, they came to a stop in front of a thick wall of intertwined ivy that had grown into the stone.

Khaja peeled back the ivy to reveal a small cave.

"Go," she urged with another smile.

Laurence looked over his shoulder at the others. "I think we're close."

"I do not hear anyone," Ian admitted.

Khaja tried pulling Laurence into the cave, almost making him stumble over his feet. Faintly, he could hear water flowing farther in, but he did not enter. Not yet.

"Sergey, lantern," Laurence instructed.

"On it!" Sergey untied the lantern from his knapsack and made quick work of summoning the flame.

Equipped with a source of light, Laurence motioned to Khaja to lead the way once more.

Her face seemed bright but there was no excitement in her expression as she jerked back more ivy and ducked into the cave.

Is she not happy to return to her tribe? Laurence's heart gave a squeeze. *I suppose, not everyone enjoys the company of their family.*

Shaking off his uncomfortable thoughts, Laurence followed her example and ducked down to get in.

The air was thick and musty. The cave entrance expanded into a room-sized space that seemed to be meticulously carved out of the stone. The grey walls were covered in finger paintings of humanoid creatures, animals, and even mountains. Some parts had hieroglyphs in a language he could not read. The most frustrating thing of all was that there were no beastmen.

Laurence lifted the lantern higher. At first glance, he found some baskets, a dead fire, wooden bowls, and a basket of berries that had shrivelled up or rotted away. Some handmade spears, with sharp stone tips tied to sturdy sticks, rested against a wall.

Khaja separated from Laurence and traced her fingertips over the text on the wall. Her lower lip quivered, so she bit down on it.

Are the beastmen gone? Did they move on? Or is this an outpost of some kind?

"What is this place, Khaja?" Laurence asked, unable to accept that there was no one around.

Khaja closed her eyes and sucked in a steadying breath. A tear rolled down her cheek as she opened them again. "Hommm."

Laurence felt the blood draining from his face. "*This* is your home? Where are the others? Khaja, we need to find your tribe!"

Ian caught Laurence by the elbow and pulled him back from the beastwoman. "It is rude to shout in someone's abode, Laurence."

Unable to contain the flurry of emotions, Laurence shook Ian off. "This cannot be it, Ian! The beastmen must be deeper in the cave structure."

"I do not hear anyone." Ian softened his harsh tone, which was an odd thing to do for an elf who was more than happy to point out everyone's flaws and lead a separate life from the group. "The Grey

Wolf and Khaja could have been the only ones here. Humans of the past did their best to eradicate them."

"But Khaja was a child until recently! Surely, there have to be other females around. Her mother, at least."

"Calm yourself!" Ian's snap brought Laurence's rising panic to a halt. "Think, observe, wait with patience. The truth will be revealed in time."

Laurence pinched the bridge of his nose. He swallowed a mouthful of air and forced his shoulders to relax. "You're right. My apologies. I lost my composure."

"Commander, should we keep going?" Sergey asked near the crack in the wall that would lead them deeper into the cave.

Khaja let out a low growl that sent a chill down Laurence's spine. Her hands morphed into claws, and she stormed over to Sergey.

Yeland, who was standing next to Sergey, nearly jumped out of his skin as his hand reached for the sword.

Before anything could happen, Laurence jumped in front of her. "What is it?"

Khaja's gaze did not leave the crevice in the wall. Grief reflected in her silver eyes and more tears came to the surface.

Pulling her against him, Laurence wrapped his arms around her and rubbed her back. Over his shoulder, he handed the lantern to Sergey and nodded to proceed into the crevice.

Sergey and Yeland left their belongings behind to be able to squeeze into the gap.

A minute later, Laurence heard Sergey shouting, "Commander, you may want to see this."

Slowly, Laurence peeled Khaja away and wiped her tears with his thumbs. "It is going to be alright."

She sniffled and nodded.

Laurence and Ian left their knapsacks against the wall and joined their comrades on the other side of the crevice.

The light from the lantern illuminated a cavern with a small stream that split it in two. The rush of the water filled Laurence's ears as he took in the mesmerising sight. Glow worms coated the ceiling and the stone walls. Their cerulean light illuminated the stalactites and the stalagmites that looked similar to the pointed teeth of an ice wolf. Shining mushrooms as large as a barrel had taken over the other side of the stream.

But that was not what held his attention the longest. It was Khaja, whose tears did not quell.

She sluggishly approached a boulder that did not seem to belong. On top of it lay dead flowers. They had long since lost their vibrancy, unlike the rest of the cavern.

Kneeling in front of the bolder, Khaja lowered her head in what seemed to be silent prayer.

Laurence's stomach sank.

Is it a grave?

No. Please, no. Don't tell me— "Khaja, is that your mother?"

The beastwoman could no longer contain her muffled sobs. She let out a loud wail overcumbered with grief. Her body quivered as she folded in on herself and wept into her hands.

Laurence was rooted to the spot. His comrades were no exception. They, too, cast their gazes to the floor in respect or uncertainty.

Our mission is a tragic failure…

33
A HEARTFELT WARNING

EMILIA

Within three days, Lady Lucienne managed to arrange for dozens of designers, tailors, jewellers, shoemakers, craftsmen, and merchants to rush to the palace to find those most suited to create the best items for Emilia's coronation.

Emilia had been measured from head to toe, prodded, poked, sketched, and praised for her beauty enough times that she wanted to bail on the whole ordeal. She knew it would not be easy. Her schedule allowed for barely four hours of sleep a night. Most servants power-walked all day to clean and prepare the palace for the visitors and guests. As plenty of items in storage were considered out of date, Lady Lucienne and Count Baudelaire offered to pay for new ones, sparing no expense. With the way things were going, half the kingdom would be spending sleepless nights alongside Emilia to meet her deadline.

While sitting behind her desk, Emilia cringed when she heard that yet another tailor had arrived to offer their services.

Lady Lucienne in her perfect composure occasionally swayed on her feet. She checked the tailor's name off her list. "Your Majesty, Madame Villeont is well known for her skill in designing the most beautiful undergarments."

Too tired to blush, the Queen waved to Sir Rowell to let the woman in. "How many more are coming today?"

Lady Lucienne skimmed her list and tapped her quill against the parchment as she counted. "Another six, Your Majesty."

I will be the first monarch to die of exhaustion before my true reign even begins. Not that I can complain when everyone else is working hard.

Sir Rowell escorted a woman and her assistant into the room. The tailor reminded Emilia more of a strict etiquette teacher than a tailor. Nothing was out of place, not even a strand of hair. Madame's nose was long, her brows plucked into thin, dark lines, and her hair reminded Emilia of a dark chocolate truffle. As amusing as the sight before her was, Emilia had no energy to even squeeze out a giggle.

Unlike the tailor, her young assistant seemed to be in her late teens. The spindly girl hugged dozens of scrolls and parchments to her chest. She dared not look at Emilia.

Madame Villeont waltzed to the middle of the room and curtsied. Her assistant, on the other hand, shuffled in behind the tailor as if trying to hide behind the woman's flamboyant dress.

Emilia nodded to Lady Lucienne who announced, "You may speak, Madame Villeont."

In a scratchy voice, Madame Villeont said, "I greet the Mistress of the Dante Kingdom, Queen Emilia Valeria Dante. It would be my highest honour to design Your Majesty's undergarments. I bring my best designs. With Your Majesty's permission, Lala will display them."

Lady Lucienne left her position at Emilia's side and approached the tailor.

Madame Villeont pinched her stupefied assistant's arm, and the assistant handed the materials to the marchioness.

Once the sketches were spread out on Emilia's desk, she studied the designs. Madame Villeont had decent skills despite her over-the-top appearance. But in every sketch, innovation was missing. When she came to the last design, the Queen's lips tugged into a smile. Instead of the typical undergarment—a chemise of varying lengths—she found a cute chemise with shoulder straps and what seemed to be the beginnings of a design for Modern Day's knickers.

"Has Your Majesty found a design she deems worthy?" Madame Villeont asked eagerly.

Emilia tapped her finger on the sketch. "I would like to order this."

The tailor glided over and peered at the chosen drawing. Her smile faltered, and she nervously glanced over her shoulder at Lala.

With an ear-grating giggle, Madame Villeont pulled out a measuring string from her pocket and returned her attention to the Queen. "Yes, of course. I will start working on a sample as soon as I take Your Majesty's measurements."

"No need. Marchioness Lucienne will provide them." After all, there was no point in constantly undressing for every tailor in the kingdom. One measurement was more than enough.

Madame's shaky smile stretched so much, that it became unnatural. "Ha-ha, of course, Your Majesty."

"This design is yours, is it not?" Emilia asked.

"Y-yes. I drew it myself only last week."

The assistant retrieved all of the drawings and retreated to the tailor's side.

As the tailor was leaving, the strut in her step was replaced with an occasional stomp.

Sir Rowell left to escort the women, but Emilia could not shake the odd feeling that forged a frown on her brow.

"Are you displeased with Madame Villeont, Your Majesty?" Lady Lucienne asked, her eyes searching Emilia's face.

"I do not think the design belongs to her."

"Do you believe she stole it?"

"Time will tell."

Sir Rowell announced yet another tailor had arrived, and Emilia nearly groaned out loud.

Covering her face with her hand, the Queen asked, "How many are left?"

"Five, Your Majesty."

Ugh, I just want to curl up in some corner with a good book.

With a drawn-out sigh, Emilia resigned herself. "Let them in."

Once the last of the tailors had left, Emilia rolled her neck from side to side. Another day at her desk and she would need to beg Ambrose for a massage.

"Your Majesty's patience is exemplary," Lady Lucienne praised with a glowing smile.

Emilia could not help smiling back. "Thank you for your hard work today, Lady Lucienne. You may retire for the night."

"I could not possibly leave my work on your shoulders."

"I shall retire early as well."

The Marchioness inclined her head in approval. "A wise decision."

Sir Rowell knocked on the office door and stuck his head inside. "Your Majesty, Lionhart is here to give his report."

Emilia smiled sheepishly at Lady Lucienne. "One more meeting and then I will finish. You may leave."

There was a hint of unhappiness in Lady Lucienne's tired eyes. She stepped away from Emilia's desk. "Please do not hesitate to call on me when you require, and I do hope that Your Majesty is able to rest soon."

With a parting 'goodbye', Lady Lucienne glided out of the office as Lionhart strode in.

Closing the door behind him, he took one look at Emilia and sighed. "You need a break."

"What I need is a body double who will do my work for me." She got up from her desk making her way over to him. Her legs had grown stiff from all the sitting, so her gait was slightly awkward at first. "Any news?"

"I've received word that Prince Thessian has arrived in Garlia." She raised a brow.

"It is my duty to stay informed for you."

He's not wrong. "Is he well?"

"My informant did not see any visible injuries or abnormalities."

Her heart filled with relief. She was beginning to miss Thessian. His presence brought a sense of ease to her as if things would be fine as long as they stayed together. With them being miles apart and with no exact meeting date set in the future, she could not help her stomach sinking with worry. Thessian could be killed like in the original novel, and she wouldn't be there to protect him.

Lionhart gave her a reassuring smile. "The prince will be fine, Emilia. He is much stronger than you think."

"I know exactly how strong he is." She let out a yawn and covered her mouth with her hand. "Is there anything else?"

His face darkened. "Be wary of Marquess Sardou."

"Did you hear back from your spies?"

"They're dead."

"All of them?"

"Three thus far." Lionhart looked away as a vein on his forehead popped out. "I believe that man is up to no good. I would go myself, but there is no one here to protect you."

She waved his comment away. "There are plenty who can keep me safe, Lionhart, but I do need you alive. We would not wish to make it four."

"Clayton is not here, Prince Thessian is headed south, Ambrose is preoccupied with the preparations for your coronation, and Lady Isobelle appears to be doing a terrible job of keeping you company."

"I've ordered Isobelle to eat something. I thought she needed a break after she nearly stabbed a tailor in the eye for questioning my taste."

"Tell me their name."

She laughed and crossed her arms. "Why? So you can make their life equally as miserable or maybe drive them out of business?"

He rubbed his shaved chin in thought. "Among other things."

"We have more important things that require your attention."

The unease about the teleporting mage did not leave Emilia. She often caught herself searching the rooms for imperfections, and it made her feel weak. So, in the end, she decided to focus on other things. Mages had their limitations, too. Their magic operated on mana. Surely, teleporting here and there required a lot of it. If Clayton could freeze a building full of soldiers, and that was considered to be powerful, the teleportation mage might not be able to leave the kingdom in one move. More likely, she would be forced to make stops or drink mana potions. Since those were expensive, she would need a lot of coin and—

"You have concerns?" he asked, bringing her back to the now.

Emilia lowered her arms. "A few."

"Care to share them?"

She felt her lips tugging into a smile. He had become a lot more open with her since he revealed his past. He had even consistently shaved, so she was once again faced with his good looks. "Have you learned anything about Clara Voylan?"

"That mage got along with the servants while never revealing anything about herself. The Mage Assembly may know more about her. I heard you instructed a representative to attend the palace."

Emilia walked back to her desk and sat on the edge of it. Using her hands for support, she contemplated how she could corner the mage representative without creating a rift between the Mage Assembly and Dante.

"Do not think too deeply about it. They may be scholars of magic, but they won't wish for Clara to be out there. If incidents of monarchs dying by a mage's hand start happening, they too will suffer. And all that positive reputation they've built over the centuries will disappear in the blink of an eye."

Emilia disagreed. "They do not need to share their information with me without an equal trade. I will know more when the representative arrives."

"And what of your coronation? Are you nervous?"

She smirked. "I am not allowed to be."

"You are more than a queen, Emilia. First and foremost, you are a person with feelings and desires. That is why there are no ideal rulers. Eventually, they succumb to their power instead of doing what is best for their people."

"I won't be here long enough to see myself get poisoned by power."

He paused. "What do you mean?"

"I plan to disappear once Thessian is crowned Emperor."

Lionhart stared at her in disbelief. Slowly, a grin spread across his mouth, and he burst out laughing.

"It can't be that funny," she said.

He wiped at the corner of his eye as his laughter began to settle down. "I suspected you wouldn't sit still, but I didn't expect this. Shall I commence the preparations for your disappearance? Where do you wish to go? South? Drovia? Vare?"

"I haven't decided yet, but I would appreciate your help."

"Anything for you, my friend. How long do I have?"

Emilia's heart fluttered at his comment, and she looked away. "Two, maybe three years."

His eyes rounded, and he turned serious. "You think you can put Thessian on the throne in two years?"

"I will try."

"Then your focus should be on the Empire and not Dante. Unless...you know something no one else does."

When she looked up at him, his dark eyes were burning holes in her head. She pushed away from her desk and rubbed her arms. "Lionhart, Thessian *must* become Emperor. There is no other choice."

"And if the current emperor is still alive?"

Emilia pursed her lips.

"Don't tell me you plan on having him assassina—"

"Of course not! He's Thessian's father."

"Then how are you so certain? It's not as if you can see the future." He chuckled at his remark and then grew very still when she did not respond in turn. "Can you?"

"Not exactly."

"Is that how you knew where those mines were when you were a child? Or when certain kingdoms would turn against each other?"

"The future I know of is...uncertain."

"So, you do know what the future holds. You've fooled me all these years!" He took a step closer to her and studied her as if she possessed the knowledge of the universe in her hands.

Since she could not be certain how much the future had changed due to her meddling, she did not want to create any more problems. "I believe we should end our meeting here for today."

"You won't tell me what makes you want to put the second prince on the throne?" He seemed hurt as he stepped back. "If I think about it, it is not uncommon for sons to kill their fathers, which means that Hellion's emperor will soon be on his deathbed." His face hardened with each realisation. "That is why you are so eager to rush your coronation. You are planning to give this kingdom to Thessian for him to become the Crown Prince."

"Lionhart, I—"

He cut her off. "You were planning to disappear from the lives of everyone who cares about you. If I did not ask, would you have kept it from me? What about the others? Will you let them know that you are playing Queen for a measly two years? Have you told Ambrose?"

She choked on her words. Nothing was willing to come out. Not even an apology.

Lionhart bowed courteously and hissed, "Have a good evening, Your *Majesty*."

He stormed out of her office.

Emilia's legs grew weak, so she grabbed her desk for support.

She never wanted to hurt anyone. All she wished for was freedom from the stifling life in the palace. Or, perhaps, she never thought she would get close enough to anyone for them to feel hurt by her decision to leave.

34
SEALED BY MAGIC

THESSIAN

After leaving the farmer's house and taking a detour to avoid the merchant's road to Garlia, Thessian and Ronne arrived at the gates to the city a day later.

A long line of people waiting to enter had their documents inspected by the city guards who wore shinier armour than the parade uniform Thessian donned for his victory parade.

They have never seen a proper fight, which means they are corrupt beyond all hope or the city is a peaceful paradise.

He assessed the passing merchants with guards protecting their wares and the adventurers who had plenty of weapons strapped to their hips.

"Not a paradise, I suppose," he concluded.

"I did not catch that," Ronne said, looking up at him.

"It's not important."

Their turn came, and Thessian handed over the identification he received from Lionhart prior to their departure.

The guard with a crooked nose and a missing front tooth looked at the parchment with dissatisfaction. Lifting his pointed stare to Thessian, he asked in a nasal voice, "What's yer business 'ere?"

"We are just passing through," Thessian informed the man.

"Hmm…" The guard patted his coin purse that hung on his hip for all to see. "These are difficult times for us guards."

Thessian stared at the man who barely reached his chest. The guard was openly asking for a bribe. Countess Fleur Morel paid no mind to what went on in her territory, it seemed.

Unless she is the one profiting from it.

Reaching into the inner pocket of his coat, Thessian fished out two silver coins. He handed them to the guard's awaiting hand. "For your troubles, good sir."

The guard grinned and handed back the papers.

Once the entry was finally permitted into Garlia, Thessian strode ahead.

Ronne pulled their horse behind them by the reins, quiet as can be.

The mud squelched beneath their boots as they squeezed in between the idle merchants, their carts, and the travellers who came for a visit. On either side of them, stalls with various wares were set up—everything from salted meats to hand-painted trinkets.

Thessian wagered that the thieves most likely operated in the area without restraint.

The air that stank of human waste and smoke had the prince wrinkling his nose. He pushed ahead, parting the crowd with his size.

A grumbling merchant stumbled backwards and stepped on Thessian's boot. The man was about to complain when he turned and spotted Thessian. His angry scowl turned into awkward apologies before the merchant stepped out of the way.

At last, they emerged on the other side of the flowing mass of bodies and waggons.

Thessian spotted a sign for a smithy. He needed a scabbard for his sword or a new sword entirely as the one he used was reaching its limit.

"Ronne, wait for me outside the smithy," Thessian instructed.

The boy nodded, his eyes searching the crowds for possible danger.

Closing the gap between him and the door to the smithy, the prince pulled the weathered door open and stepped into the shop. To his surprise, quality swords, daggers, lances, pikes, and shields lined the walls.

After a few moments of perusing the wares, he selected a longsword and tested its weight in his hand. The metal blade had good balance and appeared sharp. The grip was skilfully wrapped with dyed red leather, and the pommel had an intricate fish-tailed design that he had never seen before.

"Are you here to buy or gawk?" came a harsh snap from farther inside.

Thessian turned in the direction of the hulking woman at the counter. She had her muscular arms crossed over her chest and a mean look in her right eye that was not covered with a bandage. Her ash-coloured hair was tied into a high ponytail and a bit of grime coated her tanned face.

Thessian put the sword back on the rack and approached the counter. He unstrapped his sword from his hip and unwrapped the cloth around it. "I need a sheath for my sword. The sooner the better."

She picked up his sword and scrutinised it with her eye. "A design from Darkgate. You from there?"

He remained silent. The less information he shared with a stranger, the easier his journey to Dresgan would be.

"I guess that's supposed to be a secret." She snorted and set the sword back on the counter. "The smith you're looking for is right 'ere. If you don't want a woman making your sheath, the door's that way."

"As long as the smith is skilled, I don't care who makes the sheath."

She cocked her head to one side. "Want my advice?"

"I suspect I'll get it regardless."

She laughed at that. "Get a new sword. I'll give you a matching sheath for half the price."

My sword does need replacing... "Do you have any swords in mind?"

"Oh, I certainly do as long as you've got the coin."

"It cannot be anything too extravagant or I will be robbed blind the second I leave."

She nodded in understanding and rubbed her hands in excitement. "I've got just the sword for a man such as yourself."

The smith disappeared into the back room. After a loud clattering of metal against the floorboards and some cussing, she emerged with a wide grin.

As if presenting the treasure of the Misty Sea, she brought forth a wooden box with a sturdy iron lock on it. Once she unlocked it with a key she wore around her neck, she popped the case open to reveal a sword wrapped in black silk. She peeled back the protective material.

The sheath was made of Elderwood and painted as black as the darkest of shadows. The sword's grip was carved from the finest ivory, its pommel shaped into a sharp tooth of a beast. One strike with it would certainly kill a man.

Thessian asked, "May I take a closer look, Madam?"

"Call me Bronte."

"Bronte, then."

She pushed the sword's case towards him. "Go ahead. I've had this sword since my father's time, and he since his father's. No one ever managed to take it out of the sheath. They say it's cursed, but I don't believe it." Bronte pointed at the carefully carved embellishments on the cross guard that represented Sentrel, the ancient God of War. "In truth, I ask anyone worthy-looking of trying to free the sword. None have succeeded."

Thessian ignored the fancy story the smith was spinning. There were plenty of magical items in the world made by the Mage Assembly. Some weapons they designed had a magical locking mechanism built-in and would only allow the owner or a sword master to unsheathe the blade. To see one such sword in Garlia seemed too grand of a jest.

He lifted the sword by the grip. With the other hand, he stroked his fingers along the smooth lines of the sheath before gripping it. The craftsmanship was one of a kind. A worthy treasure that had gone unnoticed.

"I do hope this sword can leave this place. It's better than collecting dust in the store room," Bronte complained.

Thessian felt his fingers prickling where his skin touched the ivory as if a magical undercurrent passed through.

Inch by inch, the blade glided out of the sheath to the excited shrieks of Bronte. "By the Gods, it came out! It truly did!"

Once the blade was fully out in the open, Thessian noted the long lines of runes that were embedded in the steel.

His brows met. The blade had a crimson tint to it when it caught the lamplight.

Not steel. This is…

"Criadyte," Bronte wheezed. Her one eye had grown so large, Thessian thought he had to ready himself to catch it if it popped out of her skull. "My father will be kicking himself in his grave that he never got to see it." She sucked in a shaky breath. "Harder than a diamond and, if forged correctly, sharper than any blade. A weapon worthy of the gods."

Thessian sheathed the sword and put it back in its case. "How much do you want for it?"

Bronte pursed her lips as disappointment washed over her face. "Now that I know it's criadyte, how can I part with it?"

"It's not as if you can pull the sword out," he pointed out.

"True. I also haven't tried throwing it into the furnace yet."

"It's a magical item. It won't melt in the furnace," he bluffed. *Who knew if the mages made it fireproof?* As it stood, the blade was worth as much as a mansion in the Nobles' Quarter of Erehvin.

Bronte stared at the sword with longing. She blew out a heavy breath. "It will need to be sharpened…"

"It's criadyte. The blade will never dull."

"How can a sellsword from Darkgate know all of this?" She

smirked. "You are no ordinary mercenary, are you?"

"I am as ordinary as they come."

The smith rolled her eye and rested her elbows on the counter. She longingly tapped the sheath with her index finger and seemed deep in thought. After a long minute, she straightened up. "One copper coin."

"What's the catch?"

"As you've said, I can't pull the sword out, and it has no use just lying in storage, collecting dust. It's a masterpiece the world needs to see. If I made that sword, I would want the same."

Thessian accepted her explanation with a firm nod. He reached into the inner pocket of his coat and retrieved a small coin purse filled with gold coins. It would not buy her a mansion in the city, but the money should feed her for quite a while.

Tossing the leather purse on the counter, he said, "I won't accept it for free, and you can keep the old sword."

She peeked into the coin purse and let out a whistle. "I'll just melt the old one and remake it, you know."

"It has taken plenty of lives. It deserves a rest." He took his new sword out of the case and secured it to his hip. It oddly felt like an old friend, which made him wonder how Laurence was faring with his quest. To hide the hilt, he wrapped it in the cloth from his old sword.

"I thank you for your business!" Bronte sang on his way out the door.

Thessian waved goodbye over his shoulder without looking back. He exited the shop and scanned his surroundings for Ronne. The lad was busy tying their horse across the street to a pole.

Striding towards Ronne, Thessian fiddled with the pommel of his new sword. He itched to draw it and give it another good study. Magical swords were often commissioned by royalty and would come with a set of special features that only the owner was made aware of. However, he heard nothing of a sword that was crafted from criadyte. Monarchs often boasted about their new weaponry to each other in excess.

So, why was this blade kept quiet about? Unless a king did not commission it.

But who else would have the wealth and the connections with the Mage Assembly to order such a blade? Was it an experiment they conducted? A test weapon?

Then why is it in Dante? Garlia of all places.

Only the owner of the Mage Assembly could answer Thessian's question, and that man never left the island situated in the middle of the Arcane Sea.

Ronne perked up when Thessian reached him. He proudly proclaimed, "I spoke with some locals. There's an inn nearby with good security that the merchants often use to avoid being robbed in their sleep."

"An inn with good security? Are you certain they weren't directing you to a dungeon?"

Ronne's cheeks turned bright red. "I always triple-check my information when it comes to your safety, Theo."

Thessian ruffled the boy's head. "Very well. Lead the way."

With the reins of the horse back in his hand, Ronne skipped ahead and up the muddy road.

A sudden feeling of being watched made Thessian's back itch. He could not place where it was coming from or who was observing them, but his gut feeling had never been wrong. His hand rested on the hilt of his new sword.

I ended up getting something ostentatious.

35

THE VALUE OF FRIENDSHIP

EMILIA

Come morning, Emilia's mood turned foul when she learned that Lionhart had left for Marquess Sardou's territory despite her previous preference of keeping him at the palace. Not only that, he left Antonio in charge of delivering the news from the Lionhart Guild. Since Lionhart trusted the young man, Emilia had no choice but to put her faith in him, too.

By late afternoon, and having spent the day meeting with different merchants, she heard Lady Lucienne's stifled sigh.

"Is something the matter, Lady Lucienne?"

The Marchioness cleared her throat. "Your Majesty, please consider relaxing your expression. You have scared off the merchants with how fierce you appear today."

Emilia raised a brow. *It can't be that bad. Though, I do recall the last merchant quaking in his boots as if he had a sword pressed against his neck.*

The Queen ran a hand over her face and forced a smile. It only made her eye twitch, so she stopped.

Sir Rowell opened the door for Ambrose, who came in holding a tray with tea.

Ambrose smiled brightly despite the growing circles under her eyes. They were all tired. "Your Majesty, I've brought some lemongrass tea."

Emilia nodded and sat back in her seat. Turning her head, she looked out the window at the cheerful sunshine and clear skies that seemed to mock her indoor lifestyle. It was tolerable when Thessian, Clayton, and even Valerian were around. Now that all the handsome men were gone, the palace felt more like a prison.

"Should I travel to Countess Morel's territory and investigate the missing children?" Emilia let her thoughts slip out.

She heard a clatter of the cup, which drew her attention back to her aides.

"Your Majesty must not leave the palace," Ambrose said sternly as she picked up the teacup off the floor. She set it back on the tray. "Pardon me, I will bring a new cup."

Ambrose hurried out of the office.

Sir Rowell vigorously nodded his head. "It is far too dangerous. Your Majesty nearly lost her life the last time."

Taking a peek at Lady Lucienne's stubborn pout was enough to let Emilia know that she would be stuck in the palace for a long time. At least until the coronation or official business in the city.

"Perhaps Your Majesty would prefer a stroll in the garden after the next appointment?" Lady Lucienne suggested.

"Yes, that may be for the best," Emilia grumbled in defeat. "Who's next?"

"It is my favourite merchant company, The Emerald Swan. They procure only the finest of fabrics and jewels. Also, if you wish for something exotic or unique, they will do their best to acquire it. Your Majesty will not be disappointed."

Unique and exotic? Should I ask for a unicorn? Would they even know what it is? Nah, they will probably glue a horn to a horse.

Emilia was not fond of merchants. Most of them were con artists. Each ware they sold came with caveats. When she was still a princess and needed to purchase things, she had been scammed more than once, mainly because she didn't understand the new world she lived in or the value of each item. Thankfully, Lionhart and Sally taught her well, and sometimes, a dagger to the throat was enough to silence the cheat and put him back in his place.

Ambrose came back with a new teacup and effortlessly made tea for the Queen before she was called away by one of the maids. Emilia made a mental note to give everyone some time off after the Festival of Life.

Sir Rowell stepped out of her office and came back shortly after. He puffed up his chest and announced, "Mister Delphine Leferve and his adopted daughter, Miss Sacha Leferve, of the Emerald Swan have arrived, Your Majesty."

"Invite them in," Emilia replied, desperate to be done with the meetings.

The merchant and his daughter mournfully entered the office. Their eyes were cast down, their movements sluggish, and their expressions were that of grief rather than joy to see the Queen.

Maybe they don't want me on the throne.

I should be cautious no matter how many praises Lady Lucienne sang about them.

The merchants began their greetings with evident strain to maintain their smiles.

Delphine Leferve, despite being a commoner, wore clothes fit for a noble. Not that it impressed Emilia. More than anything, she disliked those who showed off their wealth.

The blonde with unusual violet eyes was what held Emilia's attention. For some reason, Emilia could not shake the peculiar feeling of familiarity. Miss Sacha's form was not that of a dainty lady. She had toned muscles under the sleeves of her dress and a knight's posture.

Is she someone who has been mentioned in the book, The Cruel Empire? Emilia raked her memory for information. The only character who vaguely resembled Sacha was Lady Clarissa von Leutten. She was

Thessian's betrothed before he left for his first war.

I must be mistaken. Lady Clarissa broke things off. Surely, she must be living the high life somewhere in the Hellion Empire. Most importantly, only Prince Thessian and Sir Laurence went to Dante in the original story. All other important characters remained in the Empire.

"I do apologise for our sullen faces, Your Majesty," Delphine said, his eyes cast downward. "We were ambushed by bandits no more than two days ago near Garlia and our dear friend died. As soon as we received word of Your Majesty's summons, we departed immediately."

Oh, that explains a lot. Emilia nodded in understanding. "I'm sorry for your loss."

The merchant's eyes seemed to widen at her words before he cleared his throat. "It's the dangers of our trade. Still, we are here to do business, and I won't be delaying Your Majesty any longer with our grief."

Emilia glanced from him to his daughter. "Does that mean you are showing your wares today, Mister Leferve?"

He rubbed his hands together and shifted awkwardly. "Perhaps, Your Majesty could tell us what it is you desire?"

Emilia glanced at Lady Lucienne, who smirked.

"Are you saying you can acquire anything I want?" Emilia asked.

"That would be correct. As long as the price is agreed upon beforehand, we will do our best," Delphine assured the Queen.

Emilia rubbed her chin in thought. Valerian promised to keep her safe, but he could turn on her at any moment. Nothing bound them together and words were cheap in her new world. "Aside from the list of jewels that Lady Lucienne will provide for you, I want a special kind of dagger."

"Special?" the merchant tilted his head to one side.

His daughter, too, seemed interested in the conversation all of a sudden. Emilia's guess must have been correct. Sacha was no ordinary woman.

"The blade should be able to cut through a god's blessing," Emilia explained, gauging their reactions.

Delphine's grief seemed briefly forgotten. His eyes burned with desire for knowledge. "Does Your Majesty seek a relic of old?"

So they exist? "Do you have one?"

"With the help of the Merchants Guild, I believe we will find one. Though, I must warn Your Majesty that the price will be—"

"The price does not matter." If she could secure a powerful weapon that could kill anyone, including those who were blessed by a higher being, she would have no trouble protecting herself. To test it, she might need to stab Valerian.

He may get a little upset if his saintess stabs him, and Sir Erenel will no doubt try to kill me for harming the Pope. Not like I have many other options in testing the weapon. I could always ask for his permission and see how far his devotion for me runs.

Delphine bowed his head. His tone came across as clear and honest when he said, "It may take some time but we will find a relic for Your Majesty."

"Wonderful." Emilia glanced at Lady Lucienne.

The Marchioness wordlessly understood the message and picked up a scroll off Emilia's desk. She brought it over to Delphine. "This is the list of jewels for Her Majesty's new crown. I expect only the best."

Delphine handed the scroll to his daughter and placed his right hand over his heart when he faced Lady Lucienne. "Of course, Marchioness Durand. Within a month or two, we will have the best—"

Lady Lucienne cut in, "The jewels must be delivered within a week."

The merchant let out a nervous laugh. "Surely, you jest, Marchioness…" Whatever he saw on Lady Lucienne's face made him stagger backwards. "A week?"

"Yes."

"Not even a month?" he muttered under his breath.

"I did not realise you have become hard of hearing since our last meeting, Mister Leferve."

He glanced back at the scroll Sacha was holding. Filled with what seemed to be newfound determination, he nodded several times. "We can do it!"

Lady Lucienne motioned to the door. "You must be eager to get started."

Delphine got the hint and shuffled backwards while bowing to the Queen. "It was a pleasure to meet Your Majesty, and, of course, to see you again, Marchioness Durand."

Sir Rowell followed closely behind the merchants.

Emilia refused to laugh at the amusing exchange until the door closed and ten seconds passed. She slapped her hand to her forehead as her chest heaved with each shaky breath. Her laughter filled her office, and she felt relieved that Marchioness Durand was on her side.

"Did the situation amuse Your Majesty?" Lady Lucienne asked, her face reflecting the kindness Emilia refused to see until recently.

"I have been working hard recently, preparing for the meeting of the lords. A good laugh is a must."

"Indeed, Your Majesty. I doubt those stifling noblemen would provide much in the way of entertaining conversation."

Emilia wiped away the tears in the corners of her eyes and stood from her seat. Her legs were almost numb from sitting all day. It made her listless as if she were trapped once again.

"Has Your Majesty had the time to read the letters?"

Emilia stretched her arms above her head and sighed in contentment. "I've read one of them." Once she made her way to the bookcases, she ran her fingers over the leather spines. "Queen Cecilia was quite the character."

For a second, Emilia thought she heard Lady Lucienne giggle. When she glanced at the Marchioness, the woman was as put-together as a marble statue.

"Why did you give me those letters?"

"It was what Cecilia would have wanted," came Lady Lucienne's reply.

So, it was all because of an old friendship?

I suppose it doesn't matter as long as I can keep Marchioness Durand's loyalty.

Shortly after, Sir Rowell returned with a shoe maker in tow, prompting a sigh from Emilia.

I wish I could go to my coronation in modern teddy pyjamas and fluffy slippers. That would be a sight...and they wouldn't even realise it was a sleeping garment. Maybe I could set a trend and make everybody wear pyjamas as outdoor clothes? Wait, there are tracksuits for that.

I must be very bored to be thinking about setting trends.

36
YEARNING OF THE HEART

LAURENCE

Each man and Khaja seemed haunted by their thoughts as they sat around the campfire. The mournful silence was only broken by the crackling of the fire Sergey and Yeland had set up in the cave. They had cut down the ivy that hid the entrance to let the air circulate and rid them of the accumulating smoke.

Laurence sat against the wall. His knees were tucked close to his chest and his arms wrapped loosely around them. He did not expect the outcome of the mission.

The beastmen were either gone or had moved on.

Khaja's parents were dead.

His mate bond could not be broken.

What's left? Do I break my vow with Calithea? Will she understand the mate bond? Will she hate me?

For every thought that riddled his mind, another sprouted and took root like poisonous vines. Khaja was alone. She trusted him enough to lead them back to her home. So, he had to honour that trust. He had to be there for her. And yet, could he shoulder taking responsibility for a beastwoman in a world where they were not welcome?

If Khaja was hidden in Prince Thessian territory, she would remain shielded from prying eyes. However, she could never learn that Thessian and Lady Riga had slain her father. Knowing her fiery personality, she would pounce on them and try to rip their heads off with her claws.

Laurence climbed to his feet, drawing everyone's attention. "I will check the perimeter for monsters."

Ian shot up and left the cave before Laurence could say anything.

"I think Sir Ian is joining you, Commander," Sergey commented.

Probably to tell me another moral tale.

Sucking in a lungful of cool air, he marched out of the cave in the direction of Ian's tracks in the snow. Passing multiple trees, Laurence suddenly came to a snow-covered sharp edge and nearly fell off before Ian caught him by the back of his coat.

Jerked back with great force, Laurence landed with his back in the snow and stared up at Ian's scowling face.

"Thank you for saving me," Laurence grumbled, sitting upright.

"I did not wish to explain to the others that their commander was careless enough to walk off a mountain."

Laurence smirked and stood. He dusted off the snow on his clothes before straightening up. "Do you wish to push me off the mountain yourself?"

"It would not benefit me."

"So, it's a matter of *when?*"

Ian's face when illuminated with the cool moonlight made him seem unnaturally pale. His white hair that framed his face reminded Laurence of the spider's shimmering threads. Elves were truly a race that was hard to understand, and they spent no effort trying to understand others in turn.

"We should return to Newburn." Ian's words were a statement rather than a request. "We have no more leads and do not have enough supplies to wander around aimlessly. Our mission is over."

Laurence studied the view of the snow-coated mountains below. Just as the previous nights, he could not hear a single monster in their vicinity, and judging by Ian's relaxed demeanour, they were safe from any predators.

"If you are not convinced." Ian added, "Sergey has a title transfer to attend, Yeland a woman to court, and Eugene will be happy to stop worrying about us being eaten by monsters."

Laurence stared into the distance. "I thought you didn't pay attention to your comrades."

"I may not show it, or say it correctly, but I never wished harm on any of you."

"There hasn't been a single monster to speak of thus far. Sometimes, Eugene worries too much."

"The lack of monsters has been unsettling. We must report our findings and continue to serve our lord."

Laurence peered back at him. "And what about Khaja? Where does she fit in all of that?"

Ian averted his eyes. "Leave her behind. She will only cause trouble for Thessian."

"After everything we have been through together, everything we have witnessed, are you planning to just *abandon* her?"

"It is the right choice. She gets to live out her life in the mountains, and we move on to our next mission. Unless..." Ian gave Laurence a judgemental stare. "Do you have feelings for the beastwoman? Are they clouding your judgement?"

Laurence's heart jolted and sped up. Heat travelled to his face and burned his cheeks against the stinging cold. He held back from swinging his fist by locking his arms to his sides. "Weren't you the one who told me to woo her?"

Ian stared blankly at Laurence and then rolled his eyes. "It is always someone else's fault with you. Admit it, you have feelings for Khaja. Her tale is tragic, so you—a man eager to please all women—could not help yourself."

This time, Laurence did take a swing, only for Ian to step out of the way and catch Laurence's wrist. His painful grip sent a shock through Laurence's bones. "Then bring her with us and call the wedding off. I thought you wanted Calithea to be your wife or has that changed?"

Laurence glowered at him and considered getting the other fist involved.

Ian smirked. He yanked Laurence toward him and then stepped aside at the last second, causing Laurence to land face-first in the snow. "Dame Calithea deserves better."

Spitting the snow out of his mouth, Laurence turned his head. "What right do you have to talk about her?"

"Same right as you. You are not yet wed, remember?"

Laurence grabbed a handful of snow and threw it at Ian's face. While the elf was momentarily distracted, Laurence caught the elf's leg and pulled it out from under him, toppling the pretentious man back into a heap of snow.

"I suppose, I deserved your anger," Ian mused without moving.

"Did you hit your head too hard? Was there a rock beneath the snow?"

Ian chuckled, which made him seem a lot more approachable once the frown creases and the unending judgement vanished from his perfectly smooth face. "No. There wasn't."

The tension in Laurence's body retreated. He sat back down on the snow and stared at the captivating view ahead. The Hollow Mountains, when not riddled with cruel monsters, were certainly a sight to behold. He wished Calithea and Thessian were there with him. After all, good things were meant to be enjoyed with friends.

"Can you feel it?" Ian asked, sitting up as well.

"Your burning stare? It often pains me."

"The mate bond with Khaja. It is supposed to be something that creates a deeper connection between the beastmen, but you are not one. I have never heard of a human becoming a mate."

"I must be *very* lucky. Ever since I came to this kingdom, my world has changed immensely. The wenches of Darkgate must have cursed me when we departed for this accursed land."

Ian was silent for a minute, making Laurence turn his head in the elf's direction.

In what appeared to be deep thought, Ian studied his hands. "I envy you, Laurence. More specifically, your freedom."

"My freedom?" Laurence scoffed. "Have you met my mother? Everything I have ever done is for the Oswald name and honour. Should I stray from that—and I believe I am well on my way to doing just that by marrying Calithea—I will probably be killed in my sleep by an assassin Mother hired. No one brings shame to the Oswald name. No one."

"Kill her first."

Laurence raised a dark brow. He hadn't considered that. He had no love for his parents, but the thought of killing them did not sit well with him. "I don't think I can."

"You are hopeless."

It was Laurence's turn to roll his eyes. "Said the banished elf."

The corner of Ian's mouth quirked upwards. "The reason I envy you is because you are able to get close to people. You do not need to question their motives every step of the—"

Laurence raised his hand to stop him. "Wait. Are you telling me you haven't spent a night with a woman in over a decade?"

"A little more than that."

"Two decades?" Laurence's voice cracked in surprise.

"I think the last time I engaged was over sixty years ago."

Laurence thought his heart would stop. Not only was Ian much older than his grandfather, he was basically a self-made eunuch. *Does it still work?* "Wow. That is… I thought your past was depressing, but this beats anything you could have thrown at me."

"I forgot that most humans do not live that long. Khaja will outlive you, Laurence, and it will break her heart as much as the loss of her parents."

Closing his eyes, Laurence felt a strange calm washing over him. Usually, he and Ian would be at each other's throats. They almost were not too long ago. "I will let her decide once she learns to speak properly."

"And Calithea?"

Laurence faltered in his response. "I will have to grovel for the rest of my days. Thankfully, I am good at that."

Ian covered his laugh with a cough and stood. "I will check the perimeter. This mountain is completely dead, almost as if it has become a graveyard."

Rising to his feet, Laurence grumbled, "I wouldn't wish to add to it if it were so, and what terrible phrasing you have."

He shook off the snow and, with a parting look at the view, made his way back to the cave.

Come daybreak, Laurence was shaken awake.

His eyes snapped open to find Ian's face so close to his, he pushed the elf away and hit the back of his head on the jagged stone wall as he rose.

"Owwww!" Laurence hissed and glared at Ian who steadied himself against the opposite wall. "What's the hurry?"

"The lords, they are under attack!" Ian shot back.

All semblance of tiredness left Laurence. He barked to Yeland and Sergey, who were huddled together for warmth under a fur blanket, "Men, on your feet! We're leaving. The lords require our assistance!"

Looking down, he saw Khaja stirring from the commotion. There was no time to debate whether to take her or leave her. He needed to leave immediately. If she came with them, another fighter was a boon. The choice remained with her, and he already knew in his heart which she would choose.

Sergey and Yeland were upright in no time. They sped through the packing and began securing their arms.

Laurence picked up his sword and turned to Ian. "How do you know they were attacked? Your hearing cannot be that good."

"I retraced our steps back to the main path and saw three men fleeing down the mountain."

Laurence offered his hand to Khaja. When she accepted it with a smile, he pulled her up and steadied her with his hand. Turning back to Ian, he demanded, "Why were they fleeing?"

"I heard it. The dragon's roar that shook the mountain. Apparently, you all slept through it." Ian's deadpan expression made Laurence's guts twist with his nerves.

Laurence raked a hand through his hair, trying to lighten the rapidly decaying mood amongst the group. "Well, Sergey did sing us a lullaby last night."

Ian scowled at the joke. "We must hurry."

Shaking his head in disapproval, the elf ventured outside.

"I thought it was funny…" Laurence glanced at Khaja and asked, "Laurence is funny, right?"

"Laurenz pretty," she countered.

"You have good eyes. I am very pretty, too." He took her hand as if it were the most natural thing to do and intertwined their fingers. "Let's save some lords in peril."

37
NOT A HERO

LAURENCE

The distance that previously took them six hours to trek was cut down to three at a speed march. Thankfully, the route they had taken was relatively plane.

Laurence's back was drenched in sweat when they reached the main path. The group stopped briefly to check their surroundings. He wiped his damp forehead with his gloved hand and looked towards the summit of the mountain. They would need to move uphill from now on.

Taking a quick assessment of his comrades, he could tell they were as worn out as he felt. Everyone except Khaja.

To his astonishment, she did not even break a sweat. When they were jogging, she sprinted ahead with minute effort, proving how weak the human race was compared to the beastmen. It was no wonder they were considered a threat.

Ian had caught his breath and approached Laurence. He pointed in the direction of the path leading to the Northern Watchtower. "The knights I saw ran that way. They must have deserted their posts when the dragon appeared."

"How do we fight a dragon?" Sergey asked. "Aren't they as big as a castle and can spit fire from their mouths?"

"And read your thoughts," Laurence offered.

Sergey's fearful expression was hard to miss. "Maybe the knights had the right idea…"

"I agree," Yeland piped in. "I would rather eat Sir Ian's cooking."

Ian ignored the jab. "We should keep going. The more time we waste, the less of a chance the lords will survive."

"Unless they are already dead," Laurence muttered.

The mountain reverberated with a tremor. The trees shook as though a giant had jumped nearby, startling the birds into fleeing. Pebbles and other loose stones rolled down the slope. Over the sudden cacophony of noise from the wildlife and moving fauna, Laurence could faintly hear the dragon's roar. It seemed different to the one he heard in the catacombs under Queen Emilia's castle. Grander. It was not the young dragon he witnessed, but the sound of a beast wrought with age and experience.

Nervously, he glanced at Ian. The elf's eyes were narrowed in the direction of the haunting roar. An air of uncertainty seemed to spread from him to the others. No one wanted to die today. Not when their mission had finally come to an end.

If Thessian was here, he wouldn't sit still when his allies were in danger. I must follow his example.

Laurence faced his comrades, his decision made. He puffed up his chest. "Men, I know this is a lot to ask. If you can't find the strength to go into battle against this beast, stay behind. As this is not part of our main mission, you are free to return."

"What about you, Commander?" Sergey asked.

Clenching his fists, Laurence announced, "I will help the lords."

Ian tore his gaze away from the mountaintop and studied Laurence's determination. "I have to join. You will find a way to cause another commotion if left to your own devices."

Sergey and Yeland chuckled.

"The only thing we are good at is following orders, Commander," Sergey said with a sheepish grin. "When we get back, I will have quite a tale to tell my family."

Yeland smirked. "Dragon slayers are more attractive to women, or so I have heard."

Laurence turned his attention to Khaja. He thought hard about how to explain the situation to her. Surely, she should have guessed where they were going by now, and she didn't look like she was trying to turn them downhill.

Ian cleared his throat, gaining Khaja's and Laurence's attention. He pointed to the summit and faked a roar. Then, he offered her his hand.

At that, Sergey and Yeland doubled over with laughter.

Laurence covered his mouth to hide his snickering. The strangling pressure was gone, and Laurence's heart lifted from the depths of paralysing despair.

We can do this. We can survive another encounter with a dragon — bigger or not.

Khaja glared at Ian's hand and took Laurence's instead, getting his attention before indicating by tilting her head towards the mountain's summit.

"I think she has made her decision," Ian said, facing away from them, but not before Laurence spied a deep blush coating the elf's face.

Laurence took off his knapsack and rummaged in it until he felt the pouch with the healing potions Thessian had entrusted to him. Slinging the strap over his shoulder and pushing his belongings behind the nearest tree, he ordered, "To arms. We will leave our supplies hidden here and collect them on our way down."

The others nodded. They followed his example and prepared for combat.

Ian picked out two daggers, claiming, "I do not want to be weighed down in battle."

Yeland longingly looked at his favourite cooking pan before

sighing and putting it back. "Too bad I cannot kill a dragon with it."

The young knight proceeded to shovel medicinal herbs and bandages into his pockets and secured a lantern to his hip, just in case.

After hiding his belongings, Sergey reached inside his coat and pulled out a silver chain with a rather ordinary-looking coin from the Empire before tucking it back under his clothes. "I need nothing else. This coin has kept me alive through every battle in Darkgate."

Laurence realised he was missing something. He separated from Khaja and dove for his bag for the last time.

"What did you forget?" Ian called.

"Something I cannot lose!" Laurence shouted back.

His fingers brushed the cool, smooth surface of Calithea's locket. With a wide smile, he pulled it out and secured the clasp around his neck. He gave it a peck before hiding it away under the layers of his clothing.

The metal warmed within a matter of seconds against his skin, and he felt as if Calithea was right there with him, preparing to have his back in battle.

I will see you again soon, Cali. That I can promise.

As they sped up the mountain, the quakes that rumbled through the First Peak wore down the steadying courage Laurence had adorned. With each roar, he could feel the shaking taking over his hands before he could regain composure.

He was no coward.

Killing on a battlefield was no simple feat that anyone could accomplish. Yet, the dragon's anger could be felt from the swirling dark clouds above, the harsh whips of the wind, to the frozen land beneath their boots.

After two more hours of an uphill climb, a cave the size of a fortress came into view which froze the quintet in astonishment. Mounds of monsters' bones were stacked so high on either side that they were almost as tall as the tip of the entrance.

Laurence swallowed. "I think we've found the missing monsters."

They got closer to the entrance. Each step was measured and filled with caution on the backdrop of silence.

"Stay focused," Ian warned. "I hear a fight inside."

Sergey's voice dipped with nerves. "For once, I am glad my hearing is not as good as Sir Ian's."

Laurence gripped the hilt of his sword while Yeland lit the lantern.

Ian took the lantern from Yeland and nodded in the direction of the entrance of the cave. "I will lead the way. My senses are superior."

Yeland stepped back with relief written on his face.

Ian looked at Laurence for the order to proceed and, with a nod, Laurence motioned for the elf to lead the way.

One by one, they followed Ian's lead. The elf took point, Laurence and Khaja right behind him while Sergey and Yeland brought up the rear.

Laurence could almost taste the musty air of the cave. The snow was gone, replaced by slippery stones and dirt. On the ground, dozens of tracks could be seen, as if a stampede had taken place there. Instead of the tracks leading out of the cave, all of them led farther in.

The dragon, it seemed, waited for the prey to come inside before pouncing. The prey, in this case, being the lords and their guards.

A cunning beast.

Their footsteps were quickly muffled by the commotion deep within the heart of the cave slowly becoming clearer with every step. Shrouded in darkness and, with the lantern's shaking light being their only solace, Laurence could not help his heart's erratic dance.

"Almost there." Ian stopped and put the lantern down. "There is light ahead. We will not need this."

"The dragon's flames?" Laurence hissed.

"It is a natural light."

Somewhat relieved, Laurence patted Ian on the shoulder. He was thankful it was the pesky elf he was with on this dreadful day and not Thessian. They were all expendable, but Thessian was the future of the Hellion Empire. They could all die today, and no one on the continent would be the wiser.

They ventured ahead.

Once the lantern's warm light could no longer reach them, the tunnel opened up into an enormous cavern. The sky could be seen through the giant hole in the ceiling, and Laurence knew exactly what made that.

Impossible...

Although greatly similar in appearance, it couldn't possibly be the dragon they had encountered in the catacombs. Instead of a hatchling that could fit under the palace, the beast before them was ten times grander. Possibly more. A single scale was on par with a man's torso.

"I think I soiled my undergarments," Sergey whispered behind Laurence.

"Sorry, beautiful women. Dragon slaying suddenly feels beyond me," Yeland whispered back.

Scattered throughout the cavern's floor were dead knights and guards, some of them in pieces. Their bodies twisted to odd angles, charred beyond recognition, or with limbs and other unrecognisable body parts strewn asunder.

The beast's golden eyes were zeroed in on a boulder that was close to a wall on the left. From what Laurence could see, the dragon could have easily moved it, yet it didn't.

It did not take long to figure out why the place held the dragon's attention. Two knights came out with their weapons drawn. They let out a courageous battle cry as they charged towards the monster.

From behind the boulder, Lord Fournier stuck his head out to assess the situation while the knights distracted the beast.

Laurence grimaced. *It's toying with them. Waiting for them to come out on their own.*

The dragon turned his head in Laurence's direction. For a second, he thought the monster smirked.

Can dragons smirk?

Ian slapped Laurence on the back. "We have no time for standing around. Laurence, Khaja, and I will distract the dragon. Sergey, Yeland, escort the lords to safety. We will buy as much time as we can. And remember, keep your mind clear of thoughts."

Sergey and Yeland nodded solemnly.

"Laurence?" Ian asked, gauging his reaction.

Laurence fired back with a cocky grin. He handed Yeland the satchel with the healing potions and pulled out his sword. His hands were clammy in his gloves and his throat felt as dry as sand. He threw his gloves away and discarded his heavy coat. "I'd rather my dance partner did not have as many sharp teeth. Well, beggars can't be choosers."

Ian led the charge, daggers in hand. "I will go to the right."

While running towards the most humongous creature Laurence had ever witnessed in his short twenty-five years, he imagined his sword making for a good toothpick after the dragon ate him whole. He then shook his head.

No, I should keep a clear head!

The dragon tilted his head to one side and careened its body towards the incoming group, Lord Fournier's knights forgotten. It let out another roar that shook the whole cavern, only this time it sounded similar to a deep echoing of laughter.

Can a dragon laugh itself to death?

On his left, Laurence noticed that Khaja's claws had come out. While he was preoccupied, she had discarded her coat and boots. Her feet became paws. Before he knew it, she ran past him with the biggest grin on her face.

She's enjoying this? Of course, she is…

Her unwavering courage and love for battle gave him strength. With the creeping tendrils of fear finally unleashing their hold on Laurence's mind, his sword had stopped shaking. He blew out a breath to steady his nerves and began to sing a song in his head.

I held the hand of a gutsy knight,

And she can get pretty rough at night.
Her hair is long,
A golden shade.
Her sapphire eyes
Will never fade.

Laurence jumped back and rolled away as the dragon swung at him with its massive claws, nearly losing his grip on his weapon. He saw that Ian had managed to get behind the dragon, and Khaja was well on her way to reaching its left leg.

Getting back up, Laurence felt the ground trembling as the dragon directed its heavy body in Ian's direction. Through the gaps in the scales of the beast's flaring throat, Laurence spotted a light blooming.

Gritting his teeth, he sprinted ahead, all the while singing another verse of his self-composed song.

I held her close on a snowy night,
And I did not let her out of my sight.
For she's a knight
In armour steel.
A single punch
Can make you kneel.

From the corner of his eye, Laurence identified one of Lord Fournier's knights. It was Captain Gagnon—a brave soul to go up against a dragon to protect his liege.

The captain signalled to Laurence, indicating with his arms that they should attack together while the lords make their escape.

Laurence gave a nod of his head in response while screaming the last verse in his head.

But she's my knight,
My golden light.
I wish I was holding her hand
In this daunting fight…

Taking a quick note of Khaja's location, he discovered that she had climbed halfway up the dragon's leg. She dug her claws into the scales, creating cracks in them as she went. The strength of her kind was truly frightening.

Once Khaja landed on the dragon's back, the dragon's head whipped around. The monster stared at her in wonder but did not attack.

It wasn't until Captain Gagnon went ahead and stabbed the fleshy gap between the dragon's toes that the creature let out an annoyed roar. The vibrations shook the cavern, with rocks and boulders falling unpredictably. Using its wing, the dragon shielded Khaja from falling debris.

Laurence cussed when he saw that Gagnon's sword was stuck and would not come out.

"Cursed dragons...and...their cursed...size," Laurence grumbled between heaving breaths.

He ran to aid Captain Gagnon and pulled the man away from the dragon's stomping foot. The second knight was not as lucky. His body became a puddle of blood and flattened metal in less than a second.

Laurence grimaced and kept pulling Captain Gagnon away. Once he sensed they were out of the beast's immediate reach, and the rocks around them stopped moving, he let go and took a quick look at the spot where Lord Fournier was originally hiding.

The lords and their remaining four knights were making their way towards the exit. Sergey and Yeland brought up the rear. Their faces were ashen with fear and for a good reason. What once was a combined force of a hundred men had dwindled to six knights and two lords. It was a miracle they had survived as long as they did.

Lord Fournier supported Lord Carrell, who was missing a part of his right arm. It must have been cut or bitten off by the dragon at some point.

The knights at their side appeared in no better shape. All heavily wounded and limping with great effort.

"Sir Laurence, we do not have much time. The dragon's flame will soon be upon us!" Captain Gagnon shouted, his face was covered in grime and dirt, eyes wild.

Laurence craned his neck and focused on the dragon's throat. A bulge had formed where the light was at its brightest. The dragon's attention was back on Khaja who simply glared back at it. "Is there another way out?"

"If there is, we could not find it," the captain replied, peering past Laurence at the lords. "They will soon reach the exit. Good."

"You are quite loyal to your lord, Captain."

The man's eyes shone with admiration. "It is my honour to serve and die for Lord Fournier."

"I'd rather we *all* made it out alive."

The captain chuckled. "As would I."

"Laurence, we need to go!" Ian sped to them. The elf was out of breath. Blood trickled down the side of his face, covering his right brow and eye.

"Go." Laurence pointed to the cave's exit. "I will get Khaja."

"Have you lost your mind?" Ian snapped. "She will follow you!"

Laurence was not certain about that. Khaja and the dragon seemed to be in a trance of some sort. They were completely still as if weighing each other's strengths and weaknesses. Which was strange since the dragon was undoubtedly more powerful.

"What are they doing?" Laurence voiced his thoughts out loud.

Ian grabbed Laurence by the shoulders and shook him. "Laurence!"

Laurence bit down on his lower lip and gave a quick nod. "Go!"

Ian's eyes hardened as he let go. The elf and Captain Gagnon started running towards the cavern's exit.

Sheathing his sword, Laurence closed his eyes briefly. "Come on, Khaja. Follow us."

With leg muscles that burned from exhaustion, he pushed his body. The distance between him and the dragon grew, just as the distance between him and Khaja increased.

Each second left like a year. His mind conjured many scenarios where Khaja met a terrible end all because he abandoned her to the black dragon.

His chest grew tight, and not from the strain his lungs were in.

I can't do it. I can't leave her.

When they were about to reach the lords who were hurrying into the tunnel, Laurence whipped around.

"Khaja!" he hollered at the top of his voice. "Come here!"

Her head snapped in his direction, breaking the staring contest with the dragon. Almost effortlessly, she jumped, sliding down the dragon's leg as if it were a snow slide.

When she landed safely on the ground, she launched in Laurence's direction with the biggest grin on her face. Bigger than the grin she sported when she was about to attack the dragon.

"I must be prettier," Laurence whispered.

The dragon shook his head and studied Khaja's retreating form. Its eyes followed her path to Laurence and then narrowed.

I have a bad feeling about this.

Laurence shouted to Lord Fournier and the rest, "Leave as fast as you can!"

They did not need to be told twice. The lords gave respectful nods to Laurence and broke into a harder sprint.

Sergey, Ian, and Yeland lagged behind despite the order.

Khaja was about to reach them when the dragon abandoned its place and chased after them. Each stomp shook the cavern, unsettling their footing.

"We need to leave!" Ian growled.

"A moment more," Laurence snapped back.

In those two seconds, the dragon was upon them, glaring down, and its sharp-toothed mouth open. Its hot breath was as stifling as the air in a desert. Its claws already mid-swing behind Khaja, who was too preoccupied with running towards Laurence to notice.

38
PROPHECY UNTOLD

EMILIA

Having spent days trapped in her office with too many merchants to count, Emilia decided she could no longer sit still. The palace was nothing more than a pretty prison cell, and she needed some air.

Dressed in a dark cloak and her commoner's disguise, Emilia stood in front of the fireplace in her bedchambers. "Ambrose, Lady Isobelle, are you ready?"

"We are prepared, Your Majesty," Lady Isobelle assured.

Emilia assessed them. While Ambrose could blend in with her plain appearance and her perfected lack of presence, Lady Isobelle was the opposite. The lady's cocky posture and beauty screamed of a noblewoman playing pretend.

It's too late to ask someone else.

Emilia pulled on the lever that put the fire out in her fireplace, and a secret passageway swung open into the catacombs. She had not dared enter them since they found a dragon under the palace, and yet, she found herself having to use them in her escape from the mundane.

"Tonight, our goal is the Temple of Holy Light," Emilia told them.

"I have prepared our horses in advance, Your Majesty," Ambrose said proudly. "We will do our best to protect you during your prayer."

"I thought this was a midnight rendezvous with the Pope," Isobelle quipped.

Emilia's cheeks warmed. It was a good thing they were in the tunnels and the only light was the one Ambrose held as she guided them. "I have my reasons for wanting to go."

Partly because I promised Luminos that I would pray once a month and partly to check on the progress Valerian has made with the preparations.

"Brother must be having a terrible time searching for that teleporting mage. They are hard to track once they leave the city," Isobelle commented. "I received word that he left for Wellens this morning."

Emilia avoided stepping on a rat by moving closer to the stone walls. She had been missing Clayton. She would give anything to snuggle up against him and breathe in his comforting smell again. Every night before bed, she would close her eyes and envision him lying beside her, keeping her safe. It had become a ritual of sorts that helped calm her fears and lulled her to sleep.

"Lord Armel will return in time," Ambrose's voice still held a bit of a strain when she mentioned him. "He would not dare leave Her Majesty alone for long."

"Not when the competition is becoming so fierce," Lady Isobelle added.

"What competition?" Emilia asked.

The two women stopped in their tracks and studied Emilia as if she were speaking in a foreign language.

"Well?" Emilia pressed.

"For Your Majesty's heart, of course," Lady Isobelle clarified with a grin on her face. "You are the woman of the season."

Ambrose placed a hand over her chest. "Should any of the suitors do anything to displease Your Majesty, I will dispose of them."

"There is no one to dispose of." Emilia urged them with her hands to keep moving.

They didn't have all night to speak of her non-existent love life. Her boyfriend was off hunting a mage, the Pope was probably trying to get close to Luminos through her, and Thessian was completely misunderstood by everyone at the palace.

"Is there nothing going on with the prince?" Isobelle inquired with slight amusement in her tone.

"No *things* of any such kind!" Though, Emilia would not mind a hug or two from her favourite character. Thessian may appear intimidating on the outside, but he was sweet and caring once she got to know him. His bravery and honest heart would make him a good emperor one day.

"His Highness will be swarmed with the single ladies when he returns to the Empire. The spring season is popular for engagements over there," Lady Isobelle added.

Emilia looked down at her feet. She never thought about who would be Thessian's empress. After all, Emilia's life's goal was to help him survive, so she could live out her life in peace. Yet, over the month they got to know each other, he became a good friend and a confidant. She wished she could tell him more, admit that she couldn't see the future. And each time those thoughts surfaced, she had to squash them.

If the fact that she lied came to pass, he would lose all trust in her.

Would he even listen to a single word of mine thereafter?

She could not risk it. Not when all she wanted was for their friendship to remain intact.

"What about you, Lady Isobelle? Have you a suitor?" Emilia asked out of curiosity and because the way Isobelle eyed Lionhart's butt the other day was still fresh on the Queen's mind.

"Me?" Isobelle let out an evil cackle. "No man would dare approach me after the last season."

"What happened?" Emilia and Ambrose asked in unison.

Isobelle's laughter settled into an unsettling grin. "I killed a man."

"What?" Emilia gasped.

"In public?" Ambrose questioned.

Isobelle snickered. "...Or I wish I did. I *accidentally* stumbled into a pushy nobleman who kept proposing to me. He fell down the longest flight of stairs in the palace, breaking his legs and arms in the process. I sent him a letter with the well-wishes and a warning that a fate far worse awaits him should we marry."

A shudder washed over Emilia. Lady Isobelle's thinking was unique when it came to ridding herself of unwanted attention. Being Isobelle's friend was better than having her as an enemy.

An hour later, they dismounted their horses at the foot of a hill beyond the walls of Newburn. A set of stone steps that reminded Emilia of a long tongue led up to the temple's large doors where Valerian and Sir Erenel were waiting for them.

The Pope's eyes twinkled in the moonlight at the sight of Emilia. Dressed in a white and gold robe, he sauntered over and smiled brightly. "I welcome Your Majesty to the sacred Temple of Holy Light." He turned to Isobelle and Ambrose and said, "May the blessings of Luminos guide you, ladies."

"May the blessings of Luminos guide Your Holiness also," they replied.

Bringing his full attention back to Emilia, Valerian offered her his arm. "Do you wish to pray right away or would you prefer a tour of the temple?"

Emilia slipped her arm around his. She couldn't get used to how easy it was for her to be herself in his presence. There was no need to lie or pretend. He could tell when she was lying anyway.

Stupid blessings!

Emilia was not about to pray and run back to the palace. She had to stretch her legs, even if it meant getting a lengthy lecture on every statue in Luminos' temple. "A tour would be lovely. Ambrose, Isobelle, there are some things I wish to discuss with His Holiness in private."

The ladies nodded.

Sir Erenel got the same message from Valerian when they approached the doors that led to the temple's grand halls.

Hundreds of candles were lit to illuminate the curving path they strolled. During King Gilebert's funeral, she didn't bother paying too much attention. Her focus was on the coffin of the king and maintaining the act of a grieving princess. With time no longer being a constraint, and an eager guide at her side, she could see how much money and love went into the temple's structure.

Everything from the lustrous sandstone floors, meticulously crafted benches and chairs, expertly sculpted statues with greater detail than what she could find even at the palace, to the reaching vaulted ceilings and chandeliers made of Elderwood was in perfect condition. The priests did not slack off on the cleaning of their holy temple.

Valerian bent down and whispered near her ear when they stopped in front of a statue of a busty woman draped in a semi-revealing robe. "I made them clean every crevice for your coronation."

Surely, he didn't get the blessing of mind-reading...

He resumed his straight posture. "It is only right that the Saintess of Luminos is welcomed into a pristine temple."

Emilia pulled away from him. *There's that term again.*

"Have I displeased you?" His voice shook with uncertainty, yet when she looked at his face, his eyes danced with amusement.

Who is the real Valerian? What's an act and what's the truth?

Valerian tucked a lock of her hair behind her ear. His warm fingers faintly brushed her skin, sending a tingling sensation to her heart.

He spoke low, his voice almost a melody that she could listen to forever. "Each time I find myself stricken by your appearance, Emilia. For a perfect being such as you, to have the heart of gold and the flawless beauty of a goddess, how can the mortal men of this world not immediately bow down and worship you at your feet?"

As if to prove a point, he knelt and pressed her hand to his forehead and then his lips. He left a soft kiss on her knuckles. She could barely feel his touch over the thumping in her chest. "Whatever you wish for, my saintess, I will bring you. And I promise that your coronation will inspire the people for centuries to come."

Emilia's hand burned where their skin touched. When she tried to move it out of his hold, he stopped her by clenching his hand around hers.

"Valerian!" she hissed his name in warning.

He released her hand and climbed back up. "What would you wish to see first?"

"Your room," she blurted out. "No, I mean—"

"My room it is!" Grabbing her by the hand and intertwining their fingers, he hurriedly pulled her after him into another hallway and then down the stairs. A long corridor stretched out ahead of them. There were no decorations or over-the-top statues. Simple wooden doors were on either side of them as they kept going.

A few priests bowed their heads to the Pope and muttered their blessings before heading to their designated rooms.

Valerian paused in front of a door no different from others and pushed it open for her. "Please, come in."

She stepped into the dark room.

He lit a candle in the iron lantern that sat on a bedside table near a single bed. There was no gold, no marble, and no expensive silk sheets. The room was simple and clean. Devoid of all luxury.

"Is this where you and Sir Erenel sleep?"

It took a moment for him to process her words, and he laughed. "That time, Klaus was only seeing if I had something in my eye."

"Regardless, I thought the priests would treat the Pope better than this."

In a room that seemed too small for two, he towered over her, invading her space. "I asked to be treated the same as any priest of Luminos during my stay here."

"Why?"

"A simple life helps to keep me from getting distracted from my goals."

"And what would those goals be?" she dared to ask.

Valerian's eyes never left hers. There was an unknown to her world behind his green eyes. If only she could see what he saw. "To complete my mission and protect you."

"In that order?"

"In any order you require, Emilia."

She could feel a powerful pull towards him. His magnetism and charisma were that of a celebrity in her previous life. Resisting him took great effort, especially when he showered her with affectionate lines every chance he got.

Emilia couldn't tell what Luminos wanted or why the Goddess put Valerian in Emilia's path. But she would not become a goddess' plaything. Instead, she would use every given opportunity to survive with her friends in her new world.

She cupped Valerian's cheek and stroked her thumb over his soft skin. His eyelashes were long and tickled the pad of her thumb.

Valerian leaned into her touch and closed his eyes. He seemed relaxed, defenceless.

If I asked for his loyalty, would he give it to me?

"I would like to see the inner sanctum," she finally said, retracting her hand.

He peeled his eyelids open. It was hard to miss the look of disappointment that soured his usual smile. "I will guide you."

They left his room, and she followed him back up a different set of stairs until they circled to almost the back of the temple while never leaving the premises. He pushed open a door which inlay a carving of a beautiful man holding a glowing sphere. Perhaps it was the old image the priests used for the God of Light.

Emilia expected the inner sanctum to be a room or a temple

within a temple. What she didn't expect was a small garden with a stone altar towards the back that had been overgrown with moss and ivy. Moonlight streamed down through the glass ceiling and a handful of candles were scattered on the mossy floor.

"I will remain here," Valerian informed her. "Please pray for as long as you wish."

He slowly closed the door behind her, its thud giving an echo of grandeur much larger than its size.

Emilia breathed in the clean air that carried a hint of wax with it. She followed the cobbled stone path to the altar and knelt in front of it.

"I wonder what Luminos is expecting exactly?" she asked no one in particular. "Here goes nothing."

Clasping her hands in front of her heart, Emilia closed her eyes and prayed out loud, "I'm here, just as you wanted, Goddess." Opening one eye to peek at her surroundings, she was disappointed to find that nothing had happened. No beams of holy light, no glowing balls in the air, and no annoying goddesses appeared.

"Am I wasting time here?" Emilia grumbled, about to get up. Patience was not her best trait. She had used up what little patience she had on hatching a plan to kill her father and the two princes.

"It takes more than an announcement of presence to summon a god." Luminos' irritable voice reverberated throughout the inner sanctum. "Humans are so impatient!"

"If you are aware that I am here for you, then why pretend to not be here?"

From behind the altar, a tiny glowing pixie-like creature floated up on four moth-like wings. The room brightened as the figure rose higher. Placing her tiny hands on her hips, the pixie landed in the middle of the altar and pointed her nose up.

The vines and fauna growing on the altar seemed to flourish and sway with her movements.

Emilia squinted to try and make out the details of the creature.

Luminos was bathed in shimmering light with golden hair and almost translucent skin. Her rose-coloured doe eyes were framed by thick blonde lashes, and a figure-fitting ivory robe adorned her shapely body.

She's kind of cute.

"You are correct in thinking that I am the most beautiful being in existence, Emily."

Emilia certainly did not miss Luminos' personality. "I wasn't—"

"Even the Goddess of Beauty cannot contain her joy when she sees me."

Emilia turned her laugh into a cough. *I can see why.* "You look different than before, and are much smaller than I expected."

Luminos ignored her comment and began to pace along the surface of the altar.

The pacing goddess made Emilia's stomach clench with nerves. "Is something the matter?"

The goddess stopped. Her wings fluttered softly behind her. "What are your thoughts on Valerian?"

"The Pope?"

"Perchance you know someone else by that name?"

Emilia sat back and crossed her arms and legs. *What kind of interrogation is this?* "He's devout."

"He has heeded your call and no longer bothers me from dusk till dawn, however, I fear that he may stray from the path."

"You wish him to pray more? Do you have a weird push-and-pull relationship with Valerian?"

Luminos seemed aghast by the idea.

"It was a joke," Emilia quickly clarified, holding her hands up in defeat. She didn't want to soothe a pouting goddess a second time. "So, about the dragon—"

"Do you not recall my words from before?"

"I didn't hear it the first time."

"You are too relaxed, Emily. There is less than four years to pass."

Emilia felt a frown setting on her face. "Four? Don't you mean two? When Kyros becomes emperor and starts killing the mages?"

"The second prophecy."

"The second prophecy?" Emilia did a double take. She was thankful she was sitting down as her legs would have given way at the news. Her arms fell to her sides and dread wormed its way into her heart. "Is there a second book?"

"Valerian must survive. He must not stray from the path."

Emilia crawled closer to the altar. Her voice rose with each word. "There's a second book? The hero saving the mages from a ruthless tyrant was not the ending? What is? What do I do?"

Luminos stepped back and kicked off into the air, her wings beating harder as she backed away. "Heed my words, Emily."

Emilia stumbled to her feet as she tried to scale the alter after Luminos. "No! No, no, no. Don't you dare disappear on m—and she's gone at a crucial time again. Argh!"

The room grew dimmer as the light that had been bathing the inner sanctum took a moment longer to leave. The vines on the altar amended as if nothing had happened.

Emilia threw her arms up in the air. Her whole being quivered with restrained rage.

Damn it, Luminos, you useless goddess!

39

THE VILLAIN

KYROS

**Year 608. Late Winter. The Duchy of Spiora, Hellion Empire.
Two weeks after Thessian's coup.**

Kyros flicked through the pages of a book that held his interest as of late. He had read it four times. Each time the scribe's words had a different meaning to them—a deeper one.

Birdsong beyond his library's windows soothed away the stress from his work day.

After only recently returning from surveying his territory, disguised as frivolous travel, he had held a ball made to amuse the nobles at his expense. The pretence was tiresome to upkeep. Not only was he acting a sickly man, but he was also spending his money whimsically.

Or so everyone thought.

He mostly purchased luxurious goods from companies he owned in secret. Their reputation had soared among the Empire's nobility, funnelling the gold back into his pocket. It was a necessary evil, in case one of his plans failed.

They cannot fail. They mustn't.

Slamming the tome shut, he pushed it back into its slot on the bookshelf and sighed. A pulsating headache from overworking had forced him to stop for the day. At his secretary's behest, he was idling in the library, feeling useless when he would rather be working.

The familiar dual knock on the door told him that Rift had arrived.

"Enter." Kyros sauntered to one of the leather armchairs where he sat down and crossed his legs, watching his advisor enter.

At barely eighteen, Rift was not a tall lad. His white hair was short and spiky. His cavernous, almond-shaped grey eyes reminded Kyros of a stormy night that would never end. Although dressed in the finest attire fit for any noble, his hunched shoulders spoke volumes of how little confidence the slender man had.

He must have been told off by someone again and took it to heart.

After paying his obeisance, Rift kept his head low. "Your Imperial Highness, I bring troublesome news."

"You know I dislike it when you bow to me. Are we not equal partners in our goals?"

Rift lifted his head. "I do apologise, Your Imperial Highness. I am trying to adjust to this new lifestyle."

Kyros waved the apology away. "What news do you bear?"

"It is a report from Dante. Prince Thessian's coup was a success..." Rift scurried over and handed Kyros the report.

Skimming over the details, Kyros' brows scrunched together the longer he read the words written by their spy in Newburn.

Kyros crumpled the letter. His headache intensified as a vein throbbed in his forehead. "That's not what should have happened!"

TO BE CONTINUED ...

THE GAME OF CROWNS

The game is played on an 8 x 8 board.

Each player has a king, an advisor, a fortification, four knights, and two archers.

Players arrange their pieces on their side of the board behind a screen before the game begins.

1. **King:** The king can move one square in any direction. If his knight or fortification is in front of him, he can move one square backwards during the same turn (**The King's Escape**).
2. **Advisor:** The advisor can move two squares diagonally. Once per game, the advisor can "**Spread False Information**" to move an opponent's knight or archer without moving itself.
3. **Fortification:** The fortification stays in place and cannot be taken by the opponent. It can be destroyed to remove it from the game by its owner which also destroys an adjacent opponent's piece (**Fortification's Crumble**).
4. **Knights:** Knights can move two squares in any direction. Once per game, a knight can be sacrificed for the king if they are within two empty squares of each other (**Oath of Loyalty**). The knight and king swap places, and the knight is then removed from the board.
5. **Archers:** Archers can move one square in any direction or two squares backwards up to three times per game (**The Retreat**). When attacking an adjacent opponent's piece, an archer can choose to stay in their square without moving.

To capture the opponent's piece, your piece needs to land directly on it (excluding archers who can also capture adjacent pieces).

Winning the Game:

You win by either capturing your opponent's king or trapping him so he cannot move.

LANGUAGE OF THE BEASTMEN

Here are some of the phrases Khaja has used in this book:
"Zaotuo yille kablenen kur kai vosie." - Pointed ear seems to like you.

BEASTMEN DICTIONARY (TO DATE)

Words and their meaning:

Jya - I
Vosie – (singular) You / Vosies - Your
Vas – (plural) You
Wo – we
Osie – they
Ose – them
Osein - their
Mir – mine
Moin – my
Nare – our
Uns – us
Elin – he / Eline – his / Elinez - him
Vast – is
Ntes – are
Eund – and
I – the
Kur – to
Wa – why
Ne – not/no
Da – yes
Mopeca – can
Ivon - have
Delte – should
Deche – make
Emberh – take
Kablenen - seem \ appear
Abei – at
Oin - one
Dei – two
Ointes – first
Deites – second

Hedu - today
Redu - yesterday
Indu – tomorrow
Kaiedes – like (similar to, hold affection for)
Kai - like (in a friendly way)
Tietna – animals
Aunen – the rest, others
Zaotuo – pointed, sharp, protruding
Yille – ear
Arikeshe – (plural) hindwalkers, a term used for humans
Arikesh – (singular) hindwalker
Werst – kill / killed – werste
Termer – Died/perished
Ukiy – hard
Ankota – attack
Heslich – happy
Fabise – weak
Sohen – go, go out, leave through
Raci – here
Paci – there
Fera – will, planning to do something
Ne fera – not will (won't)
Otarkert – marked
Zaregh – capture
Golnad – big, large
Kadachek – gift
Tsessen – kiss, kissing
Sier – bond
Nur – for
Vibezn – life
Varetz - Father
Daszik - Thank you
Yteren – respect
Druvahi – invaded
Getior – territory
Agenvir – kind (species)

Zagendier- defend
Tolle o' – daughter of
Sharte – speak
Ryin – hand / Ryine – hands
Mə'rage – revenge/vengeance
Susker – seek/want desperately
Näktue - stubborn
Keben – child
Messel – same/identical
Dechiba – fate
Ertesz – wait/await
Varthamir - formal term for Mate/Soulmate
Akatsi - a term the beastmen called their tribe.

ABOUT THE AUTHOR

May Freighter is an award-winning, internationally bestselling author from Ireland. She writes Fantasy, Urban Fantasy, Paranormal Romance, and Sci-Fi Mysteries that will keep you entertained, mystified, and hopefully craving more. Currently, she's attempting to parent two little monsters and hasn't slept in over 4 years.

Who needs sleep these days, anyway?

On days when May can join her fictional characters on an adventure, stars must align in the sky and meteors will probably rain down. So, keep an eye out.

Her hobbies are photography, drawing, plotting different ways of characters' demise, and picking up toys after her kids. Not exactly in that order, either.

For more information about the author and their work, visit their website: **www.authormayfreighter.com**

FIND OUT WHAT HAPPENS NEXT IN:

Printed in Great Britain
by Amazon

0cf77b83-4803-4dcf-a01c-8ba457cf3905R01